AF138650

Franz Kafka

Collected Works

Bibliografische Information der Deutschen Nationalbibliothek:
Die Deutsche Nationalbibliothek verzeichnet diese Publikation in der
Deutschen Nationalbibliografie; detaillierte bibliografische Daten sind im
Internet über http://dnb.dnb.de abrufbar.

Herstellung und Verlag: BoD – Books on Demand, Norderstedt

ISBN: 978-3-7386-4106-6

Table of Contents

The Metamorphosis.. 7

    I 7

    II 24

    III...43

A Country Doctor..62

A Hunger Artist 68

A Report for an Academy..79

An Imperial Message 89

Before the Law...90

In the Penal Colony 92

Jackals and Arabs.. 122

The Great Wall of China 126

The Hunter Gracchus.. 140

The Trial.. 145

    Chapter One 145

    Chapter Two...171

    Chapter Three...187

    Chapter Four 209

    Chapter Five 216

    Chapter Six...222

    Chapter Seven...241

    Chapter Eight 289

Chapter Nine...317

Chapter Ten..338

Up in the Gallery 344

The Metamorphosis

I

One morning, as Gregor Samsa was waking up from anxious dreams, he discovered that in bed he had been changed into a monstrous verminous bug. He lay on his armour-hard back and saw, as he lifted his head up a little, his brown, arched abdomen divided up into rigid bow-like sections. From this height the blanket, just about ready to slide off completely, could hardly stay in place. His numerous legs, pitifully thin in comparison to the rest of his circumference, flickered helplessly before his eyes.

"What's happened to me," he thought. It was no dream. His room, a proper room for a human being, only somewhat too small, lay quietly between the four well-known walls. Above the table, on which an unpacked collection of sample cloth goods was spread out (Samsa was a traveling salesman) hung the picture which he had cut out of an illustrated magazine a little while ago and set in a pretty gilt frame. It was a picture of a woman with a fur hat and a fur boa. She sat erect there, lifting up in the direction of the viewer a solid fur muff into which her entire forearm disappeared.

Gregor's glance then turned to the window. The dreary weather (the rain drops were falling audibly down on the metal window ledge) made him quite melancholy. "Why don't I keep sleeping for a little while longer and forget all this foolishness," he thought. But this was entirely impractical, for he was used to sleeping on his right side, and in his present state he couldn't get himself into this position. No matter how hard he threw himself onto his right side, he always rolled again onto his back. He must have tried it a hundred times, closing his eyes, so that he would not have to see the wriggling legs, and gave up only when he began to feel a light, dull pain in his side which he had never felt before.

"O God," he thought, "what a demanding job I've chosen! Day in, day out on the road. The stresses of trade are much greater than the work going on at head office, and, in addition to that, I have to deal with the problems of traveling, the worries about train connections, irregular bad food, temporary and constantly changing human relationships which never come from the heart. To hell with it all!" He felt a slight itching on the top of his abdomen. He slowly pushed himself on his back closer to the bed post so that he could lift his head more easily, found the itchy part, which was entirely covered with small white spots (he did not know what to make of them), and wanted to feel the place with a leg. But he retracted it immediately, for the contact felt like a cold shower all over him.

He slid back again into his earlier position. "This getting up early," he thought, "makes a man quite idiotic. A man must have his sleep. Other traveling salesmen live like harem women. For instance, when I come back to the inn during the course of the morning to write up the necessary orders, these gentlemen are just sitting down to breakfast. If I were to try that with my boss, I'd be thrown out on the spot. Still, who knows whether that mightn't be really good for me. If I didn't hold back for my parents' sake, I would've quit ages ago. I would've gone to the boss and told him just what I think from the bottom of my heart. He would've fallen right off his desk! How weird it is to sit up at the desk and talk down to the employee from way up there. The boss has trouble hearing, so the employee has to step up quite close to him. Anyway, I haven't completely given up that hope yet. Once I've got together the money to pay off the parents' debt to him—that should take another five or six years—I'll do it for sure. Then I'll make the big break. In any case, right now I have to get up. My train leaves at five o'clock."

And he looked over at the alarm clock ticking away by the chest of drawers. "Good God," he thought. It was half past six, and the hands were going quietly on. It was past the half hour, already nearly quarter to. Could the alarm have failed to ring? One saw from the bed that it was properly set for four o'clock. Certainly it had rung. Yes, but was it possible to sleep through this noise that made the furniture shake? Now, it's true he'd not slept quietly, but evidently he'd slept all the more deeply. Still, what should he do now? The next train left at seven o'clock. To catch that one, he would have to go in a mad rush. The sample collection wasn't packed up yet, and he really didn't feel particularly fresh and active. And even if he caught the train, there was no avoiding a blow up with the boss, because the firm's errand boy would've waited for the five o'clock train and reported the news of his absence long ago. He was the boss's minion, without backbone or intelligence. Well then, what if he reported in sick? But that would be extremely embarrassing and suspicious, because during his five years' service Gregor hadn't been sick even once. The boss would certainly come with the doctor from the health insurance company and would reproach his parents for their lazy son and cut short all objections with the insurance doctor's comments; for him everyone was completely healthy but really lazy about work. And besides, would the doctor in this case be totally wrong? Apart from a really excessive drowsiness after the long sleep, Gregor in fact felt quite well and even had a really strong appetite.

As he was thinking all this over in the greatest haste, without being able to make the decision to get out of bed (the alarm clock was indicating exactly quarter to seven) there was a cautious knock on the door by the head of the bed.

"Gregor," a voice called (it was his mother!) "it's quarter to seven. Don't you want to be on your way?" The soft voice! Gregor was startled when he heard his voice answering. It was clearly and unmistakably his earlier voice, but in it was intermingled, as if from below, an irrepressibly painful squeaking which left the words positively distinct only in the first moment and distorted them in the reverberation, so that one didn't know if one had heard correctly. Gregor wanted to answer in detail and explain everything, but in these circumstances he confined himself to saying, "Yes, yes, thank you mother. I'm getting up right away." Because of the wooden door the change in Gregor's voice was not really noticeable outside, so his mother calmed down with this explanation and shuffled off. However, as a result of the short conversation the other family members became aware of the fact that

Gregor was unexpectedly still at home, and already his father was knocking on one side door, weakly but with his fist. "Gregor, Gregor," he called out, "what's going on?" And after a short while he urged him on again in a deeper voice. "Gregor!" Gregor!" At the other side door, however, his sister knocked lightly. "Gregor? Are you all right? Do you need anything?" Gregor directed answers in both directions, "I'll be ready right away." He made an effort with the most careful articulation and by inserting long pauses between the individual words to remove everything remarkable from his voice. His father turned back to his breakfast. However, the sister whispered, "Gregor, open the door, I beg you." Gregor had no intention of opening the door, but congratulated himself on his precaution, acquired from traveling, of locking all doors during the night, even at home.

First he wanted to stand up quietly and undisturbed, get dressed, above all have breakfast, and only then consider further action, for (he noticed this clearly) by thinking things over in bed he would not reach a reasonable conclusion. He remembered that he had already often felt a light pain or other in bed, perhaps the result of an awkward lying position, which later turned out to be purely imaginary when he stood up, and he was eager to see how his present fantasies would gradually dissipate. That the change in his voice was nothing other than the onset of a real chill, an occupational illness of commercial travelers, of that he had not the slightest doubt.

It was very easy to throw aside the blanket. He needed only to push himself up a little, and it fell by itself. But to continue was difficult, particularly because he was so unusually wide. He needed arms and hands to push himself upright. Instead of these, however, he had only many small limbs which were incessantly moving with very different motions and which, in addition, he was unable to control. If he wanted to bend one of them, then it was the first to extend itself, and if he finally succeeded doing with this limb what he wanted, in the meantime all the others, as if left free, moved around in an excessively painful agitation. "But I must not stay in bed uselessly," said Gregor to himself.

At first he wanted to get of the bed with the lower part of his body, but this lower part (which he incidentally had not yet looked at and which he also couldn't picture clearly) proved itself too difficult to move. The attempt went so slowly. When, having become almost frantic, he finally hurled himself forward with all his force and without thinking, he chose his direction incorrectly, and he hit the lower bedpost hard. The violent pain he felt revealed to him that the lower part of his body was at the moment probably the most sensitive.

Thus, he tried to get his upper body out of the bed first and turned his head carefully toward the edge of the bed. He managed to do this easily, and in spite of its width and weight his body mass at last slowly followed the turning of his head. But as he finally raised his head outside the bed in the open air, he became anxious about moving forward any further in this manner, for if he allowed himself eventually to fall by this process, it would take a miracle to prevent his head from getting injured. And at all costs he must not lose consciousness right now. He preferred to remain in bed.

However, after a similar effort, while he lay there again sighing as before and once again saw his small limbs fighting one another, if anything worse than before, and didn't see any chance of imposing quiet and order on this arbitrary movement, he told himself again that he couldn't possibly remain in bed and that it might be the most reasonable thing to sacrifice everything if there was even the slightest hope of getting himself out of bed in the process. At the same moment, however, he didn't forget to remind himself from time to time of the fact that calm (indeed the calmest) reflection might be better than the most confused decisions. At such moments, he directed his gaze as precisely as he could toward the window, but unfortunately there was little confident cheer to be had from a glance at the morning mist, which concealed even the other side of the narrow street. "It's already seven o'clock" he told himself at the latest striking of the alarm clock, "already seven o'clock and still such a fog." And for a little while longer he lay quietly with weak breathing, as if perhaps waiting for normal and natural conditions to re-emerge out of the complete stillness.

But then he said to himself, "Before it strikes a quarter past seven, whatever happens I must be completely out of bed. Besides, by then someone from the office will arrive to inquire about me, because the office will open before seven o'clock." And he made an effort then to rock his entire body length out of the bed with a uniform motion. If he let himself fall out of the bed in this way, his head, which in the course of the fall he intended to lift up sharply, would probably remain uninjured. His back seemed to be hard; nothing would really happen to that as a result of the fall. His greatest reservation was a worry about the loud noise which the fall must create and which presumably would arouse, if not fright, then at least concern on the other side of all the doors. However, it had to be tried.

As Gregor was in the process of lifting himself half out of bed (the new method was more of a game than an effort; he needed only to rock with a constant rhythm) it struck him how easy all this would be if someone were to come to his aid. Two strong people (he thought of his father and the servant girl) would have been quite sufficient. They would have only had to push their arms under his arched back to get him out of the bed, to bend down with their load, and then merely to exercise patience and care that he completed the flip onto the floor, where his diminutive legs would then, he hoped, acquire a purpose. Now, quite apart from the fact that the doors were locked, should he really call out for help? In spite of all his distress, he was unable to suppress a smile at this idea.

He had already got to the point where, with a stronger rocking, he maintained his equilibrium with difficulty, and very soon he would finally have to decide, for in five minutes it would be a quarter past seven. Then there was a ring at the door of the apartment. "That's someone from the office" he told himself, and he almost froze while his small limbs only danced around all the faster. For one moment everything remained still. "They aren't opening," Gregor said to himself, caught up in some absurd hope. But of course then, as usual, the servant girl with her firm tread went to the door and opened it. Gregor needed to hear only the visitor's first word of greeting to recognize immediately who it was, the manager himself. Why was Gregor the only one condemned to work in a firm where at the slightest lapse someone immediately attracted the greatest suspicion? Were all the employees then collectively, one and all, scoundrels? Was there then among them no truly devoted person who, if he failed to use just a couple of hours in the morning for office work, would become abnormal from pangs of conscience and really be in no state to get out of bed? Was it really not enough to let an apprentice make inquiries, if such questioning was even necessary? Must the manager himself come, and in the process must it be demonstrated to the entire innocent family that the investigation of this suspicious circumstance could only be entrusted to the intelligence of the manager? And more as a consequence of the excited state in which this idea put Gregor than as a result of an actual decision, he swung himself with all his might out of the bed. There was a loud thud, but not a real crash. The fall was absorbed somewhat by the carpet and, in addition, his back was more elastic than Gregor had thought. For that reason the dull noise was not quite so conspicuous. But he had not held his head up with sufficient care and had hit it. He turned his head, irritated and in pain, and rubbed it on the carpet.

"Something has fallen in there," said the manager in the next room on the left. Gregor tried to imagine to himself whether anything similar to what was happening to him today could have also happened at some point to the manager. At least one had to concede the possibility of such a thing. However, as if to give a rough answer to this question, the manager now took a few determined steps in the next room, with a squeak of his polished boots. From the neighbouring room on the right the sister was whispering to inform Gregor: "Gregor, the manager is here." "I know," said Gregor to himself. But he did not dare make his voice loud enough so that his sister could hear.

"Gregor," his father now said from the neighbouring room on the left, "Mr. Manager has come and is asking why you have not left on the early train. We don't know what we should tell him. Besides, he also wants to speak to you personally. So please open the door. He will be good enough to forgive the mess in your room."

In the middle of all this, the manager called out in a friendly way, "Good morning, Mr. Samsa." "He is not well," said his mother to the manager, while his father was still talking at the door, "He is not well, believe me, Mr. Manager. Otherwise how would Gregor miss a train! The young man has nothing in his head except business. I'm almost angry that he never goes out at night. Right now he's been in the city eight days, but he's been at home every evening. He sits there with us at the table and reads the newspaper quietly or studies his travel schedules. It's quite a diversion for him if he busies himself with fretwork. For instance, he cut out a small frame over the course of two or three evenings. You'd be amazed how pretty it is. It's hanging right inside the room. You'll see it immediately, as soon as Gregor opens the door. Anyway, I'm happy that you're here, Mr. Manager. By ourselves, we would never have made Gregor open the door. He's so stubborn, and he's certainly not well, although he denied that this morning."

"I'm coming right away," said Gregor slowly and deliberately and didn't move, so as not to lose one word of the conversation. "My dear lady, I cannot explain it to myself in any other way," said the manager; "I hope it is nothing serious. On the other hand, I must also say that we business people, luckily or unluckily, however one looks at it, very often simply have to overcome a slight indisposition for business reasons." "So can Mr. Manager come in to see you now" asked his father impatiently and knocked once again on the door. "No," said Gregor. In the neighbouring room on the left a painful stillness descended. In the neighbouring room on the right the sister began to sob.

Why didn't his sister go to the others? She'd probably just gotten up out of bed now and hadn't even started to get dressed yet. Then why was she crying? Because he wasn't getting up and wasn't letting the manager in; because he was in danger of losing his position, and because then his boss would badger his parents once again with the old demands? Those were probably unnecessary worries right now. Gregor was still here and wasn't thinking at all about abandoning his family. At the moment he was lying right there on the carpet, and no one who knew about his condition would've seriously demanded that he let the manager in. But Gregor wouldn't be casually dismissed right way because of this small discourtesy, for which he would find an easy and suitable excuse later on. It seemed to Gregor that it might be far more reasonable to leave him in peace at the moment, instead of disturbing him with crying and conversation. But it was the very uncertainty which distressed the others and excused their behaviour.

"Mr. Samsa," the manager was now shouting, his voice raised, "what's the matter? You are barricading yourself in your room, answer with only a yes and a no, are making serious and unnecessary troubles for your parents, and neglecting (I mention this only incidentally) your commercial duties in a truly unheard of manner. I am speaking here in the name of your parents and your employer, and I am requesting you in all seriousness for an immediate and clear explanation. I am amazed. I am amazed. I thought I knew you as a calm, reasonable person, and now you appear suddenly to want to start parading around in weird moods. The Chief indicated to me earlier this very day a possible explanation for your neglect— it concerned the collection of cash entrusted to you a short while ago—but in truth I almost gave him my word of honour that this explanation could not be correct. However, now I see here your unimaginable pig headedness, and I am totally losing any desire to speak up for you in the slightest. And your position is not at all the most secure. Originally I intended to mention all this to you privately, but since you are letting me waste my time here uselessly, I don't know why the matter shouldn't come to the attention of your parents. Your productivity has also been very unsatisfactory recently. Of course, it's not the time of year to conduct exceptional business, we recognize that, but a time of year for conducting no business, there is no such thing at all, Mr. Samsa, and such a thing must never be."

"But Mr. Manager," called Gregor, beside himself and in his agitation forgetting everything else, "I'm opening the door immediately, this very moment. A slight indisposition, a dizzy spell, has prevented me from getting up. I'm still lying in bed right now. But now I'm quite refreshed once again. I'm in the midst of getting out of bed. Just have patience for a short moment! Things are not going so well as I thought. But things are all right. How suddenly this can overcome someone! Just yesterday evening everything was fine with me. My parents certainly know that. Actually just yesterday evening I had a small premonition. People must have seen that in me. Why have I not reported that to the office! But people always think that they'll get over sickness without having to stay at home. Mr. Manager! Take it easy on my parents! There is really no basis for the criticisms which you are now making against me, and really nobody has said a word to me about that. Perhaps you have not read the latest orders which I shipped. Besides, now I'm setting out on my trip on the eight o'clock train; the few hours' rest have made me stronger. Mr. Manager, do not stay. I will be at the office in person right away. Please have the goodness to say that and to convey my respects to the Chief."

While Gregor was quickly blurting all this out, hardly aware of what he was saying, he had moved close to the chest of drawers without effort, probably as a result of the practice he had already had in bed, and now he was trying to raise himself up on it. Actually, he wanted to open the door; he really wanted to let himself be seen by and to speak with the manager. He was keen to witness what the others now asking after him would say at the sight of him. If they were startled, then Gregor had no more responsibility and could be calm. But if they accepted everything quietly, then he would have no reason to get excited and, if he got a move on, could really be at the station around eight o'clock.

At first he slid down a few times from the smooth chest of drawers. But at last he gave himself a final swing and stood upright there. He was no longer at all aware of the pains in his lower body, no matter how they might still sting. Now he let himself fall against the back of a nearby chair, on the edge of which he braced himself with his thin limbs. By doing this he gained control over himself and kept quiet, for he could now hear the manager.

"Did you understand a single word?" the manager asked the parents, "Is he playing the fool with us?" "For God's sake," cried the mother already in tears, "perhaps he's very ill and we're upsetting him. Grete! Grete!" she yelled at that point. "Mother?" called the sister from the other side. They were making themselves understood through Gregor's room. "You must go to the doctor right away. Gregor is sick. Hurry to the doctor. Have you heard Gregor speak yet?" "That was an animal's voice," said the manager, remarkably quietly in comparison to the mother's cries.

"Anna! Anna!" yelled the father through the hall into the kitchen, clapping his hands, "fetch a locksmith right away!" The two young women were already running through the hall with swishing skirts (how had his sister dressed herself so quickly?) and yanked open the doors of the apartment. One couldn't hear the doors closing at all. They probably had left them open, as is customary in an apartment in which a huge misfortune has taken place.

However, Gregor had become much calmer. All right, people did not understand his words any more, although they seemed clear enough to him, clearer than previously, perhaps because his ears had gotten used to them. But at least people now thought that things were not all right with him and were prepared to help him. The confidence and assurance with which the first arrangements had been carried out made him feel good. He felt himself included once again in the circle of humanity and was expecting from both the doctor and the locksmith, without differentiating between them with any real precision, splendid and surprising results. In order to get as clear a voice as possible for the critical conversation which was imminent, he coughed a little, and certainly took the trouble to do this in a really subdued way, since it was possible that even this noise sounded like something different from a human cough. He no longer trusted himself to decide any more. Meanwhile in the next room it had become really quiet. Perhaps his parents were sitting with the manager at the table and were whispering; perhaps they were all leaning against the door and listening.

Gregor pushed himself slowly towards the door, with the help of the easy chair, let go of it there, threw himself against the door, held himself upright against it (the balls of his tiny limbs had a little sticky stuff on them), and rested there momentarily from his exertion. Then he made an effort to turn the key in the lock with his mouth. Unfortunately it seemed that he had no real teeth. How then was he to grab hold of the key? But to make up for that his jaws were naturally very strong; with their help he managed to get the key really moving, and he did not notice that he was obviously inflicting some damage on himself, for a brown fluid came out of his mouth, flowed over the key, and dripped onto the floor.

"Just listen for a moment," said the manager in the next room, "he's turning the key." For Gregor that was a great encouragement. But they all should've called out to him, including his father and mother, "Come on, Gregor," they should've shouted, "keep going, keep working on the lock." Imagining that all his efforts were being followed with suspense, he bit down frantically on the key with all the force he could muster. As the key turned more, he danced around the lock. Now he was holding himself upright only with his mouth, and he had to hang onto the key or then press it down again with the whole weight of his body, as necessary. The quite distinct click of the lock as it finally snapped really woke Gregor up. Breathing heavily he said to himself, "So I didn't need the locksmith," and he set his head against the door handle to open the door completely.

Because he had to open the door in this way, it was already open very wide without him yet being really visible. He first had to turn himself slowly around the edge of the door, very carefully, of course, if he did not want to fall awkwardly on his back right at the entrance into the room. He was still preoccupied with this difficult movement and had no time to pay attention to anything else, when he heard the manager exclaim a loud "Oh!" (it sounded like the wind whistling), and now he saw him, nearest to the door, pressing his hand against his open mouth and moving slowly back, as if an invisible constant force was pushing him away. His mother (in spite of the presence of the manager she was standing here with her hair sticking up on end, still a mess from the night) with her hands clasped was looking at his father; she then went two steps towards Gregor and collapsed right in the middle of her skirts spreading out all around her, her face sunk on her breast, completely concealed. His father clenched his fist with a hostile expression, as if he wished to push Gregor back into his room, then looked uncertainly around the living room, covered his eyes with his hands, and cried so that his mighty breast shook.

At this point Gregor did not take one step into the room, but leaned his body from the inside against the firmly bolted wing of the door, so that only half his body was visible, as well as his head, tilted sideways, with which he peeped over at the others. Meanwhile it had become much brighter. Standing out clearly from the other side of the street was a part of the endless gray-black house situated opposite (it was a hospital) with its severe regular windows breaking up the facade. The rain was still coming down, but only in large individual drops visibly and firmly thrown down one by one onto the ground. The breakfast dishes were standing piled around on the table, because for his father breakfast was the most important meal time in the day, which he prolonged for hours by reading various newspapers. Directly across on the opposite wall hung a photograph of Gregor from the time of his military service; it was a picture of him as a lieutenant, as he, smiling and worry free, with his hand on his sword, demanded respect for his bearing and uniform. The door to the hall was ajar, and since the door to the apartment was also open, one saw out into the landing of the apartment and the start of the staircase going down.

"Now," said Gregor, well aware that he was the only one who had kept his composure. "I'll get dressed right away, pack up the collection of samples, and set off. You'll allow me to set out on my way, will you not? You see, Mr. Manager, I am not pig-headed, and I am happy to work. Traveling is exhausting, but I couldn't live without it. Where are you going, Mr. Manager? To the office? Really? Will you report everything truthfully? A person can be incapable of work momentarily, but that is precisely the best time to remember the earlier achievements and to consider that later, after the obstacles have been shoved aside, the person will work all the more keenly and intensely. I am really so indebted to Mr. Chief—you know that perfectly well. On the other hand, I am concerned about my parents and my sister. I'm in a fix, but I'll work myself out of it again. Don't make things more difficult for me than they already are. Speak up on my behalf in the office! People don't like traveling salesmen. I know that. People think they earn pots of money and thus lead a fine life. People don't even have any special reason to think through this judgment more clearly. But you, Mr. Manager, you have a better perspective on the interconnections than the other people, even, I tell you in total confidence, a better perspective than Mr. Chairman himself, who in his capacity as the employer may let his judgment make casual mistakes at the expense of an employee. You also know well enough that the traveling salesman who is outside the office almost the entire year can become so easily a victim of gossip, coincidences, and groundless complaints, against which it's impossible for him to defend himself, since for the most part he doesn't hear about them at all and only then when he's exhausted after finishing a trip, and gets to feel in his own body at home the nasty consequences, which can't be thoroughly explored back to their origins. Mr. Manager, don't leave without speaking a word telling me that you'll at least concede that I'm a little in the right!"

But at Gregor's first words the manager had already turned away, and now he looked back at Gregor over his twitching shoulders with pursed lips. During Gregor's speech he was not still for a moment, but was moving away towards the door, without taking his eyes off Gregor, but really gradually, as if there was a secret ban on leaving the room. He was already in the hall, and after the sudden movement with which he finally pulled his foot out of the living room, one could have believed that he had just burned the sole of his foot. In the hall, however, he stretched out his right hand away from his body towards the staircase, as if some truly supernatural relief was waiting for him there.

Gregor realized that he must not under any circumstances allow the manager to go away in this frame of mind, especially if his position in the firm was not to be placed in the greatest danger. His parents did not understand all this very well. Over the long years, they had developed the conviction that Gregor was set up for life in his firm and, in addition, they had so much to do nowadays with their present troubles that all foresight was foreign to them. But Gregor had this foresight. The manager must be held back, calmed down, convinced, and finally won over. The future of Gregor and his family really depended on it! If only the sister had been there! She was clever. She had already cried while Gregor was still lying quietly on his back. And the manager, this friend of the ladies, would certainly let himself be guided by her. She would have closed the door to the apartment and talked him out of his fright in the hall. But the sister was not even there. Gregor must deal with it himself.

Without thinking that as yet he didn't know anything about his present ability to move and without thinking that his speech possibly (indeed probably) had once again not been understood, he left the wing of the door, pushed himself through the opening, and wanted to go over to the manager, who was already holding tight onto the handrail with both hands on the landing in a ridiculous way. But as he looked for something to hold onto, with a small scream Gregor immediately fell down onto his numerous little legs. Scarcely had this happened, when he felt for the first time that morning a general physical well being. The small limbs had firm floor under them; they obeyed perfectly, as he noticed to his joy, and strove to carry him forward in the direction he wanted. Right away he believed that the final amelioration of all his suffering was immediately at hand. But at the very moment when he lay on the floor rocking in a restrained manner quite close and directly across from his mother (apparently totally sunk into herself) she suddenly sprang right up with her arms spread far apart and her fingers extended and cried out, "Help, for God's sake, help!" She held her head bowed down, as if she wanted to view Gregor better, but ran senselessly back, contradicting that gesture, forgetting that behind her stood the table with all the dishes on it. When she reached the table, she sat down heavily on it, as if absent-mindedly, and did not appear to notice at all that next to her coffee was pouring out onto the carpet in a full stream from the large overturned container.

"Mother, mother," said Gregor quietly, and looked over towards her. The manager momentarily had disappeared completely from his mind; by contrast, at the sight of the flowing coffee he couldn't stop himself snapping his jaws in the air a few times . At that his mother screamed all over again, hurried from the table, and collapsed into the arms of his father, who was rushing towards her. But Gregor had no time right now for his parents: the manager was already on the staircase. His chin level with the banister, the manager looked back for the last time. Gregor took an initial movement to catch up to him if possible. But the manager must have suspected something, because he made a leap down over a few stairs and disappeared, still shouting "Huh!" The sound echoed throughout the entire stairwell.

Now, unfortunately this flight of the manager also seemed completely to bewilder his father, who earlier had been relatively calm, for instead of running after the manager himself or at least not hindering Gregor from his pursuit, with his right hand he grabbed hold of the manager's cane, which he had left behind with his hat and overcoat on a chair. With his left hand, his father picked up a large newspaper from the table and, stamping his feet on the floor, he set out to drive Gregor back into his room by waving the cane and the newspaper. No request of Gregor's was of any use; no request would even be understood. No matter how willing he was to turn his head respectfully, his father just stomped all the harder with his feet.

Across the room from him his mother had pulled open a window, in spite of the cool weather, and leaning out with her hands on her cheeks, she pushed her face far outside the window. Between the alley and the stair well a strong draught came up, the curtains on the window flew around, the newspapers on the table swished, and individual sheets fluttered down over the floor. The father relentlessly pressed forward pushing out sibilants, like a wild man. Now, Gregor had no practice at all in going backwards; it was really going very slowly. If Gregor only had been allowed to turn himself around, he would have been in his room right away, but he was afraid to make his father impatient by the time-consuming process of turning around, and each moment he faced the threat of a mortal blow on his back or his head from the cane in his father's hand. Finally Gregor had no other option, for he noticed with horror that he did not understand yet how to maintain his direction going backwards. And so he began, amid constantly anxious sideways glances in his father's direction, to turn himself around as quickly as possible (although in truth this was only very slowly). Perhaps his father noticed his good intentions, for he did not disrupt Gregor in this motion, but with the tip of the cane from a distance he even directed here and there Gregor's rotating movement.

If only there hadn't been his father's unbearable hissing! Because of that Gregor totally lost his head. He was already almost totally turned around, when, always with this hissing in his ear, he just made a mistake and turned himself back a little. But when he finally was successful in getting his head in front of the door opening, it became clear that his body was too wide to go through any further. Naturally his father, in his present mental state, had no idea of opening the other wing of the door a bit to create a suitable passage for Gregor to get through. His single fixed thought was that Gregor must get into his room as quickly as possible. He would never have allowed the elaborate preparations that Gregor required to orient himself and thus perhaps get through the door. On the contrary, as if there were no obstacle and with a peculiar noise, he now drove Gregor forwards. Behind Gregor the sound was at this point no longer like the voice of only a single father. Now it was really no longer a joke, and Gregor forced himself, come what might, into the door. One side of his body was lifted up. He lay at an angle in the door opening. His one flank was sore with the scraping. On the white door ugly blotches were left. Soon he was stuck fast and would have not been able to move any more on his own. The tiny legs on one side hung twitching in the air above, the ones on the other side were pushed painfully into the floor. Then his father gave him one really strong liberating push from behind, and he scurried, bleeding severely, far into the interior of his room. The door was slammed shut with the cane, and finally it was quiet.

II

Gregor first woke up from his heavy swoon-like sleep in the evening twilight. He would certainly have woken up soon afterwards without any disturbance, for he felt himself sufficiently rested and wide awake, although it appeared to him as if a hurried step and a cautious closing of the door to the hall had aroused him. The shine of the electric streetlights lay pale here and there on the ceiling and on the higher parts of the furniture, but underneath around Gregor it was dark. He pushed himself slowly toward the door, still groping awkwardly with his feelers, which he now learned to value for the first time, to check what was happening there. His left side seemed one single long unpleasantly stretched scar, and he really had to hobble on his two rows of legs. In addition, one small leg had been seriously wounded in the course of the morning incident (it was almost a miracle that only one had been hurt) and dragged lifelessly behind.

By the door he first noticed what had really lured him there: it was the smell of something to eat. For there stood a bowl filled with sweetened milk, in which swam tiny pieces of white bread. He almost laughed with joy, for he now had a much greater hunger than in the morning, and he immediately dipped his head almost up to and over his eyes down into the milk. But he soon drew it back again in disappointment, not just because it was difficult for him to eat on account of his delicate left side (he could eat only if his entire panting body worked in a coordinated way), but also because the milk, which otherwise was his favorite drink and which his sister had certainly placed there for that reason, did not appeal to him at all. He turned away from the bowl almost with aversion and crept back into the middle of the room.

In the living room, as Gregor saw through the crack in the door, the gas was lit, but where on other occasions at this time of day the father was accustomed to read the afternoon newspaper in a loud voice to his mother and sometimes also to his sister, at the moment not a sound was audible. Now, perhaps this reading aloud, about which his sister always spoken and written to him, had recently fallen out of their general routine. But it was so still all around, in spite of the fact that the apartment was certainly not empty. "What a quiet life the family leads", said Gregor to himself and, as he stared fixedly out in front of him into the darkness, he felt a great pride that he had been able to provide such a life in a beautiful apartment like this for his parents and his sister. But how would things go if now all tranquility, all prosperity, all contentment should come to a horrible end? In order not to lose himself in such thoughts, Gregor preferred to set himself moving and crawled up and down in his room.

Once during the long evening one side door and then the other door was opened just a tiny crack and quickly closed again. Someone presumably needed to come in but had then thought better of it. Gregor immediately took up a position by the living room door, determined to bring in the hesitant visitor somehow or other or at least to find out who it might be. But now the door was not opened any more, and Gregor waited in vain. Earlier, when the door had been barred, they had all wanted to come in to him; now, when he had opened one door and when the others had obviously been opened during the day, no one came any more, and the keys were stuck in the locks on the outside.

The light in the living room was turned off only late at night, and now it was easy to establish that his parents and his sister had stayed awake all this time, for one could hear clearly as all three moved away on tiptoe. Now it was certain that no one would come into Gregor any more until the morning. Thus, he had a long time to think undisturbed about how he should reorganize his life from scratch. But the high, open room, in which he was compelled to lie flat on the floor, made him anxious, without his being able to figure out the reason, for he had lived in the room for five years. With a half unconscious turn and not without a slight shame he scurried under the couch, where, in spite of the fact that his back was a little cramped and he could no longer lift up his head, he felt very comfortable and was sorry only that his body was too wide to fit completely under it.

There he remained the entire night, which he spent partly in a state of semi-sleep, out of which his hunger constantly woke him with a start, but partly in a state of worry and murky hopes, which all led to the conclusion that for the time being he would have to keep calm and with patience and the greatest consideration for his family tolerate the troubles which in his present condition he was now forced to cause them.

Already early in the morning (it was still almost night) Gregor had an opportunity to test the power of the decisions he had just made, for his sister, almost fully dressed, opened the door from the hall into his room and looked eagerly inside. She did not find him immediately, but when she noticed him under the couch (God, he had to be somewhere or other; for he could hardly fly away) she got such a shock that, without being able to control herself, she slammed the door shut once again from the outside. However, as if she was sorry for her behaviour, she immediately opened the door again and walked in on her tiptoes, as if she was in the presence of a serious invalid or a total stranger. Gregor had pushed his head forward just to the edge of the couch and was observing her. Would she really notice that he had left the milk standing, not indeed from any lack of hunger, and would she bring in something else to eat more suitable for him? If she did not do it on her own, he would sooner starve to death than call her attention to the fact, although he had a really powerful urge to move beyond the couch, throw himself at his sister's feet, and beg her for something or other good to eat. But his sister noticed right away with astonishment that the bowl was still full, with only a little milk spilled around it. She picked it up immediately (although not with her bare hands but with a rag), and took it out of the room. Gregor was extremely curious what she would bring as a substitute, and he pictured to himself different ideas about that. But he never could have guessed what his sister out of the goodness of her heart in fact did. She brought him, to test his taste, an entire selection, all spread out on an old newspaper. There were old half-rotten vegetables, bones from the evening meal, covered with a white sauce which had almost solidified, some raisins and almonds, cheese, which Gregor had declared inedible two days earlier, a slice of dry bread, a slice of salted bread smeared with butter. In addition to all this, she put down a bowl (probably designated once and for all as Gregor's) into which she had poured some water. And out of her delicacy of feeling, since she knew that Gregor would not eat in front of her, she went away very quickly and even turned the key in the lock, so that Gregor could now observe that he could make himself as comfortable as he wished. Gregor's small limbs buzzed as the time for eating had come. His wounds must, in any case, have already healed completely. He felt no handicap on that score. He was astonished at that and thought about it, how more than a month ago he had cut his finger slightly with a knife and how this wound had hurt enough even the day before yesterday.

"Am I now going to be less sensitive," he thought, already sucking greedily on the cheese, which had strongly attracted him right away, more than all the other foods. Quickly and with his eyes watering with satisfaction, he ate one after the other the cheese, the vegetables, and the sauce; the fresh food, by contrast, didn't taste good to him. He couldn't bear the smell and even carried the things he wanted to eat a little distance away. By the time his sister slowly turned the key as a sign that he should withdraw, he was long finished and now lay lazily in the same spot. The noise immediately startled him, in spite of the fact that he was already almost asleep, and he scurried back again under the couch. But it cost him great self-control to remain under the couch, even for the short time his sister was in the room, because his body had filled out somewhat on account of the rich meal and in the narrow space there he could scarcely breathe. In the midst of minor attacks of asphyxiation, he looked at her with somewhat protruding eyes, as his unsuspecting sister swept up with a broom, not just the remnants, but even the foods which Gregor had not touched at all, as if these were also now useless, and as she dumped everything quickly into a bucket, which she closed with a wooden lid, and then carried all of it out of the room. She had hardly turned around before Gregor had already dragged himself out from the couch, stretched out, and let his body expand.

In this way Gregor got his food every day, once in the morning, when his parents and the servant girl were still asleep, and a second time after the common noon meal, for his parents were, as before, asleep then for a little while, and the servant girl was sent off by his sister on some errand or other. Certainly they would not have wanted Gregor to starve to death, but perhaps they could not have endured finding out what he ate other than by hearsay. Perhaps his sister wanted to spare them what was possibly only a small grief, for they were really suffering quite enough already.

What sorts of excuses people had used on that first morning to get the doctor and the locksmith out of the house Gregor was completely unable to ascertain. Since he was not comprehensible, no one, not even his sister, thought that he might be able to understand others, and thus, when his sister was in her room, he had to be content with listening now and then to her sighs and invocations to the saints. Only later, when she had grown somewhat accustomed to everything (naturally there could never be any talk of her growing completely accustomed to it) Gregor sometimes caught a comment which was intended to be friendly or could be interpreted as such. "Well, today it tasted good to him," she said, if Gregor had really cleaned up what he had to eat; whereas, in the reverse situation, which gradually repeated itself more and more frequently, she used to say sadly, "Now everything has stopped again."

But while Gregor could get no new information directly, he did hear a good deal from the room next door, and as soon as he heard voices, he scurried right away to the relevant door and pressed his entire body against it. In the early days especially, there was no conversation which was not concerned with him in some way or other, even if only in secret. For two days at all meal times discussions on that subject could be heard on how people should now behave; but they also talked about the same subject in the times between meals, for there were always at least two family members at home, since no one really wanted to remain in the house alone and people could not under any circumstances leave the apartment completely empty. In addition, on the very first day the servant girl (it was not completely clear what and how much she knew about what had happened) on her knees had begged his mother to let her go immediately, and when she said good bye about fifteen minutes later, she thanked them for the dismissal with tears in her eyes, as if she was receiving the greatest favour which people had shown her there, and, without anyone demanding it from her, she swore a fearful oath not to betray anyone, not even the slightest bit.

Now his sister had to team up with his mother to do the cooking, although that didn't create much trouble because people were eating almost nothing. Again and again Gregor listened as one of them vainly invited another one to eat and received no answer other than "Thank you. I have enough" or something like that. And perhaps they had stopped having anything to drink, too. His sister often asked his father whether he wanted to have a beer and gladly offered to fetch it herself, and when his father was silent, she said, in order to remove any reservations he might have, that she could send the caretaker's wife to get it. But then his father finally said a resounding "No," and nothing more would be spoken about it.

Already during the first day his father laid out all the financial circumstances and prospects to his mother and to his sister as well. From time to time he stood up from the table and pulled out of the small lockbox salvaged from his business, which had collapsed five years previously, some document or other or some notebook. The sound was audible as he opened up the complicated lock and, after removing what he was looking for, locked it up again. These explanations by his father were, in part, the first enjoyable thing that Gregor had the chance to listen to since his imprisonment. He had thought that nothing at all was left over for his father from that business; at least his father had told him nothing to the contradict that view, and Gregor in any case hadn't asked him about it. At the time Gregor's only concern had been to devote everything he had in order to allow his family to forget as quickly as possible the business misfortune which had brought them all into a state of complete hopelessness. And so at that point he'd started to work with a special intensity and from an assistant had become, almost overnight, a traveling salesman, who naturally had entirely different possibilities for earning money and whose successes at work at once were converted into the form of cash commissions, which could be set out on the table at home in front of his astonished and delighted family. Those had been beautiful days, and they had never come back afterwards, at least not with the same splendour, in spite of the fact that Gregor later earned so much money that he was in a position to bear the expenses of the entire family, expenses which he, in fact, did bear. They had become quite accustomed to it, both the family and Gregor as well. They took the money with thanks, and he happily surrendered it, but the special warmth was no longer present. Only the sister had remained still close to Gregor, and it was his secret plan to send her (in contrast to Gregor she loved music very much and knew how to play the violin charmingly) next year to the conservatory, regardless of the great expense which that must necessitate and which would be made up in other ways. Now and then during Gregor's short stays in the city the conservatory was mentioned in conversations with his sister, but always only as a beautiful dream, whose realization was unimaginable, and their parents never listened to these innocent expectations with pleasure. But Gregor thought about them with scrupulous consideration and intended to explain the matter ceremoniously on Christmas Eve.

In his present situation, such futile ideas went through his head, while he pushed himself right up against the door and listened. Sometimes in his general exhaustion he couldn't listen any more and let his head bang listlessly against the door, but he immediately pulled himself together, for even the small sound which he made by this motion was heard near by and silenced everyone. " There he goes on again," said his father after a while, clearly turning towards the door, and only then would the interrupted conversation gradually be resumed again.

Gregor found out clearly enough (for his father tended to repeat himself often in his explanations, partly because he had not personally concerned himself with these matters for a long time now, and partly also because his mother did not understand everything right away the first time) that, in spite all bad luck, a fortune, although a very small one, was available from the old times, which the interest (which had not been touched) had in the intervening time gradually allowed to increase a little. Furthermore, in addition to this, the money which Gregor had brought home every month (he had kept

31

only a few florins for himself) had not been completely spent and had grown into a small capital amount. Gregor, behind his door, nodded eagerly, rejoicing over this unanticipated foresight and frugality. True, with this excess money, he could have paid off more of his father's debt to his employer and the day on which he could be rid of this position would have been a lot closer, but now things were doubtless better the way his father had arranged them.

At the moment, however, this money was nowhere near sufficient to permit the family to live on the interest payments. Perhaps it would be enough to maintain the family for one or at most two years, that's all. Thus it came only to an amount which one should not really take out and which must be set aside for an emergency. But the money to live on must be earned. Now, his father was a healthy man, although he was old, who had not worked at all for five years now and thus could not be counted on for very much. He had in these five years, the first holidays of his trouble-filled but unsuccessful life, put on a good deal of fat and thus had become really heavy. And should his old mother now maybe work for money, a woman who suffered from asthma, for whom wandering through the apartment even now was a great strain and who spent every second day on the sofa by the open window labouring for breath? Should his sister earn money, a girl who was still a seventeen-year-old child, whose earlier life style had been so very delightful that it had consisted of dressing herself nicely, sleeping in late, helping around the house, taking part in a few modest enjoyments and, above all, playing the violin? When it came to talking about this need to earn money, at first Gregor went away from the door and threw himself on the cool leather sofa beside the door, for he was quite hot from shame and sorrow.

Often he lay there all night long. He didn't sleep a moment and just scratched on the leather for hours at a time. He undertook the very difficult task of shoving a chair over to the window. Then he crept up on the window sill and, braced in the chair, leaned against the window to look out, obviously with some memory or other of the satisfaction which that used to bring him in earlier times. Actually from day to day he perceived things with less and less clarity, even those a short distance away: the hospital across the street, the all too frequent sight of which he had previously cursed, was not visible at all any more, and if he had not been precisely aware that he lived in the quiet but completely urban Charlotte Street, he could have believed that from his window he was peering out at a featureless wasteland, in which the gray heaven and the gray earth had merged and were indistinguishable. His attentive sister must have observed a couple of times that the chair stood by the window; then, after cleaning up the room, each time she pushed the chair back right against the window and from now on she even left the inner casement open.

If Gregor had only been able to speak to his sister and thank her for everything that she had to do for him, he would have tolerated her service more easily. As it was he suffered under it. The sister admittedly sought to cover up the awkwardness of everything as much as possible, and, as time went by, she naturally got more successful at it. But with the passing of time Gregor also came to understand everything more precisely. Even her entrance was terrible for him. As soon as she entered, she ran straight to the window, without taking the time to shut the door (in spite of the fact that she was otherwise very considerate in sparing anyone the sight of Gregor's room), and yanked the window open with eager hands, as if she was almost suffocating, and remained for a while by the window breathing deeply, even when it was still so cold. With this running and noise she frightened Gregor twice every day. The entire time he trembled under the couch, and yet he knew very well that she would certainly have spared him gladly if it had only been possible to remain with the window closed in a room where Gregor lived.

On one occasion (about one month had already gone by since Gregor's transformation, and there was now no particular reason any more for his sister to be startled at Gregor's appearance) she came a little earlier than usual and came upon Gregor as he was still looking out the window, immobile and well positioned to frighten someone. It would not have come as a surprise to Gregor if she had not come in, since his position was preventing her from opening the window immediately. But she not only did not step inside; she even retreated and shut the door. A stranger really could have concluded from this that Gregor had been lying in wait for her and wanted to bite her. Of course, Gregor immediately concealed himself under the couch, but he had to wait until the noon meal before his sister returned, and she seemed much less calm than usual. From this he realized that his appearance was still constantly intolerable to her and must remain intolerable in future, and that she really had to exert a lot of self-control not to run away from a glimpse of only the small part of his body which stuck out from under the couch. In order to spare her even this sight, one day he dragged the sheet on his back onto the couch (this task took him four hours) and arranged it in such a way that he was now completely concealed and his sister, even if she bent down, could not see him. If this sheet was not necessary as far as she was concerned, then she could remove it, for it was clear enough that Gregor could not derive any pleasure from isolating himself away so completely. But she left the sheet just as it was, and Gregor believed he even caught a look of gratitude when on one occasion he carefully lifted up the sheet a little with his head to check as his sister took stock of the new arrangement.

In the first two weeks his parents could not bring themselves to visit him, and he often heard how they fully acknowledged his sister's present work; whereas, earlier they had often got annoyed at his sister because she had seemed to them a somewhat useless young woman. However, now both his father and his mother often waited in front of Gregor's door while his sister cleaned up inside, and as soon as she came out she had to explain in detail how things looked in the room, what Gregor had eaten, how he had behaved this time, and whether perhaps a slight improvement was perceptible. In any event, his mother comparatively soon wanted to visit Gregor, but his father and his sister restrained her, at first with reasons which Gregor listened to very attentively and which he completely endorsed. Later, however, they had to hold her back forcefully, and when she then cried "Let me go to Gregor. He's my unlucky son! Don't you understand that I have to go to him?" Gregor then thought that perhaps it would be a good thing if his mother came in, not every day, of course, but maybe once a week. She understood everything much better than his sister, who in spite of all her courage was still a child and, in the last analysis, had perhaps undertaken such a difficult task only out of childish recklessness.

Gregor's wish to see his mother was soon realized. While during the day Gregor, out of consideration for his parents, did not want to show himself by the window, he couldn't crawl around very much on the few square metres of the floor. He found it difficult to bear lying quietly during the night, and soon eating no longer gave him the slightest pleasure. So for diversion he acquired the habit of crawling back and forth across the walls and ceiling. He was especially fond of hanging from the ceiling. The experience was quite different from lying on the floor. It was easier to breathe, a slight vibration went through his body, and in the midst of the almost happy amusement which Gregor found up there, it could happen that, to his own surprise, he let go and hit the floor. However, now he naturally controlled his body quite differently, and he did not injure himself in such a great fall. His sister noticed immediately the new amusement which Gregor had found for himself (for as he crept around he left behind here and there traces of his sticky stuff), and so she got the idea of making Gregor's creeping around as easy as possible and thus of removing the furniture which got in the way, especially the chest of drawers and the writing desk.

But she was in no position to do this by herself. She did not dare to ask her father to help, and the servant girl would certainly not have assisted her, for although this girl, about sixteen years old, had courageously remained since the dismissal of the previous cook, she had begged for the privilege of being allowed to stay permanently confined to the kitchen and of having to open the door only in answer to a special summons. Thus, his sister had no other choice but to involve his mother while his father was absent. His mother approached Gregor's room with cries of excited joy, but she fell silent at the door. Of course, his sister first checked whether everything in the room was in order. Only then did she let his mother walk in. In great haste Gregor had drawn the sheet down even further and wrinkled it more. The whole thing really looked just like a coverlet thrown carelessly over the couch. On this occasion, Gregor held back from spying out from under the sheet. Thus, he refrained from looking at his mother this time and was just happy that she had come. "Come on; he is not visible," said his sister, and evidently led his mother by the hand. Now Gregor listened as these two weak women shifted the still heavy old chest of drawers from its position, and as his sister constantly took on herself the greatest part of the work, without listening to the warnings of his mother who was afraid that she would strain herself. The work lasted a long time. After about a quarter of an hour had already gone by his mother said that it would be better if they left the chest of drawers where it was, because, in the first place, it was too heavy: they would not be finished before his father's arrival, and with the chest of drawers in the middle of the room it would block all Gregor's pathways, but, in the second place, it might not be certain that Gregor would be pleased with the removal of the furniture. To her the reverse seemed to be true; the sight of the empty walls pierced her right to the heart, and why should Gregor not feel the same, since he had been accustomed to the room furnishings for a long time and in an empty room would thus feel himself abandoned.

"And is it not the case," his mother concluded very quietly, almost whispering as if she wished to prevent Gregor, whose exact location she really didn't know, from hearing even the sound of her voice (for she was convinced that he did not understand her words), "and isn't it a fact that by removing the furniture we're showing that we're giving up all hope of an improvement and are leaving him to his own resources without any consideration? I think it would be best if we tried to keep the room exactly in the condition in which it was before, so that, when Gregor returns to us, he finds everything unchanged and can forget the intervening time all the more easily."

As he heard his mother's words Gregor realized that the lack of all immediate human contact, together with the monotonous life surrounded by the family over the course of these two months must have confused his understanding, because otherwise he couldn't explain to himself that he in all seriousness could've been so keen to have his room emptied. Was he really eager to let the warm room, comfortably furnished with pieces he had inherited, be turned into a cavern in which he would, of course, then be able to crawl about in all directions without disturbance, but at the same time with a quick and complete forgetting of his human past as well? Was he then at this point already on the verge of forgetting and was it only the voice of his mother, which he had not heard for along time, that had aroused him? Nothing was to be removed; everything must remain. In his condition he couldn't function without the beneficial influences of his furniture. And if the furniture prevented him from carrying out his senseless crawling about all over the place, then there was no harm in that, but rather a great benefit.

But his sister unfortunately thought otherwise. She had grown accustomed, certainly not without justification, so far as the discussion of matters concerning Gregor was concerned, to act as an special expert with respect to their parents, and so now the mother's advice was for his sister sufficient reason to insist on the removal, not only of the chest of drawers and the writing desk, which were the only items she had thought about at first, but also of all the furniture, with the exception of the indispensable couch. Of course, it was not only childish defiance and her recent very unexpected and hard won self-confidence which led her to this demand. She had also actually observed that Gregor needed a great deal of room to creep about; the furniture, on the other hand, as far as one could see, was not of the slightest use.

But perhaps the enthusiastic sensibility of young women of her age also played a role. This feeling sought release at every opportunity, and with it Grete now felt tempted to want to make Gregor's situation even more terrifying, so that then she would be able to do even more for him than now. For surely no one except Grete would ever trust themselves to enter a room in which Gregor ruled the empty walls all by himself. And so she did not let herself be dissuaded from her decision by her mother, who in this room seemed uncertain of herself in her sheer agitation and soon kept quiet, helping his sister with all her energy to get the chest of drawers out of the room. Now, Gregor could still do without the chest of drawers if need be, but the writing desk really had to stay. And scarcely had the women left the room with the chest of drawers, groaning as they pushed it, when Gregor stuck his head out from under the sofa to take a look how he could intervene cautiously and with as much consideration as possible. But unfortunately it was his mother who came back into the room first, while Grete had her arms wrapped around the chest of drawers in the next room and was rocking it back and forth by herself, without moving it from its position. His mother was not used to the sight of Gregor; he could have made her ill, and so, frightened, Gregor scurried backwards right to the other end of the sofa, but he could no longer prevent the sheet from moving forward a little. That was enough to catch his mother's attention. She came to a halt, stood still for a moment, and then went back to Grete.

Although Gregor kept repeating to himself over and over that really nothing unusual was going on, that only a few pieces of furniture were being rearranged, he soon had to admit to himself that the movements of the women to and fro, their quiet conversations, the scratching of the furniture on the floor affected him like a great swollen commotion on all sides, and, so firmly was he pulling in his head and legs and pressing his body into the floor, he had to tell himself unequivocally that he wouldn't be able to endure all this much longer. They were cleaning out his room, taking away from him everything he cherished; they had already dragged out the chest of drawers in which the fret saw and other tools were kept, and they were now loosening the writing desk which was fixed tight to the floor, the desk on which he, as a business student, a school student, indeed even as an elementary school student, had written out his assignments. At that moment he really didn't have any more time to check the good intentions of the two women, whose existence he had in any case almost forgotten, because in their exhaustion they were working really silently, and the heavy stumbling of their feet was the only sound to be heard.

And so he scuttled out (the women were just propping themselves up on the writing desk in the next room in order to take a breather) changing the direction of his path four times. He really didn't know what he should rescue first. Then he saw hanging conspicuously on the wall, which was otherwise already empty, the picture of the woman dressed in nothing but fur. He quickly scurried up over it and pressed himself against the glass that held it in place and which made his hot abdomen feel good. At least this picture, which Gregor at the moment completely concealed, surely no one would now take away. He twisted his head towards the door of the living room to observe the women as they came back in.

They had not allowed themselves very much rest and were coming back right away. Grete had placed her arm around her mother and held her tightly. "So what shall we take now?" said Grete and looked around her. Then her glance crossed with Gregor's from the wall. She kept her composure only because her mother was there. She bent her face towards her mother in order to prevent her from looking around, and said, although in a trembling voice and too quickly, "Come, wouldn't it be better to go back to the living room for just another moment?" Grete's purpose was clear to Gregor: she wanted to bring his mother to a safe place and then chase him down from the wall. Well, let her just attempt that! He squatted on his picture and did not hand it over. He would sooner spring into Grete's face.

But Grete's words had immediately made the mother very uneasy. She walked to the side, caught sight of the enormous brown splotch on the flowered wallpaper, and, before she became truly aware that what she was looking at was Gregor, screamed out in a high pitched raw voice "Oh God, oh God" and fell with outstretched arms, as if she was surrendering everything, down onto the couch and lay there motionless. "Gregor, you …," cried out his sister with a raised fist and an urgent glare. Since his transformation those were the first words which she had directed right at him. She ran into the room next door to bring some spirits or other with which she could revive her mother from her fainting spell. Gregor wanted to help as well (there was time enough to save the picture), but he was stuck fast on the glass and had to tear himself loose forcefully. Then he also scurried into the next room, as if he could give his sister some advice, as in earlier times, but then he had to stand there idly behind her, while she rummaged about among various small bottles. Still, she was frightened when she turned around. A bottle fell onto the floor and shattered. A splinter of glass wounded Gregor in the face, some corrosive medicine or other dripped over him. Now, without lingering any longer, Grete took as many small bottles as she could hold and ran with them into her mother. She slammed the door shut with her foot. Gregor was now shut off from his mother, who was perhaps near death, thanks to him. He could not open the door, and he did not want to chase away his sister who had to remain with her mother. At this point he had nothing to do but wait, and overwhelmed with self-reproach and worry, he began to creep and crawl over everything: walls, furniture, and ceiling,. Finally, in his despair, as the entire room started to spin around him, he fell onto the middle of the large table.

A short time elapsed. Gregor lay there limply. All around was still. Perhaps that was a good sign. Then there was ring at the door. The servant girl was naturally shut up in her kitchen, and Grete must therefore go to open the door. The father had arrived. "What's happened," were his first words. Grete's appearance had told him everything. Grete replied with a dull voice; evidently she was pressing her face into her father's chest: "Mother fainted, but she's getting better now. Gregor has broken loose." "Yes, I have expected that," said his father, "I always told you that, but you women don't want to listen."

It was clear to Gregor that his father had badly misunderstood Grete's short message and was assuming that Gregor had committed some violent crime or other. Thus, Gregor now had to find his father to calm him down, for he had neither the time nor the opportunity to clarify things for him. And so he rushed away to the door of his room and pushed himself against it, so that his father could see right away as he entered from the hall that Gregor fully intended to return at once to his room, that it was not necessary to drive him back, but that one only needed to open the door and he would disappear immediately.

But his father was not in the mood to observe such niceties. "Ah," he yelled as soon as he entered, with a tone as if he were all at once angry and pleased. Gregor pulled his head back from the door and raised it in the direction of his father. He had not really pictured his father as he now stood there. Of course, what with his new style of creeping all around, he had in the past while neglected to pay attention to what was going on in the rest of the apartment, as he had done before, and really should have grasped the fact that he would encounter different conditions. Nevertheless, nevertheless, was that still his father? Was that the same man who had lain exhausted and buried in bed in earlier days when Gregor was setting out on a business trip, who had received him on the evenings of his return in a sleeping gown and arm chair, totally incapable of standing up, who had only lifted his arm as a sign of happiness, and who in their rare strolls together a few Sundays a year and on the important holidays made his way slowly forwards between Gregor and his mother (who themselves moved slowly), always a bit more slowly than them, bundled up in his old coat, all the time setting down his walking stick carefully, and who, when he had wanted to say something, almost always stood still and gathered his entourage around him?

But now he was standing up really straight, dressed in a tight fitting blue uniform with gold buttons, like the ones servants wear in a banking company. Above the high stiff collar of his jacket his firm double chin stuck out prominently, beneath his bushy eyebrows the glance of his black eyes was freshly penetrating and alert, his otherwise disheveled white hair was combed down into a carefully exact shining part. He threw his cap, on which a gold monogram (apparently the symbol of the bank) was affixed, in an arc across the entire room onto the sofa and moved, throwing back the edge of the long coat of his uniform, with his hands in his trouser pockets and a grim face, right up to Gregor.

He really didn't know what he had in mind, but he raised his foot uncommonly high anyway, and Gregor was astonished at the gigantic size of his sole of his boot. However, he did not linger on that point. For he knew from the first day of his new life that as far as he was concerned his father considered the greatest force the only appropriate response. And so he scurried away from his father, stopped when his father remained standing, and scampered forward again when his father merely stirred. In this way they made their way around the room repeatedly, without anything decisive taking place; indeed because of the slow pace it didn't look like a chase. Gregor remained on the floor for the time being, especially as he was afraid that his father could take a flight up onto the wall or the ceiling as an act of real malice. At any event Gregor had to tell himself that he couldn't keep up this running around for a long time, because whenever his father took a single step, he had to go through an enormous number of movements. Already he was starting to suffer from a shortage of breath, just as in his earlier days his lungs had been quite unreliable. As he now staggered around in this way in order to gather all his energies for running, hardly keeping his eyes open, in his listlessness he had no notion at all of any escape other than by running and had almost already forgotten that the walls were available to him, although they were obstructed by carefully carved furniture full of sharp points and spikes— at that moment something or other thrown casually flew down close by and rolled in front of him. It was an apple; immediately a second one flew after it. Gregor stood still in fright. Further flight was useless, for his father had decided to bombard him.

From the fruit bowl on the sideboard his father had filled his pockets, and now, without for the moment taking accurate aim, was throwing apple after apple. These small red apples rolled as if electrified around on the floor and collided with each other. A weakly thrown apple grazed Gregor's back but skidded off harmlessly. However another thrown immediately after that one drove into Gregor's back really hard. Gregor wanted to drag himself off, as if the unexpected and incredible pain would go away if he changed his position. But he felt as if he was nailed in place and lay stretched out completely confused in all his senses. Only with his final glance did he notice how the door of his room was pulled open and how, right in front of his sister (who was yelling), his mother ran out in her undergarments, for his sister had undressed her in order to give her some freedom to breathe in her fainting spell, and how his mother then ran up to his father, on the way her tied up skirts one after the other slipped toward the floor, and how, tripping over her skirts, she hurled herself onto his father and, throwing her arms around him, in complete union with him—but at this moment Gregor's powers of sight gave way—as her hands reached to the back of his father's head and she begged him to spare Gregor's life.

III

Gregor's serious wound, from which he suffered for over a month (since no one ventured to remove the apple, it remained in his flesh as a visible reminder), seemed by itself to have reminded the father that, in spite of his present unhappy and hateful appearance, Gregor was a member of the family, something one should not treat as an enemy, and that it was, on the contrary, a requirement of family duty to suppress one's aversion and to endure—nothing else, just endure. And if through his wound Gregor had now apparently lost for good his ability to move and for the time being needed many many minutes to crawl across this room, like an aged invalid (so far as creeping up high was concerned, that was unimaginable), nevertheless for this worsening of his condition, in his opinion, he did get completely satisfactory compensation, because every day towards evening the door to the living room, which he was in the habit of keeping a sharp eye on even one or two hours beforehand, was opened, so that he, lying down in the darkness of his room, invisible from the living room, could see the entire family at the illuminated table and listen to their conversation, to a certain extent with their common permission, a situation quite different from what happened before.

Of course, it was no longer the animated social interaction of former times, about which Gregor in small hotel rooms had always thought about with a certain longing, when, tired out, he had to throw himself in the damp bedclothes. For the most part what went on now was very quiet. After the evening meal the father fell asleep quickly in his arm chair; the mother and sister talked guardedly to each other in the stillness. Bent far over, the mother sewed fine undergarments for a fashion shop. The sister, who had taken on a job as a salesgirl, in the evening studied stenography and French, so as perhaps later to obtain a better position. Sometimes the father woke up and, as if he was quite ignorant that he had been asleep, said to the mother "How long you have been sewing today!" and went right back to sleep, while the mother and the sister smiled tiredly to each other.

With a sort of stubbornness the father refused to take off his servant's uniform even at home, and while his sleeping gown hung unused on the coat hook, the father dozed completely dressed in his place, as if he was always ready for his responsibility and even here was waiting for the voice of his superior. As result, in spite of all the care of the mother and sister, his uniform, which even at the start was not new, grew dirty, and Gregor looked, often for the entire evening, at this clothing, with stains all over it and with its gold buttons always polished, in which the old man, although very uncomfortable, slept peacefully nonetheless.

As soon as the clock struck ten, the mother tried encouraging the father gently to wake up and then persuading him to go to bed, on the ground that he couldn't get a proper sleep here and the father, who had to report for service at six o'clock, really needed a good sleep. But in his stubbornness, which had gripped him since he had become a servant, he insisted always on staying even longer by the table, although he regularly fell asleep and then could only be prevailed upon with the greatest difficulty to trade his chair for the bed. No matter how much the mother and sister might at that point work on him with small admonitions, for a quarter of an hour he would remain shaking his head slowly, his eyes closed, without standing up. The mother would pull him by the sleeve and speak flattering words into his ear; the sister would leave her work to help her mother, but that would not have the desired effect on the father. He would settle himself even more deeply in his arm chair. Only when the two women grabbed him under the armpits would he throw his eyes open, look back and forth at the mother and sister, and habitually say "This is a life. This is the peace and quiet of my old age." And propped up by both women, he would heave himself up, elaborately, as if for him it was the greatest travail, allow himself to be led to the door by the women, wave them away there, and proceed on his own from there, while the mother quickly threw down her sewing implements and the sister her pen in order to run after the father and help him some more.

In this overworked and exhausted family who had time to worry any longer about Gregor more than was absolutely necessary? The household was constantly getting smaller. The servant girl was now let go. A huge bony cleaning woman with white hair flapping all over her head came in the morning and the evening to do the heaviest work. The mother took care of everything else in addition to her considerable sewing work. It even happened that various pieces of family jewelry, which previously the mother and sister had been overjoyed to wear on social and festive occasions, were sold, as Gregor found out in the evening from the general discussion of the prices they had fetched. But the greatest complaint was always that they could not leave this apartment, which was too big for their present means, since it was impossible to imagine how Gregor might be moved. But Gregor fully recognized that it was not just consideration for him which was preventing a move (for he could have been transported easily in a suitable box with a few air holes); the main thing holding the family back from a change in living quarters was far more their complete hopelessness and the idea that they had been struck by a misfortune like no one else in their entire circle of relatives and acquaintances.

What the world demands of poor people they now carried out to an extreme degree. The father brought breakfast to the petty officials at the bank, the mother sacrificed herself for the undergarments of strangers, the sister behind her desk was at the beck and call of customers, but the family's energies did not extend any further. And the wound in his back began to pain Gregor all over again, when now mother and sister, after they had escorted the father to bed, came back, let their work lie, moved close together, and sat cheek to cheek and when his mother would now say, pointing to Gregor's room, "Close the door, Grete," and when Gregor was again in the darkness, while close by the women mingled their tears or, quite dry eyed, stared at the table.

Gregor spent his nights and days with hardly any sleep. Sometimes he thought that the next time the door opened he would take over the family arrangements just as he had earlier. In his imagination appeared again, after a long time, his employer and supervisor and the apprentices, the excessively gormless custodian, two or three friends from other businesses, a chambermaid from a hotel in the provinces, a loving fleeting memory, a female cashier from a hat shop, whom he had seriously, but too slowly courted—they all appeared mixed in with strangers or people he had already forgotten, but instead of helping him and his family, they were all unapproachable, and he was happy to see them disappear.

But then he was in no mood to worry about his family. He was filled with sheer anger over the wretched care he was getting, even though he couldn't imagine anything for which he might have an appetite. Still, he made plans about how he could take from the larder what he at all account deserved, even if he wasn't hungry. Without thinking any more about how one might be able to give Gregor special pleasure, the sister now kicked some food or other very quickly into his room in the morning and at noon, before she ran off to her shop, and in the evening, quite indifferent about whether the food had perhaps only been tasted or, what happened most frequently, remained entirely undisturbed, she whisked it out with one sweep of her broom. The task of cleaning his room, which she now always carried out in the evening, could not be done any more quickly. Streaks of dirt ran along the walls; here and there lay tangles of dust and garbage. At first, when his sister arrived, Gregor positioned himself in a particularly filthy corner in order with this posture to make something of a protest. But he could have well stayed there for weeks without his sister's changing her ways. Indeed, she perceived the dirt as much as he did, but she had decided just to let it stay.

In this business, with a touchiness which was quite new to her and which had generally taken over the entire family, she kept watch to see that the cleaning of Gregor's room remained reserved for her. Once his mother had undertaken a major cleaning of Gregor's room, which she had only completed successfully after using a few buckets of water. But the extensive dampness made Gregor sick and he lay supine, embittered and immobile on the couch. However, the mother's punishment was not delayed for long. For in the evening the sister had hardly observed the change in Gregor's room before she ran into the living room mightily offended and, in spite of her mother's hand lifted high in entreaty, broke out in a fit of crying. Her parents (the father had, of course, woken up with a start in his arm chair) at first looked at her astonished and helpless; until they started to get agitated. Turning to his right, the father heaped reproaches on the mother that she was not to take over the cleaning of Gregor's room from the sister and, turning to his left, he shouted at the sister that she would no longer be allowed to clean Gregor's room ever again, while the mother tried to pull the father, beside himself in his excitement, into the bed room; the sister, shaken by her crying fit, pounded on the table with her tiny fists, and Gregor hissed at all this, angry that no one thought about shutting the door and sparing him the sight of this commotion.

But even when the sister, exhausted from her daily work, had grown tired of caring for Gregor as she had before, even then the mother did not have to come at all on her behalf. And Gregor did not have to be neglected. For now the cleaning woman was there. This old widow, who in her long life must have managed to survive the worst with the help of her bony frame, had no real horror of Gregor. Without being in the least curious, she had once by chance opened Gregor's door. At the sight of Gregor, who, totally surprised, began to scamper here and there, although no one was chasing him, she remained standing with her hands folded across her stomach staring at him. Since then she did not fail to open the door furtively a little every morning and evening to look in on Gregor. At first, she also called him to her with words which she presumably thought were friendly, like "Come here for a bit, old dung beetle!" or "Hey, look at the old dung beetle!" Addressed in such a manner, Gregor answered nothing, but remained motionless in his place, as if the door had not been opened at all. If only, instead of allowing this cleaning woman to disturb him uselessly whenever she felt like it, they had instead given her orders to clean up his room every day! One day in the early morning (a hard downpour, perhaps already a sign of the coming spring, struck the window panes) when the cleaning woman started up once again with her usual conversation, Gregor was so bitter that he turned towards her, as if for an attack, although slowly and weakly. But instead of being afraid of him, the cleaning woman merely lifted up a chair standing close by the door and, as she stood there with her mouth wide open, her intention was clear: she would close her mouth only when the chair in her hand had been thrown down on Gregor's back. "This goes no further, all right?" she asked, as Gregor turned himself around again, and she placed the chair calmly back in the corner.

Gregor ate hardly anything any more. Only when he chanced to move past the food which had been prepared did he, as a game, take a bit into his mouth, hold it there for hours, and generally spit it out again. At first he thought it might be his sadness over the condition of his room which kept him from eating, but he very soon became reconciled to the alterations in his room. People had grown accustomed to put into storage in his room things which they couldn't put anywhere else, and at this point there were many such things, now that they had rented one room of the apartment to three lodgers. These solemn gentlemen (all three had full beards, as Gregor once found out through a crack in the door) were meticulously intent on tidiness, not only in their own room but (since they had now rented a room here) in the entire household, and particularly in the kitchen. They simply did not tolerate any useless or shoddy stuff. Moreover, for the most part they had brought with them their own pieces of furniture. Thus, many items had become superfluous, and these were not really things one could sell or things people wanted to throw out. All these items ended up in Gregor's room, even the box of ashes and the garbage pail from the kitchen. The cleaning woman, always in a hurry, simply flung anything that was momentarily useless into Gregor's room. Fortunately Gregor generally saw only the relevant object and the hand which held it. The cleaning woman perhaps was intending, when time and opportunity allowed, to take the stuff out again or to throw everything out all at once, but in fact the things remained lying there, wherever they had ended up at the first throw, unless Gregor squirmed his way through the accumulation of junk and moved it. At first he was forced to do this because otherwise there was no room for him to creep around, but later he did it with a with a growing pleasure, although after such movements, tired to death and feeling wretched, he didn't budge for hours.

Because the lodgers sometimes also took their evening meal at home in the common living room, the door to the living room stayed shut on many evenings. But Gregor had no trouble at all going without the open door. Already on many evenings when it was open he had not availed himself of it, but, without the family noticing, was stretched out in the darkest corner of his room. However, once the cleaning woman had left the door to the living room slightly ajar, and it remained open even when the lodgers came in in the evening and the lights were put on. They sat down at the head of the table, where in earlier days the mother, the father, and Gregor had eaten, unfolded their serviettes, and picked up their knives and forks. The mother immediately appeared in the door with a dish of meat and right behind her the sister with a dish piled high with potatoes. The food gave off a lot of steam. The gentlemen lodgers bent over the plate set before them, as if they wanted to check it before eating, and in fact the one who sat in the middle (for the other two he seemed to serve as the authority) cut off a piece of meat still on the plate obviously to establish whether it was sufficiently tender and whether or not something should be shipped back to the kitchen. He was satisfied, and mother and sister, who had looked on in suspense, began to breathe easily and to smile.

The family itself ate in the kitchen. In spite of that, before the father went into the kitchen, he came into the room and with a single bow, cap in hand, made a tour of the table. The lodgers rose up collectively and murmured something in their beards. Then, when they were alone, they ate almost in complete silence. It seemed odd to Gregor that out of all the many different sorts of sounds of eating, what was always audible was their chewing teeth, as if by that Gregor should be shown that people needed their teeth to eat and that nothing could be done even with the most handsome toothless jawbone. "I really do have an appetite," Gregor said to himself sorrowfully, "but not for these things. How these lodgers stuff themselves, and I am dying."

On this very evening (Gregor didn't remember hearing the violin all through this period) it sounded from the kitchen. The lodgers had already ended their night meal, the middle one had pulled out a newspaper and had given each of the other two a page, and they were now leaning back, reading and smoking. When the violin started playing, they became attentive, got up, and went on tiptoe to the hall door, at which they remained standing pressed up against one another. They must have been audible from the kitchen, because the father called out "Perhaps the gentlemen don't like the playing? It can be stopped at once." "On the contrary," stated the lodger in the middle, "might the young woman not come into us and play in the room here where it is really much more comfortable and cheerful?" "Oh, thank you," cried out the father, as if he were the one playing the violin. The men stepped back into the room and waited. Soon the father came with the music stand, the mother with the sheet music, and the sister with the violin. The sister calmly prepared everything for the recital. The parents, who had never previously rented a room and therefore exaggerated their politeness to the lodgers, dared not sit on their own chairs. The father leaned against the door, his right hand stuck between two buttons of his buttoned up uniform. The mother, however, accepted a chair offered by one lodger. Since she left the chair sit where the gentleman had chanced to put it, she sat to one side in a corner.

The sister began to play. The father and mother, followed attentively, one on each side, the movements of her hands. Attracted by the playing, Gregor had ventured to advance a little further forward and his head was already in the living room. He scarcely wondered about the fact that recently he had had so little consideration for the others; earlier this consideration had been something he was proud of. And for that very reason he would've had at this moment more reason to hide away, because as a result of the dust which lay all over his room and flew around with the slightest movement, he was totally covered in dirt. On his back and his sides he carted around with him dust, threads, hair, and remnants of food. His indifference to everything was much too great for him to lie on his back and scour himself on the carpet, as he often had done earlier during the day. In spite of his condition he had no timidity about inching forward a bit on the spotless floor of the living room.

In any case, no one paid him any attention. The family was all caught up in the violin playing. The lodgers, by contrast, who for the moment had placed themselves, their hands in their trouser pockets, behind the music stand much too close to the sister, so that they could all see the sheet music, something that must certainly bother the sister, soon drew back to the window conversing in low voices with bowed heads, where they then remained, worriedly observed by the father. It now seemed really clear that, having assumed they were to hear a beautiful or entertaining violin recital, they were disappointed, and were allowing their peace and quiet to be disturbed only out of politeness. The way in which they all blew the smoke from their cigars out of their noses and mouths in particular led one to conclude that they were very irritated. And yet his sister was playing so beautifully. Her face was turned to the side, her gaze followed the score intently and sadly. Gregor crept forward still a little further and kept his head close against the floor in order to be able to catch her gaze if possible. Was he an animal that music so seized him? For him it was as if the way to the unknown nourishment he craved was revealing itself to him. He was determined to press forward right to his sister, to tug at her dress and to indicate to her in this way that she might still come with her violin into his room, because here no one valued the recital as he wanted to value it. He did not wish to let her go from his room any more, at least not as long as he lived. His frightening appearance would for the first time become useful for him. He wanted to be at all the doors of his room simultaneously and snarl back at the attackers. However, his sister should not be compelled but would remain with him voluntarily; she would sit next to him on the sofa, bend down her ear to him, and he would then confide in her that he firmly intended to send her to the conservatory and that, if his misfortune had not arrived in the interim, he would have declared all this last Christmas (had Christmas really already come and gone?), and would have brooked no argument. After this explanation his sister would break out in tears of emotion, and Gregor would lift himself up to her armpit and kiss her throat, which she, from the time she started going to work, had left exposed without a band or a collar.

"Mr. Samsa," called out the middle lodger to the father, and pointed his index finger, without uttering a further word, at Gregor as he was moving slowly forward. The violin fell silent. The middle lodger smiled, first shaking his head once at his friends, and then looked down at Gregor once more. Rather than driving Gregor back again, the father seemed to consider it of prime importance to calm down the lodgers, although they were not at all upset and Gregor seemed to entertain them more than the violin recital. The father hurried over to them and with outstretched arms tried to push them into their own room and simultaneously to block their view of Gregor with his own body. At this point they became really somewhat irritated, although one no longer knew whether that was because of the father's behaviour or because of knowledge they had just acquired that they had had, without knowing it, a neighbour like Gregor. They demanded explanations from his father, raised their arms to make their points, tugged agitatedly at their beards, and moved back towards their room quite slowly. In the meantime, the isolation which had suddenly fallen upon his sister after the sudden breaking off of the recital had overwhelmed her. She had held onto the violin and bow in her limp hands for a little while and had continued to look at the sheet music as if she was still playing. All at once she pulled herself together, placed the instrument in her mother's lap (the mother was still sitting in her chair having trouble breathing and with her lungs labouring) and had run into the next room, which the lodgers, pressured by the father, were already approaching more rapidly. One could observe how under the sister's practiced hands the sheets and pillows on the beds were thrown on high and arranged. Even before the lodgers had reached the room, she was finished fixing the beds and was slipping out. The father seemed so gripped once again with his stubbornness that he forgot about the respect which he always owed to his renters. He pressed on and on, until at the door of the room the middle gentleman stamped loudly with his foot and thus brought the father to a standstill. "I hereby declare," the middle lodger said, raising his hand and casting his glance both on the mother and the sister, "that considering the disgraceful conditions prevailing in this apartment and family," with this he spat decisively on the floor, "I immediately cancel my room. I will, of course, pay nothing at all for the days which I have lived here; on the contrary I shall think about whether or not I will initiate some sort of action against you, something which— believe me— will be very easy to establish." He fell silent and looked directly in front of him, as if he was waiting for something. In fact, his two friends immediately joined in with their opinions, "We also give immediate notice." At that he seized the door handle, banged the door shut, and locked it.

The father groped his way tottering to his chair and let himself fall in it. It looked as if he was stretching out for his usual evening snooze, but the heavy nodding of his head (which looked as if it was without support) showed that he was not sleeping at all. Gregor had lain motionless the entire time in the spot where the lodgers had caught him. Disappointment with the collapse of his plan and perhaps also his weakness brought on his severe hunger made it impossible for him to move. He was certainly afraid that a general disaster would break over him at any moment, and he waited. He was not even startled when the violin fell from the mother's lap, out from under her trembling fingers, and gave off a reverberating tone.

"My dear parents," said the sister banging her hand on the table by way of an introduction, "things cannot go on any longer in this way. Maybe if you don't understand that, well, I do. I will not utter my brother's name in front of this monster, and thus I say only that we must try to get rid of it. We have tried what is humanly possible to take care of it and to be patient. I believe that no one can criticize us in the slightest." "She is right in a thousand ways," said the father to himself. The mother, who was still incapable of breathing properly, began to cough numbly with her hand held up over her mouth and a manic expression in her eyes.

The sister hurried over to her mother and held her forehead. The sister's words seemed to have led the father to certain reflections. He sat upright, played with his uniform hat among the plates, which still lay on the table from the lodgers' evening meal, and looked now and then at the motionless Gregor.

"We must try to get rid of it," the sister now said decisively to the father, for the mother, in her coughing fit, wasn't listening to anything, "it is killing you both. I see it coming. When people have to work as hard as we all do, they cannot also tolerate this endless torment at home. I just can't go on any more." And she broke out into such a crying fit that her tears flowed out down onto her mother's face. She wiped them off her mother with mechanical motions of her hands.

"Child," said the father sympathetically and with obvious appreciation, "then what should we do?"

The sister only shrugged her shoulders as a sign of the perplexity which, in contrast to her previous confidence, had come over her while she was crying.

"If only he understood us," said the father in a semi-questioning tone. The sister, in the midst of her sobbing, shook her hand energetically as a sign that there was no point thinking of that.

"If he only understood us," repeated the father and by shutting his eyes he absorbed the sister's conviction of the impossibility of this point, "then perhaps some compromise would be possible with him. But as it is …"

"It must be gotten rid of," cried the sister; "That is the only way, father. You must try to get rid of the idea that this is Gregor. The fact that we have believed for so long, that is truly our real misfortune. But how can it be Gregor? If it were Gregor, he would have long ago realized that a communal life among human beings is not possible with such an animal and would have gone away voluntarily. Then we would not have a brother, but we could go on living and honour his memory. But this animal plagues us. It drives away the lodgers, will obviously take over the entire apartment, and leave us to spend the night in the alley. Just look, father," she suddenly cried out, "he's already starting up again." With a fright which was totally incomprehensible to Gregor, the sister even left the mother, pushed herself away from her chair, as if she would sooner sacrifice her mother than remain in Gregor's vicinity, and rushed behind her father who, excited merely by her behaviour, also stood up and half raised his arms in front of the sister as though to protect her.

But Gregor did not have any notion of wishing to create problems for anyone and certainly not for his sister. He had just started to turn himself around in order to creep back into his room, quite a startling sight, since, as a result of his suffering condition, he had to guide himself through the difficulty of turning around with his head, in this process lifting and banging it against the floor several times. He paused and looked around. His good intentions seem to have been recognized. The fright had only lasted for a moment. Now they looked at him in silence and sorrow. His mother lay in her chair, with her legs stretched out and pressed together; her eyes were almost shut from weariness. The father and sister sat next to one another. The sister had set her hands around the father's neck.

"Now perhaps I can actually turn myself around," thought Gregor and began the task again. He couldn't stop puffing at the effort and had to rest now and then.

Besides no one was urging him on. It was all left to him on his own. When he had completed turning around, he immediately began to wander straight back. He was astonished at the great distance which separated him from his room and did not understand in the least how in his weakness he had covered the same distance a short time before, almost without noticing it. Constantly intent only on creeping along quickly, he hardly paid any attention to the fact that no word or cry from his family interrupted him.

Only when he was already in the door did he turn his head, not completely, because he felt his neck growing stiff. At any rate he still saw that behind him nothing had changed. Only the sister was standing up. His last glimpse brushed over the mother who was now completely asleep. Hardly was he inside his room when the door was pushed shut very quickly, bolted fast, and barred. Gregor was startled by the sudden commotion behind him, so much so that his little limbs bent double under him. It was his sister who had been in such a hurry. She had stood up right away, had waited, and had then sprung forward nimbly. Gregor had not heard anything of her approach. She cried out "Finally!" to her parents, as she turned the key in the lock.

"What now?" Gregor asked himself and looked around him in the darkness. He soon made the discovery that he could no longer move at all. He was not surprised at that. On the contrary, it struck him as unnatural that he had really been able up to this point to move around with these thin little legs. Besides he felt relatively content. True, he had pains throughout his entire body, but it seemed to him that they were gradually becoming weaker and weaker and would finally go away completely. The rotten apple in his back and the inflamed surrounding area, entirely covered with white dust, he hardly noticed. He remembered his family with deep feeling and love. In this business, his own thought that he had to disappear was, if possible, even more decisive than his sister's. He remained in this state of empty and peaceful reflection until the tower clock struck three o'clock in the morning. From the window he witnessed the beginning of the general dawning outside. Then without willing it, his head sank all the way down, and from his nostrils flowed out weakly out his last breath.

Early in the morning the cleaning woman came. In her sheer energy and haste she banged all the doors (in precisely the way people had already asked her to avoid), so much so that once she arrived a quiet sleep was no longer possible anywhere in the entire apartment. In her customarily brief visit to Gregor she at first found nothing special. She thought he lay so immobile there intending to play the offended party. She gave him credit for as complete an understanding as possible. Because she happened to hold the long broom in her hand, she tried to tickle Gregor with it from the door. When that was quite unsuccessful, she became irritated and poked Gregor a little, and only when she had shoved him from his place without any resistance did she become attentive. When she quickly realized the true state of affairs, her eyes grew large, she whistled to herself, but didn't restrain herself for long. She pulled open the door of the bedroom and yelled in a loud voice into the darkness, "Come and look. It's kicked the bucket. It's lying there, totally snuffed!"

The Samsa married couple sat upright in their marriage bed and had to get over their fright at the cleaning woman before they managed to grasp her message. But then Mr. and Mrs. Samsa climbed very quickly out of bed, one on either side. Mr. Samsa threw the bedspread over his shoulders, Mrs. Samsa came out only in her night-shirt, and like this they stepped into Gregor's room. Meanwhile the door of the living room (in which Grete had slept since the lodgers had arrived on the scene) had also opened. She was fully clothed, as if she had not slept at all; her white face also seem to indicate that. "Dead?" said Mrs. Samsa and looked questioningly at the cleaning woman, although she could check everything on her own and even understand without a check. "I should say so," said the cleaning woman and, by way of proof, poked Gregor's body with the broom a considerable distance more to the side. Mrs. Samsa made a movement as if she wished to restrain the broom, but didn't do it. "Well," said Mr. Samsa, "now we can give thanks to God." He crossed himself, and the three women followed his example.

Grete, who did not take her eyes off the corpse, said, "Look how thin he was. He had eaten nothing for such a long time. The meals which came in here came out again exactly the same." In fact, Gregor's body was completely flat and dry. That was apparent really for the first time, now that he was no longer raised on his small limbs and, moreover, now that nothing else distracted one's gaze.

"Grete, come into us for a moment," said Mrs. Samsa with a melancholy smile, and Grete went, not without looking back at the corpse, behind her parents into the bed room. The cleaning woman shut the door and opened the window wide. In spite of the early morning, the fresh air was partly tinged with warmth. It was already the end of March.

The three lodgers stepped out of their room and looked around for their breakfast, astonished that they had been forgotten. "Where is the breakfast?" asked the middle one of the gentlemen grumpily to the cleaning woman. However, she laid her finger to her lips and then quickly and silently indicated to the lodgers that they could come into Gregor's room. So they came and stood around Gregor's corpse, their hands in the pockets of their somewhat worn jackets, in the room, which was already quite bright.

Then the door of the bed room opened, and Mr. Samsa appeared in his uniform, with his wife on one arm and his daughter on the other. All were a little tear stained. Now and then Grete pressed her face onto her father's arm.

"Get out of my apartment immediately," said Mr. Samsa and pulled open the door, without letting go of the women. "What do you mean?" said the middle lodger, somewhat dismayed and with a sugary smile. The two others kept their hands behind them and constantly rubbed them against each other, as if in joyful anticipation of a great squabble which must end up in their favour. "I mean exactly what I say," replied Mr. Samsa and went directly with his two female companions up to the lodger. The latter at first stood there motionless and looked at the floor, as if matters were arranging themselves in a new way in his head. "All right, then we'll go," he said and looked up at Mr. Samsa as if, suddenly overcome by humility, he was asking fresh permission for this decision. Mr. Samsa merely nodded to him repeatedly with his eyes open wide.

Following that, the lodger actually went immediately with long strides into the hall. His two friends had already been listening for a while with their hands quite still, and now they hopped smartly after him, as if afraid that Mr. Samsa could step into the hall ahead of them and disturb their reunion with their leader. In the hall all three of them took their hats from the coat rack, pulled their canes from the cane holder, bowed silently, and left the apartment. In what turned out to be an entirely groundless mistrust, Mr. Samsa stepped with the two women out onto the landing, leaned against the railing, and looked down as the three lodgers slowly but steadily made their way down the long staircase, disappeared on each floor in a certain turn of the stairwell and in a few seconds came out again. The deeper they proceeded, the more the Samsa family lost interest in them, and when a butcher with a tray on his head come to meet them and then with a proud bearing ascended the stairs high above them, Mr. Samsa., together with the women, left the banister, and they all returned, as if relieved, back into their apartment.

They decided to pass that day resting and going for a stroll. Not only had they earned this break from work, but there was no question that they really needed it. And so they sat down at the table and wrote three letters of apology: Mr. Samsa to his supervisor, Mrs. Samsa to her client, and Grete to her proprietor. During the writing the cleaning woman came in to say that she was going off, for her morning work was finished. The three people writing at first merely nodded, without glancing up. Only when the cleaning woman was still unwilling to depart, did they look up angrily. "Well?" asked Mr. Samsa. The cleaning woman stood smiling in the doorway, as if she had a great stroke of luck to report to the family but would only do it if she was asked directly. The almost upright small ostrich feather in her hat, which had irritated Mr. Samsa during her entire service, swayed lightly in all directions. "All right then, what do you really want?" asked Mrs. Samsa, whom the cleaning lady still usually respected. "Well," answered the cleaning woman (smiling so happily she couldn't go on speaking right away), "about how that rubbish from the next room should be thrown out, you mustn't worry about it. It's all taken care of." Mrs. Samsa and Grete bent down to their letters, as though they wanted to go on writing; Mr. Samsa, who noticed that the cleaning woman wanted to start describing everything in detail, decisively prevented her with an outstretched hand. But since she was not allowed to explain, she remembered the great hurry she was in, and called out, clearly insulted, "Ta ta, everyone," turned around furiously and left the apartment with a fearful slamming of the door.

"This evening she'll be let go," said Mr. Samsa, but he got no answer from either his wife or from his daughter, because the cleaning woman seemed to have upset once again the tranquility they had just attained. They got up, went to the window and remained there, with their arms about each other. Mr. Samsa turned around in his chair in their direction and observed them quietly for a while. Then he called out, "All right, come here then. Let's finally get rid of old things. And have a little consideration for me." The women attended to him at once. They rushed to him, caressed him, and quickly ended their letters.

Then all three left the apartment together, something they had not done for months now, and took the electric tram into the open air outside the city. The car in which they were sitting by themselves was totally engulfed by the warm sun. They talked to each other, leaning back comfortably in their seats, about future prospects, and they discovered that on closer observation these were not at all bad, for all three had employment, about which they had not really questioned each other at all, which was extremely favorable and with especially promising prospects. The greatest improvement in their situation at this moment, of course, had to come from a change of dwelling. Now they wanted to rent an apartment smaller and cheaper but better situated and generally more practical than the present one, which Gregor had found. While they amused themselves in this way, it struck Mr. and Mrs. Samsa almost at the same moment how their daughter, who was getting more animated all the time, had blossomed recently, in spite of all the troubles which had made her cheeks pale, into a beautiful and voluptuous young woman. Growing more silent and almost unconsciously understanding each other in their glances, they thought that the time was now at hand to seek out a good honest man for her. And it was something of a confirmation of their new dreams and good intentions when at the end of their journey the daughter first lifted herself up and stretched her young body.

A Country Doctor

I was in great difficulty. An urgent journey was facing me. A seriously ill man was waiting for me in a village ten miles distant. A severe snowstorm filled the space between him and me. I had a carriage—a light one, with large wheels, entirely suitable for our country roads. Wrapped up in furs with the bag of instruments in my hand, I was already standing in the courtyard ready for the journey; but the horse was missing—the horse. My own horse had died the previous night, as a result of over exertion in this icy winter. My servant girl was at that very moment running around the village to see if she could borrow a horse, but it was hopeless—I knew that—and I stood there useless, increasingly covered with snow, becoming all the time more immobile. The girl appeared at the gate, alone. She was swinging the lantern. Of course, who is now going to lend her his horse for such a journey? I walked once again across the courtyard. I couldn't see what to do. Distracted and tormented, I kicked my foot against the cracked door of the pig sty which had not been used for years. The door opened and banged to and fro on its hinges. A warmth and smell as if from horses came out. A dim stall lantern on a rope swayed inside. A man huddled down in the stall below showed his open blue-eyed face. "Shall I hitch up?" he asked, crawling out on all fours. I didn't know what to say and bent down to see what was still in the stall. The servant girl stood beside me. "One doesn't know the sorts of things one has stored in one's own house," she said, and we both laughed. "Hey, Brother, hey Sister," the groom cried out, and two horses, powerful animals with strong flanks, shoved their way one behind the other, legs close to the bodies, lowering their well-formed heads like camels, and getting through the door space, which they completely filled, only through the powerful movements of their rumps. But right away they stood up straight, long legged, with thick steaming bodies. "Help him," I said, and the girl obediently hurried to hand the wagon harness to the groom. But as soon as she was beside him, the groom puts his arms around her and pushes his face against hers. She screams out and runs over to me. On the girl's cheek were red marks from two rows of teeth. "You brute," I cry out in fury, "do you want the whip?". But I immediately remember that he is a stranger, that I don't know where he comes from, and that he's helping me out of his own free will, when everyone else is refusing to. As if he knows what I was thinking, he takes no offence at my threat, but turns around to me once more, still busy with the horses. Then he says, "Climb in," and, in fact, everything is ready. I notice that I have never before traveled with such a beautiful team of horses, and I climb in happily. "But I'll take the reins. You don't know the way," I say. "Of course," he says; "I'm not going with you. I'm staying with Rosa." "No," screams Rosa and runs into the house, with an accurate premonition of the inevitability of her fate. I hear the door chain rattling as she sets it in place. I hear the lock click. I see how in addition she runs down the corridor and through the rooms putting out all the lights in order to make herself impossible to find. "You're coming with me," I say to the groom, "or I'll give up the journey, no matter how urgent it is. It's not my intention to give you the girl as the price of the trip." "Giddy up," he says and claps his hands. The carriage is torn away, like a piece of wood in a current. I still hear how the door of my house is breaking down and splitting apart under the groom's on-slaught, and then my eyes and ears are filled with a roaring sound which overwhelms all my senses at once. But only for a moment. Then I am already there, as if the farm yard of my invalid opens up immediately in front of my courtyard gate. The horses stand quietly. The snowfall has stopped, moon-light all around. The sick man's parents rush out of the house, his sister behind them. They almost lift me out of the carriage. I get nothing from their confused talking. In the sick room one can hardly breathe the air. The neglected cooking stove is smoking. I want to push open the window, but first I'll look at the sick man. Thin, without fever, not cold, not warm, with empty eyes, without a shirt, the young man under the stuffed quilt heaves himself up, hangs around my throat, and whis-pers in my ear, "Doctor, let me die." I look around. No one has heard. The parents stand silently, leaning forward, and wait for my opinion. The sister has brought a stool for my handbag. I open the bag and look among my instruments. The young man constantly gropes at me from the bed to remind me of his request. I take some tweezers, test them in the candle light, and put them back. "Yes," I think blasphemously, "in such cases the gods do help. They send the missing horse, even add a second one because it's urgent, and even throw in a groom as a bonus." Now for the first time I think once more of Rosa. What am I doing? How am I saving her? How do I pull her out from under this groom, ten miles away from her, with uncontrollable horses in the front of my carriage? These horses, who have somehow loosened their straps, are pushing open the window from outside, I don't know how. Each one is sticking its head through a window and, unmoved by the crying of the family, is observing the invalid. "I'll go back right away," I think, as if the horses were ordering me to journey back, but I allow the sister, who thinks I am in a daze because of the heat, to take off my fur coat. A glass of rum is prepared for me. The old man claps me on the shoulder; the sacrifice of his treasure justifies this familiarity. I shake my head. In the narrow circle of the old man's thinking I was not well; that's the only reason I refuse to drink. The mother stands by the bed and entices me over. I follow and, as a horse neighs loudly at the ceiling, lay my head on the young man's chest, which trembles under my wet beard. That confirms what I know: the young man is healthy. His circulation is a little off, saturated with coffee by his caring mother, but he's healthy and best pushed out of bed with a shove. I'm no improver of the world and let him lie there. I am employed by the district and do my duty to the full, right to the point where it's almost too much. Badly paid, but I'm generous and ready to help the poor. I still have to look after Rosa, and then the young man may have his way, and I want to die too. What am I doing here in this endless winter! My horse is dead, and there is no one in the village who'll lend me his. I have to drag my team out of the pig sty. If they hadn't happened to be horses, I'd have had to travel with pigs. That's the way it is. And I nod to the family. They know nothing about it, and if they did know, they wouldn't believe it. Incidentally, it's easy to write prescriptions, but difficult to come to an understanding with people. Now, at this point my visit might have come to an end—they have once more called for my help unnecessarily. I'm used to that. With the help of my night bell the entire region torments me, but that this time I had to sacrifice Rosa as well, this beautiful girl, who lives in my house all year long and whom I scarcely notice—this sacrifice is too great, and I must somehow in my own head subtly rationalize it away for the moment, in order not to let loose at this family who cannot, even with their best will, give me Rosa back again. But as I am closing up by hand bag and calling for my fur coat, the family is standing together, the father sniffing the glass of rum in his hand, the mother, probably disappointed in me—what more do these people expect?—tearfully biting her lips, and the sister flapping a very bloody hand towel, I am somehow ready, in the circumstances, to concede that the young man is perhaps nonetheless sick. I go to him. He smiles up at me, as if I was bringing him the most nourishing kind of soup—ah, now both horses are whinnying, the noise is probably supposed to come from higher regions in order to illuminate my examination—and now I find out that, yes indeed, the young man is ill. On his right side, in the region of the hip, a wound the size of the palm of one's hand has opened up. Rose coloured, in many different shadings, dark in the depths, brighter on the edges, delicately grained, with uneven patches of blood, open to the light like a mine. That's what it looks like from a distance. Close up a complication is apparent. Who can look at that without whistling softly? Worms, as thick and long as my little finger, themselves rose coloured and also spattered with blood, are wriggling their white bodies with many limbs from their stronghold in the inner of the wound towards the light. Poor young man, there's no helping you. I have found out your great wound. You are dying from this flower on your side. The family is happy; they see me doing something. The sister says that to the mother, the mother tells the father, the father tells a few guests who are coming in on tip toe through the moonlight of the open door, balancing themselves with outstretched arms. "Will you save me?" whispers the young man, sobbing, quite blinded by the life inside his wound. That's how people are in my region. Always demanding the impossible from the doctor. They have lost the old faith. The priest sits at home and tears his religious robes to pieces, one after the other. But the doctor is supposed to achieve everything with his delicate surgeon's hand. Well, it's what they like to think. I have not offered myself. If they use me for sacred purposes, I let that happen to me as well. What more do I want, an old country doctor, robbed of my servant girl! And they come, the families and the village elders, and take my clothes off. A choir of school children with the teacher at the head stands in front of the house and sings an extremely simple melody with the words

> Take his clothes off, then he'll heal,
> and if he doesn't cure, then kill him.
> It's only a doctor; it's only a doctor.

Then I am stripped of my clothes and, with my fingers in my beard and my head tilted to one side, I look at the people quietly. I am completely calm and clear about everything and stay that way, too, although it is not helping me at all, for they are now taking me by the head and feet and dragging me into bed. They lay me against the wall on the side of wound. Then they all go out of the room. The door is shut. The singing stops. Clouds move in front of the moon. The bedclothes lie warmly around me. In the open space of the windows the horses' heads sway like shadows. "Do you know," I hear someone saying in my ear, "my confidence in you is very small. You were shaken out from somewhere. You don't come on your own feet. Instead of helping, you give me less room on my deathbed. The best thing would be if I scratch your eyes out." "Right," I say, "it's a disgrace. But now I'm a doctor. What am I supposed to do? Believe me, things are not easy for me either." "Should I be satisfied with this excuse? Alas, I'll probably have to be. I always have to make do. I came into the world with a beautiful wound; that was all I was furnished with." "Young friend," I say, "your mistake is that you have no perspective. I've already been in all the sick rooms, far and wide, and I tell you your wound is not so bad. Made in a tight corner with two blows from an axe. Many people offer their side and hardly hear the axe in the forest, to say nothing of the fact that it's coming closer to them." "Is that really so, or are you deceiving me in my fever?" "It is truly so. Take the word of honour of a medical doctor." He took my word and grew still. But now it was time to think about my escape. The horses were still standing loyally in place. Clothes, fur coat, and bag were quickly snatched up. I didn't want to delay by getting dressed; if the horses rushed as they had on the journey out, I should, in fact, be springing out of that bed into my own, as it were. One horse obediently pulled back from the window. I threw the bundle into the carriage. The fur coat flew too far and was caught on a hook by only one arm. Good enough. I swung myself up onto the horse. The reins dragging loosely, one horse barely harnessed to the other, the carriage swaying behind, last of all the fur coat in the snow. "Giddy up," I said, but there was no giddying up about it. We dragged through the snowy desert like old men; for a long time the fresh but inaccurate singing of the children resounded behind us:

> Enjoy yourselves, you patients.
> The doctor's laid in bed with you.

I'll never come home at this rate. My flourishing practice is lost. A successor is robbing me, but to no avail, for he cannot replace me. In my house the disgusting groom is wreaking havoc. Rosa is his victim. I will not think it through. Naked, abandoned to the frost of this unhappy age, with an earthly carriage and unearthly horses, I drive around by myself, an old man. My fur coat hangs behind the wagon, but I cannot reach it, and no one from the nimble rabble of patients lifts a finger. Betrayed! Betrayed! Once one responds to a false alarm on the night bell, there's no making it good again—not ever.

A Hunger Artist

In the last decades interest in hunger artists has declined considerably. Whereas in earlier days there was good money to be earned putting on major productions of this sort under one's own management, nowadays that is totally impossible. Those were different times. Back then the hunger artist captured the attention of the entire city. From day to day while the fasting lasted, participation increased. Everyone wanted to see the hunger artist at least daily. During the final days there were people with subscription tickets who sat all day in front of the small barred cage. And there were even viewing hours at night, their impact heightened by torchlight. On fine days the cage was dragged out into the open air, and then the hunger artist was put on display particularly for the children. While for grown-ups the hunger artist was often merely a joke, something they participated in because it was fashionable, the children looked on amazed, their mouths open, holding each other's hands for safety, as he sat there on scattered straw—spurning a chair—in a black tights, looking pale, with his ribs sticking out prominently, sometimes nodding politely, answering questions with a forced smile, even sticking his arm out through the bars to let people feel how emaciated he was, but then completely sinking back into himself, so that he paid no attention to anything, not even to what was so important to him, the striking of the clock, which was the single furnishing in the cage, merely looking out in front of him with his eyes almost shut and now and then sipping from a tiny glass of water to moisten his lips.

Apart from the changing groups of spectators there were also constant observers chosen by the public—strangely enough they were usually butchers—who, always three at a time, were given the task of observing the hunger artist day and night, so that he didn't get something to eat in some secret manner. It was, however, merely a formality, introduced to reassure the masses, for those who understood knew well enough that during the period of fasting the hunger artist would never, under any circumstances, have eaten the slightest thing, not even if compelled by force. The honour of his art forbade it. Naturally, none of the watchers understood that. Sometimes there were nightly groups of watchers who carried out their vigil very laxly, deliberately sitting together in a distant corner and putting all their attention into playing cards there, clearly intending to allow the hunger artist a small refreshment, which, according to their way of thinking, he could get from some secret supplies. Nothing was more excruciating to the hunger artist than such watchers. They depressed him. They made his fasting terribly difficult. Sometimes he overcame his weakness and sang during the time they were observing, for as long as he could keep it up, to show people how unjust their suspicions about him were. But that was little help. For then they just wondered among themselves about his skill at being able to eat even while singing. He much preferred the observers who sat down right against the bars and, not satisfied with the dim backlighting of the room, illuminated him with electric flashlights. The glaring light didn't bother him in the slightest. Generally he couldn't sleep at all, and he could always doze under any lighting and at any hour, even in an overcrowded, noisy auditorium. With such observers, he was very happily prepared to spend the entire night without sleeping. He was very pleased to joke with them, to recount stories from his nomadic life and then, in turn, to listen their stories—doing everything just to keep them awake, so that he could keep showing them once again that he had nothing to eat in his cage and that he was fasting as none of them could.

He was happiest, however, when morning came and a lavish breakfast was brought for them at his own expense, on which they hurled themselves with the appetite of healthy men after a hard night's work without sleep. True, there were still people who wanted to see in this breakfast an unfair means of influencing the observers, but that was going too far, and if they were asked whether they wanted to undertake the observers' night shift for its own sake, without the breakfast, they excused themselves. But nonetheless they stood by their suspicions.

However, it was, in general, part of fasting that these doubts were inextricably associated with it. For, in fact, no one was in a position to spend time watching the hunger artist every day and night, so no one could know, on the basis of his own observation, whether this was a case of truly uninterrupted, flawless fasting. The hunger artist himself was the only one who could know that and, at the same time, the only spectator capable of being completely satisfied with his own fasting. But the reason he was never satisfied was something different. Perhaps it was not fasting at all which made him so very emaciated that many people, to their own regret, had to stay away from his performance, because they couldn't bear to look at him. For he was also so skeletal out of dissatisfaction with himself, because he alone knew something that even initiates didn't know—how easy it was to fast. It was the easiest thing in the world. About this he did not remain silent, but people did not believe him. At best they thought he was being modest. Most of them, however, believed he was a publicity seeker or a total swindler, for whom, at all events, fasting was easy, because he understood how to make it easy, and then had the nerve to half admit it. He had to accept all that. Over the years he had become accustomed to it. But this dissatisfaction kept gnawing at his insides all the time and never yet—and this one had to say to his credit—had he left the cage of his own free will after any period of fasting.

The impresario had set the maximum length of time for the fast at forty days—he would never allow the fasting go on beyond that point, not even in the cosmopolitan cities. And, in fact, he had a good reason. Experience had shown that for about forty days one could increasingly whip up a city's interest by gradually increasing advertising, but that then the people turned away—one could demonstrate a significant decline in popularity. In this respect, there were, of course, small differences among different towns and among different countries, but as a rule it was true that forty days was the maximum length of time.

So then on the fortieth day the door of the cage—which was covered with flowers—was opened, an enthusiastic audience filled the amphitheatre, a military band played, two doctors entered the cage, in order to take the necessary measurements of the hunger artist, the results were announced to the auditorium through a megaphone, and finally two young ladies arrived, happy about the fact that they were the ones who had just been selected by lot, seeking to lead the hunger artist down a couple of steps out of the cage, where on a small table a carefully chosen hospital meal was laid out. And at this moment the hunger artist always fought back. Of course, he still freely laid his bony arms in the helpful outstretched hands of the ladies bending over him, but he did not want to stand up. Why stop right now after forty days? He could have kept going for even longer, for an unlimited length of time. Why stop right now, when he was in his best form, indeed, not yet even in his best fasting form? Why did people want to rob him of the fame of fasting longer, not just so that he could become the greatest hunger artist of all time, which he probably was already, but also so that he could surpass himself in some unimaginable way, for he felt there were no limits to his capacity for fasting. Why did this crowd, which pretended to admire him so much, have so little patience with him? If he kept going and kept fasting longer, why would they not tolerate it? Then, too, he was tired and felt good sitting in the straw. Now he was supposed to stand up straight and tall and go to eat, something which, when he just imagined it, made him feel nauseous right away. With great difficulty he repressed mentioning this only out of consideration for the women. And he looked up into the eyes of these women, apparently so friendly but in reality so cruel, and shook his excessively heavy head on his feeble neck.

But then happened what always happened. The impresario came and in silence—the music made talking impossible—raised his arms over the hunger artist, as if inviting heaven to look upon its work here on the straw, this unfortunate martyr, something the hunger artist certainly was, only in a completely different sense, then grabbed the hunger artist around his thin waist, in the process wanting with his exaggerated caution to make people believe that here he had to deal with something fragile, and handed him over—not without secretly shaking him a little, so that the hunger artist's legs and upper body swung back and forth uncontrollably—to the women, who had in the meantime turned as pale as death. At this point, the hunger artist endured everything. His head lay on his chest— it was as if it had inexplicably rolled around and just stopped there—his body was arched back, his legs, in an impulse of self-preservation, pressed themselves together at the knees, but scraped the ground, as if they were not really on the floor but were looking for the real ground, and the entire weight of his body, admittedly very small, lay against one of the women, who appealed for help with flustered breath, for she had not imagined her post of honour would be like this, and then stretched her neck as far as possible, to keep her face from the least contact with the hunger artist, but then, when she couldn't manage this and her more fortunate companion didn't come to her assistance but trembled and remained content to hold in front of her the hunger artist's hand, that small bundle of knuckles, she broke into tears, to the delighted laughter of the auditorium, and had to be relieved by an attendant who had been standing ready for some time. Then came the meal. The impresario put a little food into mouth of the hunger artist, now half unconscious, as if fainting, and kept up a cheerful patter designed to divert attention away from the hunger artist's condition. Then a toast was proposed to the public, which was supposedly whispered to the impresario by the hunger artist, the orchestra confirmed everything with a great fanfare, people dispersed, and no one had the right to be dissatisfied with the event, no one except the hunger artist—he was always the only one.

He lived this way, taking small regular breaks, for many years, apparently in the spotlight, honoured by the world, but for all that his mood was usually gloomy, and it kept growing gloomier all the time, because no one understood how to take him seriously. But how was he to find consolation? What was there left for him to wish for? And if a good-natured man who felt sorry for him ever wanted to explain to him that his sadness probably came from his fasting, then it could happen that the hunger artist responded with an outburst of rage and began to shake the bars like an animal, frightening everyone. But the impresario had a way of punishing moments like this, something he was happy to use. He would make an apology for the hunger artist to the assembled public, conceding that the irritability had been provoked only by his fasting, something quite intelligible to well-fed people and capable of excusing the behaviour of the hunger artist without further explanation. From there he would move on to speak about the equally hard to understand claim of the hunger artist that he could go on fasting for much longer than he was doing. He would praise the lofty striving, the good will, and the great self-denial no doubt contained in this claim, but then would try to contradict it simply by producing photographs, which were also on sale, for in the pictures one could see the hunger artist on the fortieth day of his fast, in bed, almost dead from exhaustion. Although the hunger artist was very familiar with this perversion of the truth, it always strained his nerves again and was too much for him. What was a result of the premature ending of the fast people were now proposing as its cause! It was impossible to fight against this lack of understanding, against this world of misunderstanding. In good faith he always listened eagerly to the impresario at the bars of his cage, but each time, once the photographs came out, he would let go of the bars and, with a sigh, sink back into the straw, and a reassured public could come up again and view him.

When those who had witnessed such scenes thought back on them a few years later, often they were unable to understand themselves. For in the meantime that change mentioned above had set it. It happened almost immediately. There may have been more profound reasons for it, but who bothered to discover what they were? At any rate, one day the pampered hunger artist saw himself abandoned by the crowd of pleasure seekers, who preferred to stream to other attractions. The impresario chased around half of Europe one more time with him, to see whether he could still re-discover the old interest here and there. It was all futile. It was as if a secret agreement against the fasting performances had developed everywhere. Naturally, it couldn't really have happened all at once, and people later remembered some things which in the days of intoxicating success they hadn't paid sufficient attention to, some inadequately suppressed indications, but now it was too late to do anything to counter them. Of course, it was certain that the popularity of fasting would return once more someday, but for those now alive that was no consolation. What was the hunger artist to do now? A man whom thousands of people had cheered on could not display himself in show booths at small fun fairs. The hunger artist was not only too old to take up a different profession, but was fanatically devoted to fasting more than anything else. So he said farewell to the impresario, an incomparable companion on his life's road, and let himself be hired by a large circus. In order to spare his own feelings, he didn't even look at the terms of his contract at all.

A large circus with its huge number of men, animals, and gimmicks, which are constantly being let go and replenished, can use anyone at any time, even a hunger artist, provided, of course, his demands are modest. Moreover, in this particular case it was not only the hunger artist himself who was engaged, but also his old and famous name. In fact, given the characteristic nature of his art, which was not diminished by his advancing age, one could never claim that a worn out artist, who no longer stood at the pinnacle of his ability, wanted to escape to a quiet position in the circus. On the contrary, the hunger artist declared that he could fast just as well as in earlier times—something that was entirely credible. Indeed, he even affirmed that if people would let him do what he wanted—and he was promised this without further ado— he would really now legitimately amaze the world for the first time, an assertion which, however, given the mood of the time, which the hunger artist in his enthusiasm easily overlooked, only brought smiles from the experts.

However, basically the hunger artist had not forgotten his sense of the way things really were, and he took it as self-evident that people would not set him and his cage up as the star attraction somewhere in the middle of the arena, but would move him outside in some other readily accessible spot near the animal stalls. Huge brightly painted signs surrounded the cage and announced what there was to look at there. During the intervals in the main performance, when the general public pushed out towards the menagerie in order to see the animals, they could hardly avoid moving past the hunger artist and stopping there a moment. They would perhaps have remained with him longer, if those pushing up behind them in the narrow passage way, who did not understand this pause on the way to the animal stalls they wanted to see, had not made a longer peaceful observation impossible. This was also the reason why the hunger artist began to tremble at these visiting hours, which he naturally used to long for as the main purpose of his life. In the early days he could hardly wait for the pauses in the performances. He had looked forward with delight to the crowd pouring around him, until he became convinced only too quickly—and even the most stubborn, almost deliberate self-deception could not hold out against the experience—that, judging by their intentions, most of these people were, again and again without exception, only visiting the menagerie. And this view from a distance still remained his most beautiful moment. For when they had come right up to him, he immediately got an earful from the shouting of the two steadily increasing groups, the ones who wanted to take their time looking at the hunger artist, not with any understanding but on a whim or from mere defiance—for him these ones were soon the more painful—and a second group of people whose only demand was to go straight to the animal stalls.

Once the large crowds had passed, the late comers would arrive, and although there was nothing preventing these people any more from sticking around for as long as they wanted, they rushed past with long strides, almost without a sideways glance, to get to the animals in time. And it was an all-too-rare stroke of luck when the father of a family came by with his children, pointed his finger at the hunger artist, gave a detailed explanation about what was going on here, and talked of earlier years, when he had been present at similar but incomparably more magnificent performances, and then the children, because they had been inadequately prepared at school and in life, always stood around still uncomprehendingly. What was fasting to them? But nonetheless the brightness of the look in their searching eyes revealed something of new and more gracious times coming. Perhaps, the hunger artist said to himself sometimes, everything would be a little better if his location were not quite so near the animal stalls. That way it would be easy for people to make their choice, to say nothing of the fact that he was very upset and constantly depressed by the stink from the stalls, the animals' commotion at night, the pieces of raw meat dragged past him for the carnivorous beasts, and the roars at feeding time. But he did not dare to approach the administration about it. In any case, he had the animals to thank for the crowds of visitors among whom, here and there, there could be one destined for him. And who knew where they would hide him if he wished to remind them of his existence and, along with that, of the fact that, strictly speaking, he was only an obstacle on the way to the menagerie.

A small obstacle, at any rate, a constantly diminishing obstacle. People got used to the strange notion that in these times they would want to pay attention to a hunger artist, and with this habitual awareness the judgment on him was pronounced. He might fast as well as he could—and he did—but nothing could save him any more. People went straight past him. Try to explain the art of fasting to anyone! If someone doesn't feel it, then he cannot be made to understand it. The beautiful signs became dirty and illegible. People tore them down, and no one thought of replacing them. The small table with the number of days the fasting had lasted, which early on had been carefully renewed every day, remained unchanged for a long time, for after the first weeks the staff grew tired of even this small task. And so the hunger artist kept fasting on and on, as he once had dreamed about in earlier times, and he had no difficulty succeeding in achieving what he had predicted back then, but no one was counting the days—no one, not even the hunger artist himself, knew how great his achievement was by this point, and his heart grew heavy. And when once in a while a person strolling past stood there making fun of the old number and talking of a swindle, that was in a sense the stupidest lie which indifference and innate maliciousness could invent, for the hunger artist was not being deceptive—he was working honestly—but the world was cheating him of his reward.

Many days went by once more, and this, too, came to an end. Finally the cage caught the attention of a supervisor, and he asked the attendant why they had left this perfectly useful cage standing here unused with rotting straw inside. Nobody knew, until one man, with the help of the table with the number on it, remembered the hunger artist. They pushed the straw around with a pole and found the hunger artist in there. "Are you still fasting?" the supervisor asked. "When are you finally going to stop?" "Forgive me everything," whispered the hunger artist. Only the supervisor, who was pressing his ear up against the cage, understood him. "Certainly," said the supervisor, tapping his forehead with his finger in order to indicate to the spectators the state the hunger artist was in, "we forgive you." "I always wanted you to admire my fasting," said the hunger artist. "But we do admire it," said the supervisor obligingly. "But you shouldn't admire it," said the hunger artist. "Well then, we don't admire it," said the supervisor, "but why shouldn't we admire it?" "Because I had to fast. I can't do anything else," said the hunger artist. "Just look at you," said the supervisor, "why can't you do anything else?" "Because," said the hunger artist, lifting his head a little and, with his lips pursed as if for a kiss, speaking right into the supervisor's ear so that he wouldn't miss anything, "because I couldn't find a food which I enjoyed. If had found that, believe me, I would not have made a spectacle of myself and would have eaten to my heart's content, like you and everyone else." Those were his last words, but in his failing eyes there was the firm, if no longer proud, conviction that he was continuing to fast.

"All right, tidy this up now," said the supervisor. And they buried the hunger artist along with the straw. But in his cage they put a young panther. Even for a person with the dullest mind it was clearly refreshing to see this wild animal throwing itself around in this cage, which had been dreary for such a long time. It lacked nothing. Without thinking about it for any length of time, the guards brought the animal food. It enjoyed the taste and never seemed to miss its freedom. This noble body, equipped with everything necessary, almost to the point of bursting, also appeared to carry freedom around with it. That seem to be located somewhere or other in its teeth, and its joy in living came with such strong passion from its throat that it was not easy for spectators to keep watching. But they controlled themselves, kept pressing around the cage, and had no desire to move on.

A Report for an Academy

Esteemed Gentlemen of the Academy!

You show me the honour of calling upon me to submit a report to the Academy concerning my previous life as an ape.

In this sense, unfortunately, I cannot comply with your request. Almost five years separate me from my existence as an ape, a short time perhaps when measured by the calendar, but endlessly long to gallop through, as I have done, at times accompanied by splendid men, advice, applause, and orchestral music, but basically alone, since all those accompanying me held themselves back a long way from the barrier, in order to preserve the image. This achievement would have been impossible if I had stubbornly wished to hold onto my origin, onto the memories of my youth.

Giving up that obstinacy was, in fact, the highest command that I gave myself. I, a free ape, submitted myself to this yoke. In so doing, however, my memories for their part constantly closed themselves off against me. If people had wanted it, my journey back at first would have been possible through the entire gateway which heaven builds over the earth, but as my development was whipped onwards, the gate simultaneously grew lower and narrower all the time. I felt myself more comfortable and more enclosed in the world of human beings. The storm which blew me out of my past eased off. Today it is only a gentle breeze which cools my heels. And the distant hole through which it comes and through which I once came has become so small that, even if I had sufficient power and will to run back there, I would have to scrape the fur off my body in order to get through. Speaking frankly, as much as I like choosing metaphors for these things—speaking frankly: your experience as apes, gentlemen—to the extent that you have something of that sort behind you—cannot be more distant from you than mine is from me. But it tickles at the heels of everyone who walks here on earth, the small chimpanzee as well as the great Achilles.

In the narrowest sense, however, I can perhaps answer your question, nonetheless, and indeed I do so with great pleasure.

The first thing I learned was to give a handshake. The handshake displays candour. Today, when I stand at the highpoint of my career, may I add to that first handshake also my candid words. For the Academy it will not provide anything essentially new and will fall far short of what people have asked of me and what with the best will I cannot speak about—but nonetheless it should demonstrate the line by which someone who was an ape was forced into the world of men and which he has continued there. Yet I would certainly not permit myself to say even the trivial things which follow if I were not completely sure of myself and if my position on all the great music hall stages of the civilized world had not established itself unassailably.

I come from the Gold Coast. For an account of how I was captured I rely on the reports of strangers. A hunting expedition from the firm of Hagenback—incidentally, since then I have already emptied a number of bottles of good red wine with the leader of that expedition—lay hidden in the bushes by the shore when I ran down in the evening in the middle of a band of apes for a drink. Someone fired a shot. I was the only one struck. I received two hits.

One was in the cheek—that was superficial. But it left behind a large hairless red scar which earned me the name Red Peter—a revolting name, completely inappropriate, presumably something invented by an ape, as if the only difference between me and the recently deceased trained ape Peter, who was well known here and there, was the red patch on my cheek. But this is only by the way.

The second shot hit me below the hip. It was serious. It's the reason that today I still limp a little. Recently I read in an article by one of the ten thousand gossipers who vent their opinions about me in the newspapers that my ape nature is not yet entirely repressed. The proof is that when visitors come I take pleasure in pulling off my trousers to show the entry wound caused by this shot. That fellow should have each finger of his writing hand shot off one by one. So far as I am concerned, I may pull my trousers down in front of anyone I like. People will not find there anything other than well cared for fur and the scar from—let us select here a precise word for a precise purpose, something that will not be misunderstood—the scar from a wicked shot. Everything is perfectly open; there is nothing to hide. When it comes to a question of the truth, every great mind discards the most subtle refinements of manners. However, if that writer were to pull down his trousers when he gets a visitor, that would certainly produce a different sight, and I'll take it as a sign of reason that he does not do that. But then he should not bother me with his delicate sensibilities.

After those shots I woke up—and here my own memory gradually begins—in a cage between decks on the Hagenbeck steamship. It was no four-sided cage with bars, but only three walls fixed to a crate, so that the crate constituted the fourth wall. The whole thing was too low to stand upright and too narrow for sitting down. So I crouched with bent knees, which shook all the time, and since at first I probably did not wish to see anyone and to remain constantly in the darkness, I turned towards the crate, while the bars of the cage cut into the flesh on my back. People consider such confinement of wild animals beneficial in the very first period of time, and today I cannot deny, on the basis of my own experience, that in a human sense that is, in fact, the case.

But at that time I didn't think about it. For the first time in my life I was without a way out—at least there was no direct way out. Right in front of me was the crate, its boards fitted closely together. Well, there was a hole running right through the boards. When I first discovered it, I welcomed it with a blissfully happy howl of ignorance. But this hole was not nearly big enough to stick my tail through, and all the power of an ape could not make it any bigger.

According to what I was told later, I am supposed to have made remarkably little noise. From that people concluded that either I must soon die or, if I succeeded in surviving the first critical period, I would be very capable of being trained. I survived this period. Muffled sobbing, painfully searching out fleas, wearily licking a coconut, banging my skull against the wall of the crate, sticking out my tongue when anyone came near—these were the first occupations in my new life. In all of them, however, there was only one feeling: no way out. Nowadays, of course, I can portray those ape-like feelings only with human words and, as a result, I misrepresent them. But even if I can no longer attain the old truth of the ape, at least it lies in the direction I have described—of that there is no doubt.

Up until then I had had so many ways out, and now I no longer had one. I was tied down. If they had nailed me down, my freedom to move would not have been any less. And why? If you scratch raw the flesh between your toes, you won't find the reason. If you press your back against the bars of the cage until it almost slices you in two, you won't find the answer. I had no way out, but I had to come up with one for myself. For without that I could not live. Always in front of that crate wall—I would inevitably have died a miserable death. But according to Hagenbeck, apes belong at the crate wall—well, that meant I had to cease being an ape. A clear and beautiful train of thought, which I must have planned somehow with my belly, since apes think with their bellies.

I'm worried that people do not understand precisely what I mean by a way out. I use the word in its most common and fullest sense. I am deliberately not saying freedom. I do not mean this great feeling of freedom on all sides. As an ape, I perhaps recognized it, and I have met human beings who yearn for it. But as far as I am concerned, I did not demand freedom either then or today. Incidentally, among human beings people all too often are deceived by freedom. And since freedom is reckoned among the most sublime feelings, the corresponding disappointment is also among the most sublime. In the variety shows, before my entrance, I have often watched a pair of artists busy on trapezes high up in the roof. They swung themselves, they rocked back and forth, they jumped, they hung in each other's arms, one held the other by clenching the hair with his teeth. "That, too, is human freedom," I thought, "self-controlled movement." What a mockery of sacred nature! At such a sight, no structure would stand up to the laughter of the apes.

No, I didn't want freedom. Only a way out—to the right or left or anywhere at all. I made no other demands, even if the way out should be only an illusion. The demand was small; the disappointment would not be any greater—to move on further, to move on further! Only not to stand still with arms raised, pressed again a crate wall.

Today I see clearly that without the greatest inner calm I would never have been able to get out. And in fact I probably owe everything that I have become to the calmness which came over me after the first days there on the ship. And, in turn, I owe that calmness to the people on the ship.

They are good people, in spite of everything. Today I still enjoy remembering the clang of their heavy steps, which used to echo then in my half sleep. They had the habit of tackling everything extremely slowly. If one of them wanted to rub his eyes, he raised his hand as if it were a hanging weight. Their jokes were gross but hearty. Their laughter was always mixed with a rasp which sounded dangerous but meant nothing. They always had something in their mouths to spit out, and they didn't care where they spat. They always complained that my fleas sprung over onto them, but they were never seriously angry at me because of it. They even knew that fleas liked being in my fur and that fleas are jumpers. They learned to live with that. When they had no duties, sometimes a few of them sat down in a semi-circle around me. They didn't speak much, but only made noises to each other and smoked their pipes, stretched out on the crates. They slapped their knees as soon as I made the slightest movement, and from time to time one of them would pick up a stick and tickle me where I liked it. If I were invited today to make a journey on that ship, I'd certainly decline the invitation, but it's equally certain that the memories I could dwell on of the time there between the decks would not be totally hateful.

The calmness which I acquired in this circle of people prevented me above all from any attempt to escape. Looking at it nowadays, it seems to me as if I had at least sensed that I had to find a way out if I wanted to live, but that this way out could not be reached by escaping. I no longer know if escape was possible, but I think it was: for an ape it should always be possible to flee. With my present teeth I have to be careful even with the ordinary task of cracking a nut, but then I must have been able, over time, to succeed in chewing through the lock on the door. I didn't do that. What would I have achieved by doing that? No sooner would I have stuck my head out, than they would have captured me again and locked me up in an even worse cage. Or I could have taken refuge unnoticed among the other animals—say, the boa constrictors opposite me—and breathed my last in their embraces. Or I could have managed to steal way up to the deck and jumped overboard. Then I'd have tossed back and forth for a while on the ocean and drowned. Acts of despair. I did not think things through in such a human way, but under the influence of my surroundings conducted myself as if I had worked things out.

I did not work things out, but I observed well in complete tranquility. I saw these men going back and forth, always the same faces, the same movements. Often it seemed to me as if there was only one man. So the man or these men went un-disturbed. A lofty purpose dawned on me. No one promised me that if I could become like them the cage would be re-moved. Such promises, apparently impossible to fulfill, were not made. But if one makes the fulfillment good, then later the promises appear precisely there where one had looked for them earlier without success. Now, these men in themselves were nothing which attracted me very much. If I had been a follower of that freedom I just mentioned, I would certainly have preferred the ocean to the way out displayed in the dull gaze of these men. But in any case, I observed them for a long time before I even thought about such things—in fact, the accumulated observations first pushed me in the proper direction.

It was so easy to imitate these people. I could already spit on the first day. We used to spit in each other's faces. The only difference was that I licked my face clean afterwards. They did not. Soon I was smoking a pipe, like an old man, and if I then pressed my thumb down into the bowl of the pipe, the entire area between decks cheered. Still, for a long time I did not understand the difference between an empty and a full pipe.

I had the greatest difficulty with the bottle of alcohol. The smell was torture to me. I forced myself with all my power, but weeks went by before I could overcome my reaction. Curiously enough, the people took this inner struggle more seriously than anything else about me. In my memories I don't distinguish the people, but there was one who always came back, alone or with comrades, day and night, at different times. He'd stand with a bottle in front of me and give me instructions. He did not understand me. He wanted to solve the riddle of my being. He used to uncork the bottle slowly and then look at me, in order to test if I had understood. I confess that I always looked at him with wildly over-eager attentiveness. No human teacher has ever found in the entire world such a student of human beings.

After he'd uncorked the bottle, he'd raise it to his mouth. I'd gaze at him, right at his throat. He would nod, pleased with me, and set the bottle to his lips. Delighted with my gradual understanding, I'd squeal and scratch myself all over, wherever it was convenient. He was happy. He'd set the bottle to his mouth and take a swallow. Impatient and desperate to emulate him, I would defecate over myself in my cage— and that again gave him great satisfaction. Then, holding the bottle at arm's length and bringing it up again with a swing, he'd drink it down with one gulp, exaggerating his backward bending as a way of instructing me. Exhausted with so much great effort, I could no longer follow and hung weakly onto the bars, while he ended the theoretical lesson by rubbing his belly and grinning.

Now the practical exercises first began. Was I not already too tired out by the theoretical part? Yes, indeed, far too weary. That's part of my fate. Nonetheless, I'd grab the proffered bottle as well as I could and uncork it trembling. Once

I'd managed to do that, new forces gradually take over. I lift the bottle—with hardly any difference between me and the original—put it to my lips—and throw it away in disgust, in disgust, although it is empty and filled only with the smell, throw it with disgust onto the floor. To the sorrow of my teacher, to my own greater sorrow. And I still do not console him or myself when, after throwing away the bottle, I do not forget to give my belly a splendid rub and to grin as I do so.

All too often, the lesson went that way. And to my teacher's credit, he was not angry with me. Well, sometimes he held his burning pipe against my fur in some place or other which I could reach only with difficulty, until it began to burn. But then he would put it out himself with his huge good hand. He wasn't angry with me. He realized that we were fighting on the same side against ape nature and that I had the more difficult part.

What a victory it was for him and for me, however, when one evening in front of a large circle of onlookers—perhaps it was a celebration, a gramophone was playing, and officer was wandering around among the people—when on this evening, at a moment when no one was watching, I grabbed a bottle of alcohol which had been inadvertently left standing in front of my cage, uncorked it just as I had been taught, amid the rising attention of the group, set it against my mouth and, without hesitating, with my mouth making no grimace, like an expert drinker, with my eyes rolling around, splashing the liquid in my throat, I really and truly drank the bottle empty, and then threw it away, no longer in despair, but like an artist. Well, I did forget to scratch my belly. But instead of that, because I couldn't do anything else, because I had to, because my senses were roaring, I cried out a short and good "Hello!" breaking out into human sounds. And with this cry I sprang into the community of human beings, and I felt its echo—"Just listen. He's talking!"—like a kiss on my entire sweat-soaked body.

I'll say it again: imitating human beings was not something which pleased me. I imitated them because I was looking for a way out, for no other reason. And even in that victory little was achieved. My voice immediately failed me again. It first came back months later. My distaste for the bottle of alcohol became even stronger. But at least my direction was given to me once and for all.

When I was handed over in Hamburg to my first trainer, I soon realized the two possibilities open to me: the Zoological Garden or the Music Hall. I did not hesitate. I said to myself: use all your energy to get into the Music Hall. That is the way out. The Zoological Garden is only a new barred cage. If you go there, you're lost.

And I learned, gentlemen. Alas, one learns when one has to. Once learns when one wants a way out. One learns ruthlessly. One supervises oneself with a whip and tears oneself apart at the slightest resistance. My ape nature ran off, head over heels, out of me, so that in the process my first teacher himself almost became an ape and soon had to give up training and be carried off to a mental hospital. Fortunately he was soon discharged again.

But I went through many teachers—indeed, even several teachers at once. As I became more confident of my abilities and the general public followed my progress and my future began to brighten, I took on teachers myself, let them sit down in five interconnected rooms, and studied with them all simultaneously, by constantly leaping from one room into another.

And such progress! The penetrating effects of the rays of knowledge from all sides on my awaking brain! I don't deny the fact—I was delighted with it. But I also confess that I did not overestimate it, not even then, even less today. With an effort which up to this point has never been repeated on earth, I have attained the average education of a European. That would perhaps not amount to much, but it is something insofar as it helped me out of the cage and created this special way out for me—the way out of human beings. There is an excellent German expression: to beat one's way through the bushes. That I have done. I have beaten my way through the bushes. I had no other way, always assuming that freedom was not a choice.

If I review my development and its goal up to this point, I do not complain. I am even satisfied. With my hands in my trouser pockets, the bottle of wine on the table, I half lie and half sit in my rocking chair and gaze out the window. If I have a visitor, I welcome him as is appropriate. My impresario sits in the parlour. If I ring, he comes and listens to what I have to say. In the evening I almost always have a performance, and my success could hardly rise any higher. When I come home late from banquets, from scientific societies, or from social gatherings in someone's home, a small half-trained female chimpanzee is waiting for me, and I take my pleasure with her the way apes do. During the day I don't want to see her. For she has in her gaze the madness of a bewildered trained animal. I'm the only one who recognizes that, and I cannot bear it.

On the whole, at any rate, I have achieved what I wished to achieve. You shouldn't say it wasn't worth the effort. In any case, I don't want any man's judgment. I only want to expand knowledge. I simply report. Even to you, esteemed gentlemen of the Academy, I have only made a report.

An Imperial Message

The Emperor—so they say—has sent a message, directly from his death bed, to you alone, his pathetic subject, a tiny shadow which has taken refuge at the furthest distance from the imperial sun. He ordered the herald to kneel down beside his bed and whispered the message in his ear. He thought it was so important that he had the herald speak it back to him. He confirmed the accuracy of verbal message by nodding his head. And in front of the entire crowd of those witnessing his death—all the obstructing walls have been broken down, and all the great ones of his empire are standing in a circle on the broad and high soaring flights of stairs—in front of all of them he dispatched his herald. The messenger started off at once, a powerful, tireless man. Sticking one arm out and then another, he makes his way through the crowd. If he runs into resistence, he points to his breast where there is a sign of the sun. So he moves forwards easily, unlike anyone else. But the crowd is so huge; its dwelling places are infinite. If there were an open field, how he would fly along, and soon you would hear the marvellous pounding of his fist on your door. But instead of that, how futile are all his efforts. He is still forcing his way through the private rooms of the innermost palace. Never will he win his way through. And if he did manage that, nothing would have been achieved. He would have to fight his way down the steps, and, if he managed to do that, nothing would have been achieved. He would have to stride through the courtyards, and after the courtyards through the second palace encircling the first, and, then again, through stairs and courtyards, and then, once again, a palace, and so on for thousands of years. And if he finally burst through the outermost door—but that can never, never happen—the royal capital city, the centre of the world, is still there in front of him, piled high and full of sediment. No one pushes his way through here, certainly not someone with a message from a dead man. But you sit at your window and dream of that message when evening comes.

Before the Law

Before the law sits a gatekeeper. To this gatekeeper comes a man from the country who asks to gain entry into the law. But the gatekeeper says that he cannot grant him entry at the moment. The man thinks about it and then asks if he will be allowed to come in later on. "It is possible," says the gatekeeper, "but not now." At the moment the gate to the law stands open, as always, and the gatekeeper walks to the side, so the man bends over in order to see through the gate into the inside. When the gatekeeper notices that, he laughs and says: "If it tempts you so much, try it in spite of my prohibition. But take note: I am powerful. And I am only the most lowly gatekeeper. But from room to room stand gatekeepers, each more powerful than the other. I can't endure even one glimpse of the third." The man from the country has not expected such difficulties: the law should always be accessible for everyone, he thinks, but as he now looks more closely at the gatekeeper in his fur coat, at his large pointed nose and his long, thin, black Tartar's beard, he decides that it would be better to wait until he gets permission to go inside. The gatekeeper gives him a stool and allows him to sit down at the side in front of the gate. There he sits for days and years. He makes many attempts to be let in, and he wears the gatekeeper out with his requests. The gatekeeper often interrogates him briefly, questioning him about his homeland and many other things, but they are indifferent questions, the kind great men put, and at the end he always tells him once more that he cannot let him inside yet. The man, who has equipped himself with many things for his journey, spends everything, no matter how valuable, to win over the gatekeeper. The latter takes it all but, as he does so, says, "I am taking this only so that you do not think you have failed to do anything." During the many years the man observes the gatekeeper almost continuously. He forgets the other gatekeepers, and this one seems to him the only obstacle for entry into the law. He curses the unlucky circumstance, in the first years thoughtlessly and out loud, later, as he grows old, he still mumbles to himself. He becomes childish and, since in the long years studying the gatekeeper he has come to know the fleas in his fur collar, he even asks the fleas to help him persuade the gatekeeper. Finally his eyesight grows weak, and he does not know whether things are really darker around him or whether his eyes are merely deceiving him. But he recognizes now in the darkness an illumination which breaks inextinguishably out of the gateway to the law. Now he no longer has much time to live. Before his death he gathers in his head all his experiences of the entire time up into one question which he has not yet put to the gatekeeper. He waves to him, since he can no longer lift up his stiffening body. The gatekeeper has to bend way down to him, for the great difference has changed things to the disadvantage of the man. "What do you still want to know, then?" asks the gatekeeper. "You are insatiable." "Everyone strives after the law," says the man, "so how is that in these many years no one except me has requested entry?" The gatekeeper sees that the man is already dying and, in order to reach his diminishing sense of hearing, he shouts at him, "Here no one else can gain entry, since this entrance was assigned only to you. I'm going now to close it."

In the Penal Colony

"It's a peculiar apparatus," said the Officer to the Traveler, gazing with a certain admiration at the device, with which he was, of course, thoroughly familiar. It appeared that the Traveler had responded to the invitation of the Commandant only out of politeness, when he had been invited to attend the execution of a soldier condemned for disobeying and insulting his superior. Of course, interest in the execution was not very high, not even in the penal colony itself. At least, here in the small, deep, sandy valley, closed in on all sides by barren slopes, apart from the Officer and the Traveler there were present only the Condemned, a vacant-looking man with a broad mouth and dilapidated hair and face, and the Soldier, who held the heavy chain to which were connected the small chains which bound the Condemned Man by his feet and wrist bones, as well as by his neck, and which were also linked to each other by connecting chains. The Condemned Man had an expression of such dog-like resignation that it looked as if one could set him free to roam around the slopes and would only have to whistle at the start of the execution for him to return.

The Traveler had little interest in the apparatus and walked back and forth behind the Condemned Man, almost visibly indifferent, while the Officer took care of the final preparations. Sometimes he crawled under the apparatus, which was built deep into the earth, and sometimes he climbed up a ladder to inspect the upper parts. These were really jobs which could have been left to a mechanic, but the Officer carried them out with great enthusiasm, maybe because he was particularly fond of this apparatus or maybe because there was some other reason why one could not trust the work to anyone else. "It's all ready now!" he finally cried and climbed back down the ladder. He was unusually tired, breathing with his mouth wide open, and he had pushed two fine lady's handkerchiefs under the collar of his uniform.

"These uniforms are really too heavy for the tropics," the Traveler said, instead of asking some questions about the apparatus, as the Officer had expected. "That's true," said the Officer. He washed the oil and grease from his dirty hands in a bucket of water standing ready, "but they mean home, and we don't want to lose our homeland." "Now, have a look at this apparatus," he added immediately, drying his hands with a towel and pointing to the device. "Up to this point I had to do some work by hand, but from now on the apparatus should work entirely on its own." The Traveler nodded and followed the Officer. The latter tried to protect himself against all eventualities by saying, "Of course, breakdowns do happen. I really hope none will occur today, but we must be prepared for it. The apparatus is supposed to keep going for twelve hours without interruption. But if any breakdowns do occur, they'll only be very minor, and we'll deal with them right away."

"Don't you want to sit down?" he asked finally, as he pulled out a chair from a pile of cane chairs and offered it to the Traveler. The latter could not refuse. He sat on the edge of the pit, into which he cast a fleeting glance. It was not very deep. On one side of the hole the piled earth was heaped up into a wall; on the other side stood the apparatus. "I don't know," the officer said, "whether the Commandant has already explained the apparatus to you." The Traveler made an vague gesture with his hand. That was good enough for the Officer, for now he could explain the apparatus himself.

"This apparatus," he said, grasping a connecting rod and leaning against it, "is our previous Commandant's invention. I also worked with him on the very first tests and took part in all the work right up to its completion. However, the credit for the invention belongs to him alone. Have you heard of our previous Commandant? No? Well, I'm not claiming too much when I say that the organization of the entire penal colony is his work. We, his friends, already knew at the time of his death that the administration of the colony was so self-contained that even if his successor had a thousand new plans in mind, he would not be able to alter anything of the old plan, at least not for several years. And our prediction has held. The New Commandant has had to recognize that. It's a shame that you didn't know the previous Commandant!"

"However," the Officer said, interrupting himself, "I'm chattering, and his apparatus stands here in front of us. As you see, it consists of three parts. With the passage of time certain popular names have been developed for each of these parts. The one underneath is called the bed, the upper one is called the inscriber, and here in the middle, this moving part is called the harrow." "The harrow?" the Traveler asked. He had not been listening with full attention. The sun was excessively strong, trapped in the shadowless valley, and one could hardly collect one's thoughts. So the Officer appeared to him all the more admirable in his tight tunic weighed down with epaulettes and festooned with braid, ready to go on parade, as he explained the matter so eagerly and, while he was talking, adjusted screws here and there with a screwdriver.

The Soldier appeared to be in a state similar to the Traveler. He had wound the Condemned Man's chain around both his wrists and was supporting himself with his hand on his weapon, letting his head hang backward, not bothering about anything. The Traveler was not surprised at that, for the Officer spoke French, and clearly neither the Soldier nor the Condemned Man understood the language. So it was all the more striking that the Condemned Man, in spite of that, did what he could to follow the Officer's explanation. With a sort of sleepy persistence he kept directing his gaze to the place where the Officer had just pointed, and when the question from the Traveler interrupted the Officer, the Condemned Man looked at the Traveler, too, just as the Officer was doing.

"Yes, the harrow," said the Officer. "The name fits. The needles are arranged as in a harrow, and the whole thing is driven like a harrow, although it stays in one place and is, in principle, much more artistic. You'll understand in a moment. The condemned is laid out here on the bed. First, I'll describe the apparatus and only then let the procedure go to work. That way you'll be able to follow it better. Also a sprocket in the inscriber is excessively worn. It really squeaks. When it's in motion one can hardly make oneself understood. Unfortunately replacement parts are difficult to come by in this place. So, here is the bed, as I said. The whole thing is completely covered with a layer of cotton wool, the purpose of which you'll find out in a moment. The condemned man is laid out on his stomach on the cotton wool—naked, of course. There are straps for the hands here, for the feet here, and for the throat here, to tie him in securely. At the head of the bed here, where the man, as I have mentioned, first lies face down, is this small protruding lump of felt, which can easily be adjusted so that it presses right into the man's mouth. Its purpose is to prevent him screaming and biting his tongue to pieces. Of course, the man has to let the felt in his mouth—otherwise the straps around his throat would break his neck." "That's cotton wool?" asked the Traveler and bent down. "Yes, it is," said the Officer smiling, "feel it for yourself."

He took the Traveler's hand and led him over to the bed. "It's a specially prepared cotton wool. That's why it looks so unrecognizable. I'll get around to mentioning its purpose in a moment." The Traveler was already being won over a little to the apparatus. With his hand over his eyes to protect them from the sun, he looked at the apparatus in the hole. It was a massive construction. The bed and the inscriber were the same size and looked like two dark chests. The inscriber was set about two metres above the bed, and the two were joined together at the corners by four brass rods, which almost reflected the sun. The harrow hung between the chests on a band of steel.

The Officer had hardly noticed the earlier indifference of the Traveler, but he did have a sense now of how the latter's interest was being aroused for the first time. So he paused in his explanation in order to allow the Traveler time to observe the apparatus undisturbed. The Condemned Man imitated the Traveler, but since he could not put his hand over his eyes, he blinked upward with his eyes uncovered.

"So now the man is lying down," said the Traveler. He leaned back in his chair and crossed his legs.

"Yes," said the Officer, pushing his cap back a little and running his hand over his hot face. "Now, listen. Both the bed and the inscriber have their own electric batteries. The bed needs them for itself, and the inscriber for the harrow. As soon as the man is strapped in securely, the bed is set in motion. It quivers with tiny, very rapid oscillations from side to side and up and down simultaneously. You will have seen similar devices in mental hospitals. Only with our bed all movements are precisely calibrated, for they must be meticulously coordinated with the movements of the harrow. But it's the harrow which has the job of actually carrying out the sentence."

"What is the sentence?" the Traveler asked. "You don't even know that?" asked the Officer in astonishment and bit his lip. "Forgive me if my explanations are perhaps confused. I really do beg your pardon. Previously it was the Commandant's habit to provide such explanations. But the New Commandant has excused himself from this honourable duty. The fact that with such an eminent visitor"—the traveler tried to deflect the honour with both hands, but the officer insisted on the expression—"that with such an eminent visitor he didn't even once make him aware of the form of our sentencing is yet again something new, which ..." He had a curse on his lips, but controlled himself and said merely: "I was not informed about it. It's not my fault. In any case, I am certainly the person best able to explain our style of sentencing, for here I am carrying"—he patted his breast pocket—"the relevant diagrams drawn by the previous Commandant."

"Diagrams made by the Commandant himself?" asked the Traveler. "Then was he in his own person a combination of everything? Was he soldier, judge, engineer, chemist, and draftsman?"

"He was indeed," said the Officer, nodding his head with a fixed and thoughtful expression. Then he looked at his hands, examining them. They didn't seem to him clean enough to handle the diagrams. So he went to the bucket and washed them again. Then he pulled out a small leather folder and said, "Our sentence does not sound severe. The law which a condemned man has violated is inscribed on his body with the harrow. This Condemned Man, for example," and the Officer pointed to the man, "will have inscribed on his body, 'Honour your superiors.'"

The Traveler had a quick look at the man. When the Officer was pointing at him, the man kept his head down and appeared to be directing all his energy into listening in order to learn something. But the movements of his thick pouting lips showed clearly that he was incapable of understanding anything. The Traveler wanted to raise various questions, but after looking at the Condemned Man he merely asked, "Does he know his sentence?" "No," said the Officer. He wished to get on with his explanation right away, but the Traveler interrupted him: "He doesn't know his own sentence?" "No," said the Officer once more. He then paused for a moment, as if he was asking the Traveler for a more detailed reason for his question, and said, "It would be useless to give him that information. He experiences it on his own body." The Traveler really wanted to keep quiet at this point, but he felt how the Condemned Man was gazing at him—he seemed to be asking whether he could approve of the process the Officer had described. So the Traveler, who had up to this point been leaning back, bent forward again and kept up his questions, "But does he nonetheless have some general idea that he's been condemned?" "Not that either," said the Officer, and he smiled at the traveler, as if he was still waiting for some strange revelations from him. "No?" said the Traveler, wiping his forehead, "then does the man also not yet know how his defence was received?" "He has had no opportunity to defend himself," said the Officer and looked away, as if he was talking to himself and wished not to embarrass the Traveler with an explanation of matters so self-evident to him. "But he must have had a chance to defend himself," said the Traveler and stood up from his chair.

The Officer recognized that he was in danger of having his explanation of the apparatus held up for a long time. So he went to the Traveler, took him by the arm, pointed with his hand at the Condemned Man, who stood there stiffly now that the attention was so clearly directed at him—the Soldier was also pulling on his chain—and said, "The matter stands like this. Here in the penal colony I have been appointed judge. In spite of my youth. For I stood at the side of our Old Commandant in all matters of punishment, and I also know the most about the apparatus. The basic principle I use for my decisions is this: Guilt is always beyond a doubt. Other courts could not follow this principle, for they are made up of many heads and, in addition, have even higher courts above them. But that is not the case here, or at least it was not that way with the previous Commandant. It's true the New Commandant has already shown a desire to get mixed up in my court, but I've succeeded so far in fending him off. And I'll continue to be successful. You want this case explained. It's simple—just like all of them. This morning a captain laid a charge that this man, who is assigned to him as a servant and who sleeps before his door, had been sleeping on duty. For his task is to stand up every time the clock strikes the hour and salute in front of the captain's door. That's certainly not a difficult duty—and it's necessary, since he is supposed to remain fresh both for guarding and for service. Yesterday night the captain wanted to check whether his servant was fulfilling his duty. He opened the door on the stroke of two and found him curled up asleep. He got his horsewhip and hit him across the face. Now, instead of standing up and begging for forgiveness, the man grabbed his master by the legs, shook him, and cried out, 'Throw away that whip or I'll eat you up.' Those are the facts. The captain came to me an hour ago. I wrote up his statement and right after that the sentence. Then I had the man chained up. It was all very simple. If I had first summoned the man and interrogated him, the result would have been confusion. He would have lied, and if I had been successful in refuting his lies, he would have replaced them with new lies, and so forth. But now I have him, and I won't release him again. Now, does that clarify everything? But time is passing. We should be starting the execution, and I haven't finished explaining the apparatus yet."

He urged the traveler to sit down in his chair, moved to the apparatus again, and started, "As you see, the shape of the harrow corresponds to the shape of a man. This is the harrow for the upper body, and here are the harrows for the legs. This small cutter is the only one designated for the head. Is that clear to you?" He leaned forward to the Traveler in a friendly way, ready to give the most comprehensive explanation.

The Traveler looked at the harrow with a wrinkled frown. The information about the judicial procedures had not satisfied him. However, he had to tell himself that here it was a matter of a penal colony, that in this place special regulations were necessary, and that one had to give precedence to military measures right down to the last detail. Beyond that, however, he had some hopes in the New Commandant, who obviously, although slowly, was intending to introduce a new procedure which the limited understanding of this Officer could not cope with.

Following this train of thought, the Traveler asked, "Will the Commandant be present at the execution?" "That is not certain," said the Officer, embarrassingly affected by the sudden question, and his friendly expression made a grimace. "That's why we need to hurry up. As much as I regret the fact, I'll have to make my explanation even shorter. But tomorrow, once the apparatus is clean again—the fact that it gets so very dirty is its only fault—I could add a detailed explanation. So now, only the most important things. When the man is lying on the bed and it starts quivering, the harrow sinks onto the body. It positions itself automatically in such a way that it touches the body only lightly with the needle tips. Once the machine is set in this position, this steel cable tightens up into a rod. And now the performance begins. Someone who is not an initiate sees no external difference among the punishments. The harrow seems to do its work uniformly. As it quivers, it sticks the tips of its needles into the body, which is also vibrating from the movement of the bed. Now, to enable someone to check on how the sentence is being carried out, the harrow is made of glass. That gave rise to certain technical difficulties with fastening the needles securely, but after several attempts we were successful. We didn't spare any efforts. And now, as the inscription is made on the body, everyone can see through the glass. Don't you want to come closer and see the needles for yourself."

The Traveler stood slowly, moved up, and bent over the harrow. "You see," the Officer said, "two sorts of needles in a multiple arrangement. Each long needle has a short one next to it. The long one inscribes, and the short one squirts water out to wash away the blood and keep the inscription always clear. The bloody water is then channeled here in small grooves and finally flows into these main gutters, and the outlet pipe takes it to the pit." The officer pointed with his finger to the exact path which the bloody water had to take. As he began to demonstrate with both hands at the mouth of the outlet pipe, in order to make his account as clear as possible, the Traveler raised his head and, feeling behind him with his hand, wanted to return to his chair. Then he saw to his horror that the Condemned Man had also, like him, accepted the Officer's invitation to inspect the arrangement of the harrow up close. He had pulled the sleeping Soldier holding the chain a little forward and was also bending over the glass. One could see how with a confused gaze he also was looking for what the two gentlemen had just observed, but how he didn't succeed because he lacked the explanation. He leaned forward this way and that. He kept running his eyes over the glass again and again. The Traveler wanted to push him back, for what he was doing was probably punishable. But the Officer held the Traveler firmly with one hand, and with the other he took a lump of earth from the wall and threw it at the Soldier. The latter opened his eyes with a start, saw what the Condemned Man had dared to do, let his weapon fall, braced his heels in the earth, and pulled the Condemned Man back, so that he immediately collapsed. The Soldier looked down at him, as he writhed around, making his chain clink. "Stand him up," cried the Officer. Then he noticed that the Condemned Man was distracting the Traveler too much. The latter was even leaning out away from the harrow, without paying any attention to it, wanting to find out what was happening to the Condemned Man. "Handle him carefully," the Officer yelled again. He ran around the apparatus, personally grabbed the Condemned Man under the armpits and, with the help of the Soldier, stood the man, whose feet kept slipping, upright.

"Now I know all about it," said the Traveler, as the Officer turned back to him again. "Except the most important thing," said the latter, grabbing the Traveler by the arm and pointing up high. "There in the inscriber is the mechanism which determines the movement of the harrow, and this mechanism is arranged according to the diagram on which the sentence is set down. I still use the diagrams of the previous Commandant. Here they are." He pulled some pages out of the leather folder. "Unfortunately I can't hand them to you. They are the most cherished thing I possess. Sit down, and I'll show you them from this distance. Then you'll be able to see it all well." He showed the first sheet. The Traveler would have been happy to say something appreciative, but all he saw was a labyrinthine series of lines, criss-crossing each other in all sort of ways. These covered the paper so thickly that only with difficulty could one make out the white spaces in between. "Read it," said the Officer. "I can't," said the Traveler. "But it's clear," said the Officer." "It's very elaborate," said the Traveler evasively, "but I can't decipher it."

"Yes," said the Officer, smiling and putting the folder back again, "it's not calligraphy for school children. One has to read it a long time. You too will finally understand it clearly. Of course, it has to be a script that isn't simple. You see, it's not supposed to kill right away, but on average over a period of twelve hours. The turning point is set for the sixth hour. There must also be many, many embellishments surrounding the basic script. The essential script moves around the body only in a narrow belt. The rest of the body is reserved for decoration. Can you now appreciate the work of the harrow and the whole apparatus? Just look at it!" He jumped up the ladder, turned a wheel, and called down, "Watch out—move to the side!" Everything started moving. If the wheel had not squeaked, it would have been marvelous. The officer threatened the wheel with his fist, as if he was surprised by the disturbance it created. Then he spread his arms, apologizing to the traveler, and quickly clambered down, in order to observe the operation of the apparatus from below.

Something was still not working properly, something only he noticed. He clambered up again and reached with both hands into the inside of the inscriber. Then, in order to descend more quickly, instead of using the ladder, he slid down on one of the poles and, to make himself understandable through the noise, strained his voice to the limit as he yelled in the traveler's ear, "Do you understand the process? The harrow is starting to write. When it's finished with the first part of the script on the man's back, the layer of cotton wool rolls and turns the body slowly onto its side to give the harrow a new area. Meanwhile those parts lacerated by the inscription are lying on the cotton wool which, because it has been specially treated, immediately stops the bleeding and prepares the script for a further deepening. Here, as the body continues to rotate, prongs on the edge of the harrow then pull the cotton wool from the wounds, throw it into the pit, and the harrow goes to work again. In this way it keeps making the inscription deeper for twelve hours. For the first six hours the condemned man goes on living almost as before. He suffers nothing but pain. After two hours, the felt is removed, for at that point the man has no more energy for screaming. Here at the head of the bed warm rice pudding is put in this electrically heated bowl. From this the man, if he feels like it, can help himself to what he can lap up with his tongue. No one passes up this opportunity. I don't know of a single one, and I have had a lot of experience. He first loses his pleasure in eating around the sixth hour. I usually kneel down at this point and observe the phenomenon. The man rarely swallows the last bit. He turns it around in his mouth and spits it into the pit. When he does that, I have to lean aside or else he'll get me in the face. But how quiet the man becomes around the sixth hour! The most stupid of them begin to understand. It starts around the eyes and spreads out from there. A look that could tempt one to lie down under the harrow. Nothing else happens. The man simply begins to decipher the inscription. He purses his lips, as if he is listening. You've seen that it's not easy to figure out the inscription with your eyes, but our man deciphers it with his wounds. True, it takes a lot of work. It requires six hours to complete. But then the harrow spits him right out and throws him into the pit, where he splashes down into the bloody water and cotton wool. Then the judgment is over, and we, the soldier and I, quickly bury him."

The Traveler had leaned his ear towards the Officer and, with his hands in his coat pockets, was observing the machine at work. The Condemned Man was also watching, but without understanding. He bent forward a little and followed the moving needles, as the Soldier, after a signal from the Officer, cut through his shirt and trousers with a knife from the back, so that they fell off the Condemned Man. He wanted to grab the falling garments to cover his bare flesh, but the Soldier held him up and shook the last rags from him. The Officer turned the machine off, and in the silence which then ensued the Condemned Man was laid out under the harrow. The chains were taken off and the straps fastened in their place. For the Condemned Man it seemed at first glance to signify almost a relief. And now the harrow sunk down a stage lower, for the Condemned was a thin man. As the needle tips touched him, a shudder went over his skin. While the Soldier was busy with the right hand, the Condemned Man stretched out his left, with no sense of its direction. But it was pointing to where the Traveler was standing. The Officer kept looking at the Traveler from the side, without taking his eyes off him, as if he was trying to read from his face the impression he was getting of the execution, which he had now explained to him, at least superficially.

The strap meant to hold the wrist ripped off. The Soldier probably had pulled on it too hard. The Soldier showed the Officer the torn-off piece of strap, wanting him to help. So the Officer went over to him and said, with his face turned towards the Traveler, "The machine is very complicated. Now and then something has to tear or break. One shouldn't let that detract from one's overall opinion. Anyway, we have an immediate replacement for the strap. I'll use a chain—even though that will affect the sensitivity of the movements for the right arm." And while he put the chain in place, he kept talking, "Our resources for maintaining the machine are very limited at the moment. Under the previous Commandant, I had free access to a cash box specially set aside for this purpose. There was a store room here in which all possible replacement parts were kept. I admit I made almost extravagant use of it. I mean earlier, not now, as the New Commandant claims. For him everything serves only as a pretext to fight against the old arrangements. Now he keeps the cash box for machinery under his own control, and if I ask him for a new strap, he demands the torn one as a piece of evidence, the new one doesn't arrive for ten days, and it's an inferior brand, of not much use to me. But how I am supposed to get the machine to work in the meantime without a strap—no one's concerned about that."

The Traveler was thinking: it's always questionable to intervene decisively in strange circumstances. He was neither a citizen of the penal colony nor a citizen of the state to which it belonged. If he wanted to condemn the execution or even hinder it, people could say to him: You're a foreigner—keep quiet. He would have nothing in response to that, but could only add that he did not understand what he was doing on this occasion, for the purpose of his traveling was merely to observe and not to alter other people's judicial systems in any way. True, at this point the way things were turning out it was very tempting. The injustice of the process and the inhumanity of the execution were beyond doubt. No one could assume that the Traveler was acting out of any sense of his own self-interest, for the Condemned Man was a stranger to him, not a countryman and not someone who invited sympathy in any way. The Traveler himself had letters of reference from high officials and had been welcomed here with great courtesy. The fact that he had been invited to this execution even seemed to indicate that people were asking for his judgment of this trial. This was all the more likely since the Commandant, as he had now heard only too clearly, was no supporter of this process and maintained an almost hostile relationship with the Officer.

Then the Traveler heard a cry of rage from the Officer. He had just shoved the stub of felt in the Condemned Man's mouth, not without difficulty, when the Condemned Man, overcome by an irresistible nausea, shut his eyes and threw up. The Officer quickly yanked him up off the stump and wanted to turn his head aside toward the pit. But it was too late. The vomit was already flowing down onto the machine. "This is all the Commandant's fault!" cried the officer and mindlessly rattled the brass rods at the front. "My machine's as filthy as a pigsty." With trembling hands he showed the Traveler what had happened. "Haven't I spent hours trying to make the Commandant understand that a day before the execution there should be no more food served. But the new lenient administration has a different opinion. Before the man is led away, the Commandant's women cram sugary things down his throat. His whole life he's fed himself on stinking fish, and now he has to eat sweets! But that would be all right—I'd have no objections—but why don't they get a new felt, the way I've been asking him for three months now? How can anyone take this felt into his mouth without feeling disgusted—something that a hundred man have sucked and bitten on it as they were dying?"

The Condemned Man had laid his head down and appeared peaceful. The Soldier was busy cleaning up the machine with the Condemned Man's shirt. The Officer went up to the Traveler, who, feeling some premonition, took a step backwards. But the Officer grasped him by the hand and pulled him aside. "I want to speak a few words to you in confidence," he said. "May I do that?" "Of course," said the Traveler and listened with his eyes lowered.

"This process and execution, which you now have an opportunity to admire, have no more open supporters in our colony. I am its only defender, just as I am the single advocate for the legacy of the Old Commandant. I can no longer think about a more extensive organization of the process—I'm using all my powers to maintain what there is at present.

When the Old Commandant was alive, the colony was full of his supporters. I have something of the Old Commandant's power of persuasion, but I completely lack his power, and as a result the supporters have gone into hiding. There are still a lot of them, but no one admits to it. If you go into a tea house today—that is to say, on a day of execution—and keep your ears open, perhaps you'll hear nothing but ambiguous remarks. They are all supporters, but under the present Commandant, considering his present views, they are totally useless to me. And now I'm asking you: Should such a life's work," he pointed to the machine, "come to nothing because of this Commandant and the women influencing him? Should people let that happen? Even if one is a foreigner and only on our island for a couple of days? But there's no time to lose. People are already preparing something against my judicial proceedings. Discussions are already taking place in the Commandant's headquarters, to which I am not invited. Even your visit today seems to me typical of the whole situation. People are cowards and send you out—a foreigner. You should have seen the executions in earlier days! The entire valley was overflowing with people, even a day before the execution. They all came merely to watch. Early in the morning the Commandant appeared with his women. Fanfares woke up the entire campsite. I delivered the news that everything was ready. The whole society—and every high official had to attend—arranged itself around the machine. This pile of cane chairs is a sorry left over from that time. The machine was freshly cleaned and glowed. For almost every execution I had new replacement parts. In front of hundreds of eyes—all the spectators stood on tip toe right up to the hills there—the condemned man was laid down under the harrow by the Commandant himself. What nowadays is done by a common soldier was then my work as the senior judge, and it was a honour for me. And then the execution began! No discordant note disturbed the work of the machine. Many people did not look any more at all, but lay down with closed eyes in the sand. They all knew: now justice was being carried out. In silence people listened to nothing but the groans of the condemned man, muffled by the felt. These days the machine no longer manages to squeeze a strong groan out of the condemned man—something the felt is not capable of smothering. But back then the needles which made the inscription dripped a caustic liquid which we are not permitted to use any more today. Well, then came the sixth hour. It was impossible to grant all the requests people made to be allowed to watch from up close. The Commandant, in his wisdom, arranged that the children should be taken care of before all the rest. Naturally, I was always allowed to stand close by, because of my official position. Often I crouched down there with two small children in my arms, on my right and left. How we all took in the expression of transfiguration on the martyred face! How we held our cheeks in the glow of this justice, finally attained and already passing away! What times we had, my friend!"

The Officer had obviously forgotten who was standing in front of him. He had put his arm around the Traveler and laid his head on his shoulder. The Traveler was extremely embarrassed. Impatiently he looked away over the Officer's head. The Soldier had ended his task of cleaning and had just shaken some rice pudding into the bowl from a tin. No sooner had the Condemned Man, who seemed to have fully recovered already, noticed this than his tongue began to lick at the pudding. The Soldier kept pushing him away, for the pudding was probably meant for a later time, but in any case it was not proper for the Soldier to reach in and grab some food with his dirty hands and eat it in front of the famished Condemned Man.

The Officer quickly collected himself. "I didn't want to upset you in any way," he said. "I know it is impossible to make someone understand those days now. Besides, the machine still works and operates on its own. It operates on its own even when it is standing alone in this valley. And at the end, the body still keeps falling in that incredibly soft flight into the pit, even if hundreds of people are not gathered like flies around the hole the way they used to be. Back then we had to erect a strong railing around the pit. It was pulled out long ago."

The Traveler wanted to turn his face away from the Officer and looked aimlessly around him. The Officer thought he was looking at the wasteland of the valley. So he grabbed his hands, turned him around in order to catch his gaze, and asked, "Do you see the shame of it?"

But the Traveler said nothing. The Officer left him alone for a while. With his legs apart and his hands on his hips, the Officer stood still and looked at the ground. Then he smiled at the Traveler cheerfully and said, "Yesterday I was nearby when the Commandant invited you. I heard the invitation. I know the Commandant. I understood right away what he intended with his invitation. Although his power might be sufficiently great to take action against me, he doesn't yet dare to. But my guess is that with you he is exposing me to the judgment of a respected foreigner. He calculates things with care. You are now in your second day on the island. You didn't know the Old Commandant and his way of thinking. You are trapped in a European way of seeing things. Perhaps you are fundamentally opposed to the death penalty in general and to this kind of mechanical style of execution in particular. Moreover, you see how the execution is a sad procedure, without any public participation, using a partially damaged machine. Now, if we take all this together (so the Commandant thinks) surely one could easily imagine that that you would not consider my procedure proper? And if you didn't consider it right, you wouldn't keep quiet about it—I'm still speaking the mind of the Commandant—for you no doubt have faith that your tried-and-true convictions are correct. It's true that you have seen many peculiar things among many peoples and have learned to respect them. Thus, you will probably not speak out against the procedure with your full power, as you would perhaps in your own homeland. But the Commandant doesn't really need that. A casual word, merely a careless remark, is enough. It doesn't have to match your convictions at all, so long as it corresponds to his wishes. I'm certain he will use all his shrewdness to interrogate you. And his women will sit around in a circle and perk up their ears. You will say something like, 'Among us the judicial procedures are different,' or 'With us the accused is questioned before the verdict,' or 'We had torture only in the Middle Ages.' For you these observations appear as correct as they are self-evident—innocent remarks which do not impugn my procedure. But how will the Commandant take them? I see him, our excellent Commandant—the way he immediately pushes his stool aside and hurries out to the balcony—I see his women, how they stream after him. I hear his voice—the women call it a thunder voice. And now he's speaking: 'A great Western explorer who has been commissioned to inspect judicial procedures in all countries has just said that our process based on old customs is inhuman. After the verdict of such a personality it is, of course, no longer possible for me to tolerate this procedure. So from this day on I am ordering … and so forth.' You want to intervene—you didn't say what he is reporting—you didn't call my procedure inhuman; by contrast, in keeping with your deep insight, you consider it most humane and most worthy of human beings. You also admire this machinery. But it is too late. You don't even go onto the balcony, which is already filled with women. You want to attract attention. You want to cry out. But a lady's hand is covering your mouth, and I and the Old Commandant's work are lost."

The Traveler had to suppress a smile. So the work which he had considered so difficult was easy. He said evasively, "You're exaggerating my influence. The Commandant has read my letters of recommendation. He knows that I am no expert in judicial processes. If I were to express an opinion, it would be that of a lay person, no more significant than the opinion of anyone else, and in any case far less significant than the opinion of the Commandant, who, as I understand it, has very extensive powers in this penal colony. If his views of this procedure are as definite as you think they are, then I'm afraid the time has come for this procedure to end, without any need for my humble opinion."

Did the Officer understand by now? No, he did not yet get it. He shook his head vigorously, briefly looked back at the Condemned Man and the Soldier, who both flinched and stopped eating the rice, went up really close up to the Traveler, without looking into his face, but gazing at parts of his jacket, and said more gently than before: "You don't know the Commandant. Where he and all of us are concerned you are—forgive the expression—to a certain extent innocent. Your influence, believe me, cannot be overestimated. In fact, I was blissfully happy when I heard that you were to be present at the execution by yourself. This order of the Commandant was aimed at me, but now I'll turn it to my advantage. Without being distracted by false insinuations and disparaging looks—which could not have been avoided with a greater number of participants at the execution—you have listened to my explanation, looked at the machine, and are now about to view the execution. Your verdict is no doubt already fixed. If some small uncertainties remain, witnessing the execution will remove them. And now I'm asking you—help me with the Commandant!"

The Traveler did not let him go on talking. "How can I do that," he cried. "It's totally impossible. I can help you as little as I can harm you."

"You could do it," said the Officer. With some apprehension the Traveler observed that the Officer was clenching his fists. "You could do it," repeated the Officer, even more emphatically. "I have a plan which must succeed. You think your influence is insufficient. I know it will be enough. But assuming you're right, doesn't saving this whole procedure require one to try even those methods which may be inadequate? So listen to my plan. To carry it out, it's necessary, above all, for you to keep as quiet as possible today in the colony about your verdict on this procedure. Unless someone asks you directly, you should not express any view whatsoever. But what you do say must be short and vague. People should notice that it's difficult for you to speak about the subject, that you feel bitter, that, if you were to speak openly, you'd have to burst out cursing on the spot. I'm not asking

you to lie, not at all. You should only give brief answers—
something like, 'Yes, I've seen the execution' or 'Yes, I've
heard the full explanation.' That's all—nothing further. For
that will be enough of an indication for people to observe in
you a certain bitterness, even if that's not what the Commandant will think. Naturally, he will completely misunderstand
the issue and interpret it in his own way. My plan is based on
that. Tomorrow a large meeting of all the higher administra-
tive officials takes place at headquarters under the chairman-
ship of the Commandant. He, of course, understands how to
turn such a meeting into a spectacle. A gallery has been built,
which is always full of spectators. I'm compelled to take part
in the discussions, though they fill me with disgust. In any
case, you will certainly be invited to the meeting. If you follow
my plan today and behave accordingly, the invitation will
become an emphatic request. But should you for some inexplicable reason still not be invited, you must make sure you
request an invitation. Then you'll receive one without question. Now, tomorrow you are sitting with the women in the
commandant's box. With frequent upward glances he reas-
sures himself that you are there. After various trivial and
ridiculous agenda items designed for the spectators—mostly
harbour construction—always harbour construction—the
judicial process comes up for discussion. If it's not raised by
the Commandant himself or does not occur soon enough, I'll
make sure that it comes up. I'll stand up and report on today's
execution. Really briefly—just the report. Such a report is not
really customary; however, I'll do it, nonetheless. The Commandant thanks me, as always, with a friendly smile. And now
he cannot restrain himself. He seizes this excellent opportunity. 'The report of the execution,' he'll say, or something like
that, 'has just been given. I would like to add to this report
only the fact that this particular execution was attended by the
great explorer whose visit confers such extraordinary honour
on our colony, as you all know. Even the significance of our
meeting today has been increased by his presence. Should we
not now ask this great explorer for his appraisal of the execution based on old customs and of the process which preceded

it?' Of course, there is the noise of applause everywhere, universal agreement. And I'm louder than anyone. The Commandant bows before you and says, 'Then in everyone's name, I'm putting the question to you.' And now you step up to the railing. Place your hands where everyone can see them. Otherwise the ladies will grab them and play with your fingers. And now finally come your remarks. I don't know how I'll bear the tension up to then. In your speech you mustn't hold back. Let truth resound. Lean over the railing and shout it out—yes, yes, roar your opinion at the Commandant, your unshakeable opinion. But perhaps you don't want to do that. It doesn't suit your character. Perhaps in your country people behave differently in such situations. That's all right. That's perfectly satisfactory. Don't stand up at all. Just say a couple of words. Whisper them so that only the officials underneath you can just hear them. That's enough. You don't even have to say anything at all about the lack of attendance at the execution or about the squeaky wheel, the torn strap, the disgusting felt. No. I'll take over all further details, and, believe me, if my speech doesn't chase him out of the room, it will force him to his knees, so he'll have to admit it: 'Old Commandant, I bow down before you.' That's my plan. Do you want to help me carry it out? But, of course, you want to. More than that—you have to."

And the officer gripped the traveler by both arms and looked at him, breathing heavily into his face. He had yelled the last sentences so loudly that even the Soldier and the Condemned Man were paying attention. Although they couldn't understand a thing, they stopped eating and looked over at the Traveler, still chewing.

From the start the Traveler had had no doubts about the answer he must give. He had experienced too much in his life to be able to waver here. Basically he was honest and unafraid. Still, with the Soldier and the Condemned Man looking at him, he hesitated a moment. But finally he said, as he had to, "No." The Officer's eyes blinked several times, but he did not take his eyes off the Traveler. "Would you like an explanation," asked the Traveler. The Officer nodded dumbly. "I am opposed to this procedure," said the Traveler. "Even before you took me into your confidence—and, of course, I will never abuse your confidence under any circumstances—I was already thinking about whether I was entitled to intervene against this procedure and whether my intervention could have the smallest chance of success. And if that was the case, it was clear to me whom I had to turn to first of all—naturally, to the Commandant. You clarified the issue for me even more, but without reinforcing my decision in any way—quite the reverse. I find your conviction genuinely moving, even if it cannot deter me."

The Officer remained quiet, turned toward the machine, grabbed one of the brass rods, and then, leaning back a little, looked up at the inscriber, as if he was checking that everything was in order. The Soldier and the Condemned Man seemed to have made friends with each other. The Condemned Man was making signs to the Soldier, although, given the tight straps on him, this was difficult for him to do. The Soldier was leaning into him. The Condemned Man whispered something to him, and the Soldier nodded. The Traveler went over to the Officer and said, "You don't yet know what I'll do. Yes, I will tell the Commandant my opinion of the procedure—not in a meeting, but in private. In addition, I won't stay here long enough to be able to get called in to some meeting or other. Early tomorrow morning I leave, or at least I go on board ship." It didn't look as if the Officer had been listening. "So the process has not convinced you," he said to himself, smiling the way an old man smiles over the silliness of a child, concealing his own true thoughts behind that smile.

"Well then, it's time," he said finally and suddenly looked at the Traveler with bright eyes which contained some sort of demand, some appeal for participation. "Time for what?" asked the Traveler uneasily. But there was no answer.

"You are free," the Officer told the Condemned Man in his own language. At first the man did not believe him. "You are free now," said the Officer. For the first time the face of the Condemned Man showed signs of real life. Was it the truth? Was it only the Officer's mood, which could change? Had the foreign Traveler brought him a reprieve? What was it? That's what the man's face seemed to be asking. But not for long. Whatever the case might be, if he could he wanted to be truly free, and he began to shake back and forth, as much as the harrow permitted.

"You're tearing my straps," cried the Officer. "Be still! We'll undo them right away." And, giving a signal to the Soldier, he set to work with him. The Condemned Man said nothing and smiled slightly to himself. He turned his face to the Officer and then to the Soldier and then back again, without ignoring the Traveler.

"Pull him out," the Officer ordered the Soldier. This process required a certain amount of care because of the harrow. The Condemned Man already had a few small wounds on his back, thanks to his own impatience.

From this point on, however, the Officer paid him hardly any attention. He went up to the Traveler, pulled out the small leather folder once more, leafed through it, finally found the sheet he was looking for, and showed it to the Traveler. "Read that," he said. "I can't," said the Traveler. "I've already told you I can't read these pages." "But take a close look at the page," said the Officer, and moved up right next to the Traveler in order to read with him. When that didn't help, he raised his little finger high up over the paper, as if the page must not be touched under any circumstances, so that using this he might make the task of reading easier for the Traveler. The Traveler also made an effort so that at least he could satisfy the Officer, but it was impossible for him. Then the Officer began to spell out the inscription and then read out once again the joined up letters. "'Be just!' it states," he said. "Now you can read it." The Traveler bent so low over the paper that the Officer, afraid that he might touch it, moved it further away. The Traveler didn't say anything more, but it was clear that he was still unable to read anything. " 'Be just!' it says," the Officer remarked once again.

"That could be," said the Traveler. "I do believe that's written there." "Good," said the Officer, at least partially satisfied. He climbed up the ladder, holding the paper. With great care he set the page in the inscriber and appeared to rotate the gear mechanism completely around. This was very tiring work. It must have required him to deal with extremely small wheels. He had to inspect the gears so closely that sometimes his head disappeared completely into the inscriber.

The Traveler followed this work from below without looking away. His neck grew stiff, and his eyes found the sunlight pouring down from the sky painful. The Soldier and the Condemned Man were keeping each other busy. With the tip of his bayonet the Soldier pulled out the Condemned Man's shirt and trousers which were lying in the hole. The shirt was horribly dirty, and the Condemned Man washed it in the bucket of water. When he was putting on his shirt and trousers, the Soldier and the Condemned Man had to laugh out loud, for the pieces of clothing were cut in two up the back. Perhaps the Condemned Man thought that it was his duty to amuse the Soldier. In his ripped-up clothes he circled around the Soldier, who crouched down on the ground, laughed, and slapped his knees. But they restrained themselves out of consideration for the two gentlemen present.

When the Officer was finally finished up on the machine, with a smile he looked over the whole thing and all its parts one more time, and this time closed the cover of the inscriber, which had been open up to this point. He climbed down, looked into the hole and then at the Condemned Man, observed with satisfaction that he had pulled out his clothes, then went to the bucket of water to wash his hands, recognized too late that it was disgustingly dirty, and was upset that now he couldn't wash his hands. Finally he pushed them into the sand. This option didn't satisfy him, but he had to do what he could in the circumstances. Then he stood up and began to unbutton the coat of his uniform. As he did this, the two lady's handkerchiefs, which he had pushed into the back of his collar, fell into his hands. "Here you have your handkerchiefs," he said and threw them over to the Condemned Man. And to the Traveler he said by way of an explanation, "Presents from the ladies."

In spite of the obvious speed with which he took off the coat of his uniform and then undressed himself completely, he handled each piece of clothing very carefully, even running his fingers over the silver braids on his tunic with special care and shaking a tassel into place. But in great contrast to this care, as soon he was finished handling an article of clothing, he immediately flung it angrily into the hole. The last items he had left were his short sword and its harness. He pulled the sword out of its scabbard, broke it in pieces, gathered up everything—the pieces of the sword, the scabbard, and the harness—and threw them away so forcefully that they rattled against each other down in the pit.

Now he stood there naked. The Traveler bit his lip and said nothing. For he was aware what would happen, but he had no right to hinder the Officer in any way. If the judicial process to which the officer clung was really so close to the point of being cancelled—perhaps as a result of the intervention of the Traveler, something to which he for his part felt duty-bound—then the Officer was now acting in a completely correct manner. In his place, the Traveler would not have acted any differently.

The Soldier and the Condemned Man at first didn't understand a thing. To begin with they didn't look, not even once. The Condemned Man was extremely happy to get the handkerchiefs back, but he couldn't enjoy them very long, for the Soldier snatched them from him with a quick grab, which he had not anticipated. The Condemned Man then tried to pull the handkerchiefs out from the Soldier's belt, where he had put them for safe keeping, but the Soldier was too wary. So they were fighting, half in jest. Only when the Officer was fully naked did they start to pay attention. The Condemned Man especially seemed to be struck by a premonition of some sort of significant transformation. What had happened to him was now taking place with the Officer. Perhaps this time the procedure would play itself out to its conclusion. The foreign Traveler had probably given the order. So that was revenge. Without having suffered all the way to the end himself, nonetheless he would be completely revenged. A wide, silent laugh now appeared on his face and did not go away.

The Officer, however, had turned towards the machine. If earlier on it had already become clear that he understood the machine thoroughly, one might well get alarmed now at the way he handled it and how it obeyed. He only had to bring his hand near the harrow for it to rise and sink several times, until it had reached the correct position to make room for him. He only had to grasp the bed by the edges, and it already began to quiver. The stump of felt moved up to his mouth. One could see how the Officer really didn't want to accept it, but his hesitation was only momentary—he immediately submitted and took it in. Everything was ready, except that the straps still hung down on the sides. But they were clearly unnecessary. The Officer did not have to be strapped down. When the Condemned Man saw the loose straps, he thought the execution would be incomplete unless they were fastened. He waved eagerly to the Soldier, and they ran over to strap in the Officer. The latter had already stuck out his foot to kick the crank designed to set the inscriber in motion. Then he saw the two men coming. So he pulled his foot back and let himself be strapped in. But now he could no longer reach the crank. Neither the Soldier nor the Condemned Man would find it, and the Traveler was determined not to touch it. But that was unnecessary. Hardly were the straps attached when the machine already started working. The bed quivered, the needles danced on his skin, and the harrow swung up and down. The Traveler had already been staring for some time before he remembered that a wheel in the inscriber was supposed to squeak. But everything was quiet, without the slightest audible hum.

Because of its silent working, the machine did not really attract attention. The Traveler looked over at the Soldier and the Condemned Man. The Condemned Man was the livelier of the two. Everything in the machine interested him. At times he bent down—at other times he stretched up, all the time pointing with his forefinger in order to show something to the Soldier. For the Traveler it was embarrassing. He was determined to remain here until the end, but he could no longer endure the sight of the two men. "Go home," he said. The Soldier might have been ready to do that, but the Condemned Man took the order as a direct punishment. With his hands folded he begged and pleaded to be allowed to stay there. And when the Traveler shook his head and was unwilling to give in, he even knelt down. Seeing that orders were of no help here, the Traveler wanted to go over and chase the two away.

Then he heard a noise from up in the inscriber. He looked up. So was the gear wheel going out of alignment? But it was something else. The lid on the inscriber was lifting up slowly. Then it fell completely open. The teeth of a cog wheel were exposed and lifted up. Soon the entire wheel appeared. It was as if some huge force was compressing the inscriber, so that there was no longer sufficient room for this wheel. The wheel rolled all the way to the edge of the inscriber, fell down, rolled upright a bit in the sand, and then fell over and lay still. But already up on the inscriber another gear wheel was moving upwards. Several others followed—large ones, small ones, ones hard to distinguish. With each of them the same thing happened. One kept thinking that now the inscriber must surely be empty, but then a new cluster with lots of parts would move up, fall down, roll in the sand, and lie still. With all this going on, the Condemned Man totally forgot the Traveler's order. The gear wheels completely delighted him. He kept wanting to grab one, and at the same time he was urging the Soldier to help him. But he kept pulling his hand back startled, for immediately another wheel followed, which, at least in its initial rolling, surprised him.

The Traveler, by contrast, was very upset. Obviously the machine was breaking up. Its quiet operation had been an illusion. He felt as if he had to look after the Officer, now that the latter could no longer look after himself. But while the falling gear wheels were claiming all his attention, he had neglected to look at the rest of the machine. However, when he now bent over the harrow, once the last gear wheel had left the inscriber, he had a new, even more unpleasant surprise. The harrow was not writing but only stabbing, and the bed was not rolling the body, but lifting it, quivering, up into the needles. The Traveler wanted to reach in to stop the whole thing, if possible. This was not the torture the Officer wished to attain. It was murder, pure and simple. He stretched out his hands. But at that point the harrow was already moving upwards and to the side, with the skewered body—just as it did in other cases, but only in the twelfth hour. Blood flowed out in hundreds of streams, not mixed with water—the water tubes had also failed to work this time. Then one last thing went wrong: the body would not come loose from the needles. Its blood streamed out, but it hung over the pit without falling. The harrow wanted to move back to its original position, but, as if it realized that it could not free itself of its load, it remained over the hole.

"Help," the Traveler yelled out to the Soldier and the Condemned Man and grabbed the Officer's feet. He wanted to push against the feet himself and have the two others grab the Officer's head from the other side, so he could be slowly taken off the needles. But now the two men could not make up their mind whether to come or not. The Condemned Man turned away at once. The Traveler had to go over to him and drag him to the Officer's head by force. At this point, almost against his will, he looked at the face of the corpse. It was as it had been in his life. He could discover no sign of the promised transfiguration. What all the others had found in the machine, the Officer had not. His lips were pressed firmly together, his eyes were open and looked as they had when he was alive, his gaze was calm and convinced. The tip of a large iron needle had gone through his forehead.

*

As the Traveler, with the Soldier and the Condemned Man behind him, came to the first houses in the colony, the Soldier pointed to one and said, "That's the tea house."

On the ground floor of one of the houses was a deep, low room, like a cave, with smoke-covered walls and ceiling. On the street side it was open along its full width. Although there was little difference between the tea house and the rest of the houses in the colony, which were all very dilapidated, except for the Commandant's palatial structure, the Traveler was struck by the impression of historical memory, and he felt the power of earlier times. Followed by his companions, he walked closer, going between the unoccupied tables, which stood in the street in front of the tea house, and took a breath of the cool, stuffy air which came from inside. "The old man is buried here," said the soldier; "a place in the cemetery was denied him by the chaplain. For a long time people were undecided where they should bury him. Finally they buried him here. Of course, the Officer explained none of that to you, for naturally he was the one most ashamed about it. A few times he even tried to dig up the old man at night, but he was always chased off." "Where is the grave?" asked the Traveler, who could not believe the Soldier. Instantly both men, the Soldier and the Condemned Man, ran in front of him and with hands outstretched pointed to the place where the grave was located. They led the Traveler to the back wall, where guests were sitting at a few tables. They were presumably dock workers, strong men with short, shiny, black beards. None of them wore coats, and their shirts were torn. They were poor, oppressed people. As the Traveler came closer, a few got up, leaned against the wall, and looked at him. A whisper went up around the Traveler—"It's a foreigner. He wants to look at the grave." They pushed one of the tables aside, under which there was a real grave stone. It was a simple stone, low enough for it to remain hidden under a table. It bore an inscription in very small letters. In order to read it the Traveler had to kneel down. It read, "Here rests the Old Commandant. His followers, who are now not permitted to have a name, buried him in this grave and erected this stone. There exists a prophecy that the Commandant will rise again after a certain number of years and from this house will lead his followers to a re-conquest of the colony. Have faith and wait!"

When the Traveler had read it and got up, he saw the men standing around him and smiling, as if they had read the inscription with him, found it ridiculous, and were asking him to share their opinion. The Traveler acted as if he hadn't noticed, distributed some coins among them, waited until the table was pushed back over the grave, left the tea house, and went to the harbour.

In the tea house the Soldier and the Condemned Man had come across some people they knew who detained them. However, they must have broken free of them soon, because by the time the Traveler found himself in the middle of a long staircase which led to the boats, they were already running after him. They probably wanted to force the Traveler at the last minute to take them with him. While the Traveler was haggling at the bottom of the stairs with a sailor about his passage out to the steamer, the two men were racing down the steps in silence, for they didn't dare cry out. But as they reached the bottom, the Traveler was already in the boat, and the sailor at once cast off from shore. They could still have jumped into the boat, but the Traveler picked up a heavy knotted rope from the boat bottom, threatened them with it, and thus prevented them from jumping in.

Jackals and Arabs

We were camping in the oasis. My companions were asleep. An Arab, tall and dressed in white, went past me. He had been tending to his camels and was going to his sleeping place.

I threw myself on my back into the grass. I wanted to sleep. I couldn't. The howling of a jackal in the distance—I sat up straight again. And what had been so far away was suddenly close by. A swarming pack of jackals around me, their eyes flashing dull gold and going out, slender bodies moving in a quick, coordinated manner, as if responding to a whip.

One of them came from behind, pushed himself under my arm, right against me, as if it needed my warmth, then stepped in front of me and spoke, almost eye to eye with me.

"I'm the oldest jackal for miles around. I'm happy I'm still able to welcome you here. I had already almost given up hope, for we've been waiting for you an infinitely long time. My mother waited, and her mother, and all her mothers, right back to the mother of all jackals. Believe me!"

"That surprises me," I said, forgetting to light the pile of wood which lay ready to keep the jackals away with its smoke, "I'm very surprised to hear that. I've come from the high north merely by chance and am in the middle of a short trip. What do you jackals want then?"

As if encouraged by this conversation, which was perhaps too friendly, they drew their circle more closely around me, all panting and snarling.

"We know," the oldest began, "that you come from the north. Our hope rests on that very point. In the north there is a way of understanding things which one cannot find here among the Arabs. You know, from their cool arrogance one cannot strike a spark of common sense. They kill animals to eat them, and they disregard rotting carcasses."

"Don't speak so loud," I said. "There are Arabs sleeping close by."

"You really are a stranger," said the jackal. "Otherwise you would know that throughout the history of the world a jackal has never yet feared an Arab. Should we fear them? Is it not misfortune enough that we have been cast out among such people?"

"Maybe—that could be," I said. "I'm not up to judging things which are so far removed from me. It seems to be a very old conflict—it's probably in the blood and so perhaps will only end with blood."

"You are very clever" said the old jackal, and they all panted even more quickly, their lungs breathing rapidly, although they were standing still. A bitter smell streamed out of their open jaws—at times I could tolerate it only by clenching my teeth. "You are very clever. What you said corresponds to our ancient doctrine. So we take their blood, and the quarrel is over."

"Oh," I said, more sharply than I intended, "they'll defend themselves. They'll shoot you down in droves with their guns."

"You do not understand us," he said, "a characteristic of human beings which has not disappeared, not even in the high north. We are not going to kill them. The Nile would not have enough water to wash us clean. The very sight of their living bodies makes us run away immediately into cleaner air, into the desert, which, for that very reason, is our home."

All the jackals surrounding us—and in the meantime many more had come up from a distance—lowered their heads between the front legs and cleaned them with their paws. It was as if they wanted to conceal an aversion which was so terrible, that I would have much preferred to take a big jump and escape beyond their circle.

"So what do you intend to do," I asked. I wanted to stand up, but I couldn't. Two young animals were holding me firmly from behind with their jaws biting my jacket and shirt. I had to remain sitting. "They are holding your train," said the old jackal seriously, by way of explanation, "a mark of respect." "They should let me go," I cried out, turning back and forth between the old one and the young ones. "Of course, they will," said the old one, "if that's what you want. But it will take a little while, for, as is our habit, they have dug their teeth in deep and must first let their jaws open gradually. Meanwhile, listen to our request." "Your conduct has not made me particularly receptive to it," I said. "Don't make us pay for our clumsiness," he said, and now for the first time he brought the plaintive tone of his natural voice to his assistance. "We are poor animals—all we have is our teeth. For everything we want to do—good and bad—the only thing available to us is our teeth." "So what do you want?" I asked, only slightly reassured.

"Sir," he cried out, and all the jackals howled. To me it sounded very remotely like a melody. "Sir, you should end the quarrel which divides the world in two. Our ancestors described a man like you as the one who will do it. We must be free of the Arabs—with air we can breathe, a view of the horizon around us clear of Arabs, no cries of pain from a sheep which an Arab has knifed, and every animal should die peacefully and be left undisturbed for us to drain it empty and clean it right down to the bones. Cleanliness—that's what we want— nothing but cleanliness." Now they were all crying and sobbing. "How can you bear it in this world, you noble heart and sweet entrails? Dirt is their white; dirt is their black; their beards are horrible; looking at the corner of their eyes makes one spit; and if they lift their arms, hell opens up in their arm pits. And that's why, sir, that's why, my dear sir, with the help of your all-capable hands you must use these scissors to slit right through their throats." He jerked his head, and in response a jackal came up carrying on its canine tooth a small pair of sewing scissors covered with old rust.

"So finally the scissors—it's time to stop!" cried the Arab leader of our caravan, who had crept up on us from downwind. Now he swung his gigantic whip.

The jackals all fled quickly, but still remained at some distance huddled closely together, many animals so close and stiff that it looked as if they were in a narrow pen with jack o' lanterns flying around them.

"So, you too, sir, have seen and heard this spectacle," said the Arab, laughing as cheerfully as the reticence of his race permitted. "So you know what the animals want," I asked. "Of course, sir," he said. "That's common knowledge—as long as there are Arabs, these scissors will wander with us through the deserts until the end of days. Every European is offered them for the great work; every European is exactly the one they think qualified to do it. These animals have an absurd hope. They're idiots, real idiots. That's why we're fond of them. They are our dogs, finer than the ones you have. Now, watch this. In the night a camel died. I have had it brought here."

Four bearers came and threw the heavy carcass right in front of us. No sooner was it lying there than the jackals raised their voices. Every one of them crept forward, its body scraping the ground, as if drawn by an irresistible rope. They had forgotten the Arabs, forgotten their hatred. The presence of a powerfully stinking dead body wiped out everything and enchanted them. One of them was already hanging at the camel's throat and with its first bite had found the artery. Like a small angry pump which—with a determination matched only by its hopelessness—seeks to put out an overpowering fire, every muscle of its body pulled and twitched in its place. Then right away all them were lying there on the corpse working in the same way, piled up like a mountain.

Then the leader cracked his sharp whip powerfully all around above them. They raised their heads, half fainting in their intoxicated state, looked at the Arab standing in front of them, started to feel the whip now hitting their muzzles, jumped away, and ran back a distance. But the camel's blood was already lying there in pools, stinking to heaven, and the body was torn wide open in several places. They could not resist. They were there again. The leader once more raised his whip. I grabbed his arm. "Sir, you are right," he said. "We'll leave them to their calling. Besides, it's time to break camp. You've seen them. Wonderful creatures, aren't they? And how they hate us!"

The Great Wall of China

The Great Wall of China was finished at its northernmost location. The construction work moved up from the southeast and south-west and joined at this point. The system of building in sections was also followed on a small scale within the two great armies of workers, the eastern and western. It was carried out in the following manner: groups of about twenty workers were formed, each of which had to take on a section of the wall, about five hundred metres. A neighbouring group then built a wall of similar length to meet it. But afterwards, when the sections were fully joined, construction was not continued on any further at the end of this thousand-metre section. Instead the groups of workers were shipped off again to build the wall in completely different regions. Naturally, with this method many large gaps arose, which were filled in only gradually and slowly, many of them not until after it had already been reported that the building of the wall was complete. In fact, there are said to be gaps which have never been built in at all, although that's merely an assertion which probably belongs among the many legends which have arisen about the structure and which, for individual people at least, are impossible to prove with their own eyes and according to their own standards, because the structure is so immense.

Now, at first one might think it would have been more advantageous in every way to build in continuous sections or at least continuously within two main sections. For the wall was conceived as a protection against the people of the north, as was commonly announced and universally known. But how can protection be provided by a wall which is not built continuously? In fact, not only can such a wall not protect, but the structure itself is in constant danger. Those parts of the wall left standing abandoned in particular regions could easily be destroyed again and again by the nomads, especially by those back then who, worried about the building of the wall, changed their place of residence with incredible speed, like grasshoppers, and thus perhaps had an even better overall view of how the construction was proceeding than we did, the people who built it.

However, there was no other way to carry out the construction except the way it happened. In order to understand this, one must consider the following: the wall was to be a protection for centuries; thus, the essential prerequisites for the work were the most careful construction, the use of the architectural wisdom of all known ages and peoples, and an enduring sense of personal responsibility in the builders. Of course, for the more humble tasks one could use ignorant day labourers from the people—the men, women, and children who offered their services for good money. But the supervision of even four day labourers required a knowledgeable man, an educated expert in construction, someone who was capable of feeling sympathy deep in his heart for what was at stake here. And the higher the challenge, the greater the demands. And such men were in fact available—if not the crowds of them which this construction could have used, at least in great numbers.

They did not set about this task recklessly. Fifty years before the start of construction it was announced throughout the whole region of China which was to be enclosed within the wall that architecture and especially masonry were the most important areas of knowledge, and everything else was recognized only to the extent that it had some relationship to those. I still remember very well how as small children who could hardly walk we stood in our teacher's little garden and had to construct a sort of wall out of pebbles, and how the teacher gathered up his coat and ran against the wall, naturally making everything collapse, and then scolded us so much for the weakness of our construction that we ran off in all directions howling to our parents. A tiny incident, but an indication of the spirit of the times.

I was lucky that at twenty years of age, when I passed the final examination of the lowest school, the construction of the wall was just starting. I say lucky because many who earlier had attained the highest limit of education available to them for years had no idea what to do with their knowledge and wandered around uselessly, with the most splendid architectural plans in their heads, and a great many of them just went downhill from there. But the ones who finally got to work as supervisors on the construction, even if they had the lowest rank, were really worthy of their position. They were masons who had given much thought to the construction and never stopped thinking about it, men who, right from the first stone which they sunk into the ground, had a sense of themselves as part of the wall. Such masons, of course, were driven not only by the desire to carry out the work as thoroughly as possible but also by impatience to see the structure standing there in its complete final perfection. Day labourers do not experience this impatience. They are driven only by their pay. The higher supervisors and, indeed, even the middle supervisors, see enough from their various perspectives on the growth of the wall to keep their spirits energized. But the subordinate supervisors, men who were mentally far above their small, more trivial tasks, had to be catered to in other ways. One could not, for example, let them lay one building block on top of another in an uninhabited region of the mountains, hundreds of miles from their homes, for months or even years at a time. The hopelessness of such a hard task, which could not be completed even in a long human lifetime, would have caused them distress and, more than anything else, made them worthless for work. For that reason they chose the system of building in sections. Five hundred metres could be completed in something like five years, by which time naturally the supervisors were as a rule too exhausted and had lost all faith in themselves, in the building, and in the world.

Thus, while they were still experiencing the elation of the celebrations for the joining up of a thousand metres of the wall, they were shipped far, far away. On their journey they saw here and there finished sections of the wall rising up; they passed through the quarters of the higher administrators, who gave them gifts as badges of honour, and they heard the rejoicing of new armies of workers streaming past them out of the depths of the land, saw forests being laid low, wood designated as scaffolding for the wall, witnessed mountains being broken up into rocks for the wall, and heard in the holy places the hymns of the pious praying for the construction to be finished. All this calmed their impatience. The quiet life of home, where they spent some time, reinvigorated them. The high regard which all those doing the building enjoyed, the devout humility with which people listened to their reports, the trust that simple quiet citizens had that the wall would be completed someday—all this tuned the strings of their souls. Then, like eternally hopeful children, they took leave of their home. The enthusiasm for labouring once again at the people's work became irresistible. They set out from their houses earlier than necessary, and half the village accompanied them for a long way. On all the roads there were groups of people, pennants, banners—they had never seen how great and rich and beautiful and endearing their country was. Every countryman was a brother for whom they were building a protective wall and who would thank him with everything he had and was for all his life. Unity! Unity! Shoulder to shoulder, a coordinated movement of the people, their blood no longer confined in the limited circulation of the body but rolling sweetly and yet still returning through the infinite extent of China.

In view of all this, the system of piecemeal building becomes understandable. But there were still other reasons, too. And there is nothing strange in the fact that I have held off on this point for so long. It is the central issue in the whole construction of the wall, no matter how unimportant it appears at first. If I want to convey the ideas and experiences of that time and make them intelligible, I cannot probe deeply enough into this particular question.

First, one must realize that at that time certain achievements were brought to fruition which rank only slightly behind the Tower of Babel, although in the pleasure they gave to God, at least by human reckoning, they made an impression exactly the opposite of that structure. I mention this because at the time construction was beginning a scholar wrote a book in which he drew this comparison very precisely. In it he tried to show that the Tower of Babel had failed to attain its goal not for the reasons commonly asserted, or at least that the most important cause was not among these well-known ones. He not only based his proofs on texts and reports, but also claimed to have carried out personal inspections of the location and thus to have found that the structure collapsed and had to collapse because of the weakness of its foundation. And it is true that in this respect our age was far superior to that one long ago. Almost every educated person in our age was a mason by profession and infallible when it came to the business of laying foundations.

But it was not at all the scholar's aim to prove this. He claimed that the great wall alone would for the first time in the age of human beings create a secure foundation for a new Tower of Babel. So first the wall and then the tower. In those days the book was in everyone's hands, but I confess that even today I do not understand exactly how he imagined this tower. How could the wall, which never once took the form of a circle but only a sort of quarter or half circle, provide the foundation for a tower? But it could be meant only in a spiritual sense. But then why the wall, which was still something real, a product of the efforts and lives of hundreds of thousands of people? And why were there plans in the book—admittedly hazy plans—sketching the tower, as well as detailed proposals about how the energies of the people could be channelled into powerfully new work.

There was a great deal of mental confusion at the time—his book is only one example—perhaps simply because so many people were trying as hard as they could to join together for a single purpose. Human nature, which is fundamentally careless and by nature like the whirling dust, endures no restraint. If it restricts itself, it will soon begin to shake the restraints madly and tear up walls, chains, and even itself all over the place.

It is possible that even these considerations, which argued against building the wall in the first place, were not ignored by the leadership when they decided on piecemeal construction. We—and here I'm really speaking on behalf of many—

actually first found out about it by spelling out the orders from the highest levels of management and learned for ourselves that without the leadership neither our school learning nor our human understanding would have been adequate for the small position we had within the enormous totality.

In the office of the leadership—where it was and who sat there no one I asked knows or knew—in this office I imagine that all human thoughts and wishes revolve in a circle, and all human aims and fulfilments in a circle going in the opposite direction. And through the window the reflection of the divine worlds fell onto the hands of the leadership as they drew up the plans. And for this reason the incorruptible observer will reject the notion that if the leadership had seriously wanted a continuous construction of the wall, they would not have been able to overcome the difficulties standing in the way. So the only conclusion left is that the leadership deliberately chose piecemeal construction. But building in sections was something merely makeshift and impractical. So the conclusion remains that the leadership wanted something impractical. An odd conclusion! True enough, and yet from another perspective it had some inherent justification.

Nowadays one can perhaps speak about it without danger. At that time for many people, even the best, there was a secret principle: Try with all your powers to understand the orders of the leadership, but only up to a certain limit—then stop thinking about them. A very reasonable principle, which incidentally found an even wider interpretation in a later often repeated comparison: Stop further thinking about it, not because it could harm you—it is not at all certain that it will harm you. In this matter one cannot speak in general about harming or not harming. What will happen to you is like a river in spring. It rises, grows stronger, eats away powerfully at the land along its shores, and still maintains its own course down into the sea and is more welcome as a fitter partner for the sea. Reflect upon the orders of the leadership as far as that. But then the river overflows its banks, loses its form and shape, slows down its forward movement, tries, contrary to its destiny, to form small seas inland, damages the fields, and yet cannot maintain its expansion long, but runs back within its banks, in fact, even dries up miserably in the hot time of year which follows. Do not reflect on the orders of the leadership to that extent.

Now, this comparison may perhaps have been extraordinarily apt during the construction of the wall, but it has at most only a limited relevance to my present report. For my investigation is only historical. There is no lightning strike flashing any more from storm clouds which have long since vanished, and thus I may seek an explanation for the piece-meal construction which goes further than the one people were satisfied with back then. The limits which my ability to think sets for me are certainly narrow enough, but the region one would have to pass through here is endless.

Against whom was the great wall to provide protection? Against the people of the north. I come from south-east China. No northern people can threaten us there. We read about them in the books of the ancients. The atrocities which their nature prompts them to commit make us heave a sigh on our peaceful porches. In the faithfully accurate pictures of artists we see the faces of this damnation, with their mouths flung open, the sharp pointed teeth stuck in their jaws, their straining eyes, which seem to be squinting for someone to seize, whom their jaws will crush and rip to pieces. When children are naughty, we hold up these pictures in front of them, and they immediately burst into tears and run into our arms. But we know nothing else about these northern lands. We have never seen them, and if we remain in our village, we never will see them, even if they charge straight at us and hunt us on their wild horses. The land is so huge, it would not permit them to reach us, and they would lose themselves in empty air.

So if things are like this, why do we leave our homes, the river and bridges, our mothers and fathers, our crying wives, our children in need of education, and go to school in the distant city, with our thoughts on the wall to the north, even further away? Why? Ask the leadership. They know us. As they mull over their immense concerns, they know about us, understand our small worries, see us all sitting together in our humble huts, and approve or disapprove of the prayer which the father of the house says in the evening surrounded by his family. And if I may be permitted such ideas about the leadership, then I must say that in my view the leadership existed even earlier. It did not come together like some high mandarins hastily summoned to a meeting by a beautiful dream of the future, something hastily concluded, a meeting which saw to it that the general population was driven from their beds by a knocking on the door so that they could carry out the decision, even if it was only to set up an lantern in honour of a god who had shown favour to the masters the day before, so that he could thrash them in some dark corner the next day, when the lantern had only just died out. On the contrary, I imagine the leadership has always existed, along with the decision to construct the wall as well. Innocent northern people believed they were the cause; the admirable innocent emperor believed he had given orders for it. We who were builders of the wall know otherwise and are silent.

Even during the construction of the wall and afterwards, right up to the present day, I have devoted myself almost exclusively to the histories of different people. There are certain questions for which one can, to some extent, get to the heart of the matter only in this way. Using this method I have found that we Chinese possess certain popular and state institutions which are uniquely clear and, then again, others which are uniquely obscure. Tracking down the reasons for these, especially for the latter phenomena, always appealed to me, and still does, and the construction of the wall is fundamentally concerned with these issues.

Now, among our most obscure institutions one can certainly include the empire itself. Of course, in Peking, right in the court, there is some clarity about it, although even this is more apparent than real. And the teachers of constitutional law and history in the schools of higher learning give out that they are precisely informed about these things and that they are able to pass this knowledge on to their students. The deeper one descends into the lower schools, understandably the more the doubts about the students' own knowledge disappear, and a superficial education surges up as high as a mountain around a few precepts drilled into them for centuries, sayings which, in fact, have lost nothing of their eternal truth, but which remain also eternally unrecognised in the mist and fog.

But, in my view, it's precisely the empire we should be asking the people about, because in them the empire has its final support. It's true that in this matter I can speak once again only about my own homeland. Other than the agricultural deities and the service to them, which so beautifully and variously fills up the entire year, our thinking concerns itself only with the emperor. But not with the present emperor. We'd rather think about the present one if we knew who he was or anything definite about him. We were naturally always trying—and it's the single curiosity which satisfies us—to find out something or other about him, but, no matter how strange this sounds, it was hardly possible to learn anything, either from pilgrims, even though they wandered through much of our land, or from the close or remote villages, or from boatmen, although they have travelled not merely on our little waterways but also on the sacred rivers. True, we heard a great deal, but could gather nothing from the many details.

Our land is so huge, that no fairy tale can adequately deal with its size. Heaven hardly covers it all. And Peking is only a point, the imperial palace only a tiny dot. It's true that, by contrast, throughout all the different levels of the world the emperor, as emperor, is great. But the living emperor, a man like us, lies on a peaceful bed, just as we do. It is, no doubt, of ample proportions, but it could be merely narrow and short. Like us, he sometime stretches out his limbs and, if he is very tired, yawns with his delicately delineated mouth. But how are we to know about that thousands of miles to the south, where we almost border on the Tibetan highlands? Besides, any report which came, even if it reached us, would get there much too late and would be long out of date. Around the emperor the glittering and yet mysterious court throngs—

malice and enmity clothed as servants and friends, the counterbalance to the imperial power, with their poisoned arrows always trying to shoot the emperor down from his side of the balance scales. The empire is immortal, but the individual emperor falls and collapses. Even entire dynasties finally sink down and breathe their one last death rattle. The people will never know anything about these struggles and sufferings. Like those who have come too late, like strangers to the city, they stand at the end of the thickly populated side alleyways, quietly living off the provisions they have brought with them, while far off in the market place right in the middle foreground the execution of their master is taking place.

There is a legend which expresses this relationship well. The Emperor—so they say—has sent a message, directly from his death bed, to you alone, his pathetic subject, a tiny shadow which has taken refuge at the furthest distance from the imperial sun. He ordered the herald to kneel down beside his bed and whispered the message into his ear. He thought it was so important that he had the herald repeat it back to him. He confirmed the accuracy of the verbal message by nodding his head. And in front of the entire crowd of those who've come to witness his death—all the obstructing walls have been broken down and all the great ones of his empire are standing in a circle on the broad and high soaring flights of stairs—in front of all of them he dispatched his herald. The messenger started off at once, a powerful, tireless man. Sticking one arm out and then another, he makes his way through the crowd. If he runs into resistance, he points to his breast where there is a sign of the sun. So he moves forward easily, unlike anyone else. But the crowd is so huge; its dwelling places are infinite. If there were an open field, how he would fly along, and soon you would hear the marvelous pounding of his fist on your door. But instead of that, how futile are all his efforts. He is still forcing his way through the private rooms of the innermost palace. He will never he win his way through. And if he did manage that, nothing would have been achieved. He would have to fight his way down the steps, and, if he managed to do that, nothing would have been achieved. He would have to stride through the courtyards, and after the courtyards the second palace encircling the first, and, then again, stairs and courtyards, and then, once again, a palace, and so on for thousands of years. And if he finally did burst through the outermost door—but that can never, never happen—the royal capital city, the centre of the world, is still there in front of him, piled high and full of sediment. No one pushes his way through here, certainly not with a message from a dead man. But you sit at your window and dream of that message when evening comes.

That's exactly how our people look at the emperor, hopelessly and full of hope. They don't know which emperor is on the throne, and there are even doubts about the name of the dynasty. In the schools they learn a great deal about things like the succession, but the common uncertainty in this respect is so great that even the best pupils are drawn into it. In our villages emperors long since dead are set on the throne, and one of them who still lives on only in songs had one of his announcements issued a little while ago, which the priest read out from the altar. Battles from our most ancient history are now fought for the first time, and with a glowing face your neighbour charges into your house with the report. The imperial wives, over indulged on silk cushions, alienated from noble customs by shrewd courtiers, swollen with thirst for power, driven by greed, excessive in their lust, are always committing their evil acts over again. The further back they are in time, the more terrible all their colours glow, and with a loud cry of grief our village eventually gets to learn how an empress thousands of years ago drank her husband's blood in lengthy gulps.

That, then, is how the people deal with the rulers from the past, but they mix up the present rulers with the dead ones. If once, once in a person's lifetime an imperial official travelling around the province comes into our village, sets out some demands or other in the name of the rulers, checks the tax lists, attends a school class, interrogates the priest about our comings and goings, and then, before climbing into his sedan chair, summarizes everything in a long sermon to the assembled local population, at that point a smile crosses every face, one man looks furtively at another and bends over his children, so as not to let the official see him. How, people think, can he speak of a dead man as if he were alive. This emperor already died a long time ago, the dynasty has been extinguished, the official is having fun with us. But we'll act as if we didn't notice, so that we don't hurt his feelings. However, in all seriousness we'll obey only our present ruler, for anything else would be a sin. And behind the official's sedan chair as it hurries away there arises from the already decomposed urn someone or other arbitrarily endorsed as ruler of the village.

Similarly, with us people are, as a rule, little affected by political revolutions and contemporary wars. Here I recall an incident from my youth. In a neighbouring but still very far distant province a rebellion broke out. I cannot remember the causes any more. Besides, they are not important here. In that province reasons for rebellion arise every new day—they are an excitable people. Well, on one occasion a rebel pamphlet was brought to my father's house by a beggar who had travelled through that province. It happened to be a holiday. Our living room was full of guests. The priest sat in their midst and studied the pamphlet. Suddenly everyone started laughing, the sheet was torn to pieces in the general confusion, and the beggar was chased out of the room with blows, although he had already been richly rewarded. Everyone scattered and ran out into the beautiful day. Why? The dialect of the neighbouring province is essentially different from ours, and these differences manifest themselves also in certain forms of the written language, which for us have an antiquated character. Well, the priest had scarcely read two pages like that, and people had already decided. Old matters heard long ago, and long since got over. And although—as I recall from my memory—a horrifying way of life seemed to speak irrefutably through the beggar, people laughed and shook their head and were unwilling to hear any more. That's how ready people are among us to obliterate the present.

If one wanted to conclude from such phenomena that we basically have no emperor at all, one would not be far from the truth. I need to say it again and again: There is perhaps no people more faithful to the emperor than we are in the south, but the emperor derives no benefits from our loyalty. It's true that on the way out of our village there stands on a little pillar the sacred dragon, which, for as long as men can remember, has paid tribute by blowing its fiery breath straight in the direction of Peking. But for the people in the village Peking itself is much stranger than living in the next world. Could there really be a village where houses stand right beside each other covering the fields and reaching further than the view from our hills, with men standing shoulder to shoulder between these houses day and night? Rather than imagining such a city, it's easier for us to believe that Peking and its emperor are one, something like a cloud, peacefully moving along under the sun as the ages pass.

Now, the consequence of such opinions is a life which is to some extent free and uncontrolled. Not in any way immoral—purity of morals like those in my homeland I have hardly ever come across in my travels. But nonetheless a life that stands under no present laws and only pays attention to the wisdom and advice which reach across to us from ancient times.

I guard again generalizations and do not claim that things like this go on in all ten thousand villages of our province or, indeed, in all five hundred provinces of China. But on the basis of the many writings which I have read concerning this subject, as well as on the basis of my many observations, especially since the construction of the wall with its human material provided an opportunity for a man of feeling to travel through the souls of almost all the provinces—on the basis of all this perhaps I may truly state that with respect to the emperor the prevailing idea again and again reveals a certain universal essential feature common to the conception in my homeland. Now, I have no desire at all to let this conception stand as a virtue—quite the contrary. It's true that in the main things the blame rests with the government, which in the oldest empire on earth right up to the present day has not been able or has, among other things, neglected to cultivate the institution of empire sufficiently clearly so that it is immediately and ceaselessly effective right up to the most remote frontiers of the empire. On the other hand, however, there is in this also a weakness in the people's power of imagining or believing, which has not succeeded in pulling the empire out of its deep contemplative state in Peking and making it something fully vital and present in the hearts of subjects, who nonetheless want nothing better than to feel its touch once and then die from the experience.

So this conception is really not a virtue. It's all the more striking that this very weakness appears to be one of the most important ways of unifying our people. Indeed, if one may go so far as to use the expression, it is the very ground itself on which we live. To provide a detailed account of why we have a flaw here would amount not just to rattling our consciences but, what is much more serious, to making our feet tremble. And therefore I do not wish to go any further in the investigation of these questions at the present time.

The Hunter Gracchus

Two boys were sitting on the wall by the jetty playing dice. A man was reading a newspaper on the steps of a monument in the shadow of a hero wielding a sabre. A young girl was filling her tub with water at a fountain. A fruit seller was lying close to his produce and looking out to sea. Through the empty openings of the door and window of a bar two men could be seen drinking wine in the back. The landlord was sitting at a table in the front dozing. A small boat glided lightly into the small harbour, as if it were being carried over the water. A man in a blue jacket climbed out onto land and pulled the ropes through the rings. Behind the man from the boat, two other men in dark coats with silver buttons carried a bier, on which, under a large silk scarf with a floral pattern and fringe, a man was obviously lying.

No one bothered with the newcomers on the jetty, even when they set the bier down to wait for their helmsman, who was still working with the ropes. No one came up to them, no one asked them any questions, no one took a closer look at them.

The helmsman was further held up a little by a woman with disheveled hair, who now appeared on deck with a child at her breast. Then he came on, pointing to a yellowish two-story house which rose close by, directly on the left near the water. The bearers took up their load and carried it through the low door furnished with slender columns. A small boy opened a window, noticed immediately how the group was disappearing into the house, and quickly shut the window again. The door closed. It had been fashioned with care out of black oak wood. A flock of doves, which up to this point had been flying around the bell tower, came down in front of the house. The doves gathered before the door, as if their food was stored inside the house. One flew right up to the first floor and pecked at the window pane. They were brightly coloured, well cared for, lively animals. With a large sweep of her hand the woman on the boat threw some seeds towards them. They ate them up and then flew over to the woman.

A man in a top hat with a mourning ribbon came down one of the small, narrow, steeply descending lanes which led to the harbour. He looked around him attentively. Everything upset him. He winced at the sight of some garbage in a corner. There were fruit peels on the steps of the monument. As he went by, he pushed them off with his cane. He knocked on the door of the house, while at the same time taking off his top hat with his black-gloved right hand. It was opened immediately, and about fifty small boys, lined up in two rows in a long corridor, bowed to him.

The helmsman came down the stairs, met the gentleman, and led him upstairs. On the first floor he accompanied him around the slight, delicately built balcony surrounding the courtyard, and, as the boys crowded behind them at a respectful distance, both men stepped into a large cool room at the back. From it one could not see a facing house, only a bare gray-black rock wall. Those who had carried the bier were busy setting up and lighting some long candles at its head. But these provided no light. They only made the previously still shadows jump and flicker across the walls. The shawl was pulled back off the bier. On it lay a man with wildly unkempt hair and beard and a brown skin—he looked rather like a hunter. He lay there motionless, apparently without breathing, his eyes closed, although his surroundings were the only the only thing indicating that it could be a corpse.

The gentleman stepped over to the bier, laid a hand on the forehead of the man lying there, then knelt down and prayed. The helmsman gave a sign to the bearers to leave the room. They went out, drove away the boys who had gathered outside, and shut the door. The gentleman, however, was apparently still not satisfied with this stillness. He looked at the helmsman. The latter understood and went through a side door into the next room. The man on the bier immediately opened his eyes, turned his face with a painful smile towards the gentleman, and said, "Who are you?" Without any surprise, the gentleman got up from his kneeling position and answered, "The burgomaster of Riva."

The man on the bier nodded, pointed to a chair by stretching his arm out feebly, and then, after the burgomaster had accepted his invitation, said, "Yes, I knew that, Burgomaster, but when I first glance around I've always forgotten it all—everything is going in circles around me, and it's better for me to ask, even when I know everything. You also presumably know that I am the hunter Gracchus."

"Of course," said the burgomaster. "I received the news today, during the night. We had been sleeping for some time. Then around midnight my wife called, 'Salvatore'—that's my name—'look at the dove in the window!' It was really a dove, but as large as a rooster. It flew up to my ear and said, 'Tomorrow the dead hunter Gracchus is coming. Welcome him in the name of the city."

The hunter nodded and pushed the tip of his tongue between his lips. "Yes, the doves fly here before me. But do you believe, Burgomaster, that I am to remain in Riva?"

"That I cannot yet say," answered the burgomaster. "Are you dead?"

"Yes," said the hunter, "as you see. Many years ago—it must have been a great many years ago—I fell from a rock in the Black Forest—that's in Germany—as I was tracking a chamois. Since then I've been dead."

"But you're also alive," said the burgomaster.

"To a certain extent," said the hunter, "to a certain extent I am also alive. My death ship lost its way—a wrong turn of the helm, a moment when the helmsman was not paying attention, a distraction from my wonderful homeland—I don't know what it was. I only know that I remain on the earth and that since that time my ship has journeyed over earthly waters. So I—who only wanted to live in my own mountains—travel on after my death through all the countries of the earth."

"And have you no share in the world beyond?" asked the burgomaster wrinkling his brow.

The hunter answered, "I am always on the immense staircase leading up to it. I roam around on this infinitely wide flight of steps, sometimes up, sometimes down, sometimes to the right, sometimes to the left, always in motion. From being a hunter I've become a butterfly. Don't laugh."

"I'm not laughing," answered the burgomaster.

"That's very considerate of you," said the hunter. "I am always moving. But when I go through the greatest upward motion and the door is shining right above me, I wake up on my old ship, still drearily stranded in some earthly stretch of water. The basic mistake of my earlier death grins at me in my cabin. Julia, the wife of the helmsman, knocks and brings to me on the bier the morning drink of the country whose coast we are sailing by at the time. I lie on a wooden plank bed, wearing—I'm no delight to look at—a filthy shroud, my hair and beard, black and gray, are inextricably intertangled, my legs covered by a large silk women's scarf, with a floral pattern and long fringes. At my head stands a church candle which illuminates me. On the wall opposite me is a small picture, evidently of a bushman aiming his spear at me and concealing himself as much as possible behind a splendidly painted shield. On board ship one comes across many stupid pictures, but this is one of the stupidest. Beyond that my wooden cage is completely empty. Through a hole in the side wall the warm air of the southern nights comes in, and I hear the water lapping against the old boat.

I have been lying here since the time when I—the still living hunter Gracchus—was pursuing a chamois to its home in the Black Forest and fell. Everything took place as it should. I followed, fell down, bled to death in a ravine, was dead, and this boat was supposed to carry me to the other side. I still remember how happily I stretched myself out here on the planking for the first time. The mountains have never heart me singing the way these four still shadowy walls did then.

I had been happy to be alive and was happy to be dead. Before I came on board, I gladly threw away my rag-tag collection of guns and bags, even the hunting rifle which I had always carried so proudly, and slipped into the shroud like a young girl into her wedding dress. There I lay down and waited. Then the accident happened."

"A nasty fate," said the burgomaster, raising his hand in a gesture of depreciation, "and you are not to blame for it in any way?"

"No," said the hunter. "I was a hunter. Is there any blame in that? I was raised to be a hunter in the Black Forest, where at that time there were still wolves. I lay in wait, shot, hit the target, removed the skin—is there any blame in that? My work was blessed. 'The great hunter of the Black Forest'—that's what they called me. Is that something bad?"

"It not up to me to decide that," said the burgomaster, "but it seems to me as well that there's no blame there. But then who is to blame?"

"The boatman," said the hunter. "No one will read what I write here, no one will come to help me. If people were assigned the task of helping me, all the doors of all the houses would remain closed, all the windows would be shut, they would all lie in bed, with sheets thrown over their heads, the entire earth would be a hostel for the night. And that makes good sense, for no one knows of me, and if he did, he would have no idea of where I was staying, and if he knew that, he would still not know how to keep me there, and so he would not know how to help me. The thought of wanting to help me is a sickness and has to be cured with bed rest.

"I know that, and so I do not cry out to summon help, even if at moments when I have no self-control, for example right now, I do think about that very seriously. But to get rid of such ideas I need only look around and recall where I am and where—and this I can assert with full confidence—I have lived for centuries.

"That's extraordinary," said the burgomaster, "extraordinary. And now are you intending to remain with us in Riva?"

"I have no intentions," said the hunter with a smile and, to make up for his mocking tone, laid a hand on the burgomaster's knee. "I am here. I don't know any more than that. There's nothing more I can do. My boat is without a helm—it journeys with the wind which blows in the deepest regions of death."

The Trial

Chapter One
Arrest – Conversation with Mrs. Grubach –
Then Miss Bürstner

Someone must have been telling lies about Josef K., he knew he had done nothing wrong but, one morning, he was arrested. Every day at eight in the morning he was brought his breakfast by Mrs. Grubach's cook – Mrs. Grubach was his landlady – but today she didn't come. That had never happened before. K. waited a little while, looked from his pillow at the old woman who lived opposite and who was watching him with an inquisitiveness quite unusual for her, and finally, both hungry and disconcerted, rang the bell. There was immediately a knock at the door and a man entered. He had never seen the man in this house before. He was slim but firmly built, his clothes were black and close-fitting, with many folds and pockets, buckles and buttons and a belt, all of which gave the impression of being very practical but without making it very clear what they were actually for. "Who are you?" asked K., sitting half upright in his bed. The man, however, ignored the question as if his arrival simply had to be accepted, and merely replied, "You rang?" "Anna should have brought me my breakfast," said K. He tried to work out who the man actually was, first in silence, just through observation and by thinking about it, but the man didn't stay still to be looked at for very long. Instead he went over to the door, opened it slightly, and said to someone who was clearly standing immediately behind it, "He wants Anna to bring him his breakfast." There was a little laughter in the neighbouring room, it was not clear from the sound of it whether there were several people laughing. The strange man could not have learned anything from it that he hadn't known already, but now he said to K., as if making his report "It is not possible." "It would be the first time that's happened," said K., as he jumped out of bed and quickly pulled on his trousers. "I want to see who that is in the next room, and why it is that Mrs. Grubach has let me be disturbed in this way." It immediately occurred to him that he needn't have said this out loud, and that he must to some extent have acknowledged their authority by doing so, but that didn't seem important to him at the time. That, at least, is how the stranger took it, as he said, "Don't you think you'd better stay where you are?" "I want neither to stay here nor to be spoken to by you until you've introduced yourself." "I meant it for your own good," said the stranger and opened the door, this time without being asked. The next room, which K. entered more slowly than he had intended, looked at first glance exactly the same as it had the previous evening. It was Mrs. Grubach's living room, over-filled with furniture, tablecloths, porcelain and photographs. Perhaps there was a little more space in there than usual today, but if so it was not immediately obvious, especially as the main difference was the presence of a man sitting by the open window with a book from which he now looked up. "You should have stayed in your room! Didn't Franz tell you?" "And what is it you want, then?" said K., looking back and forth between this new acquaintance and the one named Franz, who had remained in the doorway. Through the open window he noticed the old woman again, who had come close to the window opposite so that she could continue to see everything. She was showing an inquisitiveness that really made it seem like she was going senile. "I want to see Mrs. Grubach …," said K., making a movement as if tearing himself away from the two men – even though they were standing well away from him – and wanted to go. "No," said the man at the window, who threw his book down on a coffee table and stood up. "You can't go away when you're under arrest." "That's how it seems," said K. "And why am I under arrest?" he then asked. "That's something we're not allowed to tell you. Go into your room and wait there. Proceedings are underway and you'll learn about everything all in good time. It's not really part of my job to be friendly towards you like this, but I hope no-one, apart from Franz, will hear about it, and he's been more friendly towards you than he should have been, under the rules, himself. If you carry on having as much good luck as you have been with your arresting officers then you can reckon on things going well with you." K. wanted to sit down, but then he saw that, apart from the chair by the window, there was nowhere anywhere in the room where he could sit. "You'll get the chance to see for yourself how true all this is," said Franz and both men then walked up to K. They were significantly bigger than him, especially the second man, who frequently slapped him on the shoulder. The two of them felt K.'s nightshirt, and said he would now have to wear one that was of much lower quality, but that they would keep the nightshirt along with his other underclothes and return them to him if his case turned out well. "It's better for you if you give us the things than if you leave them in the storeroom," they said. "Things have a tendency to go missing in the storeroom, and after a certain amount of time they sell things off, whether the case involved has come to an end or not. And cases like this can last a long time, especially the ones that have been coming up lately. They'd give you the money they got for them, but it wouldn't be very much as it's not what they're offered for them when they sell them that counts, it's how much they get slipped on the side, and things like that lose their value anyway when they get passed on from hand to hand, year after year." K. paid hardly any attention to what they were saying, he did not place much value on what he may have still possessed or on who decided what happened to them. It was much more important to him to get a clear understanding of his position, but he could not think clearly while these people were here, the second policeman's belly – and they could only be policemen – looked friendly enough, sticking out towards him, but when K. looked up and saw his dry, boney face it did not seem to fit with the body. His strong nose twisted to one side as if ignoring K. and sharing an understanding with the other policeman. What sort of people were these? What were they talking about? What office did they belong to? K. was living in a free country, after all, everywhere was at peace, all laws were decent and were upheld, who was it who dared accost him in his own home? He was always inclined to take life as lightly as he could, to cross bridges when he came to them, pay no heed for the future, even when everything seemed under threat. But here that did not seem the right thing to do. He could have taken it all as a joke, a big joke set up by his colleagues at the bank for some unknown reason, or also perhaps because today was his thirtieth birthday, it was all possible of course, maybe all he had to do was laugh in the policemen's face in some way and they would laugh with him, maybe they were tradesmen from the corner of the street, they looked like they might be – but he was nonetheless determined, ever since he first caught sight of the one called Franz, not to lose any slight advantage he might have had over these people. There was a very slight risk that people would later say he couldn't understand a joke, but – although he wasn't normally in the habit of learning from experience – he might also have had a few unimportant occasions in mind when, unlike his more cautious friends, he had acted with no thought at all for what might follow and had been made to suffer for it. He didn't want that to happen again, not this time at least; if they were play-acting he would act along with them.

He still had time. "Allow me," he said, and hurried between the two policemen through into his room. "He seems sensible enough," he heard them say behind him. Once in his room, he quickly pulled open the drawer of his writing desk, everything in it was very tidy but in his agitation he was unable to find the identification documents he was looking for straight away. He finally found his bicycle permit and was about to go back to the policemen with it when it seemed to him too petty, so he carried on searching until he found his birth certificate. Just as he got back in the adjoining room the door on the other side opened and Mrs. Grubach was about to enter. He only saw her for an instant, for as soon as she recognised K. she was clearly embarrassed, asked for forgiveness and disappeared, closing the door behind her very carefully. "Do come in," K. could have said just then. But now he stood in the middle of the room with his papers in his hand and still looking at the door which did not open again.

He stayed like that until he was startled out of it by the shout of the policeman who sat at the little table at the open window and, as K. now saw, was eating his breakfast. "Why didn't she come in?" he asked. "She's not allowed to," said the big policeman. "You're under arrest, aren't you." "But how can I be under arrest? And how come it's like this?" "Now you're starting again," said the policeman, dipping a piece of buttered bread in the honeypot. "We don't answer questions like that." "You will have to answer them," said K. "Here are my identification papers, now show me yours and I certainly want to see the arrest warrant." "Oh, my God!" said the policeman. "In a position like yours, and you think you can start giving orders, do you? It won't do you any good to get us on the wrong side, even if you think it will – we're probably more on your side that anyone else you know!" "That's true, you know, you'd better believe it," said Franz, holding a cup of coffee in his hand which he did not lift to his mouth but looked at K. in a way that was probably meant to be full of meaning but could not actually be understood. K. found himself, without intending it, in a mute dialogue with Franz, but then slapped his hand down on his papers and said, "Here are my identity documents." "And what do you want us to do about it?" replied the big policeman, loudly. "The way you're carrying on, it's worse than a child. What is it you want? Do you want to get this great, bloody trial of yours over with quickly by talking about ID and arrest warrants with us? We're just coppers, that's all we are. Junior officers like us hardly know one end of an ID card from another, all we've got to do with you is keep an eye on you for ten hours a day and get paid for it. That's all we are. Mind you, what we can do is make sure that the high officials we work for find out just what sort of person it is they're going to arrest, and why he should be arrested, before they issue the warrant. There's no mistake there. Our authorities as far as I know, and I only know the lowest grades, don't go out looking for guilt among the public; it's the guilt that draws them out, like it says in the law, and they have to send us police officers out. That's the law. Where d'you think there'd be any mistake there?" "I don't know this law," said K. "So much the worse for you, then," said the policeman. "It's probably exists only in your heads," said K., he wanted, in some way, to insinuate his way into the thoughts of the policemen, to re-shape those thoughts to his benefit or to make himself at home there. But the policeman just said dismissively, "You'll find out when it affects you." Franz joined in, and said, "Look at this, Willem, he admits he doesn't know the law and at the same time insists he's innocent." "You're quite right, but we can't get him to understand a thing," said the other. K. stopped talking with them; do I, he thought to himself, do I really have to carry on getting tangled up with the chattering of base functionaries like this? – and they admit themselves that they are of the lowest position. They're talking about things of which they don't have the slightest understanding, anyway. It's only because of their stupidity that they're able to be so sure of themselves. I just need few words with someone of the same social standing as myself and everything will be incomparably clearer, much clearer than a long conversation with these two can make it. He walked up and down the free space in the room a couple of times, across the street he could see the old woman who, now, had pulled an old man, much older than herself, up to the window and had her arms around him. K. had to put an end to this display, "Take me to your superior," he said. "As soon as he wants to see you. Not before," said the policeman, the one called Willem. "And now my advice to you," he added, "is to go into your room, stay calm, and wait and see what's to be done with you. If you take our advice, you won't tire yourself out thinking about things to no purpose, you need to pull yourself together as there's a lot that's going to required of you. You've not behaved towards us the way we deserve after being so good to you, you forget that we, whatever we are, we're still free men and you're not, and that's quite an advantage. But in spite of all that we're still willing, if you've got the money, to go and get you some breakfast from the café over the road."

Without giving any answer to this offer, K. stood still for some time. Perhaps, if he opened the door of the next room or even the front door, the two of them would not dare to stand in his way, perhaps that would be the simplest way to settle the whole thing, by bringing it to a head. But maybe they would grab him, and if he were thrown down on the ground he would lose all the advantage he, in a certain respect, had over them. So he decided on the more certain solution, the way things would go in the natural course of events, and went back in his room without another word either from him or from the policemen.

He threw himself down on his bed, and from the dressing table he took the nice apple that he had put there the previous evening for his breakfast. Now it was all the breakfast he had and anyway, as he confirmed as soon as he took his first, big bite of it, it was far better than a breakfast he could have had through the good will of the policemen from the dirty café. He felt well and confident, he had failed to go into work at the bank this morning but that could easily be excused because of the relatively high position he held there. Should he really send in his explanation? He wondered about it. If nobody believed him, and in this case that would be understandable, he could bring Mrs. Grubach in as a witness, or even the old pair from across the street, who probably even now were on their way over to the window opposite. It puzzled K., at least it puzzled him looking at it from the policemen's point of view, that they had made him go into the room and left him alone there, where he had ten different ways of killing himself. At the same time, though, he asked himself, this time looking at it from his own point of view, what reason he could have to do so. Because those two were sitting there in the next room and had taken his breakfast, perhaps? It would have been so pointless to kill himself that, even if he had wanted to, the pointlessness would have made him unable. Maybe, if the policemen had not been so obviously limited in their mental abilities, it could have been supposed that they had come to the same conclusion and saw no danger in leaving him alone because of it. They could watch now, if they wanted, and see how he went over to the cupboard in the wall where he kept a bottle of good schnapps, how he first emptied a glass of it in place of his breakfast and how he then took a second glassful in order to give himself courage, the last one just as a precaution for the unlikely chance it would be needed.

Then he was so startled by a shout to him from the other room that he struck his teeth against the glass. "The supervisor wants to see you!" a voice said. It was only the shout that startled him, this curt, abrupt, military shout, that he would not have expected from the policeman called Franz. In itself, he found the order very welcome. "At last!" he called back, locked the cupboard and, without delay, hurried into the next room. The two policemen were standing there and chased him back into his bedroom as if that were a matter of course. "What d'you think you're doing?" they cried. "Think you're going to see the supervisor dressed in just your shirt, do you? He'd see to it you got a right thumping, and us and all!" "Let go of me for God's sake!" called K., who had already been pushed back as far as his wardrobe, "if you accost me when I'm still in bed you can't expect to find me in my evening dress." "That won't help you," said the policemen, who always became very quiet, almost sad, when K. began to shout, and in that way confused him or, to some extent, brought him to his senses. "Ridiculous formalities!" he grumbled, as he lifted his coat from the chair and kept it in both his hands for a little while, as if holding it out for the policemen's inspection. They shook their heads. "It's got to be a black coat," they said. At that, K. threw the coat to the floor and said – without knowing even himself what he meant by it – "Well it's not going to be the main trial, after all." The policemen laughed, but continued to insist, "It's got to be a black coat." "Well that's alright by me if it makes things go any faster," said K. He opened the wardrobe himself, spent a long time searching through all the clothes, and chose his best black suit which had a short jacket that had greatly surprised those who knew him, then he also pulled out a fresh shirt and began, carefully, to get dressed. He secretly told himself that he had succeeded in speeding things up by letting the policemen forget to make him have a bath. He watched them to see if they might remember after all, but of course it never occurred to them, although Willem did not forget to send Franz up to the supervisor with the message saying that K. was getting dressed.

Once he was properly dressed, K. had to pass by Willem as he went through the next room into the one beyond, the door of which was already wide open. K. knew very well that this room had recently been let to a typist called 'Miss Bürstner'. She was in the habit of going out to work very early and coming back home very late, and K. had never exchanged more than a few words of greeting with her. Now, her bedside table had been pulled into the middle of the room to be used as a desk for these proceedings, and the supervisor sat behind it. He had his legs crossed, and had thrown one arm over the backrest of the chair.

In one corner of the room there were three young people looking at the photographs belonging to Miss Bürstner that had been put into a piece of fabric on the wall. Hung up on the handle of the open window was a white blouse. At the window across the street, there was the old pair again, although now their number had increased, as behind them, and far taller than they were, stood a man with an open shirt that showed his chest and a reddish goatee beard which he squeezed and twisted with his fingers. "Josef K.?" asked the supervisor, perhaps merely to attract K.'s attention as he looked round the room. K. nodded. "I daresay you were quite surprised by all that's been taking place this morning," said the supervisor as, with both hands, he pushed away the few items on the bedside table – the candle and box of matches, a book and a pin cushion which lay there as if they were things he would need for his own business. "Certainly," said K., and he began to feel relaxed now that, at last, he stood in front of someone with some sense, someone with whom he would be able to talk about his situation. "Certainly I'm surprised, but I'm not in any way very surprised." "You're not very surprised?" asked the supervisor, as he positioned the candle in the middle of the table and the other things in a group around it. "Perhaps you don't quite understand me," K. hurriedly pointed out. "What I mean is …" here K. broke off what he was saying and looked round for somewhere to sit. "I may sit down, mayn't I?" he asked. "That's not usual," the supervisor answered. "What I mean is…," said K. without delaying a second time, "that, yes, I am very surprised but when you've been in the world for thirty years already and had to make your own way through everything yourself, which has been my lot, then you become hardened to surprises and don't take them too hard. Especially not what's happened today." "Why especially not what's happened today?" "I wouldn't want to say that I see all of this as a joke, you seem to have gone to too much trouble making all these arrangements for that. Everyone in the house must be taking part in it as well as all of you, that would be going beyond what could be a joke. So I don't want to say that this is a joke." "Quite right," said the supervisor, looking to see how many matches were left in the box. "But on the other hand," K. went on, looking round at everyone there and even wishing he could get the attention of the three who were looking at the photographs, "on the other hand this really can't be all that important. That follows from the fact that I've been indicted, but can't think of the slightest offence for which I could be indicted. But even that is all beside the point, the main question is: Who is issuing the indictment? What office is conducting this affair? Are you officials? None of you is wearing a uniform, unless what you are wearing" – here he turned towards Franz – "is meant to be a uniform, it's actually more of a travelling suit. I require a clear answer to all these questions, and I'm quite sure that once things have been made clear we can take our leave of each other on the best of terms." The supervisor slammed the box of matches down on the table. "You're making a big mistake," he said. "These gentlemen and I have got nothing to do with your business, in fact we know almost nothing about you. We could be wearing uniforms as proper and exact as you like and your situation wouldn't be any the worse for it. As to whether you're on a charge, I can't give you any sort of clear answer to that, I don't even know whether you are or not. You're under arrest, you're quite right about that, but I don't know any more than that. Maybe these officers have been chit-chatting with you, well if they have that's all it is, chit- chat. I can't give you an answer to your questions, but I can give you a bit of advice: You'd better think less about us and what's going to happen to you, and think a bit more about yourself. And stop making all this fuss about your sense of innocence; you don't make such a bad impression, but with all this fuss you're damaging it. And you ought to do a bit less talking, too. Almost everything you've said so far has been things we could have taken from your behaviour, even if you'd said no more than a few words. And what you have said has not exactly been in your favour."

K. stared at the supervisor. Was this man, probably younger than he was, lecturing him like a schoolmaster? Was he being punished for his honesty with a telling off? And was he to learn nothing about the reasons for his arrest or those who were arresting him? He became somewhat cross and began to walk up and down. No-one stopped him doing this and he pushed his sleeves back, felt his chest, straightened his hair, went over to the three men, said, "It makes no sense," at which these three turned round to face him and came towards him with serious expressions. He finally came again to a halt in front of the supervisor's desk. "State Attorney Hasterer is a good friend of mine," he said, "can I telephone him?" "Certainly," said the supervisor, "but I don't know what the point of that will be, I suppose you must have some private matter you want to discuss with him." "What the point is?" shouted K., more disconcerted that cross. "Who do you think you are? You want to see some point in it while you're carrying out something as pointless as it could be? It's enough to make you cry! These gentlemen first accost me, and now they sit or stand about in here and let me be hauled up in front of you. What point there would be, in telephoning a state attorney when I'm ostensibly under arrest? Very well, I won't make the telephone call." "You can call him if you want to," said the supervisor, stretching his hand out towards the outer room where the telephone was, "please, go on, do make your phone call." "No, I don't want to any more," said K., and went over to the window. Across the street, the people were still there at the window, and it was only now that K. had gone up to his window that they seemed to become uneasy about quietly watching what was going on. The old couple wanted to get up but the man behind them calmed them down. "We've got some kind of audience over there," called K. to the supervisor, quite loudly, as he pointed out with his forefinger. "Go away," he then called across to them. And the three of them did immediately retreat a few steps, the old pair even found themselves behind the man who then concealed them with the breadth of his body and seemed, going by the movements of his mouth, to be saying something incomprehensible into the distance. They did not disappear entirely, though, but seemed to be waiting for the moment when they could come back to the window without being noticed. "Intrusive, thoughtless people!" said K. as he turned back into the room. The supervisor may have agreed with him, at least K. thought that was what he saw from the corner of his eye. But it was just as possible that he had not even been listening as he had his hand pressed firmly down on the table and seemed to be comparing the length of his fingers. The two policemen were sitting on a chest covered with a coloured blanket, rubbing their knees. The three young people had put their hands on their hips and were looking round aimlessly. Everything was still, like in some office that has been forgotten about. "Now, gentlemen," called out K., and for a moment it seemed as if he was carrying all of them on his shoulders, "it looks like your business with me is over with. In my opinion, it's best now to stop wondering about whether you're proceeding correctly or incorrectly, and to bring the matter to a peaceful close with a mutual handshake. If you are of the same opinion, then please…" and he walked up to the supervisor's desk and held out his hand to him. The supervisor raised his eyes, bit his lip and looked at K.'s outstretched hand; K still believed the supervisor would do as he suggested. But instead, he stood up, picked up a hard round hat that was laying on Miss Bürstner's bed and put it carefully onto his head, using both hands as if trying on a new hat. "Everything seems so simple to you, doesn't it," he said to K. as he did so, "so you think we should bring the matter to a peaceful close, do you. No, no, that won't do. Mind you, on the other hand I certainly wouldn't want you to think there's no hope for you. No, why should you think that? You're simply under arrest, nothing more than that. That's what I had to tell you, that's what I've done and now I've seen how you've taken it. That's enough for one day and we can take our leave of each other, for the time being at least. I expect you'll want to go in to the bank now, won't you." "In to the bank?" asked K., "I thought I was under arrest." K. said this with a certain amount of defiance as, although his handshake had not been accepted, he was feeling more independent of all these people, especially since the supervisor had stood up. He was playing with them. If they left, he had decided he would run after them and offer to let them arrest him. That's why he even repeated, "How can I go in to the bank when I'm under arrest?" "I see you've misunderstood me," said the supervisor who was already at the door. "It's true that you're under arrest, but that shouldn't stop you from carrying out your job. And there shouldn't be anything to stop you carrying on with your usual life." "In that case it's not too bad, being under arrest," said K., and went up close to the supervisor. "I never meant it should be anything else," he replied. "It hardly seems to have been necessary to notify me of the arrest in that case," said K., and went even closer. The others had also come closer. All of them had gathered together into a narrow space by the door. "That was my duty," said the supervisor. "A silly duty," said K., unyielding. "Maybe so," replied the supervisor, "only don't let's waste our time talking on like this. I had assumed you'd be wanting to go to the bank. As you're paying close attention to every word I'll add this: I'm not forcing you to go to the bank, I'd just assumed you wanted to. And to make things easier for you, and to let you get to the bank with as little fuss as possible I've put these three gentlemen, colleagues of yours, at your disposal." "What's that?" exclaimed K., and looked at the three in astonishment. He could only remember seeing them in their group by the photographs, but these characterless, anaemic young people were indeed officials from his bank, not colleagues of his, that was putting it too high and it showed a gap in the omniscience of the supervisor, but they were nonetheless junior members of staff at the bank. How could K. have failed to see that? How occupied he must have been with the supervisor and the policemen not to have recognised these three! Rabensteiner, with his stiff demeanour and swinging hands, Kullich, with his blonde hair and deep-set eyes, and Kaminer, with his involuntary grin caused by chronic muscle spasms. "Good morning," said K. after a while, extending his hand to the gentlemen as they bowed correctly to him. "I didn't recognise you at all. So, we'll go into work now, shall we?" The gentlemen laughed and nodded enthusiastically, as if that was what they had been waiting for all the time, except that K. had left his hat in his room so they all dashed, one after another, into the room to fetch it, which caused a certain amount of embarrassment. K. stood where he was and watched them through the open double doorway, the last to go, of course, was the apathetic Rabensteiner who had broken into no more than an elegant trot. Kaminer got to the hat and K., as he often had to do at the bank, forcibly reminded himself that the grin was not deliberate, that he in fact wasn't able to grin deliberately. At that moment Mrs. Grubach opened the door from the hallway into the living room where all the people were. She did not seem to feel guilty about anything at all, and K., as often before, looked down at the belt of her apron which, for no reason, cut so deeply into her hefty body. Once downstairs, K., with his watch in his hand, decided to take a taxi – he had already been delayed by half an hour and there was no need to make the delay any longer. Kaminer ran to the corner to summon it, and the two others were making obvious efforts to keep K. diverted when Kullich pointed to the doorway of the house on the other side of the street where the large man with the blonde goatee beard appeared and, a little embarrassed at first at letting himself be seen in his full height, stepped back to the wall and leant against it. The old couple were probably still on the stairs. K. was cross with Kullich for pointing out this man whom he had already seen himself, in fact whom he had been expecting. "Don't look at him!" he snapped, without noticing how odd it was to speak to free men in this way. But there was no explanation needed anyway as just then the taxi arrived, they sat inside and set off. Inside the taxi, K. remembered that he had not noticed the supervisor and the policemen leaving – the supervisor had stopped him noticing the three bank staff and now the three bank staff had stopped him noticing the supervisor. This showed that K. was not very attentive, and he resolved to watch himself more carefully in this respect. Nonetheless, he gave it no thought as he twisted himself round and leant over onto the rear shelf of the car to catch sight of the supervisor and the policemen if he could. But he turned back round straight away and leant comfortably into the corner of the taxi without even having made the effort to see anyone. Although it did not seem like it, now was just the time when he needed some encouragement, but the gentlemen seemed tired just then, Rabensteiner looked out of the car to the right, Kullich to the left and only Kaminer was there with his grin at K.'s service. It would have been inhumane to make fun of that.

That spring, whenever possible, K. usually spent his evenings after work – he usually stayed in the office until nine o'clock – with a short walk, either by himself or in the company of some of the bank officials, and then he would go into a pub where he would sit at the regulars' table with mostly older men until eleven. There were, however, also exceptions to this habit, times, for instance, when K. was invited by the bank's manager (whom he greatly respected for his industry and trustworthiness) to go with him for a ride in his car or to eat dinner with him at his large house. K. would also go, once a week, to see a girl called Elsa who worked as a waitress in a wine bar through the night until late in the morning. During the daytime she only received visitors while still in bed.

That evening, though, – the day had passed quickly with a lot of hard work and many respectful and friendly birthday greetings – K. wanted to go straight home. Each time he had any small break from the day's work he considered, without knowing exactly what he had in mind, that Mrs. Grubach's flat seemed to have been put into great disarray by the events of that morning, and that it was up to him to put it back into order. Once order had been restored, every trace of those events would have been erased and everything would take its previous course once more. In particular, there was nothing to fear from the three bank officials, they had immersed themselves back into their paperwork and there was no alteration to be seen in them. K. had called each of them, separately or all together, into his office that day for no other reason than to observe them; he was always satisfied and had always been able to let them go again.

At half past nine that evening, when he arrived back in front of the building where he lived, he met a young lad in the doorway who was standing there, his legs apart and smoking a pipe. "Who are you?" immediately asked K., bringing his face close to the lad's, as it was hard to see in the half light of the landing. "I'm the landlord's son, sir," answered the lad, taking the pipe from his mouth and stepping to one side. "The landlord's son?" asked K., and impatiently knocked on the ground with his stick. "Did you want anything, sir? Would you like me to fetch my father?" "No, no," said K., there was something forgiving in his voice, as if the boy had harmed him in some way and he was excusing him. "It's alright," he said then, and went on, but before going up the stairs he turned round once more.

He could have gone directly to his room, but as he wanted to speak with Mrs. Grubach he went straight to her door and knocked. She was sat at the table with a knitted stocking and a pile of old stockings in front of her. K. apologised, a little embarrassed at coming so late, but Mrs. Grubach was very friendly and did not want to hear any apology, she was always ready to speak to him, he knew very well that he was her best and her favourite tenant. K. looked round the room, it looked exactly as it usually did, the breakfast dishes, which had been on the table by the window that morning, had already been cleared away. "A woman's hands will do many things when no-one's looking," he thought, he might himself have smashed all the dishes on the spot but certainly would not have been able to carry it all out. He looked at Mrs. Grubach with some gratitude. "Why are you working so late?" he asked. They were now both sitting at the table, and K. now and then sank his hands into the pile of stockings. "There's a lot of work to do," she said, "during the day I belong to the tenants; if I'm to sort out my own things there are only the evenings left to me." "I fear I may have caused you some exceptional work today." "How do you mean, Mr. K.?" she asked, becoming more interested and leaving her work in her lap. "I mean the men who were here this morning." "Oh, I see," she said, and went peacefully back to what she was doing, "that was no trouble, not especially." K. looked on in silence as she took up the knitted stocking once more. She seems surprised at my mentioning it, he thought, she seems to think it's improper for me to mention it. All the more important for me to do so. An old woman is the only person I can speak about it with. "But it must have caused some work for you," he said then, "but it won't happen again." "No, it can't happen again," she agreed, and smiled at K. in a way that was almost pained. "Do you mean that seriously?" asked K. "Yes," she said, more gently, "but the important thing is you mustn't take it too hard. There are so many awful things happening in the world! As you're being so honest with me, Mr. K., I can admit to you that I listened to a little of what was going on from behind the door, and that those two policemen told me one or two things as well. It's all to do with your happiness, and that's something that's quite close to my heart, perhaps more than it should be as I am, after all, only your landlady. Anyway, so I heard one or two things but I can't really say that it's about anything very serious. No. You have been arrested, but it's not in the same way as when they arrest a thief. If you're arrested in the same way as a thief, then it's bad, but an arrest like this … . It seems to me that it's something very complicated – forgive me if I'm saying something stupid – something very complicated that I don't understand, but something that you don't really need to understand anyway."

"There's nothing stupid about what you've said, Mrs. Grubach, or at least I partly agree with you, only, the way I judge the whole thing is harsher than yours, and think it's not only not something complicated but simply a fuss about nothing. I was just caught unawares, that's what happened. If I had got up as soon as I was awake without letting myself get confused because Anna wasn't there, if I'd got up and paid no regard to anyone who might have been in my way and come straight to you, if I'd done something like having my breakfast in the kitchen as an exception, asked you to bring my clothes from my room, in short, if I had behaved sensibly then nothing more would have happened, everything that was waiting to happen would have been stifled. People are so often unprepared. In the bank, for example, I am well prepared, nothing of this sort could possibly happen to me there, I have my own assistant there, there are telephones for internal and external calls in front of me on the desk, I continually receive visits from people, representatives, officials, but besides that, and most importantly, I'm always occupied with my work, that's to say I'm always alert, it would even be a pleasure for me to find myself faced with something of that sort. But now it's over with, and I didn't really even want to talk about it any more, only I wanted to hear what you, as a sensible woman, thought about it all, and I'm very glad to hear that we're in agreement. But now you must give me your hand, an agreement of this sort needs to be confirmed with a handshake."

Will she shake hands with me? The supervisor didn't shake hands, he thought, and looked at the woman differently from before, examining her. She stood up, as he had also stood up, and was a little self- conscious, she hadn't been able to understand everything that K. said. As a result of this self consciousness she said something that she certainly did not intend and certainly was not appropriate. "Don't take it so hard, Mr. K.," she said, with tears in her voice and also, of course, forgetting the handshake. "I didn't know I was taking it hard," said K., feeling suddenly tired and seeing that if this woman did agree with him it was of very little value.

Before going out the door he asked, "Is Miss Bürstner home?" "No," said Mrs. Grubach, smiling as she gave this simple piece of information, saying something sensible at last. "She's at the theatre. Did you want to see her? Should I give her a message?" "I, er, I just wanted to have a few words with her." "I'm afraid I don't know when she's coming in; she usually gets back late when she's been to the theatre." "It really doesn't matter," said K. his head hanging as he turned to the door to leave, "I just wanted to give her my apology for taking over her room today." "There's no need for that, Mr. K., you're too conscientious, the young lady doesn't know anything about it, she hasn't been home since early this morning and everything's been tidied up again, you can see for yourself." And she opened the door to Miss Bürstner's room. "Thank you, I'll take your word for it," said K, but went nonetheless over to the open door. The moon shone quietly into the unlit room. As far as could be seen, everything was indeed in its place, not even the blouse was hanging on the window handle. The pillows on the bed looked remarkably plump as they lay half in the moonlight. "Miss Bürstner often comes home late," said K., looking at Mrs. Grubach as if that were her responsibility. "That's how young people are!" said Mrs. Grubach to excuse herself. "Of course, of course," said K., "but it can be taken too far." "Yes, it can be," said Mrs. Grubach, "you're so right, Mr. K. Perhaps it is in this case. I certainly wouldn't want to say anything nasty about Miss Bürstner, she is a good, sweet girl, friendly, tidy, punctual, works hard, I appreciate all that very much, but one thing is true, she ought to have more pride, be a bit less forthcoming. Twice this month already, in the street over the way, I've seen her with a different gentleman. I really don't like saying this, you're the only one I've said this to, Mr. K., I swear to God, but I'm going to have no choice but to have a few words with Miss Bürstner about it myself. And it's not the only thing about her that I'm worried about." "Mrs. Grubach, you are on quite the wrong track," said K., so angry that he was hardly able to hide it, "and you have moreover misunderstood what I was saying about Miss Bürstner, that is not what I meant. In fact I warn you quite directly not to say anything to her, you are quite mistaken, I know Miss Bürstner very well and there is no truth at all in what you say. And what's more, perhaps I'm going to far, I don't want to get in your way, say to her whatever you see fit. Good night." "Mr. K.," said Mrs. Grubach as if asking him for something and hurrying to his door which he had already opened, "I don't want to speak to Miss Bürstner at all, not yet, of course I'll continue to keep an eye on her but you're the only one I've told what I know. And it is, after all something that everyone who lets rooms has to do if she's to keep the house decent, that's all I'm trying to do." "Decent!" called out K. through the crack in the door, "if you want to keep the house decent you'll first have to give me notice." Then he slammed the door shut, there was a gentle knocking to which he paid no more attention.

He did not feel at all like going to bed, so he decided to stay up, and this would also give him the chance to find out when Miss Bürstner would arrive home. Perhaps it would also still be possible, even if a little inappropriate, to have a few words with her. As he lay there by the window, pressing his hands to his tired eyes, he even thought for a moment that he might punish Mrs. Grubach by persuading Miss Bürstner to give in her notice at the same time as he would. But he immediately realised that that would be shockingly excessive, and there would even be the suspicion that he was moving house because of the incidents of that morning. Nothing would have been more nonsensical and, above all, more pointless and contemptible.

When he had become tired of looking out onto the empty street he slightly opened the door to the living room so that he could see anyone who entered the flat from where he was and lay down on the couch. He lay there, quietly smoking a cigar, until about eleven o'clock. He wasn't able to hold out longer than that, and went a little way into the hallway as if in that way he could make Miss Bürstner arrive sooner. He had no particular desire for her, he could not even remember what she looked like, but now he wanted to speak to her and it irritated him that her late arrival home meant this day would be full of unease and disorder right to its very end. It was also her fault that he had not had any dinner that evening and that he had been unable to visit Elsa as he had intended. He could still make up for both of those things, though, if he went to the wine bar where Elsa worked. He wanted to do so even later, after the discussion with Miss Bürstner.

It was already gone half past eleven when someone could be heard in the stairway. K., who had been lost in his thoughts in the hallway, walking up and down loudly as if it were his own room, fled behind his door. Miss Bürstner had arrived. Shivering, she pulled a silk shawl over her slender shoulders as she locked the door. The next moment she would certainly go into her room, where K. ought not to intrude in the middle of the night; that meant he would have to speak to her now, but, unfortunately, he had not put the electric light on in his room so that when he stepped out of the dark it would give the impression of being an attack and would certainly, at the very least, have been quite alarming. There was no time to lose, and in his helplessness he whispered through the crack of the door, "Miss Bürstner." It sounded like he was pleading with her, not calling to her. "Is there someone there?" asked Miss Bürstner, looking round with her eyes wide open. "It's me," said K. and came out. "Oh, Mr. K.!" said Miss Bürstner with a smile. "Good Evening," and offered him her hand. "I wanted to have a word with you, if you would allow me?" "Now?" asked Miss Bürstner, "does it have to be now? It is a little odd, isn't it?" "I've been waiting for you since nine o'clock." "Well, I was at the theatre, I didn't know anything about you waiting for me." "The reason I need to speak to you only came up today" "I see, well I don't see why not, I suppose, apart from being so tired I could drop. Come into my room for a few minutes then. We certainly can't talk out here, we'd wake everyone up and I think that would be more unpleasant for us than for them. Wait here till I've put the light on in my room, and then turn the light down out here." K. did as he was told, and then even waited until Miss Bürstner came out of her room and quietly invited him, once more, to come in. "Sit down," she said, indicating the ottoman, while she herself remained standing by the bedpost despite the tiredness she had spoken of; she did not even take off her hat, which was small but decorated with an abundance of flowers. "What is it you wanted, then? I'm really quite curious." She gently crossed her legs. "I expect you'll say," K. began, "that the matter really isn't all that urgent and we don't need to talk about it right now, but …" "I never listen to introductions," said Miss Bürstner. "That makes my job so much easier," said K. "This morning, to some extent through my fault, your room was made a little untidy, this happened because of people I did not know and against my will but, as I said, because of my fault; I wanted to apologise for it." "My room?" asked Miss Bürstner, and instead of looking round the room scrutinised K. "It is true," said K., and now, for the first time, they looked each other in the eyes, "there's no point in saying exactly how this came about." "But that's the interesting thing about it," said Miss Bürstner. "No," said K. "Well then," said Miss Bürstner, "I don't want to force my way into any secrets, if you insist that it's of no interest I won't insist. I'm quite happy to forgive you for it, as you ask, especially as I can't see anything at all that's been left untidy." With her hand laid flat on her lower hip, she made a tour around the room. At the mat where the photographs were she stopped. "Look at this!" she cried. "My photographs really have been put in the wrong places. Oh, that's horrible. Someone really has been in my room without permission." K. nodded, and quietly cursed Kaminer who worked at his bank and who was always active doing things that had neither use nor purpose. "It is odd," said Miss Bürstner, "that I'm forced to forbid you to do something that you ought to have forbidden yourself to do, namely to come into my room when I'm not here." "But I did explain to you," said K., and went over to join her by the photographs, "that it wasn't me who interfered with your photographs; but as you don't believe me I'll have to admit that the investigating committee brought along three bank employees with them, one of them must have touched your photographs and as soon as I get the chance I'll ask to have him dismissed from the bank. Yes, there was an investigating committee here," added K., as the young lady was looking at him enquiringly. "Because of you?" she asked. "Yes," answered K. "No!" the lady cried with a laugh. "Yes, they were," said K., "you believe that I'm innocent then, do you?" "Well now, innocent …" said the lady, "I don't want to start making any pronouncements that might have serious consequences, I don't really know you after all, it means they're dealing with a serious criminal if they send an investigating committee straight out to get him. But you're not in custody now – at least I take it you've not escaped from prison considering that you seem quite calm – so you can't have committed any crime of that sort." "Yes," said K., "but it might be that the investigating committee could see that I'm innocent, or not so guilty as had been supposed." "Yes, that's certainly a possibility," said Miss Bürstner, who seemed very interested. "Listen," said K., "you don't have much experience in legal matters." "No, that's true, I don't," said Miss Bürstner, "and I've often regretted it, as I'd like to know everything and I'm very interested in legal matters. There's something peculiarly attractive about the law, isn't there? But I'll certainly be perfecting my knowledge in this area, as next month I start work in a legal office." "That's very good," said K., "that means you'll be able to give me some help with my trial." "That could well be," said Miss Bürstner, "why not? I like to make use of what I know." "I mean it quite seriously," said K., "or at least, half seriously, as you do. This affair is too petty to call in a lawyer, but I could make good use of someone who could give me advice." "Yes, but if I'm to give you advice I'll have to know what it's all about," said Miss Bürstner. "That's exactly the problem," said K., "I don't know that myself." "So you have been making fun of me, then," said Miss Bürstner exceedingly disappointed, "you really ought not to try something like that on at this time of night." And she stepped away from the photographs where they had stood so long together. "Miss Bürstner, no," said K., "I'm not making fun of you. Please believe me! I've already told you everything I know. More than I know, in fact, as it actually wasn't even

167

an investigating committee, that's just what I called them because I don't know what else to call them. There was no cross questioning at all, I was merely arrested, but by a committee." Miss Bürstner sat on the ottoman and laughed again. "What was it like then?" she asked. "It was terrible" said K., although his mind was no longer on the subject, he had become totally absorbed by Miss Bürstner's gaze who was supporting her chin on one hand – the elbow rested on the cushion of the ottoman – and slowly stroking her hip with the other. "That's too vague," said Miss Bürstner. "What's too vague?" asked K. Then he remembered himself and asked, "Would you like me to show you what it was like?" He wanted to move in some way but did not want to leave. "I'm already tired," said Miss Bürstner. "You arrived back so late," said K. "Now you've started telling me off. Well I suppose I deserve it as I shouldn't have let you in here in the first place, and it turns out there wasn't even any point." "Oh, there was a point, you'll see now how important a point it was," said K. "May I move this table away from your bedside and put it here?" "What do you think you're doing?" said Miss Bürstner. "Of course you can't!" "In that case I can't show you," said K., quite upset, as if Miss Bürstner had committed some incomprehensible offence against him. "Alright then, if you need it to show what you mean, just take the bedside table then," said Miss Bürstner, and after a short pause added in a weak voice, "I'm so tired I'm allowing more than I ought to." K. put the little table in the middle of the room and sat down behind it. "You have to get a proper idea of where the people were situated, it is very interesting. I'm the supervisor, sitting over there on the chest are two policemen, standing next to the photographs there are three young people. Hanging on the handle of the window is a white blouse – I just mention that by the way. And now it begins. Ah yes, I'm forgetting myself, the most important person of all, so I'm standing here in front of the table. The supervisor is sitting extremely comfortably with his legs crossed and his arm hanging over the backrest here like some layabout. And now it really does begin. The supervisor calls out as if he had to wake me up, in fact he shouts at me, I'm afraid, if I'm to make it clear to you, I'll have to shout as well, and it's nothing more than my name that he shouts out." Miss Bürstner, laughing as she listened to him, laid her forefinger on her mouth so that K. would not shout, but it was too late. K. was too engrossed in his role and slowly called out, "Josef K.!". It was not as loud as he had threatened, but nonetheless, once he had suddenly called it out, the cry seemed gradually to spread itself all round the room.

There was a series of loud, curt and regular knocks at the door of the adjoining room. Miss Bürstner went pale and laid her hand on her heart. K. was especially startled, as for a moment he had been quite unable to think of anything other than the events of that morning and the girl for whom he was performing them. He had hardly pulled himself together when he jumped over to Miss Bürstner and took her hand. "Don't be afraid," he whispered, "I'll put everything right. But who can it be? It's only the living room next door, nobody sleeps in there." "Yes they do," whispered Miss Bürstner into K.'s ear, "a nephew of Mrs. Grubach's, an captain in the army, has been sleeping there since yesterday. There's no other room free. I'd forgotten about it too. Why did you have to shout like that? You've made me quite upset." "There is no reason for it," said K., and, now as she sank back onto the cushion, kissed her forehead. "Go away, go away," she said, hurriedly sitting back up, "get out of here, go, what is it you want, he's listening at the door he can hear everything. You're causing me so much trouble!" "I won't go," said K., "until you've calmed down a bit. Come over into the other corner of the room, he won't be able to hear us there." She let him lead her there. "Don't forget," he said, "although this might be unpleasant for you you're not in any real danger. You know how much esteem Mrs. Grubach has for me, she's the one who will make all the decisions in this, especially as the captain is her nephew, but she believes everything I say without question. What's more, she has borrowed a large sum of money from me and that makes her dependent on me. I will confirm whatever you say to explain our being here together, however inappropriate it might be, and I guarantee to make sure that Mrs. Grubach will not only say she believes the explanation in public but will believe it truly and sincerely. You will have no need to consider me in any way. If you wish to let it be known that I have attacked you then Mrs. Grubach will be informed of such and she will believe it without even losing her trust in me, that's how much respect she has for me." Miss Bürstner looked at the floor in front of her, quiet and a little sunk in on herself. "Why would Mrs. Grubach not believe that I've attacked you?" added K. He looked at her hair in front of him, parted, bunched down, reddish and firmly held in place. He thought she would look up at him, but without changing her manner she said, "Forgive me, but it was the suddenness of the knocking that startled me so much, not so much what the consequences of the captain being here might be. It was all so quiet after you'd shouted, and then there was the knocking, that's was made me so shocked, and I was sitting right by the door, the knocking was right next to me. Thank you for your suggestions, but I won't accept them. I can bear the responsibility for anything that happens in my room myself, and I can do so with anyone. I'm surprised you don't realise just how insulting your suggestions are and what they imply about me, although I certainly acknowledge your good intentions. But now, please go, leave me alone, I need you to go now even more than I did earlier. The couple of minutes you asked for have grown into half an hour, more than half an hour now." K. took hold of her hand, and then of her wrist, "You're not cross with me, though?" he said. She pulled her hand away and answered, "No, no, I'm never cross with anyone." He grasped her wrist once more, she tolerated it now and, in that way, lead him to the door. He had fully intended to leave. But when he reached the door he came to a halt as if he hadn't expected to find a door there, Miss Bürstner made use of that moment to get herself free, open the door, slip out into the hallway and gently say to K. from there, "Now, come along, please. Look," she pointed to the captain's door, from under which there was a light shining, "he's put a light on and he's laughing at us." "Alright, I'm coming," said K., moved forward, took hold of her, kissed her on the mouth and then over her whole face like a thirsty animal lapping with its tongue when it eventually finds water. He finally kissed her on her neck and her throat and left his lips pressed there for a long time. He did not look up until there was a noise from the captain's room. "I'll go now," he said, he wanted to address Miss Bürstner by her Christian name, but did not know it. She gave him a tired nod, offered him her hand to kiss as she turned away as if she did not know what she was doing, and went back into her room with her head bowed. A short while later, K. was lying in his bed. He very soon went to sleep, but before he did he thought a little while about his behaviour, he was satisfied with it but felt some surprise that he was not more satisfied; he was seriously worried about Miss Bürstner because of the captain.

Chapter Two
First Cross-examination

K. was informed by telephone that there would be a small hearing concerning his case the following Sunday. He was made aware that these cross examinations would follow one another regularly, perhaps not every week but quite frequently. On the one hand it was in everyone's interest to bring proceedings quickly to their conclusion, but on the other hand every aspect of the examinations had to be carried out thoroughly without lasting too long because of the associated stress. For these reasons, it had been decided to hold a series of brief examinations following on one after another. Sunday had been chosen as the day for the hearings so that K. would not be disturbed in his professional work. It was assumed that he would be in agreement with this, but if he wished for another date then, as far as possible, he would be accommodated. Cross-examinations could even be held in the night, for instance, but K. would probably not be fresh enough at that time. Anyway, as long as K. made no objection, the hearing would be left on Sundays. It was a matter of course that he would have to appear without fail, there was probably no need to point this out to him. He would be given the number of the building where he was to present himself, which was in a street in a suburb well away from the city centre which K. had never been to before.

Once he had received this notice, K. hung up the receiver without giving an answer; he had decided immediately to go there that Sunday, it was certainly necessary, proceedings had begun and he had to face up to it, and this first examination would probably also be the last. He was still standing in thought by the telephone when he heard the voice of the deputy director behind him – he wanted to use the telephone but K. stood in his way. "Bad news?" asked the deputy director casually, not in order to find anything out but just to get K. away from the device. "No, no," said K., he stepped to one side but did not go away entirely. The deputy director picked up the receiver and, as he waited for his connection, turned away from it and said to K., "One question, Mr. K.: Would you like to give me the pleasure of joining me on my sailing boat on Sunday morning? There's quite a few people coming, you're bound to know some of them. One of them is Hasterer, the state attorney. Would you like to come along? Do come along!" K. tried to pay attention to what the deputy director was saying. It was of no small importance for him, as this invitation from the deputy director, with whom he had never got on very well, meant that he was trying to improve his relations with him. It showed how important K. had become in the bank and how its second most important official seemed to value his friendship, or at least his impartiality. He was only speaking at the side of the telephone receiver while he waited for his connection, but in giving this invitation the deputy director was humbling himself. But K. would have to humiliate him a second time as a result, he said, "Thank you very much, but I'm afraid I will have no time on Sunday, I have a previous obligation." "Pity," said the deputy director, and turned to the telephone conversation that had just been connected. It was not a short conversation, but K., remained standing confused by the instrument all the time it was going on. It was only when the deputy director hung up that he was shocked into awareness and said, in order to partially excuse his standing there for no reason, "I've just received a telephone call, there's somewhere I need to go, but they forgot to tell me what time." "Ask them then," said the deputy director. "It's not that important," said K., although in that way his earlier excuse, already weak enough, was made even weaker. As he went, the deputy director continued to speak about other things. K. forced himself to answer, but his thoughts were mainly about that Sunday, how it would be best to get there for nine o'clock in the morning as that was the time that courts always start work on weekdays.

The weather was dull on Sunday. K. was very tired, as he had stayed out drinking until late in the night celebrating with some of the regulars, and he had almost overslept. He dressed hurriedly, without the time to think and assemble the various plans he had worked out during the week. With no breakfast, he rushed to the suburb he had been told about. Oddly enough, although he had little time to look around him, he came across the three bank officials involved in his case, Rabensteiner, Kullich and Kaminer. The first two were travelling in a tram that went across K.'s route, but Kaminer sat on the terrace of a café and leant curiously over the wall as K. came over. All of them seemed to be looking at him, surprised at seeing their superior running; it was a kind of pride that made K. want to go on foot, this was his affair and the idea of any help from strangers, however slight, was repulsive to him, he also wanted to avoid asking for anyone's help because that would initiate them into the affair even if only slightly. And after all, he had no wish at all to humiliate himself before the committee by being too punctual. Anyway, now he was running so that he would get there by nine o'clock if at all possible, even though he had no appointment for this time.

He had thought that he would recognise the building from a distance by some kind of sign, without knowing exactly what the sign would look like, or from some particular kind of activity outside the entrance. K. had been told that the building was in Juliusstrasse, but when he stood at the street's entrance it consisted on each side of almost nothing but monotonous, grey constructions, tall blocks of flats occupied by poor people. Now, on a Sunday morning, most of the windows were occupied, men in their shirtsleeves leant out smoking, or carefully and gently held small children on the sills. Other windows were piled up with bedding, above which the dishevelled head of a woman would briefly appear. People called out to each other across the street, one of the calls provoked a loud laugh about K. himself. It was a long street, and spaced evenly along it were small shops below street level, selling various kinds of foodstuffs, which you reached by going down a few steps. Women went in and out of them or stood chatting on the steps. A fruitmonger, taking his goods up to the windows, was just as inattentive as K. and nearly knocked him down with his cart. Just then, a gramophone, which in better parts of town would have been seen as worn out, began to play some murderous tune.

K. went further into the street, slowly, as if he had plenty of time now, or as if the examining magistrate were looking at him from one of the windows and therefore knew that K. had found his way there. It was shortly after nine. The building was quite far down the street, it covered so much area it was almost extraordinary, and the gateway in particular was tall and long. It was clearly intended for delivery wagons belonging to the various warehouses all round the yard which were now locked up and carried the names of companies some of which K. knew from his work at the bank. In contrast with his usual habits, he remained standing a while at the entrance to the yard taking in all these external details. Near him, there was a bare-footed man sitting on a crate and reading a newspaper. There were two lads swinging on a hand cart. In front of a pump stood a weak, young girl in a bedjacket who, as the water flowed into her can, looked at K. There was a piece of rope stretched between two windows in a corner of the yard, with some washing hanging on it to dry. A man stood below it calling out instructions to direct the work being done.

K. went over to the stairway to get to the room where the hearing was to take place, but then stood still again as besides these steps he could see three other stairway entrances, and there also seemed to be a small passageway at the end of the yard leading into a second yard. It irritated him that he had not been given more precise directions to the room, it meant they were either being especially neglectful with him or especially indifferent, and he decided to make that clear to them very loudly and very unambiguously. In the end he decided to climb up the stairs, his thoughts playing on something that he remembered the policeman, Willem, saying to him; that the court is attracted by the guilt, from which it followed that the courtroom must be on the stairway that K. selected by chance.

As he went up he disturbed a large group of children playing on the stairs who looked at him as he stepped through their rows. "Next time I come here," he said to himself, "I must either bring sweets with me to make them like me or a stick to hit them with." Just before he reached the first landing he even had to wait a little while until a ball had finished its movement, two small lads with sly faces like grown-up scoundrels held him by his trouser-legs until it had; if he were to shake them off he would have to hurt them, and he was afraid of what noise they would make by shouting.

On the first floor, his search began for real. He still felt unable to ask for the investigating committee, and so he invented a joiner called Lanz – that name occurred to him because the captain, Mrs. Grubach's nephew, was called Lanz – so that he could ask at every flat whether Lanz the joiner lived there and thus obtain a chance to look into the rooms. It turned out, though, that that was mostly possible without further ado, as almost all the doors were left open and the children ran in and out. Most of them were small, one-windowed rooms where they also did the cooking. Many women held babies in one arm and worked at the stove with the other. Half grown girls, who seemed to be dressed in just their pinafores worked hardest running to and fro. In every room, the beds were still in use by people who were ill, or still

175

asleep, or people stretched out on them in their clothes. K. knocked at the flats where the doors were closed and asked whether Lanz the joiner lived there. It was usually a woman who opened the door, heard the enquiry and turned to somebody in the room who would raise himself from the bed. "The gentleman's asking if a joiner called Lanz, lives here." "A joiner, called Lanz?" he would ask from the bed." "That's right," K. would say, although it was clear that the investigating committee was not to be found there, and so his task was at an end. There were many who thought it must be very important for K. to find Lanz the joiner and thought long about it, naming a joiner who was not called Lanz or giving a name that had some vague similarity with Lanz, or they asked neighbours or accompanied K. to a door a long way away where they thought someone of that sort might live in the back part of the building or where someone would be who could advise K. better than they could themselves. K. eventually had to give up asking if he did not want to be led all round from floor to floor in this way. He regretted his initial plan, which had at first seemed so practical to him. As he reached the fifth floor, he decided to give up the search, took his leave of a friendly, young worker who wanted to lead him on still further and went down the stairs. But then the thought of how much time he was wasting made him cross, he went back again and knocked at the first door on the fifth floor. The first thing he saw in the small room was a large clock on the wall which already showed ten o'clock. "Is there a joiner called Lanz who lives here?" he asked. "Pardon?" said a young woman with black, shining eyes who was, at that moment, washing children's underclothes in a bucket. She pointed her wet hand towards the open door of the adjoining room.

K. thought he had stepped into a meeting. A medium sized, two windowed room was filled with the most diverse crowd of people – nobody paid any attention to the person who had just entered. Close under its ceiling it was surrounded by a gallery which was also fully occupied and where the people could only stand bent down with their heads and their backs touching the ceiling. K., who found the air too stuffy, stepped out again and said to the young woman, who had probably misunderstood what he had said, "I asked for a joiner, someone by the name of Lanz." "Yes," said the woman, "please go on in." K. would probably not have followed her if the woman had not gone up to him, taken hold of the door handle and said, "I'll have to close the door after you, no-one else will be allowed in." "Very sensible," said K., "but it's too full already." But then he went back in anyway. He passed through between two men who were talking beside the door – one of them held both hands far out in front of himself making the movements of counting out money, the other looked him closely in the eyes – and someone took him by the hand. It was a small, red-faced youth. "Come in, come in," he said. K. let himself be led by him, and it turned out that there was – surprisingly in a densely packed crowd of people moving to and fro – a narrow passage which may have been the division between two factions; this idea was reinforced by the fact that in the first few rows to the left and the right of him there was hardly any face looking in his direction, he saw nothing but the backs of people directing their speech and their movements only towards members of their own side. Most of them were dressed in black, in old, long, formal frock coats that hung down loosely around them. These clothes were the only thing that puzzled K., as he would otherwise have taken the whole assembly for a local political meeting.

At the other end of the hall where K. had been led there was a little table set at an angle on a very low podium which was as overcrowded as everywhere else, and behind the table, near the edge of the podium, sat a small, fat, wheezing man who was talking with someone behind him. This second man was standing with his legs crossed and his elbows on the backrest of the chair, provoking much laughter. From time to time he threw his arm in the air as if doing a caricature of someone. The youth who was leading K. had some difficulty in reporting to the man. He had already tried twice to tell him something, standing on tip- toe, but without getting the man's attention as he sat there above him. It was only when one of the people up on the podium drew his attention to the youth that the man turned to him and leant down to hear what it was he quietly said. Then he pulled out his watch and quickly looked over at K. "You should have been here one hour and five minutes ago," he said. K. was going to give him a reply but had no time to do so, as hardly had the man spoken than a general muttering arose all over the right hand side of the hall. "You should have been here one hour and five minutes ago," the man now repeated, raising his voice this time, and quickly looked round the hall beneath him. The muttering also became immediately louder and, as the man said nothing more, died away only gradually. Now the hall was much quieter than when K. had entered. Only the people up in the gallery had not stopped passing remarks. As far as could be distinguished, up in the half-darkness, dust and haze, they seemed to be less well dressed than those below. Many of them had brought pillows that they had put between their heads and the ceiling so that they would not hurt themselves pressed against it.

K. had decided he would do more watching than talking, so he did not defend himself for supposedly having come late, and simply said, "Well maybe I have arrived late, I'm here now." There followed loud applause, once more from the right hand side of the hall. Easy people to get on your side, thought K., and was bothered only by the quiet from the left hand side which was directly behind him and from which there was applause from only a few individuals. He wondered what he could say to get all of them to support him together or, if that were not possible, to at least get the support of the others for a while.

"Yes," said the man, "but I'm now no longer under any obligation to hear your case" – there was once more a muttering, but this time it was misleading as the man waved the people's objections aside with his hand and continued – "I will, however, as an exception, continue with it today. But you should never arrive late like this again. And now, step forward!" Someone jumped down from the podium so that there would be a place free for K., and K. stepped up onto it. He stood pressed closely against the table, the press of the crowd behind him was so great that he had to press back against it if he did not want to push the judge's desk down off the podium and perhaps the judge along with it.

The judge, however, paid no attention to that but sat very comfortably on his chair and, after saying a few words to close his discussion with the man behind him, reached for a little note book, the only item on his desk. It was like an old school exercise book and had become quite misshapen from much thumbing. "Now then," said the judge, thumbing through the book. He turned to K. with the tone of someone who knows his facts and said, "you are a house painter?" "No," said K., "I am the chief clerk in a large bank." This reply was followed by laughter among the right hand faction down in the hall, it was so hearty that K. couldn't stop himself joining in with it. The people supported themselves with their hands on their knees and shook as if suffering a serious attack of coughing. Even some of those in the gallery were laughing. The judge had become quite cross but seemed to have no power over those below him in the hall, he tried to reduce what harm had been done in the gallery and jumped up threatening them, his eyebrows, until then hardly remarkable, pushed themselves up and became big, black and bushy over his eyes.

The left hand side of the hall was still quiet, though, the people stood there in rows with their faces looking towards the podium listening to what was being said there, they observed the noise from the other side of the hall with the same quietness and even allowed some individuals from their own ranks, here and there, to go forward into the other faction. The people in the left faction were not only fewer in number than the right but probably were no more important than them, although their behaviour was calmer and that made it seem like they were. When K. now began to speak he was convinced he was doing it in the same way as them.

"Your question, My Lord, as to whether I am a house painter – in fact even more than that, you did not ask at all but merely imposed it on me – is symptomatic of the whole way these proceedings against me are being carried out. Perhaps you will object that there are no proceedings against me. You will be quite right, as there are proceedings only if I acknowledge that there are. But, for the moment, I do acknowledge it, out of pity for yourselves to a large extent. It's impossible not to observe all this business without feeling pity. I don't say things are being done without due care but I would like to make it clear that it is I who make the acknowledgement."

K. stopped speaking and looked down into the hall. He had spoken sharply, more sharply than he had intended, but he had been quite right. It should have been rewarded with some applause here and there but everything was quiet, they were all clearly waiting for what would follow, perhaps the quietness was laying the ground for an outbreak of activity that would bring this whole affair to an end. It was somewhat disturbing that just then the door at the end of the hall opened, the young washerwoman, who seemed to have finished her work, came in and, despite all her caution, attracted the attention of some of the people there. It was only the judge who gave K. any direct pleasure, as he seemed to have been immediately struck by K.'s words. Until then, he had listened to him standing, as K.'s speech had taken him by surprise while he was directing his attention to the gallery. Now, in the pause, he sat down very slowly, as if he did not want anyone to notice. He took out the notebook again, probably so that he could give the impression of being calmer.

"That won't help you, sir," continued K., "even your little book will only confirm what I say." K. was satisfied to hear nothing but his own quiet words in this room full of strangers, and he even dared casually to pick up the examining judge's notebook and, touching it only with the tips of his fingers as if it were something revolting, lifted it in the air, holding it just by one of the middle pages so that the others on each side of it, closely written, blotted and yellowing, flapped down. "Those are the official notes of the examining judge," he said, and let the notebook fall down onto the desk. "You can read in your book as much as you like, sir, I really don't have anything in this charge book to be afraid of, even though I don't have access to it as I wouldn't want it in my hand, I can only touch it with two fingers." The judge grabbed the notebook from where it had fallen on the desk – which could only have been a sign of his deep humiliation, or at least that is how it must have been perceived – tried to tidy it up a little, and held it once more in front of himself in order to read from it.

The people in the front row looked up at him, showing such tension on their faces that he looked back down at them for some time. Every one of them was an old man, some of them with white beards. Could they perhaps be the crucial group who could turn the whole assembly one way or the other? They had sunk into a state of motionlessness while K. gave his oration, and it had not been possible to raise them from this passivity even when the judge was being humiliated. "What has happened to me," continued K., with less of the vigour he had had earlier, he continually scanned the faces in the first row, and this gave his address a somewhat nervous and distracted character, "what has happened to me is not just an isolated case. If it were it would not be of much importance as it's not of much importance to me, but it is a symptom of proceedings which are carried out against many. It's on behalf of them that I stand here now, not for myself alone."

Without having intended it, he had raised his voice. Somewhere in the hall, someone raised his hands and applauded him shouting, "Bravo! Why not then? Bravo! Again I say, Bravo!" Some of the men in the first row groped around in their beards, none of them looked round to see who was shouting. Not even K. thought him of any importance but it did raise his spirits; he no longer thought it at all necessary that all of those in the hall should applaud him, it was enough if the majority of them began to think about the matter and if only one of them, now and then, was persuaded.

"I'm not trying to be a successful orator," said K. after this thought, "that's probably more than I'm capable of anyway. I'm sure the examining judge can speak far better than I can, it is part of his job after all. All that I want is a public discussion of a public wrong. Listen: ten days ago I was placed under arrest, the arrest itself is something I laugh about but that's beside the point. They came for me in the morning when I was still in bed. Maybe the order had been given to arrest some house painter – that seems possible after what the judge has said – someone who is as innocent as I am, but it was me they chose. There were two police thugs occupying the next room. They could not have taken better precautions if I had been a dangerous robber. And these policemen were unprincipled riff-raff, they talked at me till I was sick of it, they wanted bribes, they wanted to trick me into giving them my clothes, they wanted money, supposedly so that they could bring me my breakfast after they had blatantly eaten my own breakfast in front of my eyes. And even that was not enough. I was led in front of the supervisor in another room. This was the room of a lady who I have a lot of respect for, and I was forced to look on while the supervisor and the policemen made quite a mess of this room because of me, although not through any fault of mine. It was not easy to stay calm, but I managed to do so and was completely calm when I asked the supervisor why it was that I was under arrest. If he were here he would have to confirm what I say. I can see him now, sitting on the chair belonging to that lady I mentioned – a picture of dull-witted arrogance. What do you think he answered? What he told me, gentlemen, was basically nothing at all; perhaps he really did know nothing, he had placed me under arrest and was satisfied. In fact he had done more than that and brought three junior employees from the bank where I work into the lady's room; they had made themselves busy interfering with some photographs that belonged to the lady and causing a mess. There was, of course, another reason for bringing these employees; they, just like my landlady and her maid, were expected to spread the news of my arrest and damage my public reputation and in particular to remove me from my position at the bank. Well they didn't succeed in any of that, not in the slightest, even my landlady, who is quite a simple person – and I will give you here her name in full respect, her name is Mrs. Grubach – even Mrs. Grubach was understanding enough to see that an arrest like this has no more significance than an attack carried out on the street by some youths who are not kept under proper control. I repeat, this whole affair has caused me nothing but unpleasantness and temporary irritation, but could it not also have had some far worse consequences?"

K. broke off here and looked at the judge, who said nothing. As he did so he thought he saw the judge use a movement of his eyes to give a sign to someone in the crowd. K. smiled and said, "And now the judge, right next to me, is giving a secret sign to someone among you. There seems to be someone among you who is taking directions from above. I don't know whether the sign is meant to produce booing or applause, but I'll resist trying to guess what its meaning is too soon. It really doesn't matter to me, and I give his lordship the judge my full and public permission to stop giving secret signs to his paid subordinate down there and give his orders in words instead; let him just say "Boo now!," and then the next time "Clap now!".

Whether it was embarrassment or impatience, the judge rocked backwards and forwards on his seat. The man behind him, whom he had been talking with earlier, leant forward again, either to give him a few general words of encouragement or some specific piece of advice. Below them in the hall the people talked to each other quietly but animatedly. The two factions had earlier seemed to hold views strongly opposed to each other but now they began to intermingle, a few individuals pointed up at K., others pointed at the judge. The air in the room was fuggy and extremely oppressive, those who were standing furthest away could hardly even be seen through it. It must have been especially troublesome for those visitors who were in the gallery, as they were forced to quietly ask the participants in the assembly what exactly was happening, albeit with timid glances at the judge. The replies they received were just as quiet, and given behind the protection of a raised hand.

"I have nearly finished what I have to say," said K., and as there was no bell available he struck the desk with his fist in a way that startled the judge and his advisor and made them look up from each other. "None of this concerns me, and I am therefore able to make a calm assessment of it, and, assuming that this so-called court is of any real importance, it will be very much to your advantage to listen to what I have to say. If you want to discuss what I say, please don't bother to write it down until later on, I don't have any time to waste and I'll soon be leaving."

There was immediate silence, which showed how well K. was in control of the crowd. There were no shouts among them as there had been at the start, no-one even applauded, but if they weren't already persuaded they seemed very close to it.

K was pleased at the tension among all the people there as they listened to him, a rustling rose from the silence which was more invigorating than the most ecstatic applause could have been. "There is no doubt," he said quietly, "that there is some enormous organisation determining what is said by this court. In my case this includes my arrest and the examination taking place here today, an organisation that employs policemen who can be bribed, oafish supervisors and judges of whom nothing better can be said than that they are not as arrogant as some others. This organisation even maintains a high-level judiciary along with its train of countless servants, scribes, policemen and all the other assistance that it needs, perhaps even executioners and torturers – I'm not afraid of using those words. And what, gentlemen, is the purpose of this enormous organisation? Its purpose is to arrest innocent people and wage pointless prosecutions against them which, as in my case, lead to no result. How are we to avoid those in office becoming deeply corrupt when everything is devoid of meaning? That is impossible, not even the highest judge would be able to achieve that for himself. That is why policemen try to steal the clothes off the back of those they arrest, that is why supervisors break into the homes of people they do not know, that is why innocent people are humiliated in front of crowds rather than being given a proper trial. The policemen only talked about the warehouses where they put the property of those they arrest, I would like to see these warehouses where the hard won possessions of people under arrest is left to decay, if, that is, it's not stolen by the thieving hands of the warehouse workers."

K. was interrupted by a screeching from the far end of the hall, he shaded his eyes to see that far, as the dull light of day made the smoke whitish and hard to see through. It was the washerwoman whom K. had recognised as a likely source of disturbance as soon as she had entered. It was hard to see now whether it was her fault or not. K. could only see that a man had pulled her into a corner by the door and was pressing himself against her. But it was not her who was screaming, but the man, he had opened his mouth wide and looked up at the ceiling. A small circle had formed around the two of them, the visitors near him in the gallery seemed delighted that the serious tone K. had introduced into the gathering had been disturbed in this way. K.'s first thought was to run over there, and he also thought that everyone would want to bring things back into order there or at least to make the pair leave the room, but the first row of people in front of him stayed were they were, no-one moved and no-one let K. through. On the contrary, they stood in his way, old men held out their arms in front of him and a hand from somewhere – he did not have the time to turn round – took hold of his collar. K., by this time, had forgotten about the pair, it seemed to him that his freedom was being limited as if his arrest was being taken seriously, and, without any thought for what he was doing, he jumped down from the podium. Now he stood face to face with the crowd. Had he judged the people properly? Had he put too much faith in the effect of his speech? Had they been putting up a pretence all the time he had been speaking, and now that he come to the end and to what must follow, were they tired of pretending? What faces they were, all around him! Dark, little eyes flickered here and there, cheeks drooped down like on drunken men, their long beards were thin and stiff, if they took hold of them it was more like they were making their hands into claws, not as if they were taking hold of their own beards. But underneath those beards – and this was the real discovery made by K. – there were badges of various sizes and colours shining on the collars of their coats. As far as he could see, every one of them was wearing one of these badges. All of them belonged to the same group, even though they seemed to be divided to the right and the left of him, and when he suddenly turned round he saw the same badge on the collar of the examining judge who calmly looked down at him with his hands in his lap. "So," called out K, throwing his arms in the air as if this sudden realisation needed more room, "all of you are working for this organisation, I see now that you are all the very bunch of cheats and liars I've just been speaking about, you've all pressed yourselves in here in order to listen in and snoop on me, you gave the impression of having formed into factions, one of you even applauded me to test me out, and you wanted to learn how to trap an innocent man! Well, I hope you haven't come here for nothing, I hope you've either had some fun from someone who expected you to defend his innocence or else – let go of me or I'll hit you," shouted K. to a quivery old man who had pressed himself especially close to him – "or else that you've actually learned something. And so I wish you good luck in your trade." He briskly took his hat from where it lay on the edge of the table and, surrounded by a silence caused perhaps by the completeness of their surprise, pushed his way to the exit. However, the examining judge seems to have moved even more quickly than K., as he was waiting for him at the doorway. "One moment," he said. K. stood where he was, but looked at the door with his hand already on its handle rather than at the judge. "I merely wanted to draw your attention," said the judge, "to something you seem not yet to be aware of: today, you have robbed yourself of the advantages that a hearing of this sort always gives to someone who is under arrest." K. laughed towards the door.

"You bunch of louts," he called, "you can keep all your hearings as a present from me," then opened the door and hurried down the steps. Behind him, the noise of the assembly rose as it became lively once more and probably began to discuss these events as if making a scientific study of them.

Chapter Three
In the empty Courtroom – The Student – The Offices

Every day over the following week, K. expected another summons to arrive, he could not believe that his rejection of any more hearings had been taken literally, and when the expected summons really had not come by Saturday evening he took it to mean that he was expected, without being told, to appear at the same place at the same time. So on Sunday, he set out once more in the same direction, going without hesitation up the steps and through the corridors; some of the people remembered him and greeted him from their doorways, but he no longer needed to ask anyone the way and soon arrived at the right door. It was opened as soon as he knocked and, paying no attention to the woman he had seen last time who was standing at the doorway, he was about to go straight into the adjoining room when she said to him "There's no session today". "What do you mean; no session?" he asked, unable to believe it. But the woman persuaded him by opening the door to the next room. It was indeed empty, and looked even more dismal empty than it had the previous Sunday. On the podium stood the table exactly as it had been before with a few books laying on it. "Can I have a look at those books?" asked K., not because he was especially curious but so that he would not have come for nothing. "No," said the woman as she re-closed the door, "that's not allowed. Those books belong to the examining judge." "I see," said K., and nodded, "those books must be law books, and that's how this court does things, not only to try people who are innocent but even to try them without letting them know what's going on." "I expect you're right," said the woman, who had not understood exactly what he meant. "I'd better go away again, then," said K. "Should I give a message to the examining judge?" asked the woman. "Do you know him, then?" asked K. "Of course I know him," said the woman, "my husband is the court usher." It was only now that K. noticed that the room, which before had held nothing but a wash-tub, had been fitted out as a living room. The woman saw how surprised he was and said, "Yes, we're allowed to live here as we like, only we have to clear the room out when the court's in session. There's lots of disadvantages to my husband's job." "It's not so much the room that surprises me," said K., looking at her crossly, "it's your being married that shocks me." "Are you thinking about what happened last time the court was in session, when I disturbed what you were saying?" asked the woman. "Of course," said K., "it's in the past now and I've nearly forgotten about it, but at the time it made me furious. And now you tell me yourself that you are a married woman." "It wasn't any disadvantage for you to have your speech interrupted. The way they talked about you after you'd gone was really bad." "That could well be," said K., turning away, "but it does not excuse you." "There's no-one I know who'd hold it against me," said the woman. "Him, who put his arms around me, he's been chasing after me for a long time. I might not be very attractive for most people, but I am for him. I've got no protection from him, even my husband has had to get used to it; if he wants to keep his job he's got to put up with it as that man's a student and he'll almost certainly be very powerful later on. He's always after me, he'd only just left when you arrived." "That fits in with everything else," said K., "I'm not surprised." "Do you want to make things a bit better here?" the woman asked slowly, watching him as if she were saying something that could be as dangerous for K. as for herself. "That's what I thought when I heard you speak, I really liked what you said. Mind you, I only heard part of it, I missed the beginning of it and at the end I was lying on the floor with the student – it's so horrible here," she said after a pause, and took hold of K.'s hand. "Do you believe you really will be able to make things better?" K. smiled and twisted his hand round a little in her soft hands. "It's really not my job to make things better here, as you put it," he said, "and if you said that to the examining judge he would laugh at you or punish you for it. I really would not have become involved in this matter if I could have helped it, and I would have lost no sleep worrying about how this court needs to be made better. But because I'm told that I have been arrested – and I am under arrest – it forces me to take some action, and to do so for my own sake. However, if I can be of some service to you in the process I will, of course, be glad to do so. And I will be glad to do so not only for the sake of charity but also because you can be of some help to me." "How could I help you, then?" said the woman. "You could, for example, show me the books on the table there." "Yes, certainly," the woman cried, and pulled K. along behind her as she rushed to them. The books were old and well worn, the cover of one of them had nearly broken through in its middle, and it was held together with a few threads. "Everything is so dirty here," said K., shaking his head, and before he could pick the books up the woman wiped some of the dust off with her apron. K. took hold of the book that lay on top and threw it open, an indecent picture appeared. A man and a woman sat naked on a sofa, the base intent of whoever drew it was easy to see but he had been so grossly lacking in skill that all that anyone could really make out were the man and the woman who dominated the picture with their bodies, sitting in overly upright postures that created a false perspective and made it difficult for them to approach each other. K. didn't thumb through that book any more, but just threw open the next one at its title page, it was a novel with the title, What Grete Suffered from her Husband, Hans. "So this is the sort of law book they study here," said K., "this is the sort of person sitting in judgement over me." "I can help you," said the woman, "would you like me to?" "Could you really do that without placing yourself in danger? You did say earlier on that your husband is wholly dependent on his superiors." "I still want to help you," said the woman, "come over here, we've got to talk about it. Don't say any more about what danger I'm in, I only fear danger where I want to fear it. Come over here." She pointed to the podium and invited him to sit down on the step with her. "You've got lovely dark eyes," she said after they had sat down, looking up into K.'s face, "people say I've got nice eyes too, but yours are much nicer. It was the first thing I noticed when you first came here. That's even why I came in here, into the assembly room, afterwards, I'd never normally do that, I'm not really even allowed to." So that's what all this is about, thought K., she's offering herself to me, she's as degenerate as everything else around here, she's had enough of the court officials, which is understandable I suppose, and so she approaches any stranger and makes compliments about his eyes. With that, K. stood up in silence as if he had spoken his thoughts out loud and thus explained his action to the woman. "I don't think you can be of any assistance to me," he said, "to be of any real assistance you would need to be in contact with high officials. But I'm sure you only know the lower employees, and there are crowds of them milling about here. I'm sure you're very familiar with them and could achieve a great deal through them, I've no doubt of that, but the most that could be done through them would have no bearing at all on the final out-come of the trial. You, on the other hand, would lose some of your friends as a result, and I have no wish of that. Carry on with these people in the same way as you have been, as it does seem to me to be something you cannot do without. I have no regrets in saying this as, in return for your compliment to me, I also find you rather attractive, especially when you look at me as sadly as you are now, although you really have no reason to do so. You belong to the people I have to combat, and you're very comfortable among them, you're even in love with the student, or if you don't love him you do at least prefer him to your husband. It's easy to see that from what you've been saying." "No!" she shouted, remained sitting where she was and grasped K.'s hand, which he failed to pull away fast enough. "You can't go away now, you can't go away when you've misjudged me like that! Are you really capable of going away now? Am I really so worthless that you won't even do me the favour of staying a little bit longer?" "You misunderstand me," said K., sitting back down, "if it's really important to you for me to stay here then I'll be glad to do so, I have plenty of time, I came here thinking there would be a trial taking place. All I meant with what I said just now was to ask you not to do anything on my behalf in the proceedings against me. But even that is nothing for you to worry about when you consider that there's nothing hanging on the outcome of this trial, and that, whatever the verdict, I will just laugh at it. And that's even presupposing it ever even reaches any conclusion, which I very much doubt. I think it's much more likely that the court officials will be too lazy, too forgetful, or even to fearful ever to continue with these proceedings and that they will soon be abandoned if they haven't been abandoned already. It's even possible that they will pretend to be carrying on with the trial in the hope of receiving a large bribe, although I can tell you now that that will be quite in vain as I pay bribes to no-one. Perhaps one favour you could do me would be to tell the examining judge, or anyone else who likes to spread important news, that I will never be induced to pay any sort of bribe through any stratagem of theirs – and I'm sure they have many stratagems at their disposal. There is no prospect of that, you can tell them that quite openly. And what's more, I expect they have already noticed themselves, or even if they haven't, this affair is really not so important to me as they think. Those gentlemen would only save some work for themselves, or at least some unpleasantness for me, which, however, I am glad to endure if I know that each piece of unpleasantness for me is a blow against them. And I will make quite sure it is a blow against them. Do you actually know the judge?" "Course I do," said the woman, "he was the first one I thought of when I offered to help you. I didn't know he's only a minor official, but if you say so it must be true. Mind you, I still think the report he gives to his superiors must have some influence. And he writes so many reports. You say these officials are lazy, but they're certainly not all lazy, especially this examining judge, he writes ever such a lot. Last Sunday, for instance, that session went on till the evening. Everyone had gone, but the examining judge, he stayed in the hall, I had to bring him a lamp in, all I had was a little kitchen lamp but he was very satisfied with it and started to write straight away. Meantime my husband arrived, he always has the day off on Sundays, we got the furniture back in and got our room sorted out and then a few of the neighbours came, we sat and talked for a bit by a candle, in short, we forgot all about the examining judge and went to bed. All of a sudden in the night, it must have been quite late in the night, I wakes up, next to the bed, there's the examining judge shading the lamp with his hand so that there's no light from it falls on my husband, he didn't need to be as careful as that, the way my husband sleeps the light wouldn't have woken him up anyway. I was quite shocked and nearly screamed, but the judge was very friendly, warned me I should be careful, he whispered to me he's been writing all this time, and now he's brought me the lamp back, and he'll never forget how I looked when he found me there asleep. What I mean, with all this, I just wanted to tell you how the examining judge really does write lots of reports, especially about you as questioning you was definitely one of the main things on the agenda that Sunday. If he writes reports as long as that they must be of some importance. And besides all that, you can see from what happened that the examining judge is after me, and it's right now, when he's first begun to notice me, that I can have a lot of influence on him. And I've got other proof I mean a lot to him, too. Yesterday, he sent that student to me, the one he really trusts and who he works with, he sent him with a present for me, silk stockings. He said it was because I clear up in the courtroom but that's only a pretence, that job's no more than what I'm supposed to do, it's what my husband gets paid for. Nice stockings, they are, look," – she stretched out her leg, drew her skirt up to her knee and looked, herself, at the stocking – "they are nice stockings, but they're too good for me, really."

She suddenly interrupted herself and lay her hand on K.'s as if she wanted to calm him down, and whispered, "Be quiet,

Berthold is watching us." K. slowly looked up. In the doorway to the courtroom stood a young man, he was short, his
legs were not quite straight, and he continually moved his
finger round in a short, thin, red beard with which he hoped
to make himself look dignified. K. looked at him with some
curiosity, he was the first student he had ever met of the
unfamiliar discipline of jurisprudence, face to face at least, a
man who would even most likely attain high office one day.
The student, in contrast, seemed to take no notice of K. at all,
he merely withdrew his finger from his beard long enough to
beckon to the woman and went over to the window, the
woman leant over to K. and whispered, "Don't be cross with
me, please don't, and please don't think ill of me either, I've
got to go to him now, to this horrible man, just look at his
bent legs. But I'll come straight back and then I'll go with you
if you'll take me, I'll go wherever you want, you can do whatever you like with me, I'll be happy if I can be away from here
for as long as possible, it'd be best if I could get away from
here for good." She stroked K.'s hand once more, jumped up
and ran over to the window. Before he realised it, K. grasped
for her hand but failed to catch it. He really was attracted to
the woman, and even after thinking hard about it could find
no good reason why he should not give in to her allure. It
briefly crossed his mind that the woman meant to entrap him
on behalf of the court, but that was an objection he had no
difficulty in fending off. In what way could she entrap him?
Was he not still free, so free that he could crush the entire
court whenever he wanted, as least where it concerned him?
Could he not have that much confidence in himself? And her
offer of help sounded sincere, and maybe it wasn't quite
worthless. And maybe there was no better revenge against the
examining judge and his cronies than to take this woman
from him and have her for himself. Maybe then, after much
hard work writing dishonest reports about K., the judge
would go to the woman's bed late one night and find it empty. And it would be empty because she belonged to K., because this woman at the window, this lush, supple, warm
body in its sombre clothes of rough, heavy material belonged

to him, totally to him and to him alone. Once he had settled his thoughts towards the woman in this way, he began to find the quiet conversation at the window was taking too long, he rapped on the podium with his knuckles, and then even with his fist. The student briefly looked away from the woman to glance at K. over his shoulder but did allow himself to be disturbed, in fact he even pressed himself close to the woman and put his arms around her. She dropped her head down low as if listening to him carefully, as she did so he kissed her right on the neck, hardly even interrupting what he was saying. K. saw this as confirmation of the tyranny the student held over the woman and which she had already complained about, he stood up and walked up and down the room. Glancing sideways at the student, he wondered what would be the quickest possible way to get rid of him, and so it was not unwelcome to him when the student, clearly disturbed by K.'s to-ing and fro-ing which K. had now developed into a stamping up and down, said to him, "You don't have to stay here, you know, if you're getting impatient. You could have gone earlier, no-one would have missed you. In fact you should have gone, you should have left as quickly as possible as soon as I got here." This comment could have caused all possible rage to break out between them, but K. also bore in mind that this was a prospective court official speaking to a disfavoured defendant, and he might well have been taking pride in speaking in this way. K. remained standing quite close to him and said with a smile, "You're quite right, I am impatient, but the easiest way to settle this impatience would be if you left us. On the other hand, if you've come here to study – you are a student, I hear – I'll be quite happy to leave the room to you and go away with the woman. I'm sure you'll still have a lot of study to do before you're made into a judge. It's true that I'm still not all that familiar with your branch of jurisprudence but I take it it involves a lot more than speaking roughly – and I see you have no shame in doing that extremely well." "He shouldn't have been allowed to move about so freely," said the student, as if he wanted to give the woman an explanation for K.'s insults, "that was a mistake. I've told the examining judge so. He should at least have been detained in his room between hearings. Sometimes it's impossible to understand what the judge thinks he's doing." "You're wasting your breath," said K., then he reached his hand out towards the woman and said, "come with me." "So that's it," said the student, "oh no, you're not going to get her," and with a strength you would not have expected from him, he glanced tenderly at her, lifted her up on one arm and, his back bent under the weight, ran with her to the door. In this way he showed, unmistakeably, that he was to some extent afraid of K., but he nonetheless dared to provoke him still further by stroking and squeezing the woman's arm with his free hand. K. ran the few steps up to him, but when he had reached him and was about to take hold of him and, if necessary, throttle him, the woman said, "It's no good, it's the examining judge who's sent for me, I daren't go with you, this little bastard…" and here she ran her hand over the student's face, "this little bastard won't let me." "And you don't want to be set free!" shouted K., laying his hand on the student's shoulder, who then snapped at it with his teeth. "No!" shouted the woman, pushing K. away with both hands, "no, no don't do that, what d'you think you're doing!? That'd be the end of me. Let go of him, please just let go of him. He's only carrying out the judge's orders, he's carrying me to him." "Let him take you then, and I want to see nothing more of you," said K., enraged by his disappointment and giving the student a thump in the back so that he briefly stumbled and then, glad that he had not fallen, immediately jumped up all the higher with his burden. K. followed them slowly. He realised that this was the first unambiguous setback he had suffered from these people. It was of course nothing to worry about, he accepted the setback only because he was looking for a fight. If he stayed at home and carried on with his normal life he would be a thousand times superior to these people and could get any of them out of his way just with a kick. And he imagined the most laughable scene possible as an example of this, if this contemptible student, this inflated child, this knock-kneed redbeard, if he were kneeling at Elsa's bed wringing his hands and begging for forgiveness. K. so enjoyed imagining this scene that he decided to take the student along to Elsa with him if ever he should get the opportunity.

K. was curious to see where the woman would be taken and he hurried over to the door, the student was not likely to carry her through the streets on his arm. It turned out that the journey was far shorter. Directly opposite the flat there was a narrow flight of wooden steps which probably led up to the attic, they turned as they went so that it was not possible to see where they ended. The student carried the woman up these steps, and after the exertions of running with her he was soon groaning and moving very slowly. The woman waved down at K. and by raising and lowering her shoulders she tried to show that she was an innocent party in this abduction, although the gesture did not show a lot of regret. K. watched her without expression like a stranger, he wanted to show neither that he was disappointed nor that he would easily get over his disappointment.

The two of them had disappeared, but K. remained standing in the doorway. He had to accept that the woman had not only cheated him but that she had also lied to him when she said she was being taken to the examining judge. The examining judge certainly wouldn't be sitting and waiting in the attic. The wooden stairs would explain nothing to him however long he stared at them. Then K. noticed a small piece of paper next to them, went across to it and read, in a childish and unpractised hand, "Entrance to the Court Offices". Were the court offices here, in the attic of this tenement, then? If that was how they were accommodated it did not attract much respect, and it was some comfort for the accused to realise how little money this court had at its disposal if it had to locate its offices in a place where the tenants of the building, who were themselves among the poorest of people, would throw their unneeded junk. On the other hand, it was possible that the officials had enough money but that they squandered it on themselves rather than use it for the court's purposes. Going by K.'s experience of them so far, that even seemed probable, except that if the court were allowed to decay in that way it would not just humiliate the accused but also give him more encouragement than if the court were simply in a state of poverty. K. also now understood that the court was ashamed to summon those it accused to the attic of this building for the initial hearing, and why it preferred to impose upon them in their own homes. What a position it was that K. found himself in, compared with the judge sitting up in the attic! K., at the bank, had a big office with an ante-room, and had an enormous window through which he could look down at the activity in the square. It was true, though, that he had no secondary income from bribes and fraud, and he couldn't tell a servant to bring him a woman up to the office on his arm. K., however, was quite willing to do without such things, in this life at least. K. was still looking at the notice when a man came up the stairs, looked through the open door into the living room where it was also possible to see the court-room, and finally asked K. whether he had just seen a woman there. "You're the court usher, aren't you?" asked K. "That's right," said the man, "oh, yes, you're defendant K., I recognise you now as well. Nice to see you here." And he offered K. his hand, which was far from what K. had expected. And when K. said nothing, he added, "There's no court session planned for today, though." "I know that," said K. as he looked at the usher's civilian coat which, beside its ordinary buttons, displayed two gilded ones as the only sign of his office and seemed to have been taken from an old army officer's coat. "I was speaking with your wife a little while ago. She is no longer here. The student has carried her off to the examining judge." "Listen to this," said the usher, "they're always carrying her away from me. It's Sunday today, and it's not part of my job to do any work today, but they send me off with some message which isn't even necessary just to get me away from here. What they do is they send me off not too far away so that I can still hope to get back on time if I really hurry. So off I go running as fast as I can, shout the message through the crack in the door of the office I've been sent to, so out of breath they'll hardly be able to understand it, run back here again, but the student's been even faster than I have

– well he's got less far to go, he's only got to run down the steps. If I wasn't so dependent on them I'd have squashed the student against the wall here a long time ago. Right here, next to the sign. I'm always dreaming of doing that. Just here, just above the floor, that's where he's crushed onto the wall, his arms stretched out, his fingers spread apart, his crooked legs twisted round into a circle and blood squirted out all around him. It's only ever been a dream so far, though." "Is there nothing else you do?" asked K. with a smile. "Nothing that I know of," said the usher. "And it's going to get even worse now, up till now he's only been carrying her off for himself, now he's started carrying her off for the judge and all, just like I'd always said he would." "Does your wife, then, not share some of the responsibility?" asked K. He had to force himself as he asked this question, as he, too, felt so jealous now. "Course she does," said the usher, "it's more her fault than theirs. It was her who attached herself to him. All he did, he just chases after any woman. There's five flats in this block alone where he's been thrown out after working his way in there. And my wife is the best looking woman in the whole building, but it's me who's not even allowed to defend himself." "If that's how things are, then there's nothing that can be done," said K. "Well why not?" asked the usher. "He's a coward that student, if he wants to lay a finger on my wife all you'd have to do is give him such a good hiding he'd never dare do it again. But I'm not allowed to do that, and nobody else is going to do me the favour as they're all afraid of his power. The only one who could do it is a man like you." "What, how could I do it?" asked K. in astonishment. "Well you're facing a charge, aren't you," said the usher. "Yes, but that's all the more reason for me to be afraid. Even if he has no influence on the outcome of the trial he probably has some on the initial examination." "Yes, exactly," said the usher, as if K.'s view had been just as correct as his own. "Only we don't usually get any trials heard here with no hope at all." "I am not of the same opinion", said K., "although that ought not to prevent me from dealing with the student if the opportunity arises." "I would be very grateful to you," said the usher of the court, somewhat formally, not really seeming to believe that his highest wish could be fulfilled. "Perhaps," continued K., "perhaps there are some other officials of yours here, perhaps all of them, who would deserve the same." "Oh yes, yes," said the usher, as if this was a matter of course. Then he looked at K. trustingly which, despite all his friendliness, he had not done until then, and added, "they're always rebelling." But the conversation seemed to have become a little uncomfortable for him, as he broke it off by saying, "now I have to report to the office. Would you like to come with me?" "There's nothing for me to do there," said K. "You'd be able to have a look at it. No-one will take any notice of you." "Is it worth seeing then?" asked K. hesitatingly, although he felt very keen to go with him. "Well," said the usher, "I thought you'd be interested in it." "Alright then," said K. finally, "I'll come with you." And, quicker than the usher himself, he ran up the steps.

At the entrance he nearly fell over, as behind the door there was another step. "They don't show much concern for the public," he said. "They don't show any concern at all," said the usher, "just look at the waiting room here." It consisted of a long corridor from which roughly made doors led out to the separate departments of the attic. There was no direct source of light but it was not entirely dark as many of the departments, instead of solid walls, had just wooden bars reaching up to the ceiling to separate them from the corridor. The light made its way in through them, and it was also possible to see individual officials through them as they sat writing at their desks or stood up at the wooden frameworks and watched the people on the corridor through the gaps. There were only a few people in the corridor, probably because it was Sunday. They were not very impressive. They sat, equally spaced, on two rows of long wooden benches which had been placed along both sides of the corridor. All of them were carelessly dressed although the expressions on their faces, their bearing, the style of their beards and many details which were hard to identify showed that they belonged to the upper classes. There were no coat hooks for them to use, and so they had placed their hats under the bench, each probably having followed the example of the others. When those who were sitting nearest the door saw K. and the usher of the court they stood up to greet them, and when the others saw that, they also thought they had to greet them, so that as the two of them went by all the people there stood up. None of them stood properly upright, their backs were bowed, their knees bent, they stood like beggars on the street. K. waited for the usher, who was following just behind him. "They must all be very dispirited," he said. "Yes," said the usher, "they are the accused, everyone you see here has been accused." "Really!" said K. "They're colleagues of mine then." And he turned to the nearest one, a tall, thin man with hair that was nearly grey. "What is it you are waiting for here?" asked K., politely, but the man was startled at being spoken to unexpectedly, which was all the more pitiful to see because the man clearly had some experience of the world and elsewhere would certainly have been able to show his superiority and would not have easily given up the advantage he had acquired. Here, though, he did not know what answer to give to such a simple question and looked round at the others as if they were under some obligation to help him, and as if noone could expect any answer from him without this help. Then the usher of the court stepped forward to him and, in order to calm him down and raise his spirits, said, "The gentleman here's only asking what it is you're waiting for. You can give him an answer." The voice of the usher was probably familiar to him, and had a better effect than K.'s. "I'm … I'm waiting …" he began, and then came to a halt. He had clearly chosen this beginning so that he could give a precise answer to the question, but now he didn't know how to continue. Some of the others waiting had come closer and stood round the group, the usher of the court said to them, "Get out the way, keep the gangway free." They moved back slightly, but not as far as where they had been sitting before. In the meantime, the man whom K. had first approached had pulled himself together and even answered him with a smile. "A month ago I made some applications for evidence to be heard in my case, and I'm waiting for it to be settled." "You certainly seem to be going to a lot of effort," said K. "Yes," said the man, "it is my affair after all." "Not everyone thinks the same way as you do," said K. "I've been indicted as well but I swear on my soul that I've neither submitted evidence nor done anything else of the sort. Do you really think that's necessary?" "I don't really know, exactly," said the man, once more totally unsure of himself; he clearly thought K. was joking with him and therefore probably thought it best to repeat his earlier answer in order to avoid making any new mistakes. With K. looking at him impatiently, he just said, "as far as I'm concerned, I've applied to have this evidence heard." "Perhaps you don't believe I've been indicted?" asked K. "Oh, please, I certainly do," said the man, stepping slightly to one side, but there was more anxiety in his answer than belief. "You don't believe me then?" asked K., and took hold of his arm, unconsciously prompted by the man's humble demeanour, and as if he wanted to force him to believe him. But he did not want to hurt the man and had only taken hold of him very lightly. Nonetheless, the man cried out as if K. had grasped him not with two fingers but with red hot tongs. Shouting in this ridiculous way finally made K. tired of him, if he didn't believe he was indicted then so much the better; maybe he even thought K. was a judge. And before leaving, he held him a lot harder, shoved him back onto the bench and walked on. "These defendants are so sensitive, most of them," said the usher of the court. Almost all of those who had been waiting had now assembled around the man who, by now, had stopped shouting and they seemed to be asking him lots of precise questions about the incident. K. was approached by a security guard, identifiable mainly by his sword, of which the scabbard seemed to be made of aluminium. This greatly surprised K., and he reached out for it with his hand. The guard had come because of the shouting and asked what had been happening. The usher of the court said a few words to try and calm him down but the guard explained that he had to look into it himself, saluted, and hurried on, walking with very short steps, probably because of gout.

K. didn't concern himself long with the guard or these people, especially as he saw a turning off the corridor, about half way along it on the right hand side, where there was no door to stop him going that way. He asked the usher whether that was the right way to go, the usher nodded, and that is the way that K. went. The usher remained always one or two steps behind K, which he found irritating as in a place like this it could give the impression that he was being driven along by someone who had arrested him, so he frequently waited for the usher to catch up, but the usher always remained behind him. In order to put an end to his discomfort, K. finally said, "Now that I've seen what it looks like here, I'd like to go." "You haven't seen everything yet," said the usher ingenuously. "I don't want to see everything," said K., who was also feeling very tired, "I want to go, what is the way to the exit?" "You haven't got lost, have you?" asked the usher in amazement, "you go down this way to the corner, then right down the corridor straight ahead as far as the door." "Come with me," said K., "show me the way, I'll miss it, there are so many different ways here." "It's the only way there is," said the usher, who had now started to sound quite reproachful, "I can't go back with you again, I've got to hand in my report, and I've already lost a lot of time because of you as it is." "Come with me!" K. repeated, now somewhat sharper as if he had finally caught the usher out in a lie. "Don't shout like that," whispered the usher, "there's offices all round us here. If you don't want to go back by yourself come on a bit further with me or else wait here till I've sorted out my report, then I'll be glad to go back with you again." "No, no," said K., "I will not wait and you must come with me now." K. had still not looked round at anything at all in the room where he found himself, and it was only when one of the many wooden doors all around him opened that he noticed it. A young woman, probably summoned by the loudness of K.'s voice, entered and asked, "What is it the gentleman wants?" In the darkness behind her there was also a man approaching. K. looked at the usher. He had, after all, said that no-one would take any notice of K., and now there were two people coming, it only needed a few and everyone in the office would become aware of him and asking for explanations as to why he was there. The only understandable and acceptable thing to say was that he was accused of something and wanted to know the date of his next hearing, but this was an explanation he did not want to give, especially as it was not true – he had only come out of curiosity. Or else, an explanation even less usable, he could say that he wanted to ascertain that the court was as revolting on the inside as it was on the outside. And it did seem that he had been quite right in this supposition, he had no wish to intrude any deeper, he was disturbed enough by what he had seen already, he was not in the right frame of mind just then to face a high official such as might appear from behind any door, and he wanted to go, either with the usher of the court or, if needs be, alone.

But he must have seemed very odd standing there in silence, and the young woman and the usher were indeed looking at him as if they thought he would go through some major metamorphosis any second which they didn't want to miss seeing. And in the doorway stood the man whom K. had noticed in the background earlier, he held firmly on to the beam above the low door swinging a little on the tips of his feet as if becoming impatient as he watched. But the young woman was the first to recognise that K.'s behaviour was caused by his feeling slightly unwell, she brought a chair and asked, "Would you not like to sit down?" K. sat down immediately and, in order to keep his place better, put his elbows on the armrests. "You're a little bit dizzy, aren't you?" she asked him. Her face was now close in front of him, it bore the severe expression that many young women have just when they're in the bloom of their youth. "It's nothing for you to worry about," she said, "that's nothing unusual here, almost everyone gets an attack like that the first time they come here. This is your first time is it? Yes, it's nothing unusual then. The sun burns down on the roof and the hot wood makes the air so thick and heavy. It makes this place rather unsuitable for offices, whatever other advantages it might offer. But the air is almost impossible to breathe on days when there's a lot of business, and that's almost every day. And when you think that there's a lot of washing put out to dry here as well – and we can't stop the tenants doing that – it's not surprising you started to feel unwell. But you get used to the air alright in the end. When you're here for the second or third time you'll hardly notice how oppressive the air is. Are you feeling any better now?" K. made no answer, he felt too embarrassed at being put at the mercy of these people by his sudden weakness, and learning the reason for feeling ill made him feel not better but a little worse. The girl noticed it straight away, and to make the air fresher for K., she took a window pole that was leaning against the wall and pushed open a small hatch directly above K.'s head that led to the outside. But so much soot fell in that the girl had to immediately close the hatch again and clean the soot off K.'s hands with her handkerchief, as K. was too tired to do that for himself. He would have liked just to sit quietly where he was until he had enough strength to leave, and the less fuss people made about him the sooner that would be. But then the girl said, "You can't stay here, we're in people's way here …" K. looked at her as if to ask whose way they were impeding. "If you like, I can take you to the sick room," and turning to the man in the doorway said, "please help me". The man immediately came over to them, but K. did not want to go to the sick room, that was just what he wanted to avoid, being led further from place to place, the further he went the more difficult it must become. So he said, "I am able to walk now," and stood up, shaking after becoming used to sitting so comfortably. But then he was unable to stay upright. "I can't manage it," he said shaking his head, and sat down again with a sigh. He remembered the usher who, despite everything, would have been able to lead him out of there but who seemed to have gone long before. K. looked out between the man and the young woman who were standing in front of him but was unable to find the usher. "I think," said the man, who was elegantly dressed and whose appearance was made especially impressive with a grey waistcoat that had two long, sharply tailored points, "the gentleman is feeling unwell because of the atmosphere here, so the best thing, and what he would most prefer, would be not to take him to the sick room but get him out of the offices altogether." "That's right," exclaimed K., with such joy that he nearly interrupted what the man was saying, "I'm sure that'll make me feel better straight away, I'm really not that weak, all I need is a little support under my arms, I won't cause you much trouble, it's not such a long way anyway, lead me to the door and then I'll sit on the stairs for a while and soon recover, as I don't suffer from attacks like this at all, I'm surprised at it myself. I also work in an office and I'm quite used to office air, but here it seems to be too strong, you've said so yourselves. So please, be so kind as to help me on my way a little, I'm feeling dizzy, you see, and it'll make me ill if I stand up by myself." And with that he raised his shoulders to make it easier for the two of them to take him by the arms.

The man, however, didn't follow this suggestion but just stood there with his hands in his trouser pockets and laughed out loud. "There, you see," he said to the girl, "I was quite right. The gentleman is only unwell here, and not in general." The young woman smiled too, but lightly tapped the man's arm with the tips of her fingers as if he had allowed himself too much fun with K. "So what do you think, then?" said the man, still laughing, "I really do want to lead the gentleman out of here." "That's alright, then," said the girl, briefly inclining her charming head. "Don't worry too much about him laughing," said the girl to K., who had become unhappy once more and stared quietly in front of himself as if needing no further explanation. "This gentleman – may I introduce you?" – (the man gave his permission with a wave of the hand) – "so, this gentleman's job is to give out information. He gives all the information they need to people who are waiting, as our court and its offices are not very well known among the public he gets asked for quite a lot. He has an answer for every question, you can try him out if you feel like it. But that's not his only distinction, his other distinction is his elegance of dress. We, that's to say all of us who work in the offices here, we decided that the information-giver would have to be elegantly dressed as he continually has to deal with the litigants and he's the first one they meet, so he needs to give a dignified first impression. The rest of us I'm afraid, as you can see just by looking at me, dress very badly and old-fashioned; and there's not much point in spending much on clothes anyway, as we hardly ever leave the offices, we even sleep here. But, as I said, we decided that the information-giver would have to have nice clothes. As the management here is rather peculiar in this respect, and they would get them for us, we had a collection – some of the litigants contributed too – and bought him these lovely clothes and some others besides. So everything would be ready for him to give a good impression, except that he spoils it again by laughing and frightening people." "That's how it is," said the man, mocking her, "but I don't understand why it is that you're explaining all our intimate facts to the gentleman, or rather why it is that you're pressing them on him, as I'm sure he's not all interested. Just look at him sitting there, it's clear he's occupied with his own affairs." K. just did not feel like contradicting him.. The girl's intention may have been good, perhaps she was under instructions to distract him or to give him the chance to collect himself, but the attempt had not worked. "I had to explain to him why you were laughing," said the girl. "I suppose it was insulting." "I think he would forgive even worse insults if I finally took him outside." K. said nothing, did not even look up, he tolerated the two of them negotiating over him like an object, that was even what suited him best. But suddenly he felt the information-giver's hand on one arm and the young woman's hand on the other. "Up you get then, weakling," said the information-giver. "Thank you both very much," said K., pleasantly surprised, as he slowly rose and personally guided these unfamiliar hands to the places where he most needed support. As they approached the corridor, the girl said quietly into K.'s ear, "I must seem to think it's very important to show the information-giver in a good light, but you shouldn't doubt what I say, I just want to say the truth. He isn't hard-hearted. It's not really his job to help litigants outside if they're unwell but he's doing it anyway, as you can see. I don't suppose any of us is hard-hearted, perhaps we'd all like to be helpful, but working for the court offices it's easy for us to give the impression we are hard-hearted and don't want to help anyone. It makes me quite sad." "Would you not like to sit down here a while?" asked the information-giver, there were already in the corridor and just in front of the defendant whom K. had spoken to earlier. K. felt almost ashamed to be seen by him, earlier he had stood so upright in front of him and now he had to be supported by two others, his hat was held up by the information-giver balanced on outstretched fingers, his hair was dishevelled and hung down onto the sweat on his forehead. But the defendant seemed to notice nothing of what was going on and just stood there humbly, as if wanting to apologise to the information-giver for being there. The information-giver looked past him. "I know," he said, "that my case can't be settled today, not yet, but I've come in anyway, I thought, I thought I could wait here anyway, it's Sunday today, I've got plenty of time, and I'm not disturbing anyone here." "There's no need to be so apologetic," said the information-giver, "it's very commendable for you to be so attentive. You are taking up space here when you don't need to but as long as you don't get in my way I will do nothing to stop you following the progress of your case as closely as you like. When one has seen so many people who shamefully neglect their cases one learns to show patience with people like you. Do sit down." "He's very good with the litigants," whispered the girl. K. nodded, but started to move off again when the information-giver repeated, "Would you not like to sit down here a while?" "No," said K., "I don't want to rest." He had said that as decisively as he could, but in fact it would have done him a lot of good to sit down. It was as if he were suffering sea-sickness. He felt as if he were on a ship in a rough sea, as if the water were hitting against the wooden walls, a thundering from the depths of the corridor as if the torrent were crashing over it, as if the corridor were swaying and the waiting litigants on each side of it rising and sinking. It made the calmness of the girl and the man leading him all the more incomprehensible. He was at their mercy, if they let go of him he would fall like a board.

Their little eyes glanced here and there, K. could feel the evenness of their steps but could not do the same, as from step to step he was virtually being carried. He finally noticed they were speaking to him but he did not understand them, all he heard was a noise that filled all the space and through which there seemed to be an unchanging higher note sounding, like a siren. "Louder," he whispered with his head sunk low, ashamed at having to ask them to speak louder when he knew they had spoken loudly enough, even if it had been, for him, incomprehensible. At last, a draught of cool air blew in his face as if a gap had been torn out in the wall in front of him, and next to him he heard someone say, "First he says he wants to go, and then you can tell him a hundred times that this is the way out and he doesn't move." K. became aware that he was standing in front of the way out, and that the young woman had opened the door. It seemed to him that all his strength returned to him at once, and to get a foretaste of freedom he stepped straight on to one of the stairs and took his leave there of his companions, who bowed to him. "Thank you very much," he repeated, shook their hands once more and did not let go until he thought he saw that they found it hard to bear the comparatively fresh air from the stairway after being so long used to the air in the offices. They were hardly able to reply, and the young woman might even have fallen over if K. had not shut the door extremely fast. K. then stood still for a while, combed his hair with the help of a pocket mirror, picked up his hat from the next stair – the information-giver must have thrown it down there – and then he ran down the steps so fresh and in such long leaps that the contrast with his previous state nearly frightened him. His normally sturdy state of health had never prepared him for surprises such as this. Did his body want to revolt and cause him a new trial as he was bearing the old one with such little effort? He did not quite reject the idea that he should see a doctor the next time he had the chance, but whatever he did – and this was something on which he could advise himself – he wanted to spend all Sunday mornings in future better than he had spent this one.

Chapter Four
Miss Bürstner's Friend

For some time after this, K. found it impossible to exchange even just a few words with Miss Bürstner. He tried to reach her in many and various ways but she always found a way to avoid it. He would come straight home from the office, remain in her room without the light on, and sit on the sofa with nothing more to distract him than keeping watch on the empty hallway. If the maid went by and closed the door of the apparently empty room he would get up after a while and open it again. He got up an hour earlier than usual in the morning so that he might perhaps find Miss Bürstner alone as she went to the office. But none of these efforts brought any success. Then he wrote her a letter, both to the office and the flat, attempting once more to justify his behaviour, offered to make whatever amends he could, promised never to cross whatever boundary she might set him and begged merely to have the chance to speak to her some time, especially as he was unable to do anything with Mrs. Grubach either until he had spoken with Miss Bürstner, he finally informed her that the following Sunday he would stay in his room all day waiting for a sign from her that there was some hope of his request being fulfilled, or at least that she would explain to him why she could not fulfil it even though he had promised to observe whatever stipulations she might make. The letters were not returned, but there was no answer either. However, on the following Sunday there was a sign that seemed clear enough. It was still early when K. noticed, through the keyhole, that there was an unusual level of activity in the hallway which soon abated. A French teacher, although she was German and called Montag, a pale and febrile girl with a slight limp who had previously occupied a room of her own, was moving into Miss Bürstner's room. She could be seen shuffling through the hallway for several hours, there was always another piece of clothing or a blanket or a book that she had forgotten and had to be fetched specially and brought into the new home.

When Mrs. Grubach brought K. his breakfast – ever since the time when she had made K. so cross she didn't trust the maid to do the slightest job – he had no choice but to speak to her, for the first time in five days. "Why is there so much noise in the hallway today?" he asked as she poured his coffee out, "Can't something be done about it? Does this clearing out have to be done on a Sunday?" K. did not look up at Mrs. Grubach, but he saw nonetheless that she seemed to feel some relief as she breathed in. Even sharp questions like this from Mr. K. she perceived as forgiveness, or as the beginning of forgiveness. "We're not clearing anything out, Mr. K.," she said, "it's just that Miss Montag is moving in with Miss Bürstner and is moving her things across." She said nothing more, but just waited to see how K. would take it and whether he would allow her to carry on speaking. But K. kept her in uncertainty, took the spoon and pensively stirred his coffee while he remained silent. Then he looked up at her and said, "What about the suspicions you had earlier about Miss Bürstner, have you given them up?" "Mr. K.," called Mrs. Grubach, who had been waiting for this very question, as she put her hands together and held them out towards him. "I just made a chance remark and you took it so badly. I didn't have the slightest intention of offending anyone, not you or anyone else. You've known me for long enough, Mr. K., I'm sure you're convinced of that. You don't know how I've been suffering for the past few days! That I should tell lies about my tenants! And you, Mr. K., you believed it! And said I should give you notice! Give you notice!" At this last outcry, Mrs. Grubach was already choking back her tears, she raised her apron to her face and blubbered out loud.

"Oh, don't cry Mrs. Grubach," said K., looking out the window, he was thinking only of Miss Bürstner and how she was accepting an unknown girl into her room. "Now don't cry," he said again as he turned his look back into the room where Mrs. Grubach was still crying. "I meant no harm either when I said that. It was simply a misunderstanding between us. That can happen even between old friends sometimes." Mrs. Grubach pulled her apron down to below her eyes to see whether K. really was attempting a reconciliation. "Well, yes, that's how it is," said K., and as Mrs. Grubach's behaviour indicated that the captain had said nothing he dared to add, "Do you really think, then, that I'd want to make an enemy of you for the sake of a girl we hardly know?" "Yes, you're quite right, Mr. K.," said Mrs. Grubach, and then, to her misfortune, as soon as she felt just a little freer to speak, she added something rather inept. "I kept asking myself why it was that Mr. K. took such an interest in Miss Bürstner. Why does he quarrel with me over her when he knows that any cross word from him and I can't sleep that night? And I didn't say anything about Miss Bürstner that I hadn't seen with my own eyes." K. said nothing in reply, he should have chased her from the room as soon as she had opened her mouth, and he didn't want to do that. He contented himself with merely drinking his coffee and letting Mrs. Grubach feel that she was superfluous. Outside, the dragging steps of Miss Montag could still be heard as she went from one side of the hallway to the other. "Do you hear that?" asked K. pointing his hand at the door. "Yes," said Mrs. Grubach with a sigh, "I wanted to give her some help and I wanted the maid to help her too but she's stubborn, she wants to move everything in herself. I wonder at Miss Bürstner. I often feel it's a burden for me to have Miss Montag as a tenant but Miss Bürstner accepts her into her room with herself." "There's nothing there for you to worry about" said K., crushing the remains of a sugar lump in his cup. "Does she cause you any trouble?" "No," said Mrs. Grubach, "in itself it's very good to have her there, it makes another room free for me and I can let my nephew, the captain, occupy it. I began to worry he might be disturbing you when I had to let him live in the living room next to you over the last few days. He's not very considerate." "What an idea!" said K. standing up, "there's no question of that. You seem to think that because I can't stand this to-ing and fro-ing of Miss Montag that I'm over-sensitive – and there she goes back again." Mrs. Grubach appeared quite powerless. "Should I tell her to leave moving the rest of her things over till later, then, Mr. K.? If that's what you want I'll do it immediately." "But she has to move in with Miss Bürstner!" said K. "Yes," said Mrs. Grubach, without quite understanding what K. meant. "So she has to take her things over there." Mrs. Grubach just nodded. K. was irritated all the more by this dumb helplessness which, seen from the outside, could have seemed like a kind of defiance on her part. He began to walk up and down the room between the window and the door, thus depriving Mrs. Grubach of the chance to leave, which she otherwise probably would have done.

Just as K. once more reached the door, someone knocked at it. It was the maid, to say that Miss Montag would like to have a few words with Mr. K., and therefore requested that he come to the dining room where she was waiting for him. K. heard the maid out thoughtfully, and then looked back at the shocked Mrs. Grubach in a way that was almost contemptuous. His look seemed to be saying that K. had been expecting this invitation for Miss Montag for a long time, and that it was confirmation of the suffering he had been made to endure that Sunday morning from Mrs. Grubach's tenants. He sent the maid back with the reply that he was on his way, then he went to the wardrobe to change his coat, and in answer to Mrs. Grubach's gentle whining about the nuisance Miss Montag was causing merely asked her to clear away the breakfast things. "But you've hardly touched it," said Mrs. Grubach. "Oh just take it away!" shouted K. It seemed to him that Miss Montag was mixed up in everything and made it repulsive to him.

As he went through the hallway he looked at the closed door of Miss Bürstner's room. But it wasn't there that he was invited, but the dining room, to which he yanked the door open without knocking.

The room was long but narrow with one window. There was only enough space available to put two cupboards at an angle in the corner by the door, and the rest of the room was entirely taken up with the long dining table which started by the door and reached all the way to the great window, which was thus made almost inaccessible. The table was already laid for a large number of people, as on Sundays almost all the tenants ate their dinner here at midday.

When K. entered, Miss Montag came towards him from the window along one side of the table. They greeted each other in silence. Then Miss Montag, her head unusually erect as always, said, "I'm not sure whether you know me." K. looked at her with a frown. "Of course I do," he said, "you've been living here with Mrs. Grubach for quite some time now." "But I get the impression you don't pay much attention to what's going on in the lodging house," said Miss Montag. "No," said K. "Would you not like to sit down?" said Miss Montag. In silence, the two of them drew chairs out from the farthest end of the table and sat down facing each other. But Miss Montag stood straight up again as she had left her hand-bag on the window sill and went to fetch it; she shuffled down the whole length of the room. When she came back, the handbag lightly swinging, she said, "I'd like just to have a few words with you on behalf of my friend. She would have come herself, but she's feeling a little unwell today. Perhaps you'll be kind enough to forgive her and listen to me instead. There's anyway nothing that she could have said that I won't. On the contrary, in fact, I think I can say even more than her because I'm relatively impartial. Would you not agree?" "What is there to say, then?" answered K., who was tired of Miss Montag continuously watching his lips. In that way she took control of what he wanted to say before he said it. "Miss Bürstner clearly refuses to grant me the personal meeting that I asked her for." "That's how it is," said Miss Montag, "or rather, that's not at all how it is, the way you put it is remarkably severe. Generally speaking, meetings are neither granted nor the opposite. But it can be that meetings are considered unnecessary, and that's how it is here. Now, after your comment, I can speak openly. You asked my friend, verbally or in writing, for the chance to speak with her. Now my friend is aware of your reasons for asking for this meeting – or at least I suppose she is – and so, for reasons I know nothing about, she is quite sure that it would be of no benefit to anyone if this meeting actually took place. Moreover, it was only yesterday, and only very briefly, that she made it clear to me that such a meeting could be of no benefit for yourself either, she feels that it can only have been a matter of chance that such an idea came to you, and that even without any explanations from her, you will very soon come to realise yourself, if you have not done so already, the futility of your idea. My answer to that is that although it may be quite right, I consider it advantageous, if the matter is to be made perfectly clear, to give you an explicit answer. I offered my services in taking on the task, and after some hesitation my friend conceded. I hope, however, also to have acted in your interests, as even the slightest uncertainty in the least significant of matters will always remain a cause of suffering and if, as in this case, it can be removed without substantial effort, then it is better if that is done without delay." "I thank you," said K. as soon as Miss Montag had finished. He stood slowly up, looked at her, then across the table, then out the window – the house opposite stood there in the sun – and went to the door. Miss Montag followed him a few paces, as if she did not quite trust him. At the door, however, both of them had to step back as it opened and Captain Lanz entered. This was the first time that K. had seen him close up. He was a large man of about forty with a tanned, fleshy face. He bowed slightly, intending it also for K., and then went over to Miss Montag and deferentially kissed her hand. He was very elegant in the way he moved. The courtesy he showed towards Miss Montag made a striking contrast with the way she had been treated by K. Nonetheless, Miss Montag did not seem to be cross with K. as it even seemed to him that she wanted to introduce the captain. K. however, did not want to be introduced, he would not have been able to show any sort of friendliness either to Miss Montag or to the captain, the kiss on the hand had, for K., bound them into a group which would keep him at a distance from Miss Bürstner whilst at the same time seeming to be totally harmless and unselfish. K. thought, however, that he saw more than that, he thought he also saw that Miss Montag had chosen a means of doing it that was good, but two-edged. She exaggerated the importance of the relationship between

K. and Miss Bürstner, and above all she exaggerated the importance of asking to speak with her and she tried at the same time to make out that K. was exaggerating everything. She would be disappointed, K. did not want to exaggerate anything, he was aware that Miss Bürstner was a little typist who would not offer him much resistance for long. In doing so he deliberately took no account of what Mrs. Grubach had told him about Miss Bürstner. All these things were going through his mind as he left the room with hardly a polite word. He wanted to go straight to his room, but a little laugh from Miss Montag that he heard from the dining room behind him brought him to the idea that he might prepare a surprise for the two of them, the captain and Miss Montag. He looked round and listened to find out if there might be any disturbance from any of the surrounding rooms, everywhere was quiet, the only thing to be heard was the conversation from the dining room and Mrs. Grubach's voice from the passage leading to the kitchen. This seemed an opportune time, K. went to Miss Bürstner's room and knocked gently. There was no sound so he knocked again but there was still no answer in reply. Was she asleep? Or was she really unwell? Or was she just pretending as she realised it could only be K. knocking so gently? K. assumed she was pretending and knocked harder, eventually, when the knocking brought no result, he carefully opened the door with the sense of doing something that was not only improper but also pointless. In the room there was no-one. What's more, it looked hardly at all like the room K. had known before. Against the wall there were now two beds behind one another, there were clothes piled up on three chairs near the door, a wardrobe stood open. Miss Bürstner must have gone out while Miss Montag was speaking to him in the dining room. K. was not greatly bothered by this, he had hardly expected to be able to find Miss Bürstner so easily and had made this attempt for little more reason than to spite Miss Montag. But that made it all the more embarrassing for him when, as he was closing the door again, he saw Miss Montag and the captain talking in the open doorway of the dining room. They had probably been standing there ever since K. had opened the door, they avoided seeming to observe K. but chatted lightly and followed his movements with glances, the absent minded glances to the side such as you make during a conversation. But these glances were heavy for K., and he rushed alongside the wall back into his own room.

Chapter Five
The whip-man

One evening, a few days later, K. was walking along one of the corridors that separated his office from the main stairway – he was nearly the last one to leave for home that evening, there remained only a couple of workers in the light of a single bulb in the dispatch department – when he heard a sigh from behind a door which he had himself never opened but which he had always thought just led into a junk room. He stood in amazement and listened again to establish whether he might not be mistaken. For a while there was silence, but then came some more sighs. His first thought was to fetch one of the servitors, it might well have been worth having a witness present, but then he was taken by an uncontrollable curiosity that make him simply yank the door open. It was, as he had thought, a junk room. Old, unusable forms, empty stone ink-bottles lay scattered behind the entrance. But in the cupboard-like room itself stood three men, crouching under the low ceiling. A candle fixed on a shelf gave them light. "What are you doing here?" asked K. quietly, but crossly and without thinking. One of the men was clearly in charge, and attracted attention by being dressed in a kind of dark leather costume which left his neck and chest and his arms exposed. He did not answer. But the other two called out, "Mr. K.! We're to be beaten because you made a complaint about us to the examining judge." And now, K. finally realised that it was actually the two policemen, Franz and Willem, and that the third man held a cane in his hand with which to beat them. "Well," said K., staring at them, "I didn't make any complaint, I only said what took place in my home. And your behaviour was not entirely unobjectionable, after all." "Mr. K.," said Willem, while Franz clearly tried to shelter behind him as protection from the third man, "if you knew how badly we get paid you wouldn't think so badly of us. I've got a family to feed, and Franz here wanted to get married, you just have to get more money where you can, you can't do it just by working hard, not however hard you try. I was sorely tempted by your fine clothes, policemen aren't allowed to do that sort of thing, course they aren't, and it wasn't right of us, but it's tradition that the clothes go to the officers, that's how it's always been, believe me; and it's understandable too, isn't it, what can things like that mean for anyone unlucky enough to be arrested? But if he starts talking about it openly then the punishment has to follow." "I didn't know about any of this that you've been telling me, and I made no sort of request that you be punished, I was simply acting on principle." "Franz," said Willem, turning to the other policeman, "didn't I tell you that the gentleman didn't say he wanted us to be punished? Now you can hear for yourself, he didn't even know we'd have to be punished." "Don't you let them persuade you, talking like that," said the third man to K., "this punishment is both just and unavoidable." "Don't listen to him," said Willem, interrupting himself only to quickly bring his hand to his mouth when it had received a stroke of the cane, "we're only being punished because you made a complaint against us. Nothing would have happened to us otherwise, not even if they'd found out what we'd done. Can you call that justice? Both of us, me especially, we'd proved our worth as good police officers over a long period – you've got to admit yourself that as far as official work was concerned we did the job well – things looked good for us, we had prospects, it's quite certain that we would've been made whipmen too, like this one, only he had the luck not to have anyone make a complaint about him, as you really don't get many complaints like that. Only that's all finished now, Mr. K., our careers are at an end, we're going to have to do work now that's far inferior to police work and besides all this we're going to get this terrible, painful beating." "Can the cane really cause so much pain, then?" asked K., testing the cane that the whip-man swang in front of him. "We're going to have to strip off totally naked," said Willem. "Oh, I see," said K., looking straight at the whip-man, his skin was burned brown like a sailor's, and his face showed health and vigour. "Is there then no possibility of sparing these two their beating?" he asked him. "No," said the whip-man, shaking his head with a laugh. "Get undressed!" he ordered the policemen. And to K. he said, "You shouldn't believe everything they tell you, it's the fear of being beaten, it's already made them a bit weak in the head. This one here, for instance," he pointed at Willem, "all that he told you about his career prospects, it's just ridiculous. Look at him, look how fat he is – the first strokes of the cane will just get lost in all that fat. Do you know what it is that's made him so fat? He's in the habit of, everyone that gets arrested by him, he eats their breakfast. Didn't he eat up your breakfast? Yeah, I thought as much. But a man with a belly like that can't be made into a whip-man and never will be, that is quite out of the question." "There are whip-men like that," Willem insisted, who had just released the belt of this trousers. "No," said the whip-man, striking him such a blow with the cane on his neck that it made him wince, "you shouldn't be listening to this, just get undressed." "I would make it well worth your while if you would let them go," said K., and without looking at the whip-man again – as such matters are best carried on with both pairs of eyes turned down – he pulled out his wallet. "And then you'd try and put in a complaint against me, too," said the whip-man, "and get me flogged. No, no!" "Now, do be reasonable," said K., "if I had wanted to get these two punished I would not now be trying to buy their freedom, would I. I could simply close the door here behind me, go home and see or hear nothing more of it. But that's not what I'm doing, it really is of much more importance to me to let them go free; if I had realised they would be punished, or even that they might be punished, I would never have named them in the first place as they are not the ones I hold responsible. It's the organisation that's to blame, the high officials are the ones to blame." "That's how it is!" shouted the policemen, who then immediately received another blow on their backs, which were by now exposed. "If you had a senior judge here beneath your stick," said K., pressing down the cane as he spoke to stop it being raised once more, "I really would do nothing to stop you, on the contrary, I would even pay you money to give you all the more strength." "Yeah, that's all very plausible, what you're saying there," said the whip-man, "only I'm not the sort of person you can bribe. It's my job to flog people, so I flog them." Franz, the policeman, had been fairly quiet so far, probably in expectation of a good result from K.'s intervention, but now he stepped forward to the door wearing just his trousers, kneeled down hanging on to K.'s arm and whispered, "Even if you can't get mercy shown for both of us, at least try and get me set free. Willem is older than me, he's less sensitive than me in every way, he even got a light beating a couple of years ago, but my record's still clean, I only did things the way I did because Willem led me on to it, he's been my teacher both for good and bad. Down in front of the bank my poor bride is waiting for me at the entrance, I'm so ashamed of myself, it's pitiful." His face was flowing over with tears, and he wiped it dry on K.'s coat. "I'm not going to wait any longer," said the whip-man, taking hold of the cane in both hands and laying in to Franz while Willem cowered back in a corner and looked on secretly, not even daring to turn his head. Then, the sudden scream that shot out from Franz was long and irrevocable, it seemed to come not from a human being but from an instrument that was being tortured, the whole corridor rang with it, it must have been heard by everyone in the building. "Don't shout like that!", called out K., unable to prevent himself, and, as he looked anxiously in the direction from which the servitor would come, he gave Franz a shove, not hard, but hard enough for him to fall down unconscious, clawing at the ground with his hands by reflex; he still did not avoid being hit; the rod still found him on the floor; the tip of the rod swung regularly up and down while he rolled to and fro under its blows. And now one of the servitors appeared in the distance, with another a few steps behind him. K. had quickly thrown the door shut, gone over to one of the windows overlooking the yard and opened it. The screams had completely stopped. So that the servitor wouldn't come in, he called out, "It's only me!" "Good evening, chief clerk," somebody called back. "Is there anything wrong?" "No, no," answered K., "it's only a dog yelping in the yard." There was no sound from the servitors so he added, "You can go back to what you were doing." He did not want to become involved with a conversation with them, and so he leant out of the window. A little while later, when he looked out in the corridor, they had already gone. Now, K. remained at the window, he did not dare go back into the junk room, and he did not want to go home either. The yard he looked down into was small and rectangular, all around it were offices, all the windows were now dark and only those at the very top caught a reflection of the moon. K tried hard to see into the darkness of one corner of the yard, where a few handcarts had been left behind one another. He felt anguish at not having been able to prevent the flogging, but that was not his fault, if Franz had not screamed like that – clearly it must have caused a great deal of pain but it's important to maintain control of oneself at important moments – if Franz had not screamed then it was at least highly probable that K. would have been able to dissuade the whip-man. If all the junior officers were contemptible why would the whip-man, whose position was the most inhumane of all, be any exception, and K. had noticed very clearly how his eyes had lit up when he saw the banknotes, he had obviously only seemed serious about the flogging to raise the level of the bribe a little. And K. had not been ungenerous, he really had wanted to get the policemen freed; if he really had now begun to do something against the degeneracy of the court then it was a matter of course that he would have to do something here as well. But of course, it became impossible for him to do anything as soon as Franz started screaming. K. could not possibly have let the junior bank staff, and perhaps even all sorts of other people, come along and catch him by surprise as he haggled with those people in the junk

220

room. Nobody could really expect that sort of sacrifice of him. If that had been his intention then it would almost have been easier, K. would have taken his own clothes off and offered himself to the whip-man in the policemen's place. The whip-man would certainly not have accepted this substitution anyway, as in that way he would have seriously violated his duty without gaining any benefit. He would most likely have violated his duty twice over, as court employees were probably under orders not to cause any harm to K. while he was facing charges, although there may have been special conditions in force here. However things stood, K. was able to do no more than throw the door shut, even though that would still do nothing to remove all the dangers he faced. It was regrettable that he had given Franz a shove, and it could only be excused by the heat of the moment.

In the distance, he heard the steps of the servitors; he did not want them to be too aware of his presence, so he closed the window and walked towards the main staircase. At the door of the junk room he stopped and listened for a little while. All was silent. The two policemen were entirely at the whip-man's mercy; he could have beaten them to death. K. reached his hand out for the door handle but drew it suddenly back. He was no longer in any position to help anyone, and the servitors would soon be back; he did, though, promise himself that he would raise the matter again with somebody and see that, as far as it was in his power, those who really were guilty, the high officials whom nobody had so far dared point out to him, received their due punishment. As he went down the main stairway at the front of the bank, he looked carefully round at everyone who was passing, but there was no girl to be seen who might have been waiting for some-body, not even within some distance from the bank. Franz's claim that his bride was waiting for him was thus shown to be a lie, albeit one that was forgivable and intended only to elicit more sympathy.

The policemen were still on K.'s mind all through the fol-lowing day; he was unable to concentrate on his work and had to stay in his office a little longer than the previous day so that he could finish it. On the way home, as he passed by the junk room again, he opened its door as if that had been his habit. Instead of the darkness he expected, he saw everything unchanged from the previous evening, and did not know how he should respond. Everything was exactly the same as he had seen it when he had opened the door the previous evening. The forms and bottles of ink just inside the doorway, the whip-man with his cane, the two policemen, still undressed, the candle on the shelf, and the two policemen began to wail and call out "Mr. K.!" K. slammed the door immediately shut, and even thumped on it with his fists as if that would shut it all the firmer. Almost in tears, he ran to the servitors working quietly at the copying machine. "Go and get that junk room cleared out!" he shouted, and, in amazement, they stopped what they were doing. "It should have been done long ago, we're sinking in dirt!" They would be able to do the job the next day, K. nodded, it was too late in the evening to make them do it there and then as he had originally intended. He sat down briefly in order to keep them near him for a little longer, looked through a few of the copies to give the impression that he was checking them and then, as he saw that they would not dare to leave at the same time as himself, went home tired and with his mind numb.

Chapter Six
K.'s uncle – Leni

One afternoon – K. was very busy at the time, getting the post ready – K.'s Uncle Karl, a small country land owner, came into the room, pushing his way between two of the staff who were bringing in some papers. K. had long expected his uncle to appear, but the sight of him now shocked K. far less than the prospect of it had done a long time before. His uncle was bound to come, K. had been sure of that for about a month. He already thought at the time he could see how his uncle would arrive, slightly bowed, his battered panama hat in his left hand, his right hand already stretched out over the desk long before he was close enough as he rushed carelessly towards K. knocking over everything that was in his way. K.'s uncle was always in a hurry, as he suffered from the unfortunate belief that he had a number things to do while he was in the big city and had to settle all of them in one day – his visits were only ever for one day – and at the same time thought he could not forgo any conversation or piece of business or pleasure that might arise by chance. Uncle Karl was K.'s former guardian, and so K. was duty-bound to help him in all of this as well as to offer him a bed for the night. 'I'm haunted by a ghost from the country', he would say.

As soon as they had greeted each other – K. had invited him to sit in the armchair but Uncle Karl had no time for that – he said he wanted to speak briefly with K. in private. "It is necessary," he said with a tired gulp, "it is necessary for my peace of mind." K. immediately sent the junior staff from the room and told them to let no-one in. "What's this that I've been hearing, Josef?" cried K.'s uncle when they were alone, as he sat on the table shoving various papers under himself without looking at them to make himself more comfortable. K. said nothing, he knew what was coming, but, suddenly relieved from the effort of the work he had been doing, he gave way to a pleasant lassitude and looked out the window at the other side of the street. From where he sat, he could see just a small, triangular section of it, part of the empty walls of houses between two shop windows. "You're staring out the window!" called out his uncle, raising his arms, "For God's sake, Josef, give me an answer! Is it true, can it really be true?" "Uncle Karl," said K., wrenching himself back from his daydreaming, "I really don't know what it is you want of me." "Josef," said his uncle in a warning tone, "as far as I know, you've always told the truth. Am I to take what you've just said as a bad sign?" "I think I know what it is you want," said K. obediently, "I expect you've heard about my trial." "That's right," answered his uncle with a slow nod, "I've heard about your trial." "Who did you hear it from, then?" asked K. "Erna wrote to me," said his uncle, "she doesn't have much contact with you, it's true, you don't pay very much attention to her,

I'm afraid to say, but she learned about it nonetheless. I got her letter today and, of course, I came straight here. And for no other reason, but it seems to me that this is reason enough. I can read you out the part of the letter that concerns you." He drew the letter out from his wallet. "Here it is. She writes; 'I have not seen Josef for a long time, I was in the bank last week but Josef was so busy that they would not let me through; I waited there for nearly an hour but then I had to go home as I had my piano lesson. I would have liked to have spoken to him, maybe there will be a chance another time. He sent me a big box of chocolates for my name-day, that was very nice and attentive of him. I forgot to tell you about it when I wrote, and I only remember now that you ask me about it. Chocolate, as I am sure you are aware, disappears straight away in this lodging house, almost as soon as you know somebody has given you chocolate it is gone. But there is something else I wanted to tell you about Josef. Like I said, they would not let me through to see him at the bank because he was negotiating with some gentleman just then. After I had been waiting quietly for quite a long time I asked one of the staff whether his meeting would last much longer. He said it might well do, as it was probably about the legal proceedings, he said, that were being conducted against him. I asked what sort of legal proceedings it was that were being conducted against the chief clerk, and whether he was not making some mistake, but he said he was not making any mistake, there were legal proceedings underway and even that they were about something quite serious, but he did not know any more about it. He would have liked to have been of some help to the chief clerk himself, as the chief clerk was a gentleman, good and honest, but he did not know what it was he could do and merely hoped there would be some influential gentlemen who would take his side. I'm sure that is what will happen and that everything will turn out for the best in the end, but in the mean time things do not look at all good, and you can see that from the mood of the chief clerk himself. Of course, I did not place too much importance on this conversation, and even did my best to put the bank clerk's mind at rest, he was quite a simple man. I told him he was not to speak to anyone else about this, and I think it is all just a rumour, but I still think it might be good if you, Dear Father, if you looked into the matter the next time you visit. It will be easy for you to find out more detail and, if it is really necessary, to do something about it through the great and influential people you know. But if it is not necessary, and that is what seems most likely, then at least your daughter will soon have the chance to embrace you and I look forward to it.' – She's a good child," said K.'s uncle when he had finished reading, and wiped a few tears from his eyes. K. nodded. With all the different disruptions he had had recently he had completely forgotten about Erna, even her birthday, and the story of the chocolates had clearly just been invented so that he wouldn't get in trouble with his aunt and uncle. It was very touching, and even the theatre tickets, which he would regularly send her from then on, would not be enough to repay her, but he really did not feel, now, that it was right for him to visit her in her lodgings and hold conversations with a little, eighteen year old schoolgirl. "And what do you have to say about that?" asked his uncle, who had forgotten all his rush and excitement as he read the letter, and seemed to be about to read it again. "Yes, Uncle," said K., "it is true." "True!" called out his uncle. "What is true? How can this be true? What sort of trial is it? Not a criminal trial, I hope?" "It's a criminal trial," answered K. "And you sit quietly here while you've got a criminal trial round your neck?" shouted his uncle, getting ever louder. "The more calm I am, the better it will be for the outcome," said K. in a tired voice, "don't worry." "How can I help worrying?!" shouted his uncle, "Josef, my Dear Josef, think about yourself, about your family, think about our good name! Up till now, you've always been our pride, don't now become our disgrace. I don't like the way you're behaving," he said, looking at K. with his head at an angle, "that's not how an innocent man behaves when he's accused of something, not if he's still got any strength in him. Just tell me what it's all about so that I can help you. It's something to do with the bank, I take it?" "No," said K. as he stood up, "and you're speaking too loud, Uncle, I expect one of the staff is listening at the door and I find that rather unpleasant. It's best if we go somewhere else, then I can answer all your questions, as far as I can. And I know very well that I have to account to the family for what I do." "You certainly do!" his uncle shouted, "Quite right, you do. Now just get a move on, Josef, hurry up now!" "I still have a few documents I need to prepare," said K., and, using the intercom, he summoned his deputy who entered a few moments later. K.'s uncle, still angry and excited, gestured with his hand to show that K. had summoned him, even though there was no need whatever to do so. K. stood in front of the desk and explained to the young man, who listened calm and attentive, what would need to be done that day in his absence, speaking in a calm voice and making use of various documents. The presence of K.'s uncle while this was going on was quite disturbing; he did not listen to what was being said, but at first he stood there with eyes wide open and nervously biting his lips. Then he began to walk up and down the room, stopped now and then at the window, or stood in front of a picture always making various exclamations such as, "That is totally incomprehensible to me!" or "Now just tell me, what are you supposed to make of that?!" The young man pretended to notice nothing of this and listened to K.'s instructions through to the end, he made a few notes, bowed to both K. and his uncle and then left the room. K.'s uncle had turned his back to him and was looking out the window, bunching up the curtains with his outstretched hands. The door had hardly closed when he called out, "At last! Now that he's stopped jumping about we can go too!" Once they were in the front hall of the bank, where several members of staff were standing about and where, just then, the deputy director was walking across, there was unfortunately no way of stopping K.'s uncle from continually asking questions about the trial. "Now then, Josef," he began, lightly acknowledging the bows from those around them as they passed, "tell me everything about this trial; what sort of trial is it?" K. made a few comments which conveyed little information, even laughed a little, and it was only when they reached the front steps that he explained to his uncle that he had not wanted to talk openly in front of those people. "Quite right," said his uncle, "but now start talking." With his head to one side, and smoking his cigar in short, impatient draughts, he listened. "First of all, Uncle," said K., "it's not a trial like you'd have in a normal courtroom." "So much the worse," said his uncle. "How's that?" asked K., looking at him. "What I mean is, that's for the worse," he repeated. They were standing on the front steps of the bank; as the doorkeeper seemed to be listening to what they were saying K. drew his uncle down further, where they were absorbed into the bustle of the street. His uncle took K.'s arm and stopped asking questions with such urgency about the trial, they walked on for a while in silence. "But how did all this come about?" he eventually asked, stopping abruptly enough to startle the people walking behind, who had to avoid walking into him. "Things like this don't come all of a sudden, they start developing a long time beforehand, there must have been warning signs of it, why didn't you write to me? You know I'd do anything for you, to some extent I am still your guardian, and until today that's something I was proud of. I'll still help you, of course I will, only now, now that the trial is already underway, it makes it very difficult. But whatever; the best thing now is for you to take a short holiday staying with us in the country. You've lost weight, I can see that now. The country life will give you strength, that will be good, there's bound to be a lot of hard work ahead of you. But besides that it'll be a way of getting you away from the court, to some extent. Here they've got every means of showing the powers at their disposal and they're automatically bound to use them against you; in the country they'll either have to delegate authority to different bodies or just have to try and bother you by letter, telegram or telephone. And that's bound to weaken the effect, it won't release you from them but it'll give you room to breathe." "You could forbid me to leave," said K., who had been drawn slightly into his uncle's way of thinking by what he had been saying. "I didn't think you would do it," said his uncle thoughtfully, "you won't suffer too much loss of power by moving away." K. grasped his uncle under the arm to prevent him stopping still and said, "I thought you'd think all this is less important than I do, and now you're taking it so hard." "Josef," called his uncle trying to disentangle himself from him so that he could stop walking, but K. did not let go, "you've completely changed, you used to be so astute, are you losing it now? Do you want to lose the trial? Do you realise what that would mean? That would mean you would be simply destroyed. And that everyone you know would be pulled down with you or at the very least humiliated, disgraced right down to the ground. Josef, pull yourself together. The way you're so indifferent about it, it's driving me mad. Looking at you I can almost believe that old saying: 'Having a trial like that means losing a trial like that'." "My dear Uncle," said K., "it won't do any good to get excited, it's no good for you to do it and it'd be no good for me to do it. The case won't be won by getting excited, and please admit that my practical experience counts for something, just as I have always and still do respect your experience, even when it surprises me. You say that the family will also be affected by this trial; I really can't see how, but that's beside the point and I'm quite willing to follow your instructions in all of this. Only, I don't see any advantage in staying in the country, not even for you, as that would indicate flight and a sense of guilt. And besides, although I am more subject to persecution if I stay in the city I can also press the matter forward better here." "You're right," said his uncle in a tone that seemed to indicate they were finally coming closer to each other, "I just made the suggestion because, as I saw it, if you stay in the city the case will be put in danger by your indifference to it, and I thought it was better if I did the work for you. But will you push things forward yourself with all your strength, if so, that will naturally be far better." "We're agreed then," said K. "And do you have any suggestions for what I should do next?" "Well, naturally I'll have to think about it," said his uncle, "you must bear in mind that I've been living in the country for twenty years now, almost without a break, you lose your ability to deal with matters like this.

But I do have some important connections with several people who, I expect, know their way around these things better
than I do, and to contact them is a matter of course. Out
there in the country I've been getting out of condition, I'm
sure you're already aware of that. It's only at times like this
that you notice it yourself. And this affair of yours came largely unexpected, although, oddly enough, I had expected something of the sort after I'd read Erna's letter, and today when I
saw your face I knew it with almost total certainty. But all that
is by the by, the important thing now is, we have no time to
lose." Even while he was still speaking, K.'s uncle had stood
on tiptoe to summon a taxi and now he pulled K. into the car
behind himself as he called out an address to the driver.
"We're going now to see Dr. Huld, the lawyer," he said, "we
were at school together. I'm sure you know the name, don't
you? No? Well that is odd. He's got a very good reputation as
a defence barrister and for working with the poor. But I esteem him especially as someone you can trust." "It's alright
with me, whatever you do," said K., although he was made
uneasy by the rushed and urgent way his uncle was dealing
with the matter. It was not very encouraging, as the accused,
be to taken to a lawyer for poor people. "I didn't know," he
said, "that you could take on a lawyer in matters like this."
"Well of course you can," said his uncle, "that goes without
saying. Why wouldn't you take on a lawyer? And now, so that
I'm properly instructed in this matter, tell me what's been
happening so far." K. instantly began telling his uncle about
what had been happening, holding nothing back – being
completely open with him was the only way that K. could
protest at his uncle's belief that the trial was a great disgrace.
He mentioned Miss Bürstner's name just once and in passing,
but that did nothing to diminish his openness about the trial
as Miss Bürstner had no connection with it. As he spoke, he
looked out the window and saw how, just then, they were
getting closer to the suburb where the court offices were. He
drew this to his uncle's attention, but he did not find the
coincidence especially remarkable. The taxi stopped in front
of a dark building. K.'s uncle knocked at the very first door at

ground level; while they waited he smiled, showing his big teeth, and whispered, "Eight o'clock; not the usual sort of time to be visiting a lawyer, but Huld won't mind it from me." Two large, black eyes appeared in the spy-hatch in the door, they stared at the two visitors for a while and then disappeared; the door, however, did not open. K. and his uncle confirmed to each other the fact that they had seen the two eyes. "A new maid, afraid of strangers," said K.'s uncle, and knocked again. The eyes appeared once more. This time they seemed almost sad, but the open gas flame that burned with a hiss close above their heads gave off little light and that may have merely created an illusion. "Open the door," called K.'s uncle, raising his fist against it, "we are friends of Dr. Huld, the lawyer!" "Dr. Huld is ill," whispered someone behind them. In a doorway at the far end of a narrow passage stood a man in his dressing gown, giving them this information in an extremely quiet voice. K.'s uncle, who had already been made very angry by the long wait, turned abruptly round and retorted, "Ill? You say he's ill?" and strode towards the gentleman in a way that seemed almost threatening, as if he were the illness himself. "They've opened the door for you, now," said the gentleman, pointing at the door of the lawyer. He pulled his dressing gown together and disappeared. The door had indeed been opened, a young girl – K. recognised the dark, slightly bulging eyes – stood in the hallway in a long white apron, holding a candle in her hand. "Next time, open up sooner!" said K.'s uncle instead of a greeting, while the girl made a slight curtsey. "Come along, Josef," he then said to K. who was slowly moving over towards the girl. "Dr. Huld is unwell," said the girl as K.'s uncle, without stopping, rushed towards one of the doors. K. continued to look at the girl in amazement as she turned round to block the way into the living room, she had a round face like a puppy's, not only the pale cheeks and the chin were round but the temples and the hairline were too. "Josef!" called his uncle once more, and he asked the girl, "It's trouble with his heart, is it?" "I think it is, sir," said the girl, who by now had found time to go ahead with the candle and open the door into the room. In one corner of the room, where the light of the candle did not reach, a face with a long beard looked up from the bed. "Leni, who's this coming in?" asked the lawyer, unable to recognise his guests because he was dazzled by the candle. "It's your old friend, Albert," said K.'s uncle. "Oh, Albert," said the lawyer, falling back onto his pillow as if this visit meant he would not need to keep up appearances. "Is it really as bad as that?" asked K.'s uncle, sitting on the edge of the bed. "I don't believe it is. It's a recurrence of your heart trouble and it'll pass over like the other times." "Maybe," said the lawyer quietly, "but it's just as much trouble as it's ever been. I can hardly breathe, I can't sleep at all and I'm getting weaker by the day." "I see," said K.'s uncle, pressing his panama hat firmly against his knee with his big hand. "That is bad news. But are you getting the right sort of care? And it's so depressing in here, it's so dark. It's a long time since I was last here, but it seemed to me friendlier then. Even your young lady here doesn't seem to have much life in her, unless she's just pretending." The maid was still standing by the door with the candle; as far as could be made out, she was watching K. more than she was watching his uncle even while the latter was still speaking about her. K. leant against a chair that he had pushed near to the girl. "When you're as ill as I am," said the lawyer, "you need to have peace. I don't find it depressing." After a short pause he added, "and Leni looks after me well, she's a good girl." But that was not enough to persuade K.'s uncle, he had visibly taken against his friend's carer and, even though he did not contradict the invalid, he persecuted her with his scowl as she went over to the bed, put the candle on the bedside table and, leaning over the bed, made a fuss of him by tidying the pillows. K.'s uncle nearly forgot the need to show any consideration for the man who lay ill in bed, he stood up, walked up and down behind the carer, and K. would not have been surprised if he had grabbed hold of her skirts behind her and dragged her away from the bed. K. himself looked on calmly, he was not even disappointed at finding the lawyer unwell, he had been able to do nothing to oppose the enthusiasm his uncle had developed for the matter, he was glad that this enthusiasm had now been distracted without his having to do anything about it. His uncle, probably simply wishing to be offensive to the lawyer's attendant, then said, "Young lady, now please leave us alone for a while, I have some personal matters to discuss with my friend." Dr. Huld's carer was still leant far over the invalid's bed and smoothing out the cloth covering the wall next to it, she merely turned her head and then, in striking contrast with the anger that first stopped K.'s uncle from speaking and then let the words out in a gush, she said very quietly, "You can see that Dr. Huld is so ill that he can't discuss any matters at all." It was probably just for the sake of convenience that she had repeated the words spoken by K.'s uncle, but an onlooker might even have perceived it as mocking him and he, of course, jumped up as if he had just been stabbed. "You damned …," in the first gurglings of his excitement his words could hardly be understood, K. was startled even though he had been expecting something of the sort and ran to his uncle with the intention, no doubt, of closing his mouth with both his hands. Fortunately, though, behind the girl, the invalid raised himself up, K.'s uncle made an ugly face as if swallowing something disgusting and then, somewhat calmer, said, "We have naturally not lost our senses, not yet; if what I am asking for were not possible I would not be asking for it. Now please, go!" The carer stood up straight by the bed directly facing K.'s uncle, K. thought he noticed that with one hand she was stroking the lawyer's hand. "You can say anything in front of Leni," said the invalid, in a tone that was unmistakably imploring. "It's not my business," said K.'s uncle, "and it's not my secrets." And he twisted himself round as if wanting to go into no more negotiations but giving himself a little more time to think. "Whose business is it then?" asked the lawyer in an exhausted voice as he leant back again. "My nephew's," said K.'s uncle, "and I've brought him along with me." And he introduced him, "Chief Clerk Josef K." "Oh!" said the invalid, now with much more life in him, and reached out his hand towards K. "Do forgive me, I didn't notice you there at all." Then he then said to his carer, "Leni, go," stretching his hand out to her as if this were a farewell that would have to last for a long time. This time the girl offered no resistance. "So you," he finally said to K.'s uncle, who had also calmed down and stepped closer, "you haven't come to visit me because I'm ill but you've come on business." The lawyer now looked so much stronger that it seemed the idea of being visited because he was ill had somehow made him weak, he remained supporting himself of one elbow, which must have been rather tiring, and continually pulled at a lock of hair in the middle of his beard. "You already look much better," said K.'s uncle, "now that that witch has gone outside." He interrupted himself, whispered, "I bet you she's listening!" and sprang over to the door. But behind the door there was no-one, K.'s uncle came back not disappointed, as her not listening seemed to him worse than if she had been, but probably somewhat embittered. "You're mistaken about her," said the lawyer, but did nothing more to defend her; perhaps that was his way of indicating that she did not need defending. But in a tone that was much more committed he went on, "As far as your nephew's affairs are concerned, this will be an extremely difficult undertaking and I'd count myself lucky if my strength lasted out long enough for it; I'm greatly afraid it won't do, but anyway I don't want to leave anything untried; if I don't last out you can always get somebody else. To be honest, this matter interests me too much, and I can't bring myself to give up the chance of taking some part in it. If my heart does totally give out then at least it will have found a worthy affair to fail in." K. believed he understood not a word of this entire speech, he looked at his uncle for an explanation but his uncle sat on the bedside table with the candle in his hand, a medicine bottle had rolled off the table onto the floor, he nodded to everything the lawyer said, agreed to everything, and now and then looked at K. urging him to show the same compliance. Maybe K.'s uncle had already told the lawyer about the trial. But that was impossible, everything that had happened so far spoke against it. So he said, "I don't understand …" "Well, maybe I've misunderstood what you've been saying," said the lawyer, just as astonished and embarrassed as K. "Perhaps I've been going too fast. What was it you wanted to speak to me about? I thought it was to do with your trial." "Of course it is," said K.'s uncle, who then asked K., "So what is it you want?" "Yes, but how is it that you know anything about me and my case?" asked K. "Oh, I see," said the lawyer with a smile. "I am a lawyer, I move in court circles, people talk about various different cases and the more interesting ones stay in your mind, especially when they concern the nephew of a friend. There's nothing very remarkable about that." "What is it you want, then?" asked K.'s uncle once more, "You seem so uneasy about it" "You move in this court's circles?" asked K. "Yes," said the lawyer. "You're asking questions like a child," said K.'s uncle. "What circles should I move in, then, if not with members of my own discipline?" the lawyer added. It sounded so indisputable that K. gave no answer at all. "But you work in the High Court, not that court in the attic," he had wanted to say but could not bring himself to actually utter it. "You have to realise," the lawyer continued, in a tone as if he were explaining something obvious, unnecessary and incidental, "you have to realise that I also derive great advantage for my clients from mixing with those people, and do so in many different ways, it's not something you can keep talking about all the time. I'm at a bit of a disadvantage now, of course, because of my illness, but I still get visits from some good friends of mine at the court and I learn one or two things. It might even be that I learn more than many of those who are in the best of health and spend all day in court. And I'm receiving a very welcome visit right now, for instance." And he pointed into a dark corner of the room. "Where?" asked K., almost uncouth in his surprise. He looked round uneasily; the little candle gave off far too little light to reach as far as the wall opposite. And then, something did indeed begin to move there in the corner. In the light of the candle held up by K.'s uncle an elderly gentleman could be seen sitting beside a small table. He had been sitting there for so long without being noticed that he could hardly have been breathing. Now he stood up with a great deal of fuss, clearly unhappy that attention had been drawn to him. It was as if, by flapping his hands about like short wings, he hoped to deflect any introductions and greetings, as if he wanted on no account to disturb the others by his presence and seemed to be exhorting them to leave him back in the dark and forget about his being there. That, however, was something that could no longer be granted him. "You took us by surprise, you see," said the lawyer in explanation, cheerfully indicating to the gentleman that he should come closer, which, slowly, hesitatingly, looking all around him, but with a certain dignity, he did. "The office director – oh, yes, forgive me, I haven't introduced you – this is my friend Albert K., this is his nephew, the chief clerk Josef K., and this is the office director – so, the office director was kind enough to pay me a visit. It's only possible to appreciate just how valuable a visit like this is if you've been let into the secret of what a pile of work the office director has heaped over him. Well, he came anyway, we were having a peaceful chat, as far as I was able when I'm so weak, and although we hadn't told Leni she mustn't let anyone in as we weren't expecting anyone, we still would rather have remained alone, but then along came you, Albert, thumping your fists on the door, the office director moved over into the corner pulling his table and chair with him, but now it turns out we might have, that is, if that's what you wish, we might have something to discuss with each other and it would be good if we can all come back together again. – Office director ...," he said with his head on one side, pointing with a humble smile to an armchair near the bed. "I'm afraid I'll only be able to stay a few minutes more," smiled the office director as he spread himself out in the armchair and looked at the clock. "Business calls. But I wouldn't want to miss the chance of meeting a friend of my friend." He inclined his head slightly toward K.'s uncle, who seemed very happy with his new acquaintance, but he was not the sort of person to express his feelings of deference and responded to the office director's words with embarrassed, but loud, laughter. A horrible sight! K. was able to quietly watch everything as nobody paid any attention to him, the office director took over as leader of the conversation as seemed to be his habit once he had been called forward, the lawyer listened attentively with his hand to his ear, his initial weakness having perhaps only had the function of driving away his new visitors, K.'s uncle served as candle-bearer – balancing the candle on his thigh while the office director frequently glanced nervously at it – and was soon free of his embarrassment and was quickly enchanted not only by the office director's speaking manner but also by the gentle, waving hand-movements with which he accompanied it. K., leaning against the bedpost, was totally ignored by the office director, perhaps deliberately, and served the old man only as audience. And besides, he had hardly any idea what the conversation was about and his thoughts soon turned to the care assistant and the ill treatment she had suffered from his uncle. Soon after, he began to wonder whether he had not seen the office director somewhere before, perhaps among the people who were at his first hearing. He may have been mistaken, but thought the office director might well have been among the old gentlemen with the thin beards in the first row.

There was then a noise that everyone heard from the hallway as if something of porcelain were being broken. "I'll go and see what's happened," said K., who slowly left the room as if giving the others the chance to stop him. He had hardly stepped into the hallway, finding his bearings in the darkness with his hand still firmly holding the door, when another small hand, much smaller than K.'s own, placed itself on his and gently shut the door. It was the carer who had been waiting there. "Nothing has happened," she whispered to him, "I just threw a plate against the wall to get you out of there." "I was thinking about you, as well," replied K. uneasily. "So much the better," said the carer. "Come with me". A few steps along, they came to a frosted glass door which the carer opened for him. "Come in here," she said. It was clearly the lawyer's office, fitted out with old, heavy furniture, as far as could be seen in the moonlight which now illuminated just a small, rectangular section of the floor by each of the three big windows. "This way," said the carer, pointing to a dark trunk with a carved, wooden backrest. When he had sat down, K. continued to look round the room, it was a large room with a high ceiling, the clients of this lawyer for the poor must have felt quite lost in it. K. thought he could see the little steps with which visitors would approach the massive desk. But then he forgot about all of this and had eyes only for the carer who sat very close beside him, almost pressing him against the armrest. "I did think," she said "you would come out here to me by yourself without me having to call you first. It was odd. First you stare at me as soon as you come in, and then you keep me waiting. And you ought to call me Leni, too," she added quickly and suddenly, as if no moment of this conversation should be lost. "Gladly," said K. "But as for its being odd, Leni, that's easy to explain. Firstly, I had to listen to what the old men were saying and couldn't leave without a good reason, but secondly I'm not a bold person, if anything I'm quite shy, and you, Leni, you didn't really look like you could be won over in one stroke, either." "That's not it," said Leni, laying one arm on the armrest and looking at K., "you didn't like me, and I don't suppose you like me now, either." "Liking wouldn't be very much," said K., evasively. "Oh!" she exclaimed with a smile, thus making use of K.'s comment to gain an advantage over him. So K. remained silent for a while. By now, he had become used to the darkness in the room and was able to make out various fixtures and fittings. He was especially impressed by a large picture hanging to the right of the door, he leant forward in order to see it better. It depicted a man wearing a judge's robes; he was sitting on a lofty throne gilded in a way that shone forth from the picture. The odd thing about the picture was that this judge was not sitting there in dignified calm but had his left arm pressed against the back and armrest, his right arm, however, was completely free and only grasped the armrest with his hand, as if about to jump up any moment in vigorous outrage and make some decisive comment or even to pass sentence. The accused was probably meant to be imagined at the foot of the steps, the top one of which could be seen in the picture, covered with a yellow carpet. "That might be my judge," said K., pointing to the picture with one finger. "I know him," said Leni looking up at the picture, "he comes here quite often. That picture is from when he was young, but he can never have looked anything like it, as he's tiny, minute almost. But despite that, he had himself made to look bigger in the picture as he's madly vain, just like everyone round here. But even I'm vain and that makes me very unhappy that you don't like me." K. replied to that last comment merely by embracing Leni and drawing her towards him, she lay her head quietly on his shoulder. To the rest of it, though, he said, "What rank is he?" "He's an examining judge," she said, taking hold of the hand with which K. held her and playing with his fingers. "Just an examining judge once again," said K. in disappointment, "the senior officials keep themselves hidden. But here he is sitting on a throne." "That's all just made up," said Leni with her face bent over K.'s hand, "really he's sitting on a kitchen chair with an old horse blanket folded over it. But do you have to be always thinking about your trial?" she added slowly. "No, not at all," said K., "I probably even think too little about it." "That's not the mistake you're making," said Leni, "you're too unyielding, that's what I've heard." "Who said that?" asked K., he felt her body against his chest and looked down on her rich, dark, tightly-bound hair. "I'd be saying too much if I told you that," answered Leni. "Please don't ask for names, but do stop making these mistakes of yours, stop being so unyielding, there's nothing you can do to defend yourself from this court, you have to confess. So confess to them as soon as you get the chance. It's only then that they give you the chance to get away, not till then. Only, without help from outside even that's impossible, but you needn't worry about getting this help as I want to help you myself." "You understand a lot about this court and what sort of tricks are needed," said K. as he lifted her, since she was pressing in much too close to him, onto his lap. "That's alright, then," she said, and made herself comfortable on his lap by smoothing out her skirt and adjusting her blouse. Then she hung both her arms around his neck, leant back and took a long look at him. "And what if I don't confess, could you not help me then?" asked K. to test her out. I'm accumulating women to help me, he thought to himself almost in amazement, first Miss Bürstner, then the court usher's wife, and now this little care assistant who seems to have some incomprehensible need for me. The way she sits on my lap as if it were her proper place! "No," answered Leni, slowly shaking her head, "I couldn't help you then. But you don't want my help anyway, it means nothing to you, you're too stubborn and won't be persuaded." Then, after a while she asked, "Do you have a lover?" "No," said K. "Oh, you must have," she said. "Well, I have really," said K. "Just think, I've even betrayed her while I'm carrying her photograph with me." Leni insisted he show her a photograph of Elsa, and then, hunched on his lap, studied the picture closely. The photograph was not one that had been taken while Elsa was posing for it, it showed her just after she had been in a wild dance such as she liked to do in wine bars, her skirt was still flung out as she span round, she had placed her hands on her firm hips and, with her neck held taut, looked to one side with a laugh; you could not see from the picture whom her laugh was intended for. "She's very tightly laced," said Leni, pointing to the place where she thought this could be seen. "I don't like her, she's clumsy and crude. But maybe she's gentle and friendly towards you, that's the impression you get from the picture. Big, strong girls like that often don't know how to be anything but gentle and friendly. Would she be capable of sacrificing herself for you, though?" "No," said K., "she isn't gentle or friendly, and nor would she be capable of sacrificing herself for me. But I've never yet asked any of those things of her. I've never looked at this picture as closely as you." "You can't think much of her, then," said Leni. "She can't be your lover after all." "Yes she is," said K., "I'm not going to take my word back on that." "Well she might be your lover now, then," said Leni, "but you wouldn't miss her much if you lost her or if you exchanged her for somebody else, me for instance." "That is certainly conceivable," said K. with a smile, "but she does have one major advantage over you, she knows nothing about my trial, and even if she did she wouldn't think about it. She wouldn't try to persuade me to be less unyielding." "Well that's no advantage," said Leni. "If she's got no advantage other than that, I can keep on hoping. Has she got any bodily defects?" "'Bodily defects'?" asked K. "Yeah," said Leni, "as I do have a bodily defect, just a little one. Look." She spread the middle and ring fingers of her right hand apart from each other. Between those fingers the flap of skin connecting them reached up almost as far as the top joint of the little finger. In the darkness, K. did not see at first what it was she wanted to show him, so she led his hand to it so that he could feel. "What a freak of nature," said K., and when he had taken a look at the whole hand he added, "What a pretty claw!" Leni looked on with a kind of pride as K. repeatedly opened and closed her two fingers in amazement, until, finally, he briefly kissed them and let go. "Oh!" she immediately exclaimed, "you kissed me!" Hurriedly, and with her mouth open, she clambered up K.'s lap with her knees. He was almost aghast as he looked up at her, now that she was so close to him there was a bitter, irritating smell from her, like pepper, she grasped his head, leant out over him, and bit and kissed his neck, even biting into his hair. "I've taken her place!" she exclaimed from time to time. "Just look, now you've taken me instead of her!" Just then, her knee slipped out and, with a little cry, she nearly fell down onto the carpet, K. tried to hold her by putting his arms around her and was pulled down with her. "Now you're mine," she said. Her last words to him as he left were, "Here's the key to the door, come whenever you want", and she planted an undirected kiss on his back. When he stepped out the front door there was a light rain falling, he was about to go to the middle of the street to see if he could still glimpse Leni at the window when K.'s uncle leapt out of a car that K., thinking of other things, had not seen waiting outside the building. He took hold of K. by both arms and shoved him against the door as if he wanted to nail him to it. "Young man," he shouted, "how could you do a thing like that?! Things were going well with this business of yours, now you've caused it terrible damage. You slip off with some dirty, little thing who, moreover, is obviously the lawyer's beloved, and stay away for hours. You don't even try to find an excuse, don't try to hide anything, no, you're quite open about it, you run off with her and stay there. And meanwhile we're sitting there, your uncle who's going to such effort for you, the lawyer who needs to be won over to your side, and above all the office director, a very important gentleman who is in direct command of your affair in its present stage. We wanted to discuss how best to help you, I had to handle the lawyer very carefully, he had to handle the office director carefully, and you had most reason of all to at least give me some support. Instead of which you stay away. Eventually we couldn't keep up the pretence any longer, but these are polite and highly capable men, they didn't say anything about it so as to spare my feelings but in the end not even they could continue to force themselves and, as they couldn't speak about the matter in hand, they became silent. We sat there for several minutes, listening to see whether you wouldn't finally come back. All in vain. In the end the office director stood up, as he had stayed far longer than he had originally intended, made his farewell, looked at me in sympathy without being able to help, he waited at the door for a long time although it's more than I can understand why he was being so good, and then he went. I, of course, was glad he'd gone, I'd been holding my breath all this time. All this had even more affect on the lawyer lying there ill, when I took my leave of him, the good man, he was quite unable to speak. You have probably contributed to his total collapse and so brought the very man who you are dependent on closer to his death. And me, your own uncle, you leave me here in the rain – just feel this, I'm wet right through – waiting here for hours, sick with worry."

Chapter Seven
Lawyer – Manufacturer – Painter

One winter morning – snow was falling in the dull light outside – K. was sitting in his office, already extremely tired despite the early hour. He had told the servitor he was engaged in a major piece of work and none of the junior staff should be allowed in to see him, so he would not be disturbed by them at least. But instead of working he turned round in his chair, slowly moved various items around his desk, but then, without being aware of it, he lay his arm stretched out on the desk top and sat there immobile with his head sunk down on his chest.

He was no longer able to get the thought of the trial out of his head. He had often wondered whether it might not be a good idea to work out a written defence and hand it in to the court. It would contain a short description of his life and explain why he had acted the way he had at each event that was in any way important, whether he now considered he had acted well or ill, and his reasons for each. There was no doubt of the advantages a written defence of this sort would have over relying on the lawyer, who was anyway not without his shortcomings. K. had no idea what actions the lawyer was taking; it was certainly not a lot, it was more than a month since the lawyer had summoned him, and none of the previous discussions had given K. the impression that this man would be able to do much for him. Most importantly, he had asked him hardly any questions. And there were so many questions here to be asked. Asking questions were the most important thing. K. had the feeling that he would be able to ask all the questions needed here himself. The lawyer, in contrast, did not ask questions but did all the talking himself or sat silently facing him, leant forward slightly over the desk, probably because he was hard of hearing, pulled on a strand of hair in the middle of his beard and looked down at the carpet, perhaps at the very spot where K. had lain with Leni. Now and then he would give K. some vague warning of the sort you give to children. His speeches were as pointless as they were boring, and K. decided that when the final bill came he would pay not a penny for them. Once the lawyer thought he had humiliated K. sufficiently, he usually started something that would raise his spirits again. He had already, he would then say, won many such cases, partly or in whole, cases which may not really have been as difficult as this one but

242

which, on the face of it, had even less hope of success. He had a list of these cases here in the drawer – here he would tap on one or other of the drawers in his desk – but could, unfortunately, not show them to K. as they dealt with official secrets. Nonetheless, the great experience he had acquired through all these cases would, of course, be of benefit to K. He had, of course, begun work straight away and was nearly ready to submit the first documents. They would be very important because the first impression made by the defence will often determine the whole course of the proceedings. Unfortunately, though, he would still have to make it clear to K. that the first documents submitted are sometimes not even read by the court. They simply put them with the other documents and point out that, for the time being, questioning and observing the accused are much more important than anything written. If the applicant becomes insistent, then they add that before they come to any decision, as soon as all the material has been brought together, with due regard, of course, to all the documents, then these first documents to have been submitted will also be checked over. But unfortunately, even this is not usually true, the first documents submitted are usually mislaid or lost completely, and even if they do keep them right to the end they are hardly read, although the lawyer only knew about this from rumour. This is all very regrettable, but not entirely without its justifications. But K. should not forget that the trial would not be public, if the court deems it necessary it can be made public but there is no law that says it has to be. As a result, the accused and his defence don't have access even to the court records, and especially not to the indictment, and that means we generally don't know – or at least not precisely – what the first documents need to be about, which means that if they do contain anything of relevance to the case it's only by a lucky coincidence. If anything about the individual charges and the reasons for them comes out clearly or can be guessed at while the accused is being questioned, then it's possible to work out and submit documents that really direct the issue and present proof, but not before. Conditions like this, of course, place the defence in a very unfavourable and difficult position. But that is what they intend. In fact, defence is not really allowed under the law, it's only tolerated, and there is even some dispute about whether the relevant parts of the law imply even that. So strictly speaking, there is no such thing as a counsel acknowledged by the court, and anyone who comes before this court as counsel is basically no more than a barrack room lawyer. The effect of all this, of course, is to remove the dignity of the whole procedure, the next time K. is in the court offices he might like to have a look in at the lawyers' room, just so that he's seen it. He might well be quite shocked by the people he sees assembled there. The room they've been allocated, with its narrow space and low ceiling, will be enough to show what contempt the court has for these people. The only light in the room comes through a little window that is so high up that, if you want to look out of it, you first have to get one of your colleagues to support you on his back, and even then the smoke from the chimney just in front of it will go up your nose and make your face black. In the floor of this room – to give yet another example of the conditions there – there is a hole that's been there for more than a year, it's not so big that a man could fall through, but it is big enough for your foot to disappear through it. The lawyers' room is on the second floor of the attic; if your foot does go through it will hang down into the first floor of the attic underneath it, and right in the corridor where the litigants are waiting. It's no exaggeration when lawyers say that conditions like that are a disgrace. Complaints to the management don't have the slightest effect, but the lawyers are strictly forbidden to alter anything in the room at their own expense. But even treating the lawyers in this way has its reasons. They want, as far as possible, to prevent any kind of defence, everything should be made the responsibility of the accused. Not a bad point of view, basically, but nothing could be more mistaken than to think from that that lawyers are not necessary for the accused in this court. On the contrary, there is no court where they are less needed than here. This is because proceedings are generally kept secret not only from the public but also from the accused. Only as far as that is possible, of course, but it is possible to a very large extent. And the accused doesn't get to see the court records either, and it's very difficult to infer what's in the court records from what's been said during questioning based on them, especially for the accused who is in a difficult situation and is faced with every possible worry to distract him. This is when the defence begins. Counsel for the defence are not normally allowed to be present while the accused is being questioned, so afterwards, and if possible still at the door of the interview room, he has to learn what he can about it from him and extract whatever he can that might be of use, even though what the accused has to report is often very confused. But that is not the most important thing, as there's really not a lot that can be learned in this way, although in this, as with anything else, a competent man will learn more than another. Nonetheless, the most important thing is the lawyer's personal connections, that's where the real value of taking counsel lies. Now K. will most likely have already learned from his own experience that, among its very lowest orders, the court organisation does have its imperfections, the court is strictly closed to the public, but staff who forget their duty or who take bribes do, to some extent, show where the gaps are. This is where most lawyers will push their way in, this is where bribes are paid and information extracted, there have even, in earlier times at least, been incidents where documents have been stolen. There's no denying that some surprisingly favourable results have been attained for the accused in this way, for a limited time, and these petty advocates then strut to and fro on the basis of them and attract new clients, but for the further course of the proceedings it signifies either nothing or nothing good. The only things of real value are honest personal contacts, contacts with higher officials, albeit higher officials of the lower grades, you understand. That is the only way the progress of the trial can be influenced, hardly noticeable at first, it's true, but from then on it becomes more and more visible. There are, of course, not many lawyers who can do this, and K. has made a very good choice in this matter. There were probably no more than one or two who had as many contacts as Dr. Huld, but they don't bother with the company of the lawyers' room and have nothing to do with it. This means they have all the less contact with the court officials. It is not at all necessary for Dr. Huld to go to the court, wait in the ante-rooms for the examining judges to turn up, if they turn up, and try to achieve something which, according to the judges' mood is usually more apparent than real and most often not even that. No, K. has seen for himself that the court officials, including some who are quite high up, come forward without being asked, are glad to give information which is fully open or at least easy to understand, they discuss the next stages in the proceedings, in fact in some cases they can be won over and are quite willing to adopt the other person's point of view. However, when this happens, you should never trust them too far, as however firmly they may have declared this new point of view in favour of the defendant they might well go straight back to their offices and write a report for the court that says just the opposite, and might well be even harder on the defendant than the original view, the one they insist they've been fully dissuaded from. And, of course, there's no way of defending yourself from this, something said in private is indeed in private and cannot then be used in public, it's not something that makes it easy for the defence to keep those gentlemen's favour. On the other hand, it's also true that the gentlemen don't become involved with the defence – which will of course be done with great expertise – just for philanthropic reasons or in order to be friendly, in some respects it would be truer to say that they, too, have it allocated to them. This is where the disadvantages of a court structure that, right from the start, stipulates that all proceedings take place in private, come into force. In normal, mediocre trials its officials have contact with the public, and they're very well equipped for it, but here they don't; normal trials run their course all by themselves, almost, and just need a nudge here and there; but when they're faced with cases that are especially difficult they're as lost as they often are with ones that are very simple; they're forced to spend all their time, day and night, with their laws, and so they don't have the right feel for human relationships, and that's a serious shortcoming in cases like this. That's when they come for advice to the lawyer, with a servant behind them carrying the documents which normally are kept so secret. You could have seen many gentlemen at this window, gentlemen of whom you would least expect it, staring out this window in despair on the street below while the lawyer is at his desk studying the documents so that he can give them good advice. And at times like that it's also possible to see how exceptionally seriously these gentlemen take their professions and how they are thrown into great confusion by difficulties which it's just not in their natures to overcome. But they're not in an easy position, to regard their positions as easy would be to do them an injustice. The different ranks and hierarchies of the court are endless, and even someone who knows his way around them cannot always tell what's going to happen. But even for the junior officials, the proceedings in the courtrooms are usually kept secret, so they are hardly able to see how the cases they work with proceed, court affairs appear in their range of vision often without their knowing where they come from and they move on further without their learning where they go. So civil servants like this are not able to learn the things you can learn from studying the successive stages that individual trials go through, the final verdict or the reasons for it. They're only allowed to deal with that part of the trial which the law allocates them, and they usually know less about the results of their work after it's left them than the defence does, even though the defence will usually stay in contact with the accused until the trial is nearly at its end, so that the court officials can learn many useful things from the defence. Bearing all this in mind, does it still surprise K. that the officials are irritated and often express themselves about the litigants in unflattering ways – which is an experience shared by everyone. All the officials are irritated, even when they appear calm. This causes many difficulties for the junior advocates, of course. There is a story, for instance, that has very much the ring of truth about it. It goes like this: One of the older officials, a good and peaceful man, was dealing with a difficult matter for the court which had become very confused, especially thanks to the contributions from the lawyers. He had been studying it for a day and a night without a break – as these officials are indeed hard working, no-one works as hard as they do. When it was nearly morning, and he had been working for twenty-four hours with probably very little result, he went to the front entrance, waited there in ambush, and every time a lawyer tried to enter the building he would throw him down the steps. The lawyers gathered together down in front of the steps and discussed with each other what they should do; on the one hand they had actually no right to be allowed into the building so that there was hardly anything that they could legally do to the official and, as I've already mentioned, they would have to be careful not to set all the officials against them. On the other hand, any day not spent in court is a day lost for them and it was a matter of some importance to force their way inside. In the end, they agreed that they would try to tire the old man out. One lawyer after another was sent out to run up the steps and let himself be thrown down again, offering what resistance he could as long as it was passive resistance, and his colleagues would catch him at the bottom of the steps. That went on for about an hour until the old gentleman, who was already exhausted from working all night, was very tired and went back to his office. Those who were at the bottom of the steps could not believe it at first, so they sent somebody out to go and look behind the door to see if there really was no-one there, and only then did they all gather together and probably didn't even dare to complain, as it's far from being the lawyers' job to introduce any improvements in the court system, or even to want to. Even the most junior lawyer can understand the relationship there to some extent, but one significant point is that almost every defendant, even very simple people, begins to think of suggestions for improving the court as soon as his proceedings have begun, many of them often even spend time and energy on the matter that could be spent far better elsewhere. The only right thing to do is to learn how to deal with the situation as it is. Even if it were possible to improve any detail of it – which is anyway no more than superstitious nonsense – the best that they could achieve, although doing themselves incalculable harm in the process, is that they will have attracted the special attention of the officials for any case that comes up in the future, and the officials are always ready to seek revenge. Never attract attention to yourself! Stay calm, however much it goes against your character! Try to gain some insight into the size of the court organism and how, to some extent, it remains in a state of suspension, and that even if you alter something in one place you'll draw the ground out from under your feet and might fall, whereas if an enormous organism like the court is disrupted in any one place it finds it easy to provide a substitute for itself somewhere else. Everything is connected with everything else and will continue without any change or else, which is quite probable, even more closed, more attentive, more strict, more malevolent. So it's best to leave the work to the lawyers and not to keep disturbing them. It doesn't do much good to make accusations, especially if you can't make it clear what they're based on and their full significance, but it must be said that K. caused a great deal of harm to his own case by his behaviour towards the office director, he was a very influential man but now he might as well be struck off the list of those who might do anything for K. If the trial is mentioned, even just in passing, it's quite obvious that he's ignoring it. These officials are in many ways just like children. Often, something quite harmless – although K.'s behaviour could unfortunately not be called harmless – will leave them feeling so offended that they will even stop talking with good friends of theirs, they turn away when they see them and do everything they can to oppose them. But then, with no particular reason, surprisingly enough, some little joke that was only ever attempted because everything seemed so hopeless will make them laugh and they'll be reconciled. It's both difficult and hard at the same time to deal with them, and there's hardly any reason for it. It's sometimes quite astonishing that a single, average life is enough to encompass so much that it's at all possible ever to have any success in one's work here. On the other hand, there are also dark moments, such as everyone has, when you think you've achieved nothing at all, when it seems that the only trials to come to a good end are those that were determined to have a good end from the start and would do so without any help, while all the others are lost despite all the running to and fro, all the effort, all the little, apparent successes that gave such joy. Then you no longer feel very sure of anything and, if asked about a trial that was doing well by its own nature but which was turned for the worse because you assisted in it, would not even dare deny that. And even that is a kind of self- confidence, but then it's the only one that's left. Lawyers are especially vulnerable to fits of depression of that sort – and they are no more than fits of depression of course – when a case is suddenly taken out of their hands after they've been conducting it satisfactorily for some time. That's probably the worst that can happen to a lawyer. It's not that the accused takes the case away from him, that hardly ever happens, once a defendant has taken on a certain lawyer he has to stay with him whatever happens. How could he ever carry on by himself after he's taken on help from a lawyer? No, that just doesn't happen, but what does sometimes happen is that the trial takes on a course where the lawyer may not go along with it. Client and trial are both simply taken away from the lawyer; and then even contact with the court officials won't help, however good they are, as they don't know anything themselves. The trial will have entered a stage where no more help can be given, where it's being processed in courts to which no-one has any access, where the defendant cannot even be contacted by his lawyer. You come home one day and find all the documents you've submitted, which you've worked hard to create and which you had the best hopes for, lying on the desk, they've been sent back as they can't be carried through to the next stage in the trial, they're just worthless scraps of paper. It doesn't mean that the case has been lost, not at all, or at least there is no decisive reason for supposing so, it's just that you don't know anything more about the case and won't be told anything of what's happening. Well, cases like that are the exceptions, I'm glad to say, and even if K.'s trial is one of them, it's still, for the time being, a long way off. But there was still plenty of opportunity for lawyers to get to work, and K. could be sure they would be made use of. As he had said, the time for submitting documents was still in the future and there was no rush to prepare them, it was much more important to start the initial discussions with the appropriate officials, and they had already taken place. With varying degrees of success, it must be said. It was much better not to give away any details before their time, as in that way K. could only be influenced unfavourably and his hopes might be raised or he might be made too anxious, better just to say that some individuals have spoken very favourably and shown themselves very willing to help, although others have spoken less favourably, but even they have not in any way refused to help. So all in all, the results are very encouraging, only you should certainly not draw any particular conclusions as all preliminary proceedings begin in the same way and it was only the way they developed further that would show what the value of these preliminary proceedings has been. Anyway, nothing has been lost yet, and if we can succeed in getting the office director, despite everything, on our side – and several actions have been undertaken to this end – then everything is a clean wound, as a surgeon would say, and we can wait for the results with some comfort.

When he started talking on in this way the lawyer was quite tireless. He went through it all again every time K. went to see him. There was always some progress, but he could never be told what sort of progress it was. The first set of documents to be submitted were being worked on but still not ready, which usually turned out to be a great advantage the next time K. went to see him as the earlier occasion would have been a very bad time to put them in, which they could not then have known. If K., stupefied from all this talking, ever pointed out that even considering all these difficulties progress was very slow, the lawyer would object that progress was not slow at all, but that they might have progressed far further if K. had come to him at the right time. But he had come to him late and that lateness would bring still further difficulties, and not only where time was concerned. The only welcome interruption during these visits was always when Leni contrived to bring the lawyer his tea while K. was there. Then she would stand behind K. – pretending to watch the lawyer as he bent greedily over his cup, poured the tea in and drank – and secretly let K. hold her hand. There was always complete silence. The lawyer drank. K. squeezed Leni's hand and Leni would sometimes dare to gently stroke K.'s hair. "Still here, are you?" the lawyer would ask when he was ready. "I wanted to take the dishes away," said Leni, they would give each other's hands a final squeeze, the lawyer would wipe his mouth and then start talking at K. again with renewed energy.

Was the lawyer trying to comfort K. or to confuse him? K. could not tell, but it seemed clear to him that his defence was not in good hands. Maybe everything the lawyer said was quite right, even though he obviously wanted to make himself as conspicuous as possible and probably had never even taken on a case as important as he said K.'s was. But it was still suspicious how he continually mentioned his personal contacts with the civil servants. Were they to be exploited solely for K.'s benefit? The lawyer never forgot to mention that they were dealing only with junior officials, which meant officials who were dependent on others, and the direction taken in each trial could be important for their own furtherment. Could it be that they were making use of the lawyer to turn trials in a certain direction, which would, of course, always be at the cost of the defendant? It certainly did not mean that they would do that in every trial, that was not likely at all, and there were probably also trials where they gave the lawyer advantages and all the room he needed to turn it in the direction he wanted, as it would also be to their advantage to keep his reputation intact. If that really was their relationship, how would they direct K.'s trial which, as the lawyer had explained, was especially difficult and therefore important enough to attract great attention from the very first time it came to court? There could not be much doubt about what they would do. The first signs of it could already be seen in the fact that the first documents still had not been submitted even though the trial had already lasted several months, and that, according to the lawyer, everything was still in its initial stages, which was very effective, of course, in making the defendant passive and keeping him helpless. Then he could be suddenly surprised with the verdict, or at least with a notification that the hearing had not decided in his favour and the matter would be passed on to a higher office.

It was essential that K. take a hand in it himself. On winter's mornings such as this, when he was very tired and everything dragged itself lethargically through his head, this belief of his seemed irrefutable. He no longer felt the contempt for the trial that he had had earlier. If he had been alone in the world it would have been easy for him to ignore it, although it was also certain that, in that case, the trial would never have arisen in the first place. But now, his uncle had already dragged him to see the lawyer, he had to take account of his family; his job was no longer totally separate from the progress of the trial, he himself had carelessly – with a certain, inexplicable complacency – mentioned it to acquaintances and others had learned about it in ways he did not know, his relationship with Miss Bürstner seemed to be in trouble because of it. In short, he no longer had any choice whether he would accept the trial or turn it down, he was in the middle of it and had to defend himself. If he was tired, then that was bad.

But there was no reason to worry too much before he needed to. He had been capable of working himself up to his high position in the bank in a relatively short time and to retain it with respect from everyone, now he simply had to apply some of the talents that had made that possible for him to the trial, and there was no doubt that it had to turn out well. The most important thing, if something was to be achieved, was to reject in advance any idea that he might be in any way guilty. There was no guilt. The trial was nothing but a big piece of business, just like he had already concluded to the benefit of the bank many times, a piece of business that concealed many lurking dangers waiting in ambush for him, as they usually did, and these dangers would need to be defended against. If that was to be achieved then he must not entertain any idea of guilt, whatever he did, he would need to look after his own interests as closely as he could. Seen in this way, there was no choice but to take his representation away from the lawyer very soon, at best that very evening. The lawyer had told him, as he talked to him, that that was something unheard of and would probably do him a great deal of harm, but K. could not tolerate any impediment to his efforts where his trial was concerned, and these impediments were probably caused by the lawyer himself. But once he had shaken off the lawyer the documents would need to be submitted straight away and, if possible, he would need to see to it that they were being dealt with every day. It would of course not be enough, if that was to be done, for K. to sit in the corridor with his hat under the bench like the others. Day after day, he himself, or one of the women or somebody else on his behalf, would have to run after the officials and force them to sit at their desks and study K.'s documents instead of looking out on the corridor through the grating. There could be no let-up in these efforts, everything would need to be organised and supervised, it was about time that the court came up against a defendant who knew how to defend and make use of his rights.

But when K. had the confidence to try and do all this the difficulty of composing the documents was too much for him. Earlier, just a week or so before, he could only have felt shame at the thought of being made to write out such documents himself; it had never entered his head that the task could also be difficult. He remembered one morning when, already piled up with work, he suddenly shoved everything to one side and took a pad of paper on which he sketched out some of his thoughts on how documents of this sort should proceed. Perhaps he would offer them to that slow-witted lawyer, but just then the door of the manager's office opened and the deputy-director entered the room with a loud laugh. K. was very embarrassed, although the deputy-director, of course, was not laughing at K.'s documents, which he knew nothing about, but at a joke he had just heard about the stock-exchange, a joke which needed an illustration if it was to be understood, and now the deputy- director leant over K.'s desk, took his pencil from his hand, and drew the illustration on the writing pad that K. had intended for his ideas about his case.

K. now had no more thoughts of shame, the documents had to be prepared and submitted. If, as was very likely, he could find no time to do it in the office he would have to do it at home at night. If the nights weren't enough he would have to take a holiday. Above all, he could not stop half way, that was nonsense not only in business but always and everywhere. Needless to say, the documents would mean an almost endless amount of work. It was easy to come to the belief, not only for those of an anxious disposition, that it was impossible ever to finish it. This was not because of laziness or deceit, which were the only things that might have hindered the lawyer in preparing it, but because he did not know what the charge was or even what consequences it might bring, so that he had to remember every tiny action and event from the whole of his life, looking at them from all sides and checking and reconsidering them. It was also a very disheartening job. It would have been more suitable as a way of passing the long days after he had retired and become senile. But now, just when K. needed to apply all his thoughts to his work, when he was still rising and already posed a threat to the deputy-director, when every hour passed so quickly and he wanted to enjoy the brief evenings and nights as a young man, this was the time he had to start working out these documents. Once more, he began to feel resentment. Almost involuntarily, only to put an end to it, his finger felt for the button of the electric bell in the ante-room. As he pressed it he glanced up to the clock. It was eleven o'clock, two hours, he had spent a great deal of his costly time just dreaming and his wits were, of course, even more dulled than they had been before. But the time had, nonetheless, not been wasted, he had come to some decisions that could be of value. As well as various pieces of mail, the servitors brought two visiting cards from gentlemen who had already been waiting for K. for some time. They were actually very important clients of the bank who should not really have been kept waiting under any circumstances. Why had they come at such an awkward time, and why, the gentlemen on the other side of the closed door seemed to be asking, was the industrious K. using up the best business time for his private affairs? Tired from what had gone before, and tired in anticipation of what was to follow, K. stood up to receive the first of them.

He was a short, jolly man, a manufacturer who K. knew well. He apologised for disturbing K. at some important work, and K., for his part, apologised for having kept the manufacturer waiting for so long. But even this apology was spoken in such a mechanical way and with such false intonation that the manufacturer would certainly have noticed if he had not been fully preoccupied with his business affairs. Instead, he hurriedly pulled calculations and tables out from all his pockets, spread them out in front of K., explained several items, corrected a little mistake in the arithmetic that he noticed as he quickly glanced over it all, and reminded K. of a similar piece of business he'd concluded with him about a year before, mentioning in passing that this time there was another bank spending great effort to get his business, and finally stopped speaking in order to learn K.'s opinion on the matter. And K. had indeed, at first, been closely following what the manufacturer was saying, he too was aware of how important the deal was, but unfortunately it did not last, he soon stopped listening, nodded at each of the manufacturer's louder exclamations for a short while, but eventually he stopped doing even that and did no more than stare at the bald head bent over the papers, asking himself when the manufacturer would finally realise that everything he was saying was useless. When he did stop talking, K. really thought at first that this was so that he would have the chance to confess that he was incapable of listening. Instead, seeing the anticipation on the manufacturer's face, obviously ready to counter any objections made, he was sorry to realise that the business discussion had to be continued. So he bent his head as if he'd been given an order and began slowly to move his pencil over the papers, now and then he would stop and stare at one of the figures. The manufacturer thought there must be some objection, perhaps his figures weren't really sound, perhaps they weren't the decisive issue, whatever he thought, the manufacturer covered the papers with his hand and began once again, moving very close to K., to explain what the deal was all about. "It is difficult," said K., pursing his lips. The only thing that could offer him any guidance were the papers, and the manufacturer had covered them from his view, so he just sank back against the arm of the chair. Even when the door of the manager's office opened and revealed not very clearly, as if through a veil, the deputy director, he did no more than look up weakly. K. thought no more about the matter, he merely watched the immediate effect of the deputy director's appearance and, for him, the effect was very pleasing; the manufacturer immediately jumped up from his seat and hurried over to meet the deputy director, although K. would have liked to make him ten times livelier as he feared the deputy director might disappear again. He need not have worried, the two gentlemen met each other, shook each other's hand and went together over to K.'s desk. The manufacturer said he was sorry to find the chief clerk so little inclined to do business, pointing to K. who, under the view of the deputy director, had bent back down over the papers. As the two men leant over the desk and the manufacturer made some effort to gain and keep the deputy director's attention, K. felt as if they were much bigger than they really were and that their negotiations were about him. Carefully and slowly turning his eyes upwards, he tried to learn what was taking place above him, took one of the papers from his desk without looking to see what it was, lay it on the flat of his hand and raised it slowly up as he rose up to the level of the two men himself. He had no particular plan in mind as he did this, but merely felt this was how he would act if only he had finished preparing that great document that was to remove his burden entirely. The deputy director had been paying all his attention to the conversation and did no more than glance at the paper, he did not read what was written on it at all as what was important for the chief clerk was not important for him, he took it from K.'s hand saying, "Thank you, I'm already familiar with everything", and lay it calmly back on the desk. K. gave him a bitter, sideways look. But the deputy director did not notice this at all, or if he did notice it it only raised his spirits, he frequently laughed out loud, one time he clearly embarrassed the manufacturer when he raised an objection in a witty way but drew him immediately back out of his embarrassment by commenting adversely on himself, and finally invited him into his office where they could bring the matter to its conclusion. "It's a very important matter," said the manufacturer. "I understand that completely. And I'm sure the chief clerk …" – even as he said this he was actually speaking only to the manufacturer – "will be very glad to have us take it off his hands. This is something that needs calm consideration. But he seems to be over-burdened today, there are even some people in the room outside who've been waiting there for hours for him." K. still had enough control of himself to turn away from the deputy director and direct his friendly, albeit stiff, smile only at the manufacturer, he made no other retaliation, bent down slightly and supported himself with both hands on his desk like a clerk, and watched as the two gentlemen, still talking, took the papers from his desk and disappeared into the manager's office. In the doorway, the manufacturer turned and said he wouldn't make his farewell with K. just yet, he would of course let the chief clerk know about the success of his discussions but he also had a little something to tell him about.

At last, K. was by himself. It did not enter his head to show anyone else into his office and only became vaguely aware of how nice it was that the people outside thought he was still negotiating with the manufacturer and, for this reason, he could not let anyone in to see him, not even the servitor. He went over to the window, sat down on the ledge beside it, held firmly on to the handle and looked down onto the square outside. The snow was still falling, the weather still had not brightened up at all.

He remained a long time sitting in this way, not knowing what it actually was that made him so anxious, only occasionally did he glance, slightly startled, over his shoulder at the door to the outer room where, mistakenly, he thought he'd heard some noise. No-one came, and that made him feel calmer, he went over to the wash stand, rinsed his face with cold water and, his head somewhat clearer, went back to his place by the window. The decision to take his defence into his own hands now seemed more of a burden than he had originally assumed. All the while he had left his defence up to the lawyer his trial had had little basic affect on him, he had observed it from afar as something that was scarcely able to reach him directly, when it suited him he looked to see how things stood but he was also able to draw his head back again whenever he wanted. Now, in contrast, if he was to conduct his defence himself, he would have to devote himself entirely to the court – for the time being, at least – success would mean, later on, his complete and conclusive liberation, but if he was to achieve this he would have to place himself, to start with, in far greater danger than he had been in so far. If he ever felt tempted to doubt this, then his experience with the deputy director and the manufacturer that day would be quite enough to convince him of it. How could he have sat there totally convinced of the need to do his own defence? How would it be later? What would his life be like in the days ahead? Would he find the way through it all to a happy conclusion? Did a carefully worked out defence – and any other sort would have made no sense – did a carefully worked out defence not also mean he would need to shut himself off from everything else as much as he could? Would he survive that? And how was he to succeed in conducting all this at the bank? It involved much more than just submitting some documents that he could probably prepare in a few days' leave, although it would have been great temerity to ask for time off from the bank just at that time, it was a whole trial and there was no way of seeing how long it might last. This was an enormous difficulty that had suddenly been thrown into K.'s life!

And was he supposed to be doing the bank's work at a time like this? He looked down at his desk. Was he supposed to let people in to see him and go into negotiations with them at a time like this? While his trial trundled on, while the court officials upstairs in the attic room sat looking at the papers for this trial, should he be worrying about the business of the bank? Did this not seem like a kind of torture, acknowledged by the court, connected with the trial and which followed him around? And is it likely that anyone in the bank, when judging his work, would take any account of his peculiar situation? No- one and never. There were those who knew about his trial, although it was not quite clear who knew about it or how much. But he hoped rumours had not reached as far as the deputy director, otherwise he would obviously soon find a way of making use of it to harm K., he would show neither comradeship nor humaneness. And what about the director? It was true that he was well disposed towards K., and as soon as he heard about the trial he would probably try to do every-thing he could to make it easier for him, but he would certain-ly not devote himself to it. K. at one time had provided the counter-balance to what the deputy director said but the director was now coming more and more under his influence, and the deputy director would also exploit the weakened condition of the director to strengthen his own power. So what could K. hope for? Maybe considerations of this sort weakened his power of resistance, but it was still necessary not to deceive oneself and to see everything as clearly as it could be seen at that moment.

For no particular reason, just to avoiding returning to his desk for a while, he opened the window. It was difficult to open and he had to turn the handle with both his hands. Then, through the whole height and breadth of the window, the mixture of fog and smoke was drawn into the room, filling it with a slight smell of burning. A few flakes of snow were blown in with it. "It's a horrible autumn," said the man-ufacturer, who had come into the room unnoticed after see-ing the deputy director and now stood behind K. K. nodded and looked uneasily at the manufacturer's briefcase, from which he would now probably take the papers and inform K. of the result of his negotiations with the deputy director. However, the manufacturer saw where K. was looking, knocked on his briefcase and without opening it said, "You'll be wanting to hear how things turned out. I've already got the contract in my pocket, almost. He's a charming man, your deputy director – he's got his dangers, though." He laughed as he shook K.'s hand and wanted to make him laugh with him. But to K., it once more seemed suspicious that the manufacturer did not want to show him the papers and saw nothing about his comments to laugh at. "Chief clerk," said the manufacturer, "I expect the weather's been affecting your mood, has it? You're looking so worried today." "Yes," said K., raising his hand and holding the temple of his head, "headaches, worries in the family." "Quite right," said the manufacturer, who was always in a hurry and could never listen to anyone for very long, "everyone has his cross to bear." K. had unconsciously made a step towards the door as if wanting to show the manufacturer out, but the manufacturer said, "Chief clerk, there's something else I'd like to mention to you. I'm very sorry if it's something that'll be a burden to you today of all days but I've been to see you twice already, lately, and each time I forgot all about it. If I delay it any longer it might well lose its point altogether. That would be a pity, as I think what I've got to say does have some value." Before K. had had the time to answer, the manufacturer came up close to him, tapped his knuckle lightly on his chest and said quietly, "You've got a trial going on, haven't you?" K. stepped back and immediately exclaimed, "That's what the deputy director's been telling you!" "No, no," said the manufacturer, "how would the deputy director know about it?" "And what about you?" asked K., already more in control of himself. "I hear things about the court here and there," said the manufacturer, "and that even applies to what it is that I wanted to tell you about." "There are so many people who have connections with the court!" said K. with lowered head, and he led the manufacturer over to his desk. They sat down where they had been before, and the manufacturer said, "I'm afraid it's not very much that I've got to tell you about. Only, in matters like this, it's best not to overlook the tiniest details. Besides, I really want to help you in some way, however modest my help might be. We've been good business partners up till now, haven't we? Well then." K. wanted to apologise for his behaviour in the conversation earlier that day, but the manufacturer would tolerate no interruption, shoved his briefcase up high in his armpit to show that he was in a hurry, and carried on. "I know about your case through a certain Titorelli. He's a painter, Titorelli's just his artistic name, I don't even know what his real name is. He's been coming to me in my office for years from time to time, and brings little pictures with him which I buy more or less just for the sake of charity as he's hardly more than a beggar. And they're nice pictures, too, moorland landscapes and that sort of thing. We'd both got used to doing business in this way and it always went smoothly. Only, one time these visits became a bit too frequent, I began to tell him off for it, we started talking and I became interested how it was that he could earn a living just by painting, and then I learned to my amazement that his main source of income was painting portraits. 'I work for the court,' he said, 'what court?' said I. And that's when he told me about the court. I'm sure you can imagine how amazed I was at being told all this. Ever since then I learn something new about the court every time he comes to visit, and so little by little I get to understand something of how it works. Anyway, Titorelli talks a lot and I often have to push him away, not only because he's bound to be lying but also, most of all, because a businessman like me who's already close to breaking point under the weight of his own business worries can't pay too much attention to other people's. But all that's just by the by. Perhaps – this is what I've been thinking – perhaps Titorelli might be able to help you in some small way, he knows lots of judges and even if he can't have much influence himself he can give you some advice about how to get some influential people on your side. And even if this advice doesn't turn out to make all the difference I still think it'll be very important once you've got it. You're nearly a lawyer yourself. That's what I always say, Mr. K. the chief clerk is nearly a lawyer. Oh I'm sure this trial of yours will turn out all right. So do you want to go and see Titorelli, then? If I ask him to he'll certainly do everything he possibly can. I really do think you ought to go. It needn't be today, of course, just some time, when you get the chance. And anyway – I want to tell you this too – you don't actually have to go and see Titorelli, this advice from me doesn't place you under any obligation at all. No, if you think you can get by without Titorelli it'll certainly be better to leave him completely out of it. Maybe you've already got a clear idea of what you're doing and Titorelli could upset your plans. No, if that's the case then of course you shouldn't go there under any circumstances! And it certainly won't be easy to take advice from a lad like that. Still, it's up to you. Here's the letter of recommendation and here's the address."

Disappointed, K. took the letter and put it in his pocket. Even at best, the advantage he might derive from this recommendation was incomparably smaller than the damage that lay in the fact of the manufacturer knowing about his trial, and that the painter was spreading the news about. It was all he could manage to give the manufacturer, who was already on his way to the door, a few words of thanks. "I'll go there," he said as he took his leave of the manufacturer at the door, "or, as I'm very busy at present, I'll write to him, perhaps he would like to come to me in my office some time." "I was sure you'd find the best solution," said the manufacturer. "Although I had thought you'd prefer to avoid inviting people like this Titorelli to the bank and talking about the trial here. And it's not always a good idea to send letters to people like Titorelli, you don't know what might happen to them. But you're bound to have thought everything through and you know what you can and can't do." K. nodded and accompanied the manufacturer on through the ante-room. But despite seeming calm on the outside he was actually very shocked; he had told the manufacturer he would write to Titorelli only to show him in some way that he valued his recommendations and would consider the opportunity to speak with Titorelli without delay, but if he had thought Titorelli could offer any worthwhile assistance he would not have delayed. But it was only the manufacturer's comment that made K. realise what dangers that could lead to. Was he really able to rely on his own understanding so little? If it was possible that he might invite a questionable character into the bank with a clear letter, and ask advice from him about his trial, separated from the deputy director by no more than a door, was it not possible or even very likely that there were also other dangers he had failed to see or that he was even running towards? There was not always someone beside him to warn him. And just now, just when he would have to act with all the strength he could muster, now a number of doubts of a sort he had never before known had presented themselves and affected his own vigilance! The difficulties he had been feeling in carrying out his office work; were they now going to affect the trial too? Now, at least, he found himself quite unable to understand how he could have intended to write to Titorelli and invite him into the bank.

He shook his head at the thought of it once more as the servitor came up beside him and drew his attention to the three gentlemen who were waiting on a bench in the ante-room. They had already been waiting to see K. for a long time. Now that the servitor was speaking with K. they had stood up and each of them wanted to make use of the opportunity to see K. before the others. It had been negligent of the bank to let them waste their time here in the waiting room, but none of them wanted to draw attention to this. "Mr. K., …" one of them was saying, but K. had told the servitor to fetch his winter coat and said to the three of them, as the servitor helped him to put it on, "Please forgive me, gentlemen, I'm afraid I have no time to see you at present. Please do forgive me but I have some urgent business to settle and have to leave straight away. You've already seen yourselves how long I've been delayed. Would you be so kind as to come back tomorrow or some time? Or perhaps we could settle your affairs by telephone? Or perhaps you would like to tell me now, briefly, what it's about and I can then give you a full answer in writing. Whatever, the best thing will be for you to come here again." The gentlemen now saw that their wait had been totally pointless, and these suggestions of K.'s left them so astounded that they looked at each other without a word. "That's agreed then, is it?" asked K., who had turned toward the servitor bringing him his hat. Through the open door of K.'s office they could see that the snowfall outside had become much heavier. So K. turned the collar of his coat up and buttoned it up high under his chin. Just then the deputy director came out of the adjoining room, smiled as he saw K. negotiating with the gentlemen in his winter coat, and asked, "Are you about to go out?" "Yes," said K., standing more upright, "I have to go out on some business." But the deputy director had already turned towards the gentlemen. "And what about these gentlemen?" he asked. "I think they've already been waiting quite a long time." "We've already come to an understanding," said K. But now the gentlemen could be held back no longer, they surrounded K. and explained that they would not have been waiting for hours if it had not been about something important that had to be discussed now, at length and in private. The deputy director listened to them for a short while, he also looked at K. as he held his hat in his hand cleaning the dust off it here and there, and then he said, "Gentlemen, there is a very simple way to solve this. If you would prefer it, I'll be very glad to take over these negotiations instead of the chief clerk. Your business does, of course, need to be discussed without delay. We are businessmen like yourselves and know the value of a businessman's time. Would you like to come this way?" And he opened the door leading to the ante-room of his own office.

The deputy director seemed very good at appropriating everything that K. was now forced to give up! But was K. not giving up more than he absolutely had to? By running off to some unknown painter, with, as he had to admit, very little hope of any vague benefit, his renown was suffering damage that could not me repaired. It would probably be much better to take off his winter coat again and, at the very least, try to win back the two gentlemen who were certainly still waiting in the next room. If K. had not then glimpsed the deputy director in his office, looking for something from his bookshelves as if they were his own, he would probably even have made the attempt. As K., somewhat agitated, approached the door the deputy director called out, "Oh, you've still not left!" He turned his face toward him – its many deep folds seemed to show strength rather than age – and immediately began once more to search. "I'm looking for a copy of a contract," he said, "which this gentleman insists you must have. Could you help me look for it, do you think?" K. made a step forward, but the deputy director said, "thank you, I've already found it," and with a big package of papers, which certainly must have included many more documents than just the copy of the contract, he turned and went back into his own office.

"I can't deal with him right now," K. said to himself, "but once my personal difficulties have been settled, then he'll certainly be the first to get the effect of it, and he certainly won't like it." Slightly calmed by these thoughts, K. gave the servitor, who had already long been holding the door to the corridor open for him, the task of telling the director, when he was able, that K. was going out of the bank on a business matter. As he left the bank he felt almost happy at the thought of being able to devote more of himself to his own business for a while.

He went straight to the painter, who lived in an outlying part of town which was very near to the court offices, although this area was even poorer, the houses were darker, the streets were full of dirt that slowly blew about over the half-melted snow. In the great gateway to the building where the painter lived only one of the two doors was open, a hole had been broken open in the wall by the other door, and as K. approached it a repulsive, yellow, steaming liquid shot out causing some rats to scurry away into the nearby canal. Down by the staircase there was a small child lying on its belly crying, but it could hardly be heard because of the noise from a metal-workshop on the other side of the entrance hall, drowning out any other sound. The door to the workshop was open, three workers stood in a circle around some piece of work that they were beating with hammers. A large tin plate hung on the wall, casting a pale light that pushed its way in between two of the workers, lighting up their faces and their work-aprons. K. did no more than glance at any of these things, he wanted to get things over with here as soon as possible, to exchange just a few words to find out how things stood with the painter and go straight back to the bank. Even if he had just some tiny success here it would still have a good effect on his work at the bank for that day. On the third floor he had to slow down his pace, he was quite out of breath – the steps, just like the height of each floor, were much higher than they needed to be and he'd been told that the painter lived right up in the attic. The air was also quite oppressive, there was no proper stairwell and the narrow steps were closed in by walls on both sides with no more than a small, high window here and there. Just as K. paused for a while some young girls ran out of one of the flats and rushed higher up the stairs, laughing. K. followed them slowly, caught up with one of the girls who had stumbled and been left behind by the others, and asked her as they went up side by side, "Is there a painter, Titorelli, who lives here?" The girl, hardly thirteen years old and somewhat hunchbacked, jabbed him with her elbow and looked at him sideways. Her youth and her bodily defects had done nothing to stop her being already quite depraved. She did not smile once, but looked at K. earnestly, with sharp, acquisitive eyes. K. pretended not to notice her behaviour and asked, "Do you know Titorelli, the painter?" She nodded and asked in reply, "What d'you want to see him for?" K. thought it would be to his advantage quickly to find out something more about Titorelli. "I want to have him paint my portrait," he said. "Paint your portrait?" she asked, opening her mouth too wide and lightly hitting K. with her hand as if he had said something extraordinarily surprising or clumsy, with both hands she lifted her skirt, which was already very short, and, as fast as she could, she ran off after the other girls whose indistinct shouts lost themselves in the heights. At the next turn of the stairs, however, K. encountered all the girls once more. The hunchbacked girl had clearly told them about K.'s intentions and they were waiting for him. They stood on both sides of the stairs, pressing themselves against the wall so that K. could get through between them, and smoothed their aprons down with their hands. All their faces, even in this guard of honour, showed a mixture of childishness and depravity. Up at the head of the line of girls, who now, laughing, began to close in around K., was the hunchback who had taken on the role of leader. It was thanks to her that K. found the right direction without delay – he would have continued up the stairs straight in front of him, but she showed him that to reach Titorelli he would need to turn off to one side. The steps that led up to the painter were especially narrow, very long without any turning, the whole length could be seen in one glance and, at the top, at Titorelli's closed door, it came to its end. This door was much better illuminated than the rest of the stairway by the light from a small skylight set obliquely above it, it had been put together from unpainted planks of wood and the name 'Titorelli' was painted on it in broad, red brushstrokes. K. was no more than half way up the steps, accompanied by his retinue of girls, when, clearly the result of the noise of all those footsteps, the door opened slightly and in the crack a man who seemed to be dressed in just his nightshirt appeared. "Oh!" he cried, when he saw the approaching crowd, and vanished. The hunchbacked girl clapped her hands in glee and the other girls crowded in behind K. to push him faster forward.

They still had not arrived at the top, however, when the painter up above them suddenly pulled the door wide open and, with a deep bow, invited K. to enter. The girls, on the other hand, he tried to keep away, he did not want to let any of them in however much they begged him and however much they tried to get in – if they could not get in with his permission they would try to force their way in against his will. The only one to succeed was the hunchback when she slipped through under his outstretched arm, but the painter chased after her, grabbed her by the skirt, span her once round and set her down again by the door with the other girls who, unlike the first, had not dared to cross the doorstep while the painter had left his post. K. did not know what he was to make of all this, as they all seemed to be having fun. One behind the other, the girls by the door stretched their necks up high and called out various words to the painter which were meant in jest but which K. did not understand, and even the painter laughed as the hunchback whirled round in his hand. Then he shut the door, bowed once more to K., offered him his hand and introduced himself, saying, "Titorelli, painter". K. pointed to the door, behind which the girls were whispering, and said, "You seem to be very popular in this building." "Ach, those brats!" said the painter, trying in vain to fasten his nightshirt at the neck. He was also barefooted and, apart from that, was wearing nothing more than a loose pair of yellowish linen trousers held up with a belt whose free end whipped to and fro. "Those kids are a real burden for me," he continued. The top button of his nightshirt came off and he gave up trying to fasten it, fetched a chair for K. and made him sit down on it. "I painted one of them once – she's not here today – and ever since then they've been following me about. If I'm here they only come in when I allow it, but as soon as I've gone out there's always at least one of them in here. They had a key made to my door and lend it round to each other. It's hard to imagine what a pain that is. Suppose I come back home with a lady I'm going to paint, I open the door with my own key and find the hunchback there or something, by the table painting her lips red with my paintbrush, and meanwhile her little sisters will be keeping guard for her, moving about and causing chaos in every corner of the room. Or else, like happened yesterday, I might come back home late in the evening – please forgive my appearance and the room being in a mess, it is to do with them – so, I might come home late in the evening and want to go to bed, then I feel something pinching my leg, look under the bed and pull another of them out from under it. I don't know why it is they bother me like this, I expect you've just seen that I do nothing to encourage them to come near me. And they make it hard for me to do my work too, of course. If I didn't get this studio for nothing I'd have moved out a long time ago." Just then, a little voice, tender and anxious, called out from under the door, "Titorelli, can we come in now?" "No," answered the painter. "Not even just me, by myself?" the voice asked again. "Not even just you," said the painter, as he went to the door and locked it.

Meanwhile, K. had been looking round the room, if it had not been pointed out it would never have occurred to him that this wretched little room could be called a studio. It was hardly long enough or broad enough to make two steps. Everything, floor, walls and ceiling, was made of wood, between the planks narrow gaps could be seen. Across from where K. was, the bed stood against the wall under a covering of many different colours. In the middle of the room a picture stood on an easel, covered over with a shirt whose arms dangled down to the ground. Behind K. was the window through which the fog made it impossible to see further than the snow covered roof of the neighbouring building.

The turning of the key in the lock reminded K. that he had not wanted to stay too long. So he drew the manufacturer's letter out from his pocket, held it out to the painter and said, "I learned about you from this gentleman, an acquaintance of yours, and it's on his advice that I've come here". The painter glanced through the letter and threw it down onto the bed. If the manufacturer had not said very clearly that Titorelli was an acquaintance of his, a poor man who was dependent on his charity, then it would really have been quite possible to believe that Titorelli did not know him or at least that he could not remember him. This impression was augmented by the painter's asking, "Were you wanting to buy some pictures or did you want to have yourself painted?" K. looked at the painter in astonishment. What did the letter actually say? K. had taken it as a matter of course that the manufacturer had explained to the painter in his letter that K. wanted nothing more with him than to find out more about his trial. He had been far too rash in coming here! But now he had to give the painter some sort of answer and, glancing at the easel, said, "Are you working on a picture currently?" "Yes," said the painter, and he took the shirt hanging over the easel and threw it onto the bed after the letter. "It's a portrait. Quite a good piece of work, although it's not quite finished yet." This was a convenient coincidence for K., it gave him a good opportunity to talk about the court as the picture showed, very clearly, a judge. What's more, it was remarkably similar to the picture in the lawyer's office, although this one showed a quite different judge, a heavy man with a full beard which was black and bushy and extended to the sides far up the man's cheeks. The lawyer's picture was also an oil painting, whereas this one had been made with pastel colours and was pale and unclear. But everything else about the picture was similar, as this judge, too, was holding tightly to the arm of his throne and seemed ominously about to rise from it. At first K. was about to say, "He certainly is a judge," but he held himself back for the time being and went closer to the picture as if he wanted to study it in detail. There was a large figure shown in middle of the throne's back rest which K. could not understand and asked the painter about it. That'll need some more work done on it, the painter told him, and taking a pastel crayon from a small table he added a few strokes to the edges of the figure but without making it any clearer as far as K. could make out. "That's the figure of justice," said the painter, finally. "Now I see," said K., "here's the blindfold and here are the scales. But aren't those wings on her heels, and isn't she moving?" "Yes," said the painter, "I had to paint it like that according to the contract. It's actually the figure of justice and the goddess of victory all in one." "That is not a good combination," said K. with a smile. "Justice needs to remain still, otherwise the scales will move about and it won't be possible to make a just verdict." "I'm just doing what the client wanted," said the painter. "Yes, certainly," said K., who had not meant to criticise anyone by that comment. "You've painted the figure as it actually appears on the throne." "No," said the painter, "I've never seen that figure or that throne, it's all just invention, but they told me what it was I had to paint." "How's that?" asked K. pretending not fully to understand what the painter said. "That is a judge sitting on the judge's chair, isn't it?" "Yes," said the painter, "but that judge isn't very high up and he's never sat on any throne like that." "And he has himself painted in such a grand pose? He's sitting there just like the president of the court." "Yeah, gentlemen like this are very vain," said the painter. "But they have permission from higher up to get themselves painted like this. It's laid down quite strictly just what sort of portrait each of them can get for himself. Only it's a pity that you can't make out the details of his costume and pose in this picture, pastel colours aren't really suitable for showing people like this." "Yes," said K., "it does seem odd that it's in pastel colours." "That's what the judge wanted," said the painter, "it's meant to be for a woman." The sight of the picture seemed to make him feel like working, he rolled up his shirtsleeves, picked up a few of the crayons, and K. watched as a reddish shadow built up around the head of the judge under their quivering tips and radiated out the to edges of the picture. This shadow play slowly surrounded the head like a decoration or lofty distinction. But around the figure of Justice, apart from some coloration that was barely noticeable, it remained light, and in this brightness the figure seemed to shine forward so that it now looked like neither the God of Justice nor the God of Victory, it seemed now, rather, to be a perfect depiction of the God of the Hunt. K. found the painter's work more engrossing than he had wanted; but finally he reproached himself for staying so long without having done anything relevant to his own affair. "What's the name of this judge?" he asked suddenly. "I'm not allowed to tell you that," the painter answered. He was bent deeply over the picture and clearly neglecting his guest who, at first, he had received with such care. K. took this to be just a foible of the painter's, and it irritated him as it made him lose time. "I take it you must be a trustee of the court," he said. The painter immediately put his crayons down, stood upright, rubbed his hands together and looked at K. with a smile. "Always straight out with the truth," he said. "You want to learn something about the court, like it says in your letter of recommendation, but then you start talking about my pictures to get me on your side.

Still, I won't hold it against you, you weren't to know that that was entirely the wrong thing to try with me. Oh, please!" he said sharply, repelling K.'s attempt to make some objection. He then continued, "And besides, you're quite right in your comment that I'm a trustee of the court." He made a pause, as if wanting to give K. the time to come to terms with this fact. The girls could once more be heard from behind the door. They were probably pressed around the keyhole, perhaps they could even see into the room through the gaps in the planks. K. forewent the opportunity to excuse himself in some way as he did not wish to distract the painter from what he was saying, or else perhaps he didn't want him to get too far above himself and in this way make himself to some extent unattainable, so he asked, "Is that a publicly acknowledged position?" "No," was the painter's curt reply, as if the question prevented him saying any more. But K. wanted him to continue speaking and said, "Well, positions like that, that aren't officially acknowledged, can often have more influence than those that are." "And that's how it is with me," said the painter, and nodded with a frown. "I was talking about your case with the manufacturer yesterday, and he asked me if I wouldn't like to help you, and I answered: 'He can come and see me if he likes', and now I'm pleased to see you here so soon. This business seems to be quite important to you, and, of course, I'm not surprised at that. Would you not like to take your coat off now?" K. had intended to stay for only a very short time, but the painter's invitation was nonetheless very welcome. The air in the room had slowly become quite oppressive for him, he had several times looked in amazement at a small, iron stove in the corner that certainly could not have been lit, the heat of the room was inexplicable. As he took off his winter overcoat and also unbuttoned his frock coat the painter said to him in apology, "I must have warmth. And it is very cosy here, isn't it. This room's very good in that respect." K. made no reply, but it was actually not the heat that made him uncomfortable but, much more, the stuffiness, the air that almost made it more difficult to breathe, the room had probably not been ventilated for a long time. The unpleasantness of this was made all the stronger for K. when the painter invited him to sit on the bed while he himself sat down on the only chair in the room in front of the easel. The painter even seemed to misunderstand why K. remained at the edge of the bed and urged K. to make himself comfortable, and as he hesitated he went over to the bed himself and pressed K. deep down into the bedclothes and pillows. Then he went back to his seat and at last he asked his first objective question, which made K. forget everything else. "You're innocent, are you?" he asked. "Yes," said K. He felt a simple joy at answering this question, especially as the answer was given to a private individual and therefore would have no consequences. Up till then no-one had asked him this question so openly. To make the most of his pleasure he added, "I am totally innocent." "So," said the painter, and he lowered his head and seemed to be thinking. Suddenly he raised his head again and said, "Well if you're innocent it's all very simple." K. began to scowl, this supposed trustee of the court was talking like an ignorant child. "My being innocent does not make things simple," said K. Despite everything, he couldn't help smiling and slowly shook his head. "There are many fine details in which the court gets lost, but in the end it reaches into some place where originally there was nothing and pulls enormous guilt out of it." "Yeah, yeah, sure," said the painter, as if K. had been disturbing his train of thought for no reason. "But you are innocent, aren't you?" "Well of course I am," said K. "That's the main thing," said the painter. There was no counter-argument that could influence him, but although he had made up his mind it was not clear whether he was talking this way because of conviction or indifference. K., then, wanted to find out and said therefore, "I'm sure you're more familiar with the court than I am, I know hardly more about it than what I've heard, and that's been from many very different people. But they were all agreed on one thing, and that was that when ill thought-out accusations are made they are not ignored, and that once the court has made an accusation it is convinced of the guilt of the defendant and it's very hard to make it think otherwise."

274

"Very hard?" the painter asked, throwing one hand up in the air. "It's impossible to make it think otherwise. If I painted all the judges next to each other here on canvas, and you were trying to defend yourself in front of it, you'd have more success with them than you'd ever have with the real court." "Yes," said K. to himself, forgetting that he had only gone there to investigate the painter.

One of the girls behind the door started up again, and asked, "Titorelli, is he going to go soon?" "Quiet!" shouted the painter at the door, "Can't you see I'm talking with the gentleman?" But this was not enough to satisfy the girl and she asked, "You going to paint his picture?" And when the painter didn't answer she added, "Please don't paint him, he's an 'orrible bloke." There followed an incomprehensible, interwoven babble of shouts and replies and calls of agreement. The painter leapt over to the door, opened it very slightly – the girls' clasped hands could be seen stretching through the crack as if they wanted something – and said, "If you're not quiet I'll throw you all down the stairs. Sit down here on the steps and be quiet." They probably did not obey him immediately, so that he had to command, "Down on the steps!" Only then it became quiet.

"I'm sorry about that," said the painter as he returned to K. K. had hardly turned towards the door, he had left it completely up to the painter whether and how he would place him under his protection if he wanted to. Even now, he made hardly any movement as the painter bent over him and, whispering into his ear in order not to be heard outside, said, "These girls belong to the court as well." "How's that?" asked K., as he leant his head to one side and looked at the painter. But the painter sat back down on his chair and, half in jest, half in explanation, "Well, everything belongs to the court." "That is something I had never noticed until now," said K. curtly, this general comment of the painter's made his comment about the girls far less disturbing. Nonetheless, K. looked for a while at the door, behind which the girls were now sitting quietly on the steps. Except, that one of them had pushed a drinking straw through a crack between the planks and was moving it slowly up and down. "You still don't seem to have much general idea of what the court's about", said the painter, who had stretched his legs wide apart and was tapping loudly on the floor with the tip of his foot. "But as you're innocent you won't need it anyway. I'll get you out of this by myself." "How do you intend to do that?" asked K. "You did say yourself not long ago that it's quite impossible to go to the court with reasons and proofs." "Only impossible for reasons and proofs you take to the court yourself" said the painter, raising his forefinger as if K. had failed to notice a fine distinction. "It goes differently if you try to do something behind the public court, that's to say in the consultation rooms, in the corridors or here, for instance, in my studio." K. now began to find it far easier to believe what the painter was saying, or rather it was largely in agreement with what he had also been told by others. In fact it was even quite promising. If it really was so easy to influence the judges through personal contacts as the lawyer had said then the painter's contacts with these vain judges was especially important, and at the very least should not be undervalued. And the painter would fit in very well in the circle of assistants that K. was slowly gathering around himself. He had been noted at the bank for his talent in organising, here, where he was placed entirely on his own resources, would be a good opportunity to test that talent to its limits. The painter observed the effect his explanation had had on K. and then, with a certain unease, said, "Does it not occur to you that the way I'm speaking is almost like a lawyer? It's the incessant contact with the gentlemen of the court has that influence on me. I gain a lot by it, of course, but I lose a lot, artistically speaking." "How did you first come into contact with the judges, then?" asked K., he wanted first to gain the painter's trust before he took him into his service. "That was very easy," said the painter, "I inherited these contacts. My father was court painter before me. It's a position that's always inherited. They can't use new people for it, the rules governing how the various grades of officials are painted are so many and varied, and, above all, so secret that no- one outside of certain families even knows them. In the drawer there, for instance, I've got my father's notes, which I don't show to anyone. But you're only able to paint judges if you know what they say. Although, even if I lost them no-one could ever dispute my position because of all the rules I just carry round in my head. All the judges want to be painted like the old, great judges were, and I'm the only one who can do that." "You are to be envied," said K., thinking of his position at the bank. "Your position is quite unassailable, then?" "Yes, quite unassailable," said the painter, and he raised his shoulders in pride. "That's how I can even afford to help some poor man facing trial now and then." "And how do you do that?" asked K., as if the painter had not just described him as a poor man. The painter did not let himself be distracted, but said, "In your case, for instance, as you're totally innocent, this is what I'll do." The repeated mention of K.'s innocence was becoming irksome to him. It sometimes seemed to him as if the painter was using these comments to make a favourable outcome to the trial a precondition for his help, which of course would make the help itself unnecessary. But despite these doubts K. forced himself not to interrupt the painter. He did not want to do without the painter's help, that was what he had decided, and this help did not seem in any way less questionable than that of the lawyer. K. valued the painter's help far more highly because it was offered in a way that was more harmless and open.

The painter had pulled his seat closer to the bed and continued in a subdued voice: "I forgot to ask you; what sort of acquittal is it you want? There are three possibilities; absolute acquittal, apparent acquittal and deferment. Absolute acquittal is the best, of course, only there's nothing I could do to get that sort of outcome. I don't think there's anyone at all who could do anything to get an absolute acquittal. Probably the only thing that could do that is if the accused is innocent. As you are innocent it could actually be possible and you could depend on your innocence alone. In that case you won't need me or any other kind of help."

At first, K. was astonished at this orderly explanation, but then, just as quietly as the painter, he said, "I think you're contradicting yourself." "How's that?" asked the painter patiently, leaning back with a smile. This smile made K. feel as if he were examining not the words of the painter but seeking out inconsistencies in the procedures of the court itself. Nonetheless, he continued unabashed and said, "You remarked earlier that the court cannot be approached with reasoned proofs, you later restricted this to the open court, and now you go so far as to say that an innocent man needs no assistance in court. That entails a contradiction. Moreover, you said earlier that the judges can be influenced personally but now you insist that an absolute acquittal, as you call it, can never be attained through personal influence. That entails a second contradiction." "It's quite easy to clear up these contradictions," said the painter. "We're talking about two different things here, there's what it says in the law and there's what I know from my own experience, you shouldn't get the two confused. I've never seen it in writing, but the law does, of course, say on the one hand that the innocent will be set free, but on the other hand it doesn't say that the judges can be influenced. But in my experience it's the other way round. I don't know of any absolute acquittals but I do know of many times when a judge has been influenced. It's possible, of course, that there was no innocence in any of the cases I know about. But is that likely? Not a single innocent defendant in so many cases? When I was a boy I used to listen closely to my father when he told us about court cases at home, and the judges that came to his studio talked about the court, in our circles nobody talks about anything else; I hardly ever got the chance to go to court myself but always made use of it when I could, I've listened to countless trials at important stages in their development, I've followed them closely as far as they could be followed, and I have to say that I've never seen a single acquittal." "So. Not a single acquittal," said K., as if talking to himself and his hopes. "That confirms the impression I already have of the court. So there's no point in it from this side either. They could replace the whole court with a single hangman." "You shouldn't generalise," said the painter, dissatisfied, "I've only been talking about my own experience." "Well that's enough," said K., "or have you heard of any acquittals that happened earlier?" "They say there have been some acquittals earlier," the painter answered, "but it's very hard to be sure about it. The courts don't make their final conclusions public, not even the judges are allowed to know about them, so that all we know about these earlier cases are just legends. But most of them did involve absolute acquittals, you can believe that, but they can't be proved. On the other hand, you shouldn't forget all about them either, I'm sure there is some truth to them, and they are very beautiful, I've painted a few pictures myself depicting these legends." "My assessment will not be altered by mere legends," said K. "I don't suppose it's possible to cite these legends in court, is it?" The painter laughed. "No, you can't cite them in court," he said. "Then there's no point in talking about them," said K., he wanted, for the time being, to accept anything the painter told him, even if he thought it unlikely or contradicted what he had been told by others. He did not now have the time to examine the truth of everything the painter said or even to disprove it, he would have achieved as much as he could if the painter would help him in any way even if his help would not be decisive. As a result, he said, "So let's pay no more attention to absolute acquittal, but you mentioned two other possibilities." "Apparent acquittal and deferment. They're the only possibilities," said the painter. "But before we talk about them, would you not like to take your coat off? You must be hot." "Yes," said K., who until then had paid attention to nothing but the painter's explanations, but now that he had had the heat pointed out to him his brow began to sweat heavily. "It's almost unbearable." The painter nodded as if he understood K.'s discomfort very well. "Could we not open the window?" asked K. "No," said the painter. "It's only a fixed pane of glass, it can't be opened." K. now realised that all this time he had been hoping the painter would suddenly go over to the window and pull it open. He had prepared himself even for the fog that he would breathe in through his open mouth. The thought that here he was entirely cut off from the air made him feel dizzy.

He tapped lightly on the bedspread beside him and, with a weak voice, said, "That is very inconvenient and unhealthy." "Oh no," said the painter in defence of his window, "as it can't be opened this room retains the heat better than if the window were double glazed, even though it's only a single pane. There's not much need to air the room as there's so much ventilation through the gaps in the wood, but when I do want to I can open one of my doors, or even both of them." K. was slightly consoled by this explanation and looked around to see where the second door was. The painter saw him do so and said, "It's behind you, I had to hide it behind the bed." Only then was K. able to see the little door in the wall. "It's really much too small for a studio here," said the painter, as if he wanted to anticipate an objection K. would make. "I had to arrange things as well as I could. That's obviously a very bad place for the bed, in front of the door. For instance when the judge I'm painting at present comes he always comes through the door by the bed, and I've even given him a key to this door so that he can wait for me here in the studio when I'm not home. Although nowadays he usually comes early in the morning when I'm still asleep. And of course, it always wakes me up when I hear the door opened beside the bed, however fast asleep I am. If you could hear the way I curse him as he climbs over my bed in the morning you'd lose all respect for judges. I suppose I could take the key away from him but that'd only make things worse. It only takes a tiny effort to break any of the doors here off their hinges." All the time the painter was speaking, K. was considering whether he should take off his coat, but he finally realised that, if he didn't do so, he would be quite unable to stay here any longer, so he took off his frock coat and lay it on his knee so that he could put it back on again as soon as the conversation was over. He had hardly done this when one of the girls called out, "Now he's taken his coat off!" and they could all be heard pressing around the gaps in the planks to see the spectacle for themselves. "The girls think I'm going to paint your portrait," said the painter, "and that's why you're taking your coat off." "I see," said K., only slightly amused by this, as he felt little better than he had before even though he now sat in his shirtsleeves. With some irritation he asked, "What did you say the two other possibilities were?" He had already forgotten the terms used. "Apparent acquittal and deferment," said the painter. "It's up to you which one you choose. You can get either of them if I help you, but it'll take some effort of course, the difference between them is that apparent acquittal needs concentrated effort for a while and that deferment takes much less effort but it has to be sustained. Now then, apparent acquittal. If that's what you want I'll write down an assertion of your innocence on a piece of paper. The text for an assertion of this sort was passed down to me from my father and it's quite unassailable. I take this assertion round to the judges I know. So I'll start off with the one I'm currently painting, and put the assertion to him when he comes for his sitting this evening. I'll lay the assertion in front of him, explain that you're innocent and give him my personal guarantee of it. And that's not just a superficial guarantee, it's a real one and it's binding." The painter's eyes seemed to show some reproach of K. for wanting to impose that sort of responsibility on him. "That would be very kind of you", said K. "And would the judge then believe you and nonetheless not pass an absolute acquittal?" "It's like I just said," answered the painter. "And anyway, it's not entirely sure that all the judges would believe me, many of them, for instance, might want me to bring you to see them personally. So then you'd have to come along too. But at least then, if that happens, the matter is half way won, especially as I'd teach you in advance exactly how you'd need to act with the judge concerned, of course. What also happens, though, is that there are some judges who'll turn me down in advance, and that's worse. I'll certainly make several attempts, but still, we'll have to forget about them, but at least we can afford to do that as no one judge can pass the decisive verdict. Then when I've got enough judges' signatures on this document I take it to the judge who's concerned with your case. I might even have his signature already, in which case things develop a bit quicker than they would do otherwise.

But there aren't usually many hold ups from then on, and that's the time that the defendant can feel most confident. It's odd, but true, that people feel more confidence in this time than they do after they've been acquitted. There's no particular exertion needed now. When he has the document asserting the defendant's innocence, guaranteed by a number of other judges, the judge can acquit you without any worries, and although there are still several formalities to be gone through there's no doubt that that's what he'll do as a favour to me and several other acquaintances. You, however, walk out the court and you're free." "So, then I'll be free," said K., hesitantly. "That's right," said the painter, "but only apparently free or, to put it a better way, temporarily free, as the most junior judges, the ones I know, they don't have the right to give the final acquittal. Only the highest judge can do that, in the court that's quite out of reach for you, for me and for all of us. We don't know how things look there and, incidentally, we don't want to know. The right to acquit people is a major privilege and our judges don't have it, but they do have the right to free people from the indictment. That's to say, if they're freed in this way then for the time being the charge is withdrawn but it's still hanging over their heads and it only takes an order from higher up to bring it back into force. And as I'm in such good contact with the court I can also tell you how the difference between absolute and apparent acquittal is described, just in a superficial way, in the directives to the court offices. If there's an absolute acquittal all proceedings should stop, everything disappears from the process, not just the indictment but the trial and even the acquittal disappears, everything just disappears. With an apparent acquittal it's different. When that happens, nothing has changed except that the case for your innocence, for your acquittal and the grounds for the acquittal have been made stronger. Apart from that, proceedings go on as before, the court offices continue their business and the case gets passed to higher courts, gets passed back down to the lower courts and so on, backwards and forwards, sometimes faster, sometimes slower, to and fro. It's impossible to know exactly what's happening while this is going on. Seen from outside it can sometimes seem that everything has been long since forgotten, the documents have been lost and the acquittal is complete. No-one familiar with the court would believe it. No documents ever get lost, the court forgets nothing. One day – no-one expects it – some judge or other picks up the documents and looks more closely at them, he notices that this particular case is still active, and orders the defendant's immediate arrest. I've been talking here as if there's a long delay between apparent acquittal and re-arrest, that is quite possible and I do know of cases like that, but it's just as likely that the defendant goes home after he's been acquitted and finds somebody there waiting to re-arrest him. Then, of course, his life as a free man is at an end." "And does the trial start over again?" asked K., finding it hard to believe. "The trial will always start over again," said the painter, "but there is, once again as before, the possibility of getting an apparent acquittal. Once again, the accused has to muster all his strength and mustn't give up." The painter said that last phrase possibly as a result of the impression that K., whose shoulders had dropped somewhat, gave on him. "But to get a second acquittal," asked K., as if in anticipation of further revelations by the painter, "is that not harder to get than the first time?" "As far as that's concerned," answered the painter, "there's nothing you can say for certain. You mean, do you, that the second arrest would have an adverse influence on the judge and the verdict he passes on the defendant? That's not how it happens. When the acquittal is passed the judges are already aware that re-arrest is likely. So when it happens it has hardly any effect. But there are countless other reasons why the judges' mood and their legal acumen in the case can be altered, and efforts to obtain the second acquittal must therefore be suited to the new conditions, and generally just as vigorous as the first." "But this second acquittal will once again not be final," said K., shaking his head. "Of course not," said the painter, "the second acquittal is followed by the third arrest, the third acquittal by the fourth arrest and so on. That's what is meant by the term apparent acquittal." K. was silent. "You clearly don't think an apparent acquittal offers much advantage," said the painter, "perhaps deferment would suit you better. Would you like me to explain what deferment is about?" K. nodded. The painter had leant back and spread himself out in his chair, his nightshirt was wide open, he had pushed his hand inside and was stroking his breast and his sides. "Deferment," said the painter, looking vaguely in front of himself for a while as if trying to find a perfectly appropriate explanation, "deferment consists of keeping proceedings permanently in their earliest stages. To do that, the accused and those helping him need to keep in continuous personal contact with the court, especially those helping him. I repeat, this doesn't require so much effort as getting an apparent acquittal, but it probably requires a lot more attention. You must never let the trial out of your sight, you have to go and see the appropriate judge at regular intervals as well as when something in particular comes up and, whatever you do, you have to try and remain friendly with him; if you don't know the judge personally you have to influence him through the judges you do know, and you have to do it without giving up on the direct discussions. As long as you don't fail to do any of these things you can be reasonably sure the trial won't get past its first stages. The trial doesn't stop, but the defendant is almost as certain of avoiding conviction as if he'd been acquitted. Compared with an apparent acquittal, deferment has the advantage that the defendant's future is less uncertain, he's safe from the shock of being suddenly re-arrested and doesn't need to fear the exertions and stress involved in getting an apparent acquittal just when everything else in his life would make it most difficult. Deferment does have certain disadvantages of its own though, too, and they shouldn't be under-estimated. I don't mean by this that the defendant is never free, he's never free in the proper sense of the word with an apparent acquittal either. There's another disadvantage. Proceedings can't be prevented from moving forward unless there are some at least ostensible reasons given. So something needs to seem to be happening when looked at from the outside. This means that from time to time various injunctions have to be obeyed, the accused has to be questioned, investigations have to take place and so on. The trial's been artificially constrained inside a tiny circle, and it has to be continuously spun round within it. And that, of course, brings with it certain unpleasantnesses for the accused, although you shouldn't imagine they're all that bad. All of this is just for show, the interrogations, for instance, they're only very short, if you ever don't have the time or don't feel like going to them you can offer an excuse, with some judges you can even arrange the injunctions together a long time in advance, in essence all it means is that, as the accused, you have to report to the judge from time to time." Even while the painter was speaking those last words K. had laid his coat over his arm and had stood up. Immediately, from outside the door, there was a cry of 'He's standing up now!'. "Are you leaving already?" asked the painter, who had also stood up. "It must be the air that's driving you out. I'm very sorry about that. There's still a lot I need to tell you. I had to put everything very briefly but I hope at least it was all clear." "Oh yes," said K., whose head was aching from the effort of listening. Despite this affirmation the painter summed it all up once more, as if he wanted to give K. something to console him on his way home. "Both have in common that they prevent the defendant being convicted," he said. "But they also prevent his being properly acquitted," said K. quietly, as if ashamed to acknowledge it. "You've got it, in essence," said the painter quickly. K. placed his hand on his winter overcoat but could not bring himself to put it on. Most of all he would have liked to pack everything together and run out to the fresh air. Not even the girls could induce him to put his coat on, even though they were already loudly telling each other that he was doing so. The painter still had to interpret K.'s mood in some way, so he said, "I expect you've deliberately avoided deciding between my suggestions yet. That's good. I would even have advised against making a decision straight away. There's no more than a hair's breadth of difference between the advantages and disadvantages. Everything has to be carefully weighed up. But the most important thing is you shouldn't lose too much time." "I'll come back here again soon," said K., who had suddenly decided to put his frock coat on, threw his overcoat over his shoulder and hurried over to the door behind which the girls now began to scream. K. thought he could even see the screaming girls through the door. "Well, you'll have to keep your word," said the painter, who had not followed him, "otherwise I'll come to the bank to ask about it myself." "Will you open this door for me," said K. pulling at the handle which, as he noticed from the resistance, was being held tightly by the girls on the other side. "Do you want to be bothered by the girls?" asked the painter. "It's better if you use the other way out," he said, pointing to the door behind the bed. K. agreed to this and jumped back to the bed. But instead of opening that door the painter crawled under the bed and from underneath it asked K., "Just a moment more, would you not like to see a picture I could sell to you?" K. did not want to be impolite, the painter really had taken his side and promised to help him more in the future, and because of K.'s forgetfulness there had been no mention of any payment for the painter's help, so K. could not turn him down now and allowed him to show him the picture, even though he was quivering with impatience to get out of the studio. From under the bed, the painter withdrew a pile of unframed paintings. They were so covered in dust that when the painter tried to blow it off the one on top the dust swirled around in front of K.'s eyes, robbing him of breath for some time. "Moorland landscape," said the painter passing the picture to K. It showed two sickly trees, well separated from each other in dark grass. In the background there was a multi-coloured sunset. "That's nice," said K. "I'll buy it." K. expressed himself in this curt way without any thought, so he was glad when the painter did not take this amiss and picked up a second painting from the floor. "This is a counterpart to the first picture," said the painter. Perhaps it had been intended as a counterpart, but there was not the slightest difference to be seen between it and the first picture, there were the trees, there the grass and there the sunset. But this was of little importance to K. "They are beautiful landscapes," he said,

"I'll buy them both and hang them in my office." "You seem to like this subject," said the painter, picking up a third painting, "good job I've still got another, similar picture here." The picture though, was not similar, rather it was exactly the same moorland landscape. The painter was fully exploiting this opportunity to sell off his old pictures. "I'll take this one too," said K. "How much do the three paintings cost?" "We can talk about that next time," said the painter. "You're in a hurry now, and we'll still be in contact. And besides, I'm glad you like the paintings, I'll give you all the paintings I've got down here. They're all moorland landscapes, I've painted a lot of moorland landscapes. A lot of people don't like that sort of picture because they're too gloomy, but there are others, and you're one of them, who love gloomy themes." But K. was not in the mood to hear about the professional experiences of this painter cum beggar. "Wrap them all up!" he called out, interrupting the painter as he was speaking, "my servant will come to fetch them in the morning." "There's no need for that," said the painter. "I expect I can find a porter for you who can go with you now." And, at last, he leant over the bed and unlocked the door. "Just step on the bed, don't worry about that," said the painter, "that's what everyone does who comes in here." Even without this invitation, K. had shown no compunction in already placing his foot in the middle of the bed covers, then he looked out through the open door and drew his foot back again. "What is that?" he asked the painter. "What are you so surprised at?" he asked, surprised in his turn. "Those are court offices. Didn't you know there are court offices here? There are court offices in almost every attic, why should this building be any different? Even my studio is actually one of the court offices but the court put it at my disposal." It was not so much finding court offices even here that shocked K., he was mainly shocked at himself, at his own naïvety in court matters. It seemed to him that one of the most basic rules governing how a defendant should behave was always to be prepared, never allow surprises, never to look, unsuspecting, to the right when the judge stood beside him to his left – and this was the very basic rule that he was continually violating. A long corridor extended in from of him, air blew in from it which, compared with the air in the studio, was refreshing. There were benches set along each side of the corridor just as in the waiting area for the office he went to himself. There seemed to be precise rules governing how offices should be equipped. There did not seem to be many people visiting the offices that day. There was a man there, half sitting, half laying, his face was buried in his arm on the bench and he seemed to be sleeping; another man was standing in the half-dark at the end of the corridor. K. now climbed over the bed, the painter followed him with the pictures. They soon came across a servant of the court – K. was now able to recognise all the servants of the court from the gold buttons they wore on their civilian clothes below the normal buttons – and the painter instructed him to go with K. carrying the pictures. K. staggered more than he walked, his handkerchief pressed over his mouth. They had nearly reached the exit when the girls stormed in on them, so K. had not been able to avoid them. They had clearly seen that the second door of the studio had been opened and had gone around to impose themselves on him from this side. "I can't come with you any further!" called out the painter with a laugh as the girls pressed in. "Goodbye, and don't hesitate too long!" K. did not even look round at him. Once on the street he took the first cab he came across. He now had to get rid of the servant, whose gold button continually caught his eye even if it caught no-one else's. As a servant, the servant of the court was going to sit on the coach-box. But K. chased him down from there. It was already well into the afternoon when K. arrived in front of the bank. He would have liked to leave the pictures in the cab but feared there might be some occasion when he would have to let the painter see he still had them. So he had the pictures taken to his office and locked them in the lowest drawer of his desk so that he could at least keep them safe from the deputy director's view for the next few days.

Chapter Eight
Block, the businessman – Dismissing the lawyer

K. had at last made the decision to withdraw his defence from the lawyer. It was impossible to remove his doubts as to whether this was the right decision, but this was outweighed by his belief in its necessity. This decision, on the day he intended to go to see the lawyer, took a lot of the strength he needed for his work, he worked exceptionally slowly, he had to remain in his office a long time, and it was already past ten o'clock when he finally stood in front of the lawyer's front door. Even before he rang he considered whether it might not be better to give the lawyer notice by letter or telephone, a personal conversation would certainly be very difficult. Nonetheless, K. did not actually want to do without it, if he gave notice by any other means it would be received in silence or with a few formulated words, and unless Leni could discover anything K. would never learn how the lawyer had taken his dismissal and what its consequences might be, in the lawyer's not unimportant opinion. But sitting in front of him and taken by surprise by his dismissal, K. would be able easily to infer everything he wanted from the lawyer's face and behaviour, even if he could not be induced to say very much. It was not even out of the question that K. might, after all, be persuaded that it would be best to leave his defence to the lawyer and withdraw his dismissal.

As usual, there was at first no response to K.'s ring at the door. "Leni could be a bit quicker," thought K. But he could at least be glad there was nobody else interfering as usually happened, be it the man in his nightshirt or anyone else who might bother him. As K. pressed on the button for the second time he looked back at the other door, but this time it, too, remained closed. At last, two eyes appeared at the spyhatch in the lawyer's door, although they weren't Leni's eyes. Someone unlocked the door, but kept himself pressed against it as he called back inside, "It's him!", and only then did he open the door properly. K. pushed against the door, as behind him he could already hear the key being hurriedly turned in the lock of the door to the other flat. When the door in front of him finally opened, he stormed straight into the hallway. Through the corridor which led between the rooms he saw Leni, to whom the warning cry of the door opener had been directed, still running away in her nightshirt. He looked at her for a moment and then looked round at the person who had opened the door. It was a small, wizened man with a full beard, he held a candle in his hand. "Do you work here?" asked K. "No," answered the man, "I don't belong here at all, the lawyer is only representing me, I'm here on legal business." "Without your coat?" asked K., indicating the man's deficiency of dress with a gesture of his hand. "Oh, do forgive me!" said the man, and he looked at himself in the light of the candle he was holding as if he had not known about his appearance until then. "Is Leni your lover?" asked K. curtly. He had set his legs slightly apart, his hands, in which he held his hat, were behind his back. Merely by being in possession of a thick overcoat he felt his advantage over this thin little man. "Oh God," he said and, shocked, raised one hand in front of his face as if in defence, "no, no, what can you be thinking?" "You look honest enough," said K. with a smile, "but come along anyway." K. indicated with his hat which way the man was to go and let him go ahead of him. "What is your name then?" asked K. on the way. "Block. I'm a businessman," said the small man, twisting himself round as he thus introduced himself, although K. did not allow him to stop moving. "Is that your real name?" asked K. "Of course it is," was the man's reply, "why do you doubt it?" "I thought you might have some reason to keep your name secret," said K. He felt himself as much at liberty as is normally only felt in foreign parts when speaking with people of lower standing, keeping everything about himself to himself, speaking only casually about the interests of the other, able to raise him to a level above one's own, but also able, at will, to let him drop again. K. stopped at the door of the lawyer's office, opened it and, to the businessman who had obediently gone ahead, called, "Not so fast! Bring some light here!" K. thought Leni might have hidden in here, he let the businessman search in every corner, but the room was empty. In front of the picture of the judge K. took hold of the businessman's braces to stop him moving on. "Do you know him?" he asked, pointing upwards with his finger. The businessman lifted the candle, blinked as he looked up and said, "It's a judge." "An important judge?" asked K., and stood to the side and in front of the business-man so that he could observe what impression the picture had on him. The businessman was looking up in admiration. "He's an important judge." "You don't have much insight," said K. "He is the lowest of the lowest examining judges." "I remember now," said the businessman as he lowered the candle, "that's what I've already been told." "Well of course you have," called out K., "I'd forgotten about it, of course you would already have been told." "But why, why?" asked the businessman as he moved forwards towards the door, propelled by the hands of K. Outside in the corridor K. said, "You know where Leni's hidden, do you?" "Hidden?" said the businessman, "No, but she might be in the kitchen cook-ing soup for the lawyer." "Why didn't you say that immediate-ly?" asked K. "I was going to take you there, but you called me back again," answered the businessman, as if confused by the contradictory commands. "You think you're very clever, don't you," said K, "now take me there!" K. had never been in the kitchen, it was surprisingly big and very well equipped. The stove alone was three times bigger than normal stoves, but it was not possible to see any detail beyond this as the kitchen was at the time illuminated by no more than a small lamp hanging by the entrance. At the stove stood Leni, in a white apron as always, breaking eggs into a pot standing on a spirit lamp. "Good evening, Josef," she said with a glance sideways. "Good evening," said K., pointing with one hand to a chair in a corner which the businessman was to sit on, and he did indeed sit down on it. K. however went very close behind Leni's back, leant over her shoulder and asked, "Who is this man?" Leni put one hand around K. as she stirred the soup with the other, she drew him forward toward herself and said, "He's a pitiful character, a poor businessman by the

name of Block. Just look at him." The two of them looked
back over their shoulders. The businessman was sitting on the
chair that K. had directed him to, he had extinguished the
candle whose light was no longer needed and pressed on the
wick with his fingers to stop the smoke. "You were in your
nightshirt," said K., putting his hand on her head and turning
it back towards the stove. She was silent. "Is he your lover?"
asked K. She was about to take hold of the pot of soup, but
K. took both her hands and said, "Answer me!" She said,
"Come into the office, I'll explain everything to you." "No,"
said K., "I want you to explain it here." She put her arms
around him and wanted to kiss him. K., though, pushed her
away and said, "I don't want you to kiss me now." "Josef,"
said Leni, looking at K. imploringly but frankly in the eyes,
"you're not going to be jealous of Mr. Block now, are you?
Rudi," she then said, turning to the businessman, "help me
out will you, I'm being suspected of something, you can see
that, leave the candle alone." It had looked as though Mr.
Block had not been paying attention but he had been following closely. "I don't even know why you might be jealous," he
said ingenuously. "Nor do I, actually," said K., looking at the
businessman with a smile. Leni laughed out loud and while K.
was not paying attention took the opportunity of embracing
him and whispering, "Leave him alone, now, you can see
what sort of person he is. I've been helping him a little bit
because he's an important client of the lawyer's, and no other
reason. And what about you? Do you want to speak to the
lawyer at this time of day? He's very unwell today, but if you
want I'll tell him you're here. But you can certainly spend the
night with me. It's so long since you were last here, even the
lawyer has been asking about you. Don't neglect your case!
And I've got some things to tell you that I've learned about.
But now, before anything else, take your coat off!" She helped
him off with his coat, took the hat off his head, ran with the
things into the hallway to hang them up, then she ran back
and saw to the soup. "Do you want me to tell him you're here
straight away or take him his soup first?" "Tell him I'm here
first," said K. He was in a bad mood, he had originally in-

tended a detailed discussion of his business with Leni, especially the question of his giving the lawyer notice, but now he no longer wanted to because of the presence of the businessman. Now he considered his affair too important to let this little businessman take part in it and perhaps change some of his decisions, and so he called Leni back even though she was already on her way to the lawyer. "Bring him his soup first," he said, "I want him to get his strength up for the discussion with me, he'll need it." "You're a client of the lawyer's too, aren't you," said the businessman quietly from his corner as if he were trying to find this out. It was not, however, taken well. "What business is that of yours?" said K., and Leni said, "Will you be quiet. – I'll take him his soup first then, shall I?" And she poured the soup into a dish. "The only worry then is that he might go to sleep soon after he's eaten." "What I've got to say to him will keep him awake," said K., who still wanted to intimate that he intended some important negotiations with the lawyer, he wanted Leni to ask him what it was and only then to ask her advice. But instead, she just promptly carried out the order he had given her. When she went over to him with the dish she deliberately brushed against him and whispered, "I'll tell him you're here as soon as he's eaten the soup so that I can get you back as soon as possible." "Just go," said K., "just go." "Be a bit more friendly," she said and, still holding the dish, turned completely round once more in the doorway.

K. watched her as she went; the decision had finally been made that the lawyer was to be dismissed, it was probably better that he had not been able to discuss the matter any more with Leni beforehand; she hardly understood the complexity of the matter, she would certainly have advised him against it and perhaps would even have prevented him from dismissing the lawyer this time, he would have remained in doubt and unease and eventually have carried out his decision after a while anyway as this decision was something he could not avoid. The sooner it was carried out the more harm would be avoided. And moreover, perhaps the businessman had something to say on the matter.

K. turned round, the businessman hardly noticed it as he was about to stand up. "Stay where you are," said K. and pulled up a chair beside him. "Have you been a client of the lawyer's for a long time?" asked K. "Yes," said the businessman, "a very long time." "How many years has he been representing you so far, then?" asked K. "I don't know how you mean," said the businessman, "he's been my business lawyer – I buy and sell cereals – he's been my business lawyer since I took the business over, and that's about twenty years now, but perhaps you mean my own trial and he's been representing me in that since it started, and that's been more than five years. Yes, well over five years," he then added, pulling out an old briefcase, "I've got everything written down; I can tell you the exact dates if you like. It's so hard to remember everything. Probably, my trial's been going on much longer than that, it started soon after the death of my wife, and that's been more than five and a half years now." K. moved in closer to him. "So the lawyer takes on ordinary legal business, does he?" he asked. This combination of criminal and commercial business seemed surprisingly reassuring for K. "Oh yes," said the businessman, and then he whispered, "They even say he's more efficient in jurisprudence than he is in other matters." But then he seemed to regret saying this, and he laid a hand on K.'s shoulder and said, "Please don't betray me to him, will you." K. patted his thigh to reassure him and said, "No, I don't betray people." "He can be so vindictive, you see," said the businessman. "I'm sure he won't do anything against such a faithful client as you," said K. "Oh, he might do," said the businessman, "when he gets cross it doesn't matter who it is, and anyway, I'm not really faithful to him." "How's that then?" asked K. "I'm not sure I should tell you about it," said the businessman hesitantly. "I think it'll be alright," said K. "Well then," said the businessman, "I'll tell you about some of it, but you'll have to tell me a secret too, then we can support each other with the lawyer." "You are very careful," said K., "but I'll tell you a secret that will set your mind completely at ease. Now tell me, in what way have you been unfaithful to the lawyer?" "I've ..." said the businessman hesitantly, and in a tone as if he were confessing something dishonourable, "I've taken on other lawyers besides him." "That's not so serious," said K., a little disappointed. "It is, here," said the businessman, who had had some difficulty breathing since making his confession but who now, after hearing K.'s comment, began to feel more trust for him. "That's not allowed. And it's allowed least of all to take on petty lawyers when you've already got a proper one. And that's just what I have done, besides him I've got five petty lawyers." "Five!" exclaimed K., astonished at this number, "Five lawyers besides this one?" The businessman nodded. "I'm even negotiating with a sixth one." "But why do you need so many lawyers?" asked K. "I need all of them," said the businessman. "Would you mind explaining that to me?" asked K. "I'd be glad to," said the businessman. "Most of all, I don't want to lose my case, well that's obvious. So that means I mustn't neglect anything that might be of use to me; even if there's very little hope of a particular thing being of any use I can't just throw it away. So everything I have I've put to use in my case. I've taken all the money out of my business, for example, the offices for my business used to occupy nearly a whole floor, but now all I need is a little room at the back where I work with one apprentice. It wasn't just using up the money that caused the difficulty, of course, it was much more to do with me not working at the business as much as I used to. If you want to do something about your trial you don't have much time for anything else." "So you're also working at the court yourself?" asked K. "That's just what I want to learn more about." "I can't tell you very much about that," said the businessman, "at first I tried to do that too but I soon had to give it up again. It wears you out too much, and it's really not much use. And it turned out to be quite impossible to work there yourself and to negotiate, at least for me it was. It's a heavy strain there just sitting and waiting. You know yourself what the air is like in those offices." "How do you know I've been there, then?" asked K. "I was in the waiting room myself when you went through." "What a coincidence that is!" exclaimed K., totally engrossed and forgetting how ridiculous the businessman had seemed to him earlier. "So you saw me! You were in the waiting room when I went through. Yes, I did go through it one time." "It isn't such a big coincidence," said the businessman, "I'm there nearly every day." "I expect I'll have to go there quite often myself now," said K., "although I can hardly expect to be shown the same respect as I was then. They all stood up for me. They must have thought I was a judge." "No," said the businessman, "we were greeting the servant of the court. We knew you were a defendant. That sort of news spreads very quickly." "So you already knew about that," said K., "the way I behaved must have seemed very arrogant to you. Did you criticise me for it afterwards?" "No," said the businessman, "quite the opposite. That was just stupidity." "What do you mean, 'stupidity'?" asked K. "Why are you asking about it?" said the businessman in some irritation. "You still don't seem to know the people there and you might take it wrong. Don't forget in proceedings like this there are always lots of different things coming up to talk about, things that you just can't understand with reason alone, you just get too tired and distracted for most things and so, instead, people rely on superstition. I'm talking about the others, but I'm no better myself. One of these superstitions, for example, is that you can learn a lot about the outcome of a defendant's case by looking at his face, especially the shape of his lips. There are lots who believe that, and they said they could see from the shape of your lips that you'd definitely be found guilty very soon. I repeat that all this is just a ridiculous superstition, and in most cases it's completely disproved by the facts, but when you live in that society it's hard to hold yourself back from beliefs like that. Just think how much effect that superstition can have. You spoke to one of them there, didn't you? He was hardly able to give you an answer. There are lots of things there that can make you confused, of course, but one of them, for him, was the appearance of your lips. He told us all later he thought he could see something in your lips that meant he'd be convicted himself." "On my lips?" asked K., pulling out a pocket mirror and examining himself. "I can see nothing special about my lips. Can you?"

"Nor can I," said the businessman, "nothing at all." "These people are so superstitious!" exclaimed K. "Isn't that what I just told you?" asked the businessman. "Do you then have that much contact with each other, exchanging each other's opinions?" said K. "I've kept myself completely apart so far." "They don't normally have much contact with each other," said the businessman, "that would be impossible, there are so many of them. And they don't have much in common either. If a group of them ever thinks they have found something in common it soon turns out they were mistaken. There's nothing you can do as a group where the court's concerned. Each case is examined separately, the court is very painstaking. So there's nothing to be achieved by forming into a group, only sometimes an individual will achieve something in secret; and it's only when that's been done the others learn about it; nobody knows how it was done. So there's no sense of togetherness, you meet people now and then in the waiting rooms, but we don't talk much there. The superstitious beliefs were established a long time ago and they spread all by themselves." "I saw those gentlemen in the waiting room," said K., "it seemed so pointless for them to be waiting in that way." "Waiting is not pointless," said the businessman, "it's only pointless if you try and interfere yourself. I told you just now I've got five lawyers besides this one. You might think – I thought it myself at first – you might think I could leave the whole thing entirely up to them now. That would be entirely wrong. I can leave it up to them less than when I had just the one. Maybe you don't understand that, do you?" "No," said K., and to slow the businessman down, who had been speaking too fast, he laid his hand on the businessman's to reassure him, "but I'd like just to ask you to speak a little more slowly, these are many very important things for me, and I can't follow exactly what you're saying." "You're quite right to remind me of that," said the businessman, "you're new to all this, a junior. Your trial is six months old, isn't it? Yes, I've heard about it. Such a new case! But I've already thought all these things through countless times, to me they're the most obvious things in the world." "You must be glad your trial has already progressed so far, are you?" asked K., he did not wish to ask directly how the businessman's affairs stood, but received no clear answer anyway. "Yes, I've been working at my trial for five years now," said the businessman as his head sank, "that's no small achievement." Then he was silent for a while. K. listened to hear whether Leni was on her way back. On the one hand he did not want her to come back too soon as he still had many questions to ask and did not want her to find him in this intimate discussion with the businessman, but on the other hand it irritated him that she stayed so long with the lawyer when K. was there, much longer than she needed to give him his soup. "I still remember it exactly," the businessman began again, and K. immediately gave him his full attention, "when my case was as old as yours is now. I only had this one lawyer at that time but I wasn't very satisfied with him." Now I'll find out everything, thought K., nodding vigorously as if he could thereby encourage the businessman to say everything worth knowing. "My case," the businessman continued, "didn't move on at all, there were some hearings that took place and I went to every one of them, collected materials, handed all my business books to the court – which I later found was entirely unnecessary – I ran back and forth to the lawyer, and he submitted various documents to the court too ..." "Various documents?" asked K. "Yes, that's right," said the businessman. "That's very important for me," said K., "in my case he's still working on the first set of documents. He still hasn't done anything. I see now that he's been neglecting me quite disgracefully." "There can be lots of good reasons why the first documents still aren't ready," said the businessman, "and anyway, it turned out later on that the ones he submitted for me were entirely worthless. I even read one of them myself, one of the officials at the court was very helpful. It was very learned, but it didn't actually say anything. Most of all, there was lots of Latin, which I can't understand, then pages and pages of general appeals to the court, then lots of flattery for particular officials, they weren't named, these officials, but anyone familiar with the court must have been able to guess who they were, then there was self-praise by the lawyer where he humiliated himself to the court in a way that was downright dog-like, and then endless investigations of cases from the past which were supposed to be similar to mine. Although, as far as I was able to follow them, these investigations had been carried out very carefully. Now, I don't mean to criticise the lawyer's work with all of this, and the document I read was only one of many, but even so, and this is something I will say, at that time I couldn't see any progress in my trial at all." "And what sort of progress had you been hoping for?" asked K. "That's a very sensible question," said the businessman with a smile, "it's only very rare that you see any progress in these proceedings at all. But I didn't know that then. I'm a businessman, much more in those days than now, I wanted to see some tangible progress, it should have all been moving to some conclusion or at least should have been moving on in some way according to the rules. Instead of which there were just more hearings, and most of them went through the same things anyway; I had all the answers off pat like in a church service; there were messengers from the court coming to me at work several times a week, or they came to me at home or anywhere else they could find me; and that was very disturbing of course (but at least now things are better in that respect, it's much less disturbing when they contact you by telephone), and rumours about my trial even started to spread among some of the people I do business with, and especially my relations, so I was being made to suffer in many different ways but there was still not the slightest sign that even the first hearing would take place soon. So I went to the lawyer and complained about it. He explained it all to me at length, but refused to do anything I asked for, no-one has any influence on the way the trial proceeds, he said, to try and insist on it in any of the documents submitted – like I was asking – was simply unheard of and would do harm to both him and me. I thought to myself: What this lawyer can't or won't do another lawyer will. So I looked round for other lawyers. And before you say anything: none of them asked for a definite date for the main trial and none of them got one, and anyway, apart from one exception which I'll talk about in a minute, it really is impossible, that's one thing this lawyer didn't mislead me about; but besides, I had no reason to regret turning to other lawyers. Perhaps you've already heard how Dr. Huld talks about the petty lawyers, he probably made them sound very contemptible to you, and he's right, they are contemptible. But when he talks about them and compares them with himself and his colleagues there's a small error running through what he says, and, just for your interest, I'll tell you about it. When he talks about the lawyers he mixes with he sets them apart by calling them the 'great lawyers'. That's wrong, anyone can call himself 'great' if he wants to, of course, but in this case only the usage of the court can make that distinction. You see, the court says that besides the petty lawyers there are also minor lawyers and great lawyers. This one and his colleagues are only minor lawyers, and the difference in rank between them and the great lawyers, who I've only ever heard about and never seen, is incomparably greater than between the minor lawyers and the despised petty lawyers." "The great lawyers?" asked K. "Who are they then? How do you contact them?" "You've never heard about them, then?" said the businessman. "There's hardly anyone who's been accused who doesn't spend a lot of time dreaming about the great lawyers once he's heard about them. It's best if you don't let yourself be misled in that way. I don't know who the great lawyers are, and there's probably no way of contacting them. I don't know of any case I can talk about with certainty where they've taken any part. They do defend a lot of people, but you can't get hold of them by your own efforts, they only defend those who they want to defend. And I don't suppose they ever take on cases that haven't already got past the lower courts. Anyway, it's best not to think about them, as if you do it makes the discussions with the other lawyers, all their advice and all that they do manage to achieve, seem so unpleasant and useless, I had that experience myself, just wanted to throw everything away and lay at home in bed and hear nothing more about it. But that, of course, would be the stupidest thing you could do, and you wouldn't be left in peace in bed for very long either." "So you weren't thinking about the great lawyers at that time?" asked K. "Not for very long," said the businessman, and smiled again, "you can't forget about them entirely, I'm afraid, especially in the night when these thoughts come so easily. But I wanted immediate results in those days, so I went to the petty lawyers."

"Well look at you two sat huddled together!" called Leni as she came back with the dish and stood in the doorway. They were indeed sat close together, if either of them turned his head even slightly it would have knocked against the other's, the businessman was not only very small but also sat hunched down, so that K. was also forced to bend down low if he wanted to hear everything. "Not quite yet!" called out K., to turn Leni away, his hand, still resting on the businessman's hand, twitching with impatience. "He wanted me to tell him about my trial," said the businessman to Leni. "Carry on, then, carry on," she said. She spoke to the businessman with affection but, at the same time, with condescension. K. did not like that, he had begun to learn that the man was of some value after all, he had experience at least, and he was willing to share it. Leni was probably wrong about him. He watched her in irritation as Leni now took the candle from the businessman's hand – which he had been holding on to all this time – wiped his hand with her apron and then knelt beside him to scratch off some wax that had dripped from the candle onto his trousers. "You were about to tell me about the petty lawyers," said K., shoving Leni's hand away with no further comment. "What's wrong with you today?" asked Leni, tapped him gently and carried on with what she had been doing. "Yes, the petty lawyers," said the businessman, putting his hand to his brow as if thinking hard. K. wanted to help him and said, "You wanted immediate results and so went to the petty lawyers." "Yes, that's right," said the businessman, but did not continue with what he'd been saying. "Maybe he doesn't want to speak about it in front of Leni," thought K., suppressing his impatience to hear the rest straight away, and stopped trying to press him.

"Have you told him I'm here?" he asked Leni. "Course I have," she said, "he's waiting for you. Leave Block alone now, you can talk to Block later, he'll still be here." K. still hesitated. "You'll still be here?" he asked the businessman, wanting to hear the answer from him and not wanting Leni to speak about the businessman as if he weren't there, he was full of secret resentment towards Leni today. And once more it was only Leni who answered. "He often sleeps here." "He sleeps here?" exclaimed K., he had thought the businessman would just wait there for him while he quickly settled his business with the lawyer, and then they would leave together to discuss everything thoroughly and undisturbed. "Yes," said Leni, "not everyone's like you, Josef, allowed to see the lawyer at any time you like. Do don't even seem surprised that the lawyer, despite being ill, still receives you at eleven o'clock at night. You take it far too much for granted, what your friends do for you. Well, your friends, or at least I do, we like to do things for you. I don't want or need any more thanks than that you're fond of me." "Fond of you?" thought K. at first, and only then it occurred to him, "Well, yes, I am fond of her." Nonetheless, what he said, forgetting all the rest, was, "He receives me because I am his client. If I needed anyone else's help I'd have to beg and show gratitude whenever I do anything." "He's really nasty today, isn't he?" Leni asked the businessman. "Now it's me who's not here," thought K., and nearly lost his temper with the businessman when, with the same rudeness as Leni, he said, "The lawyer also has other reasons to receive him. His case is much more interesting than mine. And it's only in its early stages too, it probably hasn't progressed very far so the lawyer still likes to deal with him. That'll all change later on." "Yeah, yeah," said Leni, looking at the businessman and laughing. "He doesn't half talk!" she said, turning to face K. "You can't believe a word he says. He's as talkative as he is sweet. Maybe that's why the lawyer can't stand him. At least, he only sees him when he's in the right mood. I've already tried hard to change that but it's impossible. Just think, there are times when I tell him Block's here and he doesn't receive him until three days later. And if

Block isn't on the spot when he's called then everything's lost and it all has to start all over again. That's why I let Block sleep here, it wouldn't be the first time Dr. Huld has wanted to see him in the night. So now Block is ready for that. Sometimes, when he knows Block is still here, he'll even change his mind about letting him in to see him." K. looked questioningly at the businessman. The latter nodded and, although he had spoken quite openly with K. earlier, seemed to be confused with shame as he said, "Yes, later on you become very dependent on your lawyer." "He's only pretending to mind," said Leni. "He likes to sleep here really, he's often said so." She went over to a little door and shoved it open. "Do you want to see his bedroom?" she asked. K. went over to the low, windowless room and looked in from the doorway. The room contained a narrow bed which filled it completely, so that to get into the bed you would need to climb over the bedpost. At the head of the bed there was a niche in the wall where, fastidiously tidy, stood a candle, a bottle of ink, and a pen with a bundle of papers which were probably to do with the trial. "You sleep in the maid's room?" asked K., as he went back to the businessman. "Leni's let me have it," answered the businessman, "it has many advantages." K. looked long at him; his first impression of the businessman had perhaps not been right; he had experience as his trial had already lasted a long time, but he had paid a heavy price for this experience. K. was suddenly unable to bear the sight of the businessman any longer. "Bring him to bed, then!" he called out to Leni, who seemed to understand him. For himself, he wanted to go to the lawyer and, by dismissing him, free himself from not only the lawyer but also from Leni and the businessman. But before he had reached the door the businessman spoke to him gently. "Excuse me, sir," he said, and K. looked round crossly. "You've forgotten your promise," said the businessman, stretching his hand out to K. imploringly from where he sat. "You were going to tell me a secret." "That is true," said K., as he glanced at Leni, who was watching him carefully, to check on her. "So listen; it's hardly a secret now anyway. I'm going to see the lawyer now to sack him." "He's sacking him!" yelled the businessman, and he jumped up from his chair and ran around the kitchen with his arms in the air. He kept on shouting, "He's sacking his lawyer!" Leni tried to rush at K. but the businessman got in her way so that she shoved him away with her fists. Then, still with her hands balled into fists, she ran after K. who, however, had been given a long start. He was already inside the lawyer's room by the time Leni caught up with him. He had almost closed the door behind himself, but Leni held the door open with her foot, grabbed his arm and tried to pull him back. But he put such pressure on her wrist that, with a sigh, she was forced to release him. She did not dare go into the room straight away, and K. locked the door with the key.

"I've been waiting for you a very long time," said the lawyer from his bed. He had been reading something by the light of a candle but now he laid it onto the bedside table and put his glasses on, looking at K. sharply through them. Instead of apologising K. said, "I'll be leaving again soon." As he had not apologised the lawyer ignored what K. said, and replied, "I won't let you in this late again next time." "I find that quite acceptable," said K. The lawyer looked at him quizzically. "Sit down," he said. "As you wish," said K., drawing a chair up to the bedside table and sitting down. "It seemed to me that you locked the door," said the lawyer. "Yes," said K., "it was because of Leni." He had no intention of letting anyone off lightly. But the lawyer asked him, "Was she being importunate again?" "Importunate?" asked K. "Yes," said the lawyer, laughing as he did so, had a fit of coughing and then, once it had passed, began to laugh again. "I'm sure you must have noticed how importunate she can be sometimes," he said, and patted K.'s hand which K. had rested on the bedside table and which he now snatched back. "You don't attach much importance to it, then," said the lawyer when K. was silent, "so much the better. Otherwise I might have needed to apologise to you. It is a peculiarity of Leni's. I've long since forgiven her for it, and I wouldn't be talking of it now, if you hadn't locked the door just now. Anyway, perhaps I should at least explain this peculiarity of hers to you, but you seem rather disturbed, the way you're looking at me, and so that's why I'll do it, this peculiarity of hers consists in this; Leni finds most of the accused attractive. She attaches herself to each of them, loves each of them, even seems to be loved by each of them; then she sometimes entertains me by telling me about them when I allow her to. I am not so astonished by all of this as you seem to be. If you look at them in the right way the accused really can be attractive, quite often. But that is a remarkable and to some extent scientific phenomenon. Being indicted does not cause any clear, precisely definable change in a person's appearance, of course. But it's not like with other legal matters, most of them remain in their usual way of life and, if they have a good lawyer looking after them, the trial doesn't get in their way. But there are nonetheless those who have experience in these matters who can look at a crowd, however big, and tell you which among them is facing a charge. How can they do that, you will ask. My answer will not please you. It is simply that those who are facing a charge are the most attractive. It cannot be their guilt that makes them attractive as not all of them are guilty – at least that's what I, as a lawyer, have to say – and nor can it be the proper punishment that has made them attractive as not all of them are punished, so it can only be that the proceedings levelled against them take some kind of hold on them. Whatever the reason, some of these attractive people are indeed very attractive. But all of them are attractive, even Block, pitiful worm that he is." As the lawyer finished what he was saying, K. was fully in control of himself, he had even nodded conspicuously at his last few words in order to confirm to himself the view he had already formed; that the lawyer was trying to confuse him, as he always did, by making general and irrelevant observations, and thus distract him from the main question of what he was actually doing for K.'s trial. The lawyer must have noticed that K. was offering him more resistance than before, as he became silent, giving K. the chance to speak himself, and then, as K. also remained silent, he asked, "Did you have a particular reason for coming to see me today?" "Yes," said K., putting his hand up to slightly shade his eyes from the light of the candle so that he could see the lawyer better, "I wanted to tell you that I'm withdrawing my representation from you, with immediate effect." "Do I understand you rightly?" asked the lawyer as he half raised himself in his bed and supported himself with one hand on the pillow. "I think you do," said K., sitting stiffly upright as if waiting in ambush. "Well we can certainly discuss this plan of yours," said the lawyer after a pause. "It's not a plan any more," said K. "That may be," said the lawyer, "but we still mustn't rush anything." He used the word 'we', as if he had no intention of letting K. go free, and as if, even if he could no longer represent him, he could still at least continue as his adviser. "Nothing is being rushed," said K., standing slowly up and going behind his chair, "everything has been well thought out and probably even for too long. The decision is final." "Then allow me to say a few words," said the lawyer, throwing the bed cover to one side and sitting on the edge of the bed. His naked, white-haired legs shivered in the cold. He asked K. to pass him a blanket from the couch. K. passed him the blanket and said, "You are running the risk of catching cold for no reason." "The circumstances are important enough," said the lawyer as he wrapped the bed cover around the top half of his body and then the blanket around his legs. "Your uncle is my friend and in the course of time I've become fond of you as well. I admit that quite openly. There's nothing in that for me to be ashamed of." It was very unwelcome for K. to hear the old man speak in this touching way, as it forced him to explain himself more fully, which he would rather have avoided, and he was aware that it also confused him even though it could never make him reverse his decision. "Thank you for feeling so friendly toward me," he said, "and I also realise how deeply involved you've been in my case, as deeply as possible for yourself and to bring as much advantage as possible to me. Nonetheless, I have recently come to the conviction that it is not enough. I would naturally never attempt, considering that you are so much older and more experienced than I am, to convince you of my opinion; if I have ever unintentionally done so then I beg your forgiveness, but, as you have just said yourself, the circumstances are important enough and it is my belief that my trial needs to be approached with much more vigour than has so far been the case." "I see," said the lawyer, "you've become impatient." "I am not impatient," said K., with some irritation and he stopped paying so much attention to his choice of words. "When I first came here with my uncle you probably noticed I wasn't greatly concerned about my case, and if I wasn't reminded of it by force, as it were, I would forget about it completely. But my uncle insisted I should allow you to represent me and I did so as a favour to him. I could have expected the case to be less of a burden than it had been, as the point of taking on a lawyer is that he should take on some of its weight. But what actually happened was the opposite. Before, the trial was never such a worry for me as it has been since you've been representing me. When I was by myself I never did anything about my case, I was hardly aware of it, but then, once there was someone representing me, everything was set for something to happen, I was always, without cease, waiting for you to do something, getting more and more tense, but you did nothing. I did get some information about the court from you that I probably could not have got anywhere else, but that can't be enough when the trial, supposedly in secret, is getting closer and closer to me." K. had pushed the chair away and stood erect, his hands in the pockets of his frock coat. "After a certain point in the proceedings," said the lawyer quietly and calmly, "nothing new of any importance ever happens. So many litigants, at the same stage in their trials, have stood before me just like you are now and spoken in the same way." "Then these other litigants," said K., "have all been right, just as I am. That does not show that I'm not." "I wasn't trying to show that you were mistaken," said the lawyer, "but I wanted to add that I expected better judgement from you than from the others, especially as I've given you more insight into the workings of the court and my own activities than I normally do. And now I'm forced to accept that, despite everything, you have too little trust in me. You don't make it easy for me." How the lawyer was humiliating himself to K.! He was showing no regard for the dignity of his position, which on this point, must have been at its most sensitive. And why did he do that? He did seem to be very busy as a lawyer as well a rich man, neither the loss of income nor the loss of a client could have been of much importance to him in themselves. He was moreover unwell and should have been thinking of passing work on to others. And despite all that he held on tightly to K. Why? Was it something personal for his uncle's sake, or did he really see K.'s case as one that was exceptional and hoped to be able to distinguish himself with it, either for K.'s sake or – and this possibility could never be excluded – for his friends at the court? It was not possible to learn anything by looking at him, even though K. was scrutinizing him quite brazenly. It could almost be supposed he was deliberately hiding his thoughts as he waited to see what effect his words would have. But he clearly deemed K.'s silence to be favourable for himself and he continued, "You will have noticed the size of my office, but that I don't employ any staff to help me. That used to be quite different, there was a time when several young lawyers were working for me but now I work alone. This is partly to do with changes in the way I do business, in that I concentrate nowadays more and more on matters such as your own case, and partly to do with the ever deeper understanding that I acquire from these legal matters. I found that I could never let anyone else deal with this sort of work unless I wanted to harm both the client and the job I had taken on. But the decision to do all the work myself had its obvious result: I was forced to turn almost everyone away who asked me to represent them and could only accept those I was especially interested in – well there are enough creatures who leap at every crumb I throw down, and they're not so very far away. Most importantly, I became ill from over-work. But despite that I don't regret my decision, quite possibly I should have turned more cases away than I did, but it did turn out to be entirely necessary for me to devote myself fully to the cases I did take on, and the successful results showed that it was worth it. I once read a description of the difference between representing someone in ordinary legal matters and in legal matters of this sort, and the writer expressed it very well. This is what he said: some lawyers lead their clients on a thread until judgement is passed, but there are others who immediately lift their clients onto their shoulders and carry them all the way to the judgement and beyond. That's just how it is. But it was quite true when I said I never regret all this work. But if, as in your case, they are so fully misunderstood, well, then I come very close to regretting it." All this talking did more to make K. impatient than to persuade him. From the way the lawyer was speaking, K. thought he could hear what he could expect if he gave in, the delays and excuses would begin again, reports of how the documents were progressing, how the mood of the court officials had improved, as well as all the enormous difficulties – in short all that he had heard so many times before would be brought out again even more fully, he would try to mislead K. with hopes that were never specified and to make him suffer with threats that were never clear. He had to put a stop to that, so he said, "What will you undertake on my behalf if you continue to represent me?" The lawyer quietly accepted even this insulting question, and answered, "I should continue with what I've already been doing for you." "That's just what I thought," said K., "and now you don't need to say another word." "I will make one more attempt," said the lawyer as if whatever had been making K. so annoyed was affecting him too. "You see, I have the impression that you have not only misjudged the legal assistance I have given you but also that that misjudgement has led you to behave in this way, you seem, although you are the accused, to have been treated too well or, to put it a better way, handled with neglect, with apparent neglect. Even that has its reason; it is often better to be in chains than to be free. But I would like to show you how other defendants are treated, perhaps you will succeed in learning something from it. What I will do is I will call Block in, unlock the door and sit down here beside the bedside table." "Be glad to," said K., and did as the lawyer suggested; he was always ready to learn something new. But to make sure of himself for any event he added, "but you do realise that you are no longer to be my lawyer, don't you?" "Yes," said the lawyer. "But you can still change your mind today if you want to." He lay back down in the bed, pulled the quilt up to his chin and turned to face the wall. Then he rang.

Leni appeared almost the moment he had done so. She looked hurriedly at K. and the lawyer to try and find out what had happened; she seemed to be reassured by the sight of K. sitting calmly at the lawyer's bed. She smiled and nodded to K., K. looked blankly back at her. "Fetch Block," said the lawyer. But instead of going to fetch him, Leni just went to the door and called out, "Block! To the lawyer!" Then, probably because the lawyer had turned his face to the wall and was paying no attention, she slipped in behind K.'s chair. From then on, she bothered him by leaning forward over the back of the chair or, albeit very tenderly and carefully, she would run her hands through his hair and over his cheeks. K. eventually tried to stop her by taking hold of one hand, and after some resistance Leni let him keep hold of it. Block came as soon as he was called, but he remained standing in the doorway and seemed to be wondering whether he should enter or not. He raised his eyebrows and lowered his head as if listening to find out whether the order to attend the lawyer would be repeated. K. could have encouraged to enter, but he had decided to make a final break not only with the lawyer but with everything in his home, so he kept himself motionless. Leni was also silent. Block noticed that at least no-one was chasing him away, and, on tiptoe, he entered the room, his face was tense, his hands were clenched behind his back. He left the door open in case he needed to go back again. K. did not even glance at him, he looked instead only at the thick quilt under which the lawyer could not be seen as he had squeezed up very close to the wall. Then his voice was heard: "Block here?" he asked. Block had already crept some way into the room but this question seemed to give him first a shove in the breast and then another in the back, he seemed about to fall but remained standing, deeply bowed, and said, "At your service, sir." "What do you want?" asked the lawyer, "you've come at a bad time." "Wasn't I summoned?" asked

Block, more to himself than the lawyer. He held his hands in front of himself as protection and would have been ready to run away any moment. "You were summoned," said the lawyer, "but you have still come at a bad time." Then, after a pause he added, "You always come at a bad time." When the lawyer started speaking Block had stopped looking at the bed but stared rather into one of the corners, just listening, as if the light from the speaker were brighter than Block could bear to look at. But it was also difficult for him to listen, as the lawyer was speaking into the wall and speaking quickly and quietly. "Would you like me to go away again, sir?" asked Block. "Well you're here now," said the lawyer. "Stay!" It was as if the lawyer had not done as Block had wanted but instead threatened him with a stick, as now Block really began to shake. "I went to see," said the lawyer, "the third judge yesterday, a friend of mine, and slowly brought the conversation round to the subject of you. Do you want to know what he said?" "Oh, yes please," said Block. The lawyer did not answer immediately, so Block repeated his request and lowered his head as if about to kneel down. But then K. spoke to him: "What do you think you're doing?" he shouted. Leni had wanted to stop him from calling out and so he took hold of her other hand. It was not love that made him squeeze it and hold on to it so tightly, she sighed frequently and tried to disengage her hands from him. But Block was punished for K.'s outburst, as the lawyer asked him, "Who is your lawyer?" "You are, sir," said Block. "And who besides me?" the lawyer asked. "No-one besides you, sir," said Block. "And let there be no-one besides me," said the lawyer. Block fully understood what that meant, he glowered at K., shaking his head violently. If these actions had been translated into words they would have been coarse insults. K. had been friendly and willing to discuss his own case with someone like this! "I won't disturb you any more," said K., leaning back in his chair. "You can kneel down or creep on all fours, whatever you like. I won't bother with you any more." But Block still had some sense of pride, at least where K. was concerned, and he went towards him waving his fists, shouting as loudly as he dared while the lawyer was there. "You shouldn't speak to me like that, that's not allowed. Why are you insulting me? Especially here in front of the lawyer, where both of us, you and me, we're only tolerated because of his charity. You're not a better person than me, you've been accused of something too, you're facing a charge too. If, in spite of that, you're still a gentleman then I'm just as much a gentleman as you are, if not even more so. And I want to be spoken to as a gentleman, especially by you. If you think being allowed to sit there and quietly listen while I creep on all fours as you put it makes you something better than me, then there's an old legal saying you ought to bear in mind: If you're under suspicion it's better to be moving than still, as if you're still you can be in the pan of the scales without knowing it and be weighed along with your sins." K. said nothing. He merely looked in amazement at this distracted being, his eyes completely still. He had gone through such changes in just the last few hours! Was it the trial that was throwing him from side to side in this way and stopped him knowing who was friend and who was foe? Could he not see the lawyer was deliberately humiliating him and had no other purpose today than to show off his power to K., and perhaps even thereby subjugate K.? But if Block was incapable of seeing that, or if he so feared the lawyer that no such insight would even be of any use to him, how was it that he was either so sly or so bold as to lie to the lawyer and conceal from him the fact that he had other lawyers working on his behalf? And how did he dare to attack K., who could betray his secret any time he liked? But he dared even more than this, he went to the lawyer's bed and began there to make complaints about K. "Dr. Huld, sir," he said, "did you hear the way this man spoke to me? You can count the length of his trial in hours, and he wants to tell me what to do when I've been involved in a legal case for five years. He even insults me. He doesn't know anything, but he insults me, when I, as far as my weak ability allows, when I've made a close study of how to behave with the court, what we ought to do and what the court practices are." "Don't let anyone bother you," said the lawyer, "and do what seems to you to be right." "I will," said Block, as if speaking to himself to give himself courage, and with a quick glance to the side he kneeled down close beside the bed. "I'm kneeling now Dr. Huld, sir," he said. But the lawyer remained silent. With one hand, Block carefully stroked the bed cover. In the silence while he did so, Leni, as she freed herself from K.'s hands, said, "You're hurting me. Let go of me. I'm going over to Block." She went over to him and sat on the edge of the bed. Block was very pleased at this and with lively, but silent, gestures he immediately urged her to intercede for him with the lawyer. It was clear that he desperately needed to be told something by the lawyer, although perhaps only so that he could make use of the information with his other lawyers. Leni probably knew very well how the lawyer could be brought round, pointed to his hand and pursed her lips as if making a kiss. Block immediately performed the hand-kiss and, at further urging from Leni, repeated it twice more. But the lawyer continued to be silent. Then Leni leant over the lawyer, as she stretched out, the attractive shape of her body could be seen, and, bent over close to his face, she stroked his long white hair. That now forced him to give an answer. "I'm rather wary of telling him," said the lawyer, and his head could be seen shaking slightly, perhaps so that he would feel the pressure of Leni's hand better. Block listened closely with his head lowered, as if by listening he were breaking an order. "What makes you so wary about it?" asked Leni. K. had the feeling he was listening to a contrived dialogue that had been repeated many times, that would be repeated many times more, and that for Block alone it would never lose its freshness. "What has his behaviour been like today?" asked the lawyer instead of an answer. Before Leni said anything she looked down at Block and watched him a short while as he raised his hands towards her and rubbed them together imploringly. Finally she gave a serious nod, turned back to the lawyer and said, "He's been quiet and industrious." This was an elderly businessman, a man whose beard was long, and he was begging a young girl to speak on his behalf. Even if there was some plan behind what he did, there was nothing that could reinstate him in the eyes of his fellow man. K. could not understand how the lawyer could have thought this performance would win him over. Even if he had done nothing earlier to make him want to leave then this scene would have done so. It was almost humiliating even for the onlooker. So these were the lawyer's methods, which K. fortunately had not been exposed to for long, to let the client forget about the whole world and leave him with nothing but the hope of reaching the end of his trial by this deluded means. He was no longer a client, he was the lawyer's dog. If the lawyer had ordered him to crawl under the bed as if it were a kennel and to bark out from under it, then he would have done so with enthusiasm. K. listened to all of this, testing it and thinking it over as if he had been given the task of closely observing everything spoken here, inform a higher office about it and write a report. "And what has he been doing all day?" asked the lawyer. "I kept him locked in the maid's room all day," said Leni, "so that he wouldn't stop me doing my work. That's where he usually stays. From time to time I looked in through the spyhole to see what he was doing, and each time he was kneeling on the bed and reading the papers you gave him, propped up on the window sill. That made a good impression on me; as the window only opens onto an air shaft and gives hardly any light. It showed how obedient he is that he was even reading in those conditions." "I'm pleased to hear it," said the lawyer. "But did he understand what he was reading?" While this conversation was going on, Block continually moved his lips and was clearly formulating the answers he hoped Leni would give. "Well I can't give you any certain answer to that of course," said Leni, "but I could see that he was reading thoroughly. He spent all day reading the same page, running his finger along the lines. Whenever I looked in on him he sighed as if this reading was a lot of work for him. I expect the papers you gave him were very hard to understand." "Yes," said the lawyer, "they certainly are that. And I really don't think he understood anything of them. But they should at least give him some inkling of just how hard a struggle it is and how much work it is for me to defend him.

And who am I doing all this hard work for? I'm doing it – it's laughable even to say it – I'm doing it for Block. He ought to realise what that means, too. Did he study without a pause?" "Almost without a pause," answered Leni. "Just the once he asked me for a drink of water, so I gave him a glassful through the window. Then at eight o'clock I let him out and gave him something to eat." Block glanced sideways at K., as if he were being praised and had to impress K. as well. He now seemed more optimistic, he moved more freely and rocked back and forth on his knees. This made his astonishment all the more obvious when he heard the following words from the lawyer: "You speak well of him," said the lawyer, "but that's just what makes it difficult for me. You see, the judge did not speak well of him at all, neither about Block nor about his case." "Didn't speak well of him?" asked Leni. "How is that possible?" Block looked at her with such tension he seemed to think that although the judge's words had been spoken so long before she would be able to change them in his favour. "Not at all," said the lawyer. "In fact he became quite cross when I started to talk about Block to him. 'Don't talk to me about Block,' he said. 'He is my client,' said I. 'You're letting him abuse you,' he said. 'I don't think his case is lost yet,' said I. 'You're letting him abuse you,' he repeated. 'I don't think so,' said I. 'Block works hard in his case and always knows where it stands. He practically lives with me so that he always knows what's happening. You don't always find such enthusiasm as that. He's not very pleasant personally, I grant you, his manners are terrible and he's dirty, but as far as the trial's concerned he's quite immaculate.' I said immaculate, but I was deliberately exaggerating. Then he said, 'Block is sly, that's all. He's accumulated plenty of experience and knows how to delay proceedings. But there's more that he doesn't know than he does. What do you think he'd say if he learned his trial still hasn't begun, if you told him they haven't even rung the bell to announce the start of proceedings?' Alright Block, alright," said the lawyer, as at these words Block had begun to raise himself on his trembling knees and clearly wanted to plead for some explanation. It was the first time the lawyer had spoken any clear words directly to Block. He looked down with his tired eyes, half blankly and half at Block, who slowly sank back down on his knees under this gaze. "What the judge said has no meaning for you," said the lawyer. "You needn't be frightened at every word. If you do it again I won't tell you anything else at all. It's impossible to start a sentence without you looking at me as if you were receiving your final judgement. You should be ashamed of yourself here in front of my client! And you're destroying the trust he has for me. Just what is it you want? You're still alive, you're still under my protection. There's no point in worrying! Somewhere you've read that the final judgement can often come without warning, from anyone at any time. And, in the right circumstances, that's basically true, but it's also true that I dislike your anxiety and fear and see that you don't have the trust in me you should have. Now what have I just said? I repeated something said by one of the judges. You know that there are so many various opinions about the procedure that they form into a great big pile and nobody can make any sense of them. This judge, for instance, sees proceedings as starting at a different point from where I do. A difference of opinion, nothing more. At a certain stage in the proceedings tradition has it that a sign is given by ringing a bell. This judge sees that as the point at which proceedings begin. I can't set out all the opinions opposed to that view here, and you wouldn't understand it anyway, suffice it to say that there are many reasons to disagree with him." Embarrassed, Block ran his fingers through the pile of the carpet, his anxiety about what the judge had said had let him forget his inferior status towards the lawyer for a while, he thought only about himself and turned the judges words round to examine them from all sides. "Block," said Leni, as if reprimanding him, and, taking hold of the collar of his coat, pulled him up slightly higher. "Leave the carpet alone and listen to what the lawyer is saying."

This chapter was left unfinished.

Chapter Nine
In the Cathedral

A very important Italian business contact of the bank had come to visit the city for the first time and K. was given the task of showing him some of its cultural sights. At any other time he would have seen this job as an honour but now, when he was finding it hard even to maintain his current position in the bank, he accepted it only with reluctance. Every hour that he could not be in the office was a cause of concern for him, he was no longer able to make use of his time in the office anything like as well as he had previously, he spent many hours merely pretending to do important work, but that only increased his anxiety about not being in the office. Then he sometimes thought he saw the deputy director, who was always watching, come into K.'s office, sit at his desk, look through his papers, receive clients who had almost become old friends of K., and lure them away from him, perhaps he even discovered mistakes, mistakes that seemed to threaten K. from a thousand directions when he was at work now, and which he could no longer avoid. So now, if he was ever asked to leave the office on business or even needed to make a short business trip, however much an honour it seemed – and tasks of this sort happened to have increased substantially recently – there was always the suspicion that they wanted to get him out of his office for a while and check his work, or at least the idea that they thought he was dispensable. It would not have been difficult for him to turn down most of these jobs, but he did not dare to do so because, if his fears had the slightest foundation, turning the jobs down would have been an acknowledgement of them. For this reason, he never demurred from accepting them, and even when he was asked to go on a tiring business trip lasting two days he said nothing about having to go out in the rainy autumn weather when he had a severe chill, just in order to avoid the risk of not being asked to go. When, with a raging headache, he arrived back from this trip he learned that he had been chosen to accompany the Italian business contact the following day. The temptation for once to turn the job down was very great, especially as it had no direct connection with business, but there was no denying that social obligations towards this business contact were in themselves important enough, only not for K., who knew quite well that he needed some successes at work if he was to maintain his position there and that, if he failed in that, it would not help him even if this Italian somehow found him quite charming; he did not want to be removed from his workplace for even one day, as the fear of not being allowed back in was too great, he knew full well that the fear was exaggerated but it still made him anxious. However, in this case it was almost impossible to think of an acceptable excuse, his knowledge of Italian was not great but still good enough; the deciding factor was that K. had earlier known a little about art history and this had become widely known around the bank in extremely exaggerated form, and that K. had been a member of the Society for the Preservation of City Monuments, albeit only for business reasons. It was said that this Italian was an art lover, so the choice of K. to accompany him was a matter of course.

It was a very rainy and stormy morning when K., in a foul temper at the thought of the day ahead of him, arrived early at seven o'clock in the office so that he could at least do some work before his visitor would prevent him. He had spent half the night studying a book of Italian grammar so that he would be somewhat prepared and was very tired; his desk was less attractive to him than the window where he had spent far too much time sitting of late, but he resisted the temptation and sat down to his work. Unfortunately, just then the servitor came in and reported that the director had sent him to see whether the chief clerk was already in his office; if he was, then would he please be so kind as to come to his reception room as the gentleman from Italy was already there. "I'll come straight away," said K. He put a small dictionary in his pocket, took a guide to the city's tourist sites under his arm that he had compiled for strangers, and went through the deputy director's office into that of the director. He was glad he had come into the office so early and was able to be of service immediately, nobody could seriously have expected that of him. The deputy director's office was, of course, still as empty as the middle of the night, the servitor had probably been asked to summon him too but without success. As K. entered the reception room two men stood up from the deep armchairs where they had been sitting. The director gave him a friendly smile, he was clearly very glad that K. was there, he immediately introduced him to the Italian who shook K.'s hand vigorously and joked that somebody was an early riser. K. did not quite understand whom he had in mind, it was moreover an odd expression to use and it took K. a little while to guess its meaning. He replied with a few bland phrases which the Italian received once more with a laugh, passing his hand nervously and repeatedly over his blue-grey, bushy moustache. This moustache was obviously perfumed, it was almost tempting to come close to it and sniff. When they had all sat down and begun a light preliminary conversation, K. was disconcerted to notice that he understood no more than fragments of what the Italian said. When he spoke very calmly he understood almost everything, but that was very infrequent, mostly the words gushed from his mouth and he seemed to be enjoying himself so much his head shook. When he was talking in this way his speech was usually wrapped up in some kind of dialect which seemed to K. to have nothing to do with Italian but which the director not only understood but also spoke, although K. ought to have foreseen this as the Italian came from the south of his country where the director had also spent several years. Whatever the cause, K. realised that the possibility of communicating with the Italian had been largely taken from him, even his French was difficult to understand, and his moustache concealed the movements of his lips which might have offered some help in understanding what he said. K. began to anticipate many difficulties, he gave up trying to understand what the Italian said – with the director there, who could understand him so easily, it would have been pointless effort – and for the time being did no more than scowl at the Italian as he relaxed sitting deep but comfortable in the armchair, as he frequently

pulled at his short, sharply tailored jacket and at one time
lifted his arms in the air and moved his hands freely to try and
depict something that K. could not grasp, even though he was
leaning forward and did not let the hands out of his sight. K.
had nothing to occupy himself but mechanically watch the
exchange between the two men and his tiredness finally made
itself felt, to his alarm, although fortunately in good time, he
once caught himself nearly getting up, turning round and
leaving. Eventually the Italian looked at the clock and jumped
up. After taking his leave from the director he turned to K.,
pressing himself so close to him that K. had to push his chair
back just so that he could move. The director had, no doubt,
seen the anxiety in K.'s eyes as he tried to cope with this
dialect of Italian, he joined in with this conversation in a way
that was so adroit and unobtrusive that he seemed to be add-
ing no more than minor comments, whereas in fact he was
swiftly and patiently breaking into what the Italian said so that
K. could understand. K. learned in this way that the Italian
first had a few business matters to settle, that he unfortunately
had only a little time at his disposal, that he certainly did not
intend to rush round to see every monument in the city, that
he would much rather – at least as long as K. would agree, it
was entirely his decision – just see the cathedral and to do so
thoroughly. He was extremely pleased to be accompanied by
someone who was so learned and so pleasant – by this he
meant K., who was occupied not with listening to the Italian
but the director – and asked if he would be so kind, if the
time was suitable, to meet him in the cathedral in two hours'
time at about ten o'clock. He hoped he would certainly be
able to be there at that time. K. made an appropriate reply,
the Italian shook first the director's hand and then K.'s, then
the director's again and went to the door, half turned to the
two men who followed him and continuing to talk without a
break. K. remained together with the director for a short
while, although the director looked especially unhappy today.
He thought he needed to apologise to K. for something and
told him – they were standing intimately close together – he
had thought at first he would accompany the Italian himself,

but then – he gave no more precise reason than this – then he decided it would be better to send K. with him. He should not be surprised if he could not understand the Italian at first, he would be able to very soon, and even if he really could not understand very much he said it was not so bad, as it was really not so important for the Italian to be understood. And anyway, K.'s knowledge of Italian was surprisingly good, the director was sure he would get by very well. And with that, it was time for K. to go. He spent the time still remaining to him with a dictionary, copying out obscure words he would need to guide the Italian round the cathedral. It was an extremely irksome task, servitors brought him the mail, bank staff came with various queries and, when they saw that K. was busy, stood by the door and did not go away until he had listened to them, the deputy director did not miss the opportunity to disturb K. and came in frequently, took the dictionary from his hand and flicked through its pages, clearly for no purpose, when the door to the ante-room opened even clients would appear from the half darkness and bow timidly to him – they wanted to attract his attention but were not sure whether he had seen them – all this activity was circling around K. with him at its centre while he compiled the list of words he would need, then looked them up in the dictionary, then wrote them out, then practised their pronunciation and finally tried to learn them by heart. The good intentions he had had earlier, though, seemed to have left him completely, it was the Italian who had caused him all this effort and sometimes he became so angry with him that he buried the dictionary under some papers firmly intending to do no more preparation, but then he realised he could not walk up and down in the cathedral with the Italian without saying a word, so, in an even greater rage, he pulled the dictionary back out again.

At exactly half past nine, just when he was about to leave, there was a telephone call for him, Leni wished him good morning and asked how he was, K. thanked her hurriedly and told her it was impossible for him to talk now as he had to go to the cathedral. "To the cathedral?" asked Leni. "Yes, to the cathedral." "What do you have to go to the cathedral for?" said Leni. K. tried to explain it to her briefly, but he had hardly begun when Leni suddenly said, "They're harassing you." One thing that K. could not bear was pity that he had not wanted or expected, he took his leave of her with two words, but as he put the receiver back in its place he said, half to himself and half to the girl on the other end of the line who could no longer hear him, "Yes, they're harassing me."

By now the time was late and there was almost a danger he would not be on time. He took a taxi to the cathedral, at the last moment he had remembered the album that he had had no opportunity to give to the Italian earlier and so took it with him now. He held it on his knees and drummed impatiently on it during the whole journey. The rain had eased off slightly but it was still damp chilly and dark, it would be difficult to see anything in the cathedral but standing about on cold flagstones might well make K.'s chill much worse. The square in front of the cathedral was quite empty, K. remembered how even as a small child he had noticed that nearly all the houses in this narrow square had the curtains at their windows closed most of the time, although today, with the weather like this, it was more understandable. The cathedral also seemed quite empty, of course no-one would think of going there on a day like this. K. hurried along both the side naves but saw no-one but an old woman who, wrapped up in a warm shawl, was kneeling at a picture of the Virgin Mary and staring up at it. Then, in the distance, he saw a church official who limped away through a doorway in the wall. K. had arrived on time, it had struck ten just as he was entering the building, but the Italian still was not there. K. went back to the main entrance, stood there indecisively for a while, and then walked round the cathedral in the rain in case the Italian was waiting at another entrance. He was nowhere to be found. Could the director have misunderstood what time they had agreed on? How could anyone understand someone like that properly anyway? Whatever had happened, K. would have to wait for him for at least half an hour. As he was tired he wanted to sit down, he went back inside the cathedral, he found something like a small carpet on one of the steps, he moved it with his foot to a nearby pew, wrapped himself up tighter in his coat, put the collar up and sat down. To pass the time he opened the album and flicked through the pages a little but soon had to give up as it became so dark that when he looked up he could hardly make out anything in the side nave next to him.

In the distance there was a large triangle of candles flickering on the main altar, K. was not certain whether he had seen them earlier. Perhaps they had only just been lit. Church staff creep silently as part of their job, you don't notice them. When K. happened to turn round he also saw a tall, stout candle attached to a column not far behind him. It was all very pretty, but totally inadequate to illuminate the pictures which were usually left in the darkness of the side altars, and seemed to make the darkness all the deeper. It was discourteous of the Italian not to come but it was also sensible of him, there would have been nothing to see, they would have had to content themselves with seeking out a few pictures with K.'s electric pocket torch and looking at them one small part at a time. K. went over to a nearby side chapel to see what they could have hoped for, he went up a few steps to a low marble railing and leant over it to look at the altar picture by the light of his torch. The eternal light hung disturbingly in front of it. The first thing that K. partly saw and partly guessed at was a large knight in armour who was shown at the far edge of the painting. He was leaning on his sword that he had stuck into the naked ground in front of him where only a few blades of grass grew here and there. He seemed to be paying close attention to something that was being played out in front of him. It was astonishing to see how he stood there without going any closer. Perhaps it was his job to stand guard. It was a long time since K. had looked at any pictures and he studied the knight for a long time even though he had continually to blink as he found it difficult to bear the green light of his torch. Then when he moved the light to the other parts of the picture he found an interment of Christ shown in the usual way, it was also a comparatively new painting. He put his torch away and went back to his place.

There seemed to be no point in waiting for the Italian any longer, but outside it was certainly raining heavily, and as it was not so cold in the cathedral as K. had expected he decided to stay there for the time being. Close by him was the great pulpit, there were two plain golden crosses attached to its little round roof which were lying almost flat and whose tips crossed over each other. The outside of the pulpit's balustrade was covered in green foliage which continued down to the column supporting it, little angels could be seen among the leaves, some of them lively and some of them still. K. walked up to the pulpit and examined it from all sides, its stonework had been sculpted with great care, it seemed as if the foliage had trapped a deep darkness between and behind its leaves and held it there prisoner, K. lay his hand in one of these gaps and cautiously felt the stone, until then he had been totally unaware of this pulpit's existence. Then K. happened to notice one of the church staff standing behind the next row of pews, he wore a loose, creased, black cassock, he held a snuff box in his left hand and he was watching K. Now what does he want? thought K. Do I seem suspicious to him? Does he want a tip? But when the man in the cassock saw that K. had noticed him he raised his right hand, a pinch of snuff still held between two fingers, and pointed in some vague direction. It was almost impossible to understand what this behaviour meant, K. waited a while longer but the man in the cassock did not stop gesturing with his hand and even augmented it by nodding his head. "Now what does he want?" asked K. quietly, he did not dare call out loud here; but then he drew out his purse and pushed his way through the nearest pews to reach the man. He, however, immediately gestured to turn down this offer, shrugged his shoulders and limped away. As a child K. had imitated riding on a horse with the same sort of movement as this limp. "This old man is like a child," thought K., "he doesn't have the sense for anything more than serving in a church. Look at the way he stops when I stop, and how he waits to see whether I'll continue." With a smile, K. followed the old man all the way up the side nave and almost as far as the main altar, all this time the old man continued to point at something but K. deliberately avoided looking round, he was only pointing in order to make it harder for K. to follow him. Eventually, K. did stop following, he did not want to worry the old man too much, and he also did not want to frighten him away completely in case the Italian turned up after all.

When he entered the central nave to go back to where he had left the album, he noticed a small secondary pulpit on a column almost next to the stalls by the altar where the choir sat. It was very simple, made of plain white stone, and so small that from a distance it looked like an empty niche where the statue of a saint ought to have been. It certainly would have been impossible for the priest to take a full step back from the balustrade, and, although there was no decoration on it, the top of the pulpit curved in exceptionally low so that a man of average height would not be able stand upright and would have to remain bent forward over the balustrade. In all, it looked as if it had been intended to make the priest suffer, it was impossible to understand why this pulpit would be needed as there were also the other ones available which were large and so artistically decorated.

And K. would certainly not have noticed this little pulpit if there had not been a lamp fastened above it, which usually meant there was a sermon about to be given. So was a sermon to be given now? In this empty church? K. looked down at the steps which, pressed close against the column, led up to the pulpit. They were so narrow they seemed to be there as decoration on the column rather than for anyone to use. But under the pulpit – K. grinned in astonishment – there really was a priest standing with his hand on the handrail ready to climb the steps and looking at K. Then he nodded very slightly, so that K. crossed himself and genuflected as he should have done earlier. With a little swing, the priest went up into the pulpit with short fast steps. Was there really a sermon about to begin? Maybe the man in the cassock had not been really so demented, and had meant to lead K.'s way to the preacher, which in this empty church would have been very necessary. And there was also, somewhere in front of a picture of the Virgin Mary, an old woman who should have come to hear the sermon. And if there was to be a sermon why had it not been introduced on the organ? But the organ remained quiet and merely looked out weakly from the darkness of its great height.

K. now considered whether he should leave as quickly as possible, if he did not do it now there would be no chance of doing so during the sermon and he would have to stay there for as long as it lasted, he had lost so much time when he should have been in his office, there had long been no need for him to wait for the Italian any longer, he looked at his watch, it was eleven. But could there really be a sermon given? Could K. constitute the entire congregation? How could he when he was just a stranger who wanted to look at the church? That, basically, was all he was. The idea of a sermon, now, at eleven o'clock, on a workday, in hideous weather, was nonsense. The priest – there was no doubt that he was a priest, a young man with a smooth, dark face – was clearly going up there just to put the lamp out after somebody had lit it by mistake.

But there had been no mistake, the priest seemed rather to check that the lamp was lit and turned it a little higher, then he slowly turned to face the front and leant down on the balustrade gripping its angular rail with both hands. He stood there like that for a while and, without turning his head, looked around. K. had moved back a long way and leant his elbows on the front pew. Somewhere in the church – he could not have said exactly where – he could make out the man in the cassock hunched under his bent back and at peace, as if his work were completed. In the cathedral it was now very quiet! But K. would have to disturb that silence, he had no intention of staying there; if it was the priest's duty to preach at a certain time regardless of the circumstances then he could, and he could do it without K.'s taking part, and K.'s presence would do nothing to augment the effect of it. So K. began slowly to move, felt his way on tiptoe along the pew, arrived at the broad aisle and went along it without being disturbed, except for the sound of his steps, however light, which rang out on the stone floor and resounded from the vaulting, quiet but continuous at a repeating, regular pace. K. felt slightly abandoned as, probably observed by the priest, he walked by himself between the empty pews, and the size of the cathedral seemed to be just at the limit of what a man could bear. When he arrived back at where he had been sitting he did not hesitate but simply reached out for the album he had left there and took it with him. He had nearly left the area covered by pews and was close to the empty space between himself and the exit when, for the first time, he heard the voice of the priest. A powerful and experienced voice. It pierced through the reaches of the cathedral ready waiting for it! But the priest was not calling out to the congregation, his cry was quite unambiguous and there was no escape from it, he called "Josef K.!"

K. stood still and looked down at the floor. In theory he was still free, he could have carried on walking, through one of three dark little wooden doors not far in front of him and away from there. It would simply mean he had not understood, or that he had understood but chose not to pay attention to it. But if he once turned round he would be trapped, then he would have acknowledged that he had understood perfectly well, that he really was the Josef K. the priest had called to and that he was willing to follow. If the priest had called out again K. would certainly have carried on out the door, but everything was silent as K. also waited, he turned his head slightly as he wanted to see what the priest was doing now. He was merely standing in the pulpit as before, but it was obvious that he had seen K. turn his head. If K. did not now turn round completely it would have been like a child playing hide and seek. He did so, and the priest beckoned him with his finger. As everything could now be done openly he ran – because of curiosity and the wish to get it over with – with long flying leaps towards the pulpit. At the front pews he stopped, but to the priest he still seemed too far away, he reached out his hand and pointed sharply down with his finger to a place immediately in front of the pulpit. And K. did as he was told, standing in that place he had to bend his head a long way back just to see the priest. "You are Josef K.," said the priest, and raised his hand from the balustrade to make a gesture whose meaning was unclear. "Yes," said K., he considered how freely he had always given his name in the past, for some time now it had been a burden to him, now there were people who knew his name whom he had never seen before, it had been so nice first to introduce yourself and only then for people to know who you were. "You have been accused," said the priest, especially gently. "Yes," said K., "so I have been informed." "Then you are the one I am looking for," said the priest. "I am the prison chaplain." "I see," said K. "I had you summoned here," said the priest, "because I wanted to speak to you." "I knew nothing of that," said K. "I came here to show the cathedral to a gentleman from Italy." "That is beside the point," said the priest. "What are you holding in your hand? Is it a prayer book?" "No," answered K., "it's an album of the city's tourist sights." "Put it down," said the priest. K. threw it away with such force that it flapped open and rolled across the floor, tearing its pages. "Do you know your case is going badly?" asked the priest. "That's how it seems to me too," said K. "I've expended a lot of effort on it, but so far with no result. Although I do still have some documents to submit." "How do you imagine it will end?" asked the priest. "At first I thought it was bound to end well," said K., "but now I have my doubts about it. I don't know how it will end. Do you know?" "I don't," said the priest, "but I fear it will end badly. You are considered guilty. Your case will probably not even go beyond a minor court. Provisionally at least, your guilt is seen as proven." "But I'm not guilty," said K., "there's been a mistake. How is it even possible for someone to be guilty. We're all human beings here, one like the other." "That is true," said the priest, "but that is how the guilty speak." "Do you presume I'm guilty too?" asked K. "I make no presumptions about you," said the priest. "I thank you for that," said K. "but everyone else involved in these proceedings has something against me and presumes I'm guilty. They even influence those who aren't involved. My position gets harder all the time." "You don't understand the facts," said the priest, "the verdict does not come suddenly, proceedings continue until a verdict is reached gradually." "I see," said K., lowering his head. "What do you intend to do about your case next?" asked the priest. "I still need to find help," said K., raising his head to see what the priest thought of this. "There are still certain possibilities I haven't yet made use of." "You look for too much help from people you don't know," said the priest disapprovingly, "and especially from women. Can you really not see that's not the help you need?" "Sometimes, in fact quite often, I could believe you're right," said K., "but not always. Women have a lot of power. If I could persuade some of the women I know to work together with me then I would be certain to succeed. Especially in a court like this that seems to consist of nothing but woman-chasers. Show the examining judge a woman in the distance and he'll run right over the desk, and the accused, just to get to her as soon as he can." The priest lowered his head down to the balustrade, only now did the roof over the pulpit seem to press him down. What sort of dreadful weather could it be outside? It was no longer just a dull day, it was deepest night. None of the stained glass in the main window shed even a flicker of light on the darkness of the walls. And this was the moment when the man in the cassock chose to put out the candles on the main altar, one by one. "Are you cross with me?" asked K. "Maybe you don't know what sort of court it is you serve." He received no answer. "Well, it's just my own experience," said K. Above him there was still silence. "I didn't mean to insult you," said K. At that, the priest screamed down at K.: "Can you not see two steps in front of you?" He shouted in anger, but it was also the scream of one who sees another fall and, shocked and without thinking, screams against his own will.

The two men, then, remained silent for a long time. In the darkness beneath him, the priest could not possibly have seen K. distinctly, although K. was able to see him clearly by the light of the little lamp. Why did the priest not come down?

He had not given a sermon, he had only told K. a few things which, if he followed them closely, would probably cause him more harm than good. But the priest certainly seemed to mean well, it might even be possible, if he would come down and cooperate with him, it might even be possible for him to obtain some acceptable piece of advice that could make all the difference, it might, for instance, be able to show him not so much to influence the proceedings but how to break free of them, how to evade them, how to live away from them. K. had to admit that this was something he had had on his mind quite a lot of late. If the priest knew of such a possibility he might, if K. asked him, let him know about it, even though he was part of the court himself and even though, when K. had criticised the court, he had held down his gentle nature and actually shouted at K.

"Would you not like to come down here?" asked K. "If you're not going to give a sermon come down here with me." "Now I can come down," said the priest, perhaps he regretted having shouted at K. As he took down the lamp from its hook he said, "to start off with I had to speak to you from a distance. Otherwise I'm too easily influenced and forget my duty."

K. waited for him at the foot of the steps. While he was still on one of the higher steps as he came down them the priest reached out his hand for K. to shake. "Can you spare me a little of your time?" asked K. "As much time as you need," said the priest, and passed him the little lamp for him to carry. Even at close distance the priest did not lose a certain solemnity that seemed to be part of his character. "You are very friendly towards me," said K., as they walked up and down beside each other in the darkness of one of the side naves. "That makes you an exception among all those who belong to the court. I can trust you more than any of the others I've seen. I can speak openly with you." "Don't fool yourself," said the priest. "How would I be fooling myself?" asked K. "You fool yourself in the court," said the priest, "it talks about this self-deceit in the opening paragraphs to the law. In front of the law there is a doorkeeper. A man from the countryside comes up to the door and asks for entry. But the doorkeeper says he can't let him in to the law right now. The man thinks about this, and then he asks if he'll be able to go in later on. 'That's possible,' says the doorkeeper, 'but not now'. The gateway to the law is open as it always is, and the doorkeeper has stepped to one side, so the man bends over to try and see in. When the doorkeeper notices this he laughs and says, 'If you're tempted give it a try, try and go in even though I say you can't. Careful though: I'm powerful. And I'm only the lowliest of all the doormen. But there's a door-keeper for each of the rooms and each of them is more pow-erful than the last. It's more than I can stand just to look at the third one.' The man from the country had not expected difficulties like this, the law was supposed to be accessible for anyone at any time, he thinks, but now he looks more closely at the doorkeeper in his fur coat, sees his big hooked nose, his long thin tartar-beard, and he decides it's better to wait until he has permission to enter. The doorkeeper gives him a stool and lets him sit down to one side of the gate. He sits there for days and years. He tries to be allowed in time and again and tires the doorkeeper with his requests. The doorkeeper often questions him, asking about where he's from and many other things, but these are disinterested questions such as great men ask, and he always ends up by telling him he still can't let him in. The man had come well equipped for his journey, and uses everything, however valuable, to bribe the doorkeeper. He accepts everything, but as he does so he says, 'I'll only accept this so that you don't think there's anything you've failed to do'. Over many years, the man watches the doorkeeper al-most without a break. He forgets about the other doormen, and begins to think this one is the only thing stopping him from gaining access to the law. Over the first few years he curses his unhappy condition out loud, but later, as he be-comes old, he just grumbles to himself. He becomes senile, and as he has come to know even the fleas in the doorkeep-er's fur collar over the years that he has been studying him he even asks them to help him and change the doorkeeper's mind. Finally his eyes grow dim, and he no longer knows whether it's really getting darker or just his eyes that are deceiving him. But he seems now to see an inextinguishable light begin to shine from the darkness behind the door. He doesn't have long to live now. Just before he dies, he brings together all his experience from all this time into one question which he has still never put to the doorkeeper. He beckons to him, as he's no longer able to raise his stiff body. The doorkeeper has to bend over deeply as the difference in their sizes has changed very much to the disadvantage of the man. 'What is it you want to know now?' asks the doorkeeper, 'You're insatiable.' 'Everyone wants access to the law,' says the man, 'how come, over all these years, no- one but me has asked to be let in?' The doorkeeper can see the man's come to his end, his hearing has faded, and so, so that he can be heard, he shouts to him: 'Nobody else could have got in this way, as this entrance was meant only for you. Now I'll go and close it'."

"So the doorkeeper cheated the man," said K. immediately, who had been captivated by the story. "Don't be too quick," said the priest, "don't take somebody else's opinion without checking it. I told you the story exactly as it was written. There's nothing in there about cheating." "But it's quite clear," said K., "and your first interpretation of it was quite correct. The doorkeeper gave him the information that would release him only when it could be of no more use." "He didn't ask him before that," said the priest, "and don't forget he was only a doorkeeper, and as doorkeeper he did his duty." "What makes you think he did his duty?" asked K., "He didn't. It might have been his duty to keep everyone else away, but this man is who the door was intended for and he ought to have let him in." "You're not paying enough attention to what was written and you're changing the story," said the priest. "According to the story, there are two important things that the doorkeeper explains about access to the law, one at the beginning, one at the end. At one place he says he can't allow him in now, and at the other he says this entrance was intended for him alone. If one of the statements contradicted the other you would be right and the doorkeeper would have cheated the man from the country. But there is no contradiction. On the contrary, the first statement even hints at the second. You could almost say the doorkeeper went beyond his duty in that he offered the man some prospect of being admitted in the future. Throughout the story, his duty seems to have been merely to turn the man away, and there are many commentators who are surprised that the doorkeeper offered this hint at all, as he seems to love exactitude and keeps strict guard over his position. He stays at his post for many years and doesn't close the gate until the very end, he's very conscious of the importance of his service, as he says, 'I'm powerful,' he has respect for his superiors, as he says, 'I'm only the lowliest of the doormen', he's not talkative, as through all these years the only questions he asks are 'disinterested', he's not corruptible, as when he's offered a gift he says, 'I'll only accept this so that you don't think there's anything you've failed to do,' as far as fulfilling his duty goes he can be neither ruffled nor begged, as it says about the man that, 'he tires the doorkeeper with his requests', even his external appearance suggests a pedantic character, the big hooked nose and the long, thin, black tartar-beard. How could any doorkeeper be more faithful to his duty? But in the doorkeeper's character there are also other features which might be very useful for those who seek entry to the law, and when he hinted at some possibility in the future it always seemed to make it clear that he might even go beyond his duty. There's no denying he's a little simple minded, and that makes him a little conceited. Even if all he said about his power and the power of the other doorkeepers and how not even he could bear the sight of them – I say even if all these assertions are right, the way he makes them shows that he's too simple and arrogant to understand properly. The commentators say about this that, 'correct understanding of a matter and a misunderstanding of the same matter are not mutually exclusive'. Whether they're right or not, you have to concede that his simplicity and arrogance, however little they show, do weaken his function of guarding the entrance, they are defects in the doorkeeper's character. You also have to consider that the doorkeeper seems to be friendly by nature, he isn't always just an official. He makes a joke right at the beginning, in that he invites the man to enter at the same time as maintaining the ban on his entering, and then he doesn't send him away but gives him, as it says in the text, a stool to sit on and lets him stay by the side of the door. The patience with which he puts up with the man's requests through all these years, the little questioning sessions, accepting the gifts, his politeness when he puts up with the man cursing his fate even though it was the doorkeeper who caused that fate – all these things seem to want to arouse our sympathy. Not every doorkeeper would have behaved in the same way. And finally, he lets the man beckon him and he bends deep down to him so that he can put his last question. There's no more than some slight impatience – the doorkeeper knows everything's come to its end – shown in the words, 'You're insatiable'. There are many commentators who go even further in explaining it in this way and think the words, 'you're insatiable' are an expression of friendly admiration, albeit with some condescension. However you look at it the figure of the doorkeeper comes out differently from how you might think." "You know the story better than I do and you've known it for longer," said K. They were silent for a while. And then K. said, "So you think the man was not cheated, do you?" "Don't get me wrong," said the priest, "I'm just pointing out the different opinions about it. You shouldn't pay too much attention to people's opinions. The text cannot be altered, and the various opinions are often no more than an expression of despair over it. There's even one opinion which says it's the doorkeeper who's been cheated." "That does seem to take things too far," said K. "How can they argue the doorkeeper has been cheated?" "Their argument," answered the priest, "is based on the simplicity of the doorkeeper. They say the doorkeeper doesn't know the inside of the law, only the way into it where he just walks up and down. They see his ideas of what's inside the law as rather childish, and suppose he's afraid himself of what he wants to make the man frightened of. Yes, he's more afraid of it than the man, as the man wants nothing but to go inside the law, even after he's heard about the terrible doormen there, in contrast to the doorkeeper who doesn't want to go in, or at least we don't hear anything about it. On the other hand, there are those who say he must have already been inside the law as he has been taken on into its service and that could only have been done inside. That can be countered by supposing he could have been given the job of doorkeeper by somebody calling out from inside, and that he can't have gone very far inside as he couldn't bear the sight of the third doorkeeper. Nor, through all those years, does the story say the doorkeeper told the man anything about the inside, other than his comment about the other doorkeepers. He could have been forbidden to do so, but he hasn't said anything about that either. All this seems to show he doesn't know anything about what the inside looks like or what it means, and that that's why he's being deceived. But he's also being deceived by the man from the country as he's this man's subordinate and doesn't know it. There's a lot to indicate that he treats the man as his subordinate, I expect you remember, but those who hold this view would say it's very clear that he really is his subordinate. Above all, the free man is superior to the man who has to serve another. Now, the man really is free, he can go wherever he wants, the only thing forbidden to him is entry into the law and, what's more, there's only one man forbidding him to do so – the doorkeeper. If he takes the stool and sits down beside the door and stays there all his life he does this of his own free will, there's nothing in the story to say he was forced to do it. On the other hand, the doorkeeper is kept to his post by his employment, he's not allowed to go away from it and it seems he's not allowed to go inside either, not even if he wanted to. Also, although he's in the service of the law he's only there for this one entrance, therefore he's there only in the service of this one man who the door's intended for. This is another way in which he's his subordinate. We can take it that he's been performing this somewhat empty service for many years, through the whole of a man's life, as it says that a man will come, that means someone old enough to be a man. That means the doorkeeper will have to wait a long time before his function is fulfilled, he will have to wait for as long as the man liked, who came to the door of his own free will. Even the end of the doorkeeper's service is determined by when the man's life ends, so the doorkeeper remains his subordinate right to the end. And it's pointed out repeatedly that the doorkeeper seems to know nothing of any of this, although this is not seen as anything remarkable, as those who hold this view see the doorkeeper as deluded in a way that's far worse, a way that's to do with his service. At the end, speaking about the entrance he says, 'Now I'll go and close it', although at the beginning of the story it says the door to the law is open as it always is, but if it's always open – always – that means it's open independently of the lifespan of the man it's intended for, and not even the doorkeeper will be able to close it. There are various opinions about this, some say the door-keeper was only answering a question or showing his devotion to duty or, just when the man was in his last moments, the doorkeeper wanted to cause him regret and sorrow. There are many who agree that he wouldn't be able to close the door. They even believe, at the end at least, the doorkeeper is aware, deep down, that he's the man's subordinate, as the man sees the light that shines out of the entry to the law whereas the doorkeeper would probably have his back to it and says nothing at all to show there's been any change."

"That is well substantiated," said K., who had been repeating some parts of the priest's explanation to himself in a whisper. "It is well substantiated, and now I too think the doorkeeper must have been deceived. Although that does not mean I've abandoned what I thought earlier as the two versions are, to some extent, not incompatible. It's not clear whether the doorkeeper sees clearly or is deceived. I said the man had been cheated. If the doorkeeper understands clearly, then there could be some doubt about it, but if the doorkeeper has been deceived then the man is bound to believe the same thing. That would mean the doorkeeper is not a cheat but so simple-minded that he ought to be dismissed from his job immediately; if the doorkeeper is mistaken it will do him no harm but the man will be harmed immensely." "There you've found another opinion," said the priest, "as there are many who say the story doesn't give anyone the right to judge the doorkeeper. However he might seem to us he is still in the service of the law, so he belongs to the law, so he's beyond what man has a right to judge. In this case we can't believe the doorkeeper is the man's subordinate. Even if he has to stay at the entrance into the law his service makes him incomparably more than if he lived freely in the world. The man has come to the law for the first time and the doorkeeper is already there. He's been given his position by the law, to doubt his worth would be to doubt the law." "I can't say I'm in complete agreement with this view," said K. shaking his head, "as if you accept it you'll have to accept that everything said by the doorkeeper is true. But you've already explained very fully that that's not possible." "No," said the priest, "you don't need to accept everything as true, you only have to accept it as necessary." "Depressing view," said K. "The lie made into the rule of the world."

K. said that as if it were his final word but it was not his conclusion. He was too tired to think about all the ramifications of the story, and the sort of thoughts they led him into were not familiar to him, unrealistic things, things better suited for officials of the court to discuss than for him. The simple story had lost its shape, he wanted to shake it off, and the priest who now felt quite compassionate allowed this and accepted K.'s remarks without comment, even though his view was certainly very different from K.'s.

In silence, they carried on walking for some time, K. stayed close beside the priest without knowing where he was. The lamp in his hand had long since gone out. Once, just in front of him, he thought he could see the statue of a saint by the glitter of the silver on it, although it quickly disappeared back into the darkness. So that he would not remain entirely dependent on the priest, K. asked him, "We're now near the main entrance, are we?" "No," said the priest, "we're a long way from it. Do you already want to go?" K. had not thought of going until then, but he immediately said, "Yes, certainly, I have to go. I'm the chief clerk in a bank and there are people waiting for me, I only came here to show a foreign business contact round the cathedral." "Alright," said the priest offering him his hand, "go then." "But I can't find my way round in this darkness by myself," said K. "Go to your left as far as the wall," said the priest, "then continue alongside the wall without leaving it and you'll find a way out." The priest had only gone a few paces from him, but K. was already shouting loudly, "Please, wait!" "I'm waiting," said the priest. "Is there anything else you want from me?" asked K. "No," said the priest. "You were so friendly to me earlier on," said K., "and you explained everything, but now you abandon me as if I were nothing to you." "You have to go," said the priest. "Well, yes," said K., "you need to understand that." "First, you need to understand who I am," said the priest. "You're the prison chaplain," said K., and went closer to the priest, it was not so important for him to go straight back to the bank as he had made out, he could very well stay where he was. "So that means I belong to the court," said the priest. "So why would I want anything from you? the court doesn't want anything from you. It accepts you when you come and it lets you go when you leave."

Chapter Ten
End

The evening before K.'s thirty-first birthday – it was about nine o'clock in the evening, the time when the streets were quiet – two men came to where he lived. In frock coats, pale and fat, wearing top hats that looked like they could not be taken off their heads. After some brief formalities at the door of the flat when they first arrived, the same formalities were repeated at greater length at K.'s door. He had not been notified they would be coming, but K. sat in a chair near the door, dressed in black as they were, and slowly put on new gloves which stretched tightly over his fingers and behaved as if he were expecting visitors. He immediately stood up and looked at the gentlemen inquisitively. "You've come for me then, have you?" he asked. The gentlemen nodded, one of them indicated the other with the top hand now in his hand. K. told them he had been expecting a different visitor. He went to the window and looked once more down at the dark street. Most of the windows on the other side of the street were also dark already, many of them had the curtains closed. In one of the windows on the same floor where there was a light on, two small children could be seen playing with each other inside a playpen, unable to move from where they were, reaching out for each other with their little hands. "Some ancient, unimportant actors – that's what they've sent for me," said K. to himself, and looked round once again to confirm this to himself. "They want to sort me out as cheaply as they can." K. suddenly turned round to face the two men and asked, "What theatre do you play in?" "Theatre?" asked one of the gentlemen, turning to the other for assistance and pulling in the corners of his mouth. The other made a gesture like someone who was dumb, as if he were struggling with some organism causing him trouble. "You're not properly prepared to answer questions," said K. and went to fetch his hat.

As soon as they were on the stairs the gentlemen wanted to take K.'s arms, but K. said "Wait till we're in the street, I'm not ill." But they waited only until the front door before they took his arms in a way that K. had never experienced before. They kept their shoulders close behind his, did not turn their arms in but twisted them around the entire length of K.'s arms and took hold of his hands with a grasp that was formal, experienced and could not be resisted. K. was held stiff and upright between them, they formed now a single unit so that if any one of them had been knocked down all of them must have fallen. They formed a unit of the sort that normally can be formed only by matter that is lifeless.

Whenever they passed under a lamp K. tried to see his companions more clearly, as far as was possible when they were pressed so close together, as in the dim light of his room this had been hardly possible. "Maybe they're tenors," he thought as he saw their big double chins. The cleanliness of their faces disgusted him. He could see the hands that cleaned them, passing over the corners of their eyes, rubbing at their upper lips, scratching out the creases on those chins.

When K. noticed that, he stopped, which meant the others had to stop too; they were at the edge of an open square, devoid of people but decorated with flower beds. "Why did they send you, of all people!" he cried out, more a shout than a question. The two gentleman clearly knew no answer to give, they waited, their free arms hanging down, like nurses when the patient needs to rest. "I will go no further," said K. as if to see what would happen. The gentlemen did not need to make any answer, it was enough that they did not loosen their grip on K. and tried to move him on, but K. resisted them. "I'll soon have no need of much strength, I'll use all of it now," he thought. He thought of the flies that tear their legs off struggling to get free of the flypaper. "These gentleman will have some hard work to do".

Just then, Miss Bürstner came up into the square in front of them from the steps leading from a small street at a lower level. It was not certain that it was her, although the similarity was, of course, great. But it did not matter to K. whether it was certainly her anyway, he just became suddenly aware that there was no point in his resistance. There would be nothing heroic about it if he resisted, if he now caused trouble for these gentlemen, if in defending himself he sought to enjoy his last glimmer of life. He started walking, which pleased the gentlemen and some of their pleasure conveyed itself to him. Now they permitted him to decide which direction they took, and he decided to take the direction that followed the young woman in front of them, not so much because he wanted to catch up with her, nor even because he wanted to keep her in sight for as long as possible, but only so that he would not forget the reproach she represented for him. "The only thing I can do now," he said to himself, and his thought was confirmed by the equal length of his own steps with the steps of the two others, "the only thing I can do now is keep my common sense and do what's needed right till the end. I always wanted to go at the world and try and do too much, and even to do it for something that was not too cheap. That was wrong of me. Should I now show them I learned nothing from facing trial for a year? Should I go out like someone stupid? Should I let anyone say, after I'm gone, that at the start of the proceedings I wanted to end them, and that now that they've ended I want to start them again? I don't want anyone to say that. I'm grateful they sent these unspeaking, uncomprehending men to go with me on this journey, and that it's been left up to me to say what's necessary".

Meanwhile, the young woman had turned off into a side street, but K. could do without her now and let his companions lead him. All three of them now, in complete agreement, went over a bridge in the light of the moon, the two gentlemen were willing to yield to each little movement made by K. as he moved slightly towards the edge and directed the group in that direction as a single unit. The moonlight glittered and quivered in the water, which divided itself around a small island covered in a densely-piled mass of foliage and trees and bushes. Beneath them, now invisible, there were gravel paths with comfortable benches where K. had stretched himself out on many summer's days. "I didn't actually want to stop here," he said to his companions, shamed by their compliance with his wishes. Behind K.'s back one of them seemed to quietly criticise the other for the misunderstanding about stopping, and then they went on. The went on up through several streets where policemen were walking or standing here and there; some in the distance and then some very close. One of them with a bushy moustache, his hand on the grip of his sword, seemed to have some purpose in approaching the group, which was hardly unsuspicious. The two gentlemen stopped, the policeman seemed about to open his mouth, and then K. drove his group forcefully forward. Several times he looked back cautiously to see if the policeman was following; but when they had a corner between themselves and the policeman K. began to run, and the two gentlemen, despite being seriously short of breath, had to run with him.

In this way they quickly left the built up area and found themselves in the fields which, in this part of town, began almost without any transition zone. There was a quarry, empty and abandoned, near a building which was still like those in the city. Here the men stopped, perhaps because this had always been their destination or perhaps because they were too exhausted to run any further. Here they released their hold on K., who just waited in silence, and took their top hats off while they looked round the quarry and wiped the sweat off their brows with their handkerchiefs. The moonlight lay everywhere with the natural peace that is granted to no other light.

After exchanging a few courtesies about who was to carry out the next tasks – the gentlemen did not seem to have been allocated specific functions – one of them went to K. and took his coat, his waistcoat, and finally his shirt off him. K. made an involuntary shiver, at which the gentleman gave him a gentle, reassuring tap on the back. Then he carefully folded the things up as if they would still be needed, even if not in the near future. He did not want to expose K. to the chilly night air without moving though, so he took him under the arm and walked up and down with him a little way while the other gentleman looked round the quarry for a suitable place. When he had found it he made a sign and the other gentleman escorted him there. It was near the rockface, there was a stone lying there that had broken loose. The gentlemen sat K. down on the ground, leant him against the stone and settled his head down on the top of it. Despite all the effort they went to, and despite all the co-operation shown by K., his demeanour seemed very forced and hard to believe. So one of the gentlemen asked the other to grant him a short time while he put K. in position by himself, but even that did nothing to make it better. In the end they left K. in a position that was far from the best of the ones they had tried so far. Then one of the gentlemen opened his frock coat and from a sheath hanging on a belt stretched across his waistcoat he withdrew a long, thin, double-edged butcher's knife which he held up in the light to test its sharpness. The repulsive courtesies began once again, one of them passed the knife over K. to the other, who then passed it back over K. to the first. K. now knew it would be his duty to take the knife as it passed from hand to hand above him and thrust it into himself. But he did not do it, instead he twisted his neck, which was still free, and looked around. He was not able to show his full worth, was not able to take all the work from the official bodies, he lacked the rest of the strength he needed and this final shortcoming was the fault of whoever had denied it to him. As he looked round, he saw the top floor of the building next to the quarry. He saw how a light flickered on and the two halves of a window opened out, somebody, made weak and thin by the height and the distance, leant suddenly far out from it and stretched his arms out even further. Who was that? A friend? A good person? Somebody who was taking part? Somebody who wanted to help? Was he alone? Was it everyone? Would anyone help? Were there objections that had been forgotten? There must have been some. The logic cannot be refuted, but someone who wants to live will not resist it. Where was the judge he'd never seen? Where was the high court he had never reached? He raised both hands and spread out all his fingers.

But the hands of one of the gentleman were laid on K.'s throat, while the other pushed the knife deep into his heart and twisted it there, twice. As his eyesight failed, K. saw the two gentlemen cheek by cheek, close in front of his face, watching the result. "Like a dog!" he said, it was as if the shame of it should outlive him.

Up in the Gallery

If some frail tubercular lady circus rider were to be driven in circles around and around the arena for months and months without interruption in front of a tireless public on a swaying horse by a merciless whip-wielding master of ceremonies, spinning on the horse, throwing kisses and swaying at the waist, and if this performance, amid the incessant roar of the orchestra and the ventilators, were to continue into the ever-expanding, gray future, accompanied by applause, which died down and then swelled up again, from hands which were really steam hammers, perhaps then a young visitor to the gallery might rush down the long stair case through all the levels, burst into the ring, and cry "Stop!" through the fanfares of the constantly adjusting orchestra.

But since things are not like that—since a beautiful woman, in white and red, flies in through curtains which proud men in livery open in front of her, since the director, devotedly seeking her eyes, breathes in her direction, behaving like an animal, and, as a precaution, lifts her up on the dapple-gray horse, as if she were his grand daughter, the one he loved more than anything else, as she starts a dangerous journey, but he cannot decide to give the signal with his whip and finally, controlling himself, gives it a crack, runs right beside the horse with his mouth open, follows the rider's leaps with a sharp gaze, hardly capable of comprehending her skill, tries to warn her by calling out in English, furiously castigating the grooms holding hoops, telling them to pay the most scrupulous attention, and begs the orchestra, with upraised arms, to be quiet before the great jump, finally lifts the small woman down from the trembling horse, kisses her on both cheeks, considers no public tribute adequate, while she herself, leaning on him, high on the tips of her toes, with dust swirling around her, arms outstretched and head thrown back, wants to share her luck with the entire circus—since this is how things are, the visitor to the gallery puts his face on the railing and, sinking into the final march as if into a difficult dream, weeps, without realizing it.